Queen of the Mardi Gras Ball

by

Lynn Shurr

The Mardi Gras Series

Queen of the Mardi Gras Ball

Cover Art by *Diana Carlile*

The Wild Rose Press, Inc.
PO Box 708
Adams Basin, NY 14410-0708
Visit us at www.thewildrosepress.com

Publishing History
previously published by L & L Dreamspell, 2012
First Mainstream Historical Edition, 2015
Print ISBN 978-1-62830-873-0
Digital ISBN 978-1-62830-874-7

The Mardi Gras Series
Published in the United States of America

"Doing a good business today, Anna-Marie?" she heard her masked man ask.

"No rest for the wicked, Doctor Pierre. Eh, you want a room? I won't tell JoJo. He don't count the sheets I wash. Lucky number seven, she's all made up and ready to go. I got the key right here. Some lagnaippe for taking care of my girl when she got the clap." The yellow woman tossed her load of soiled linens into a basket and took a set of fresh sheets from a pile stacked on one of the bar's bentwood chairs. Draping her burden over one arm, she fished in her apron for the key and dangled it before him.

"Not today, *Senora*, but you have my thanks."

"Yes," said Roz as she came up behind him. "Yes, we want the key."

She stroked the dark hair at the nape of his neck and recognized the same small shiver she had gotten out of him on the balcony of the Yacht Club.

"Ah, you should take the room. It's Mardi Gras, and who knows when you will have another chance with the gypsy lady, eh?" Anna-Marie said, still dangling temptation.

"You're sure. You must be sure," he said to Roz so seriously, his breath hot against her cheek.

She took the key for him and led the way to number seven.

Praise for Lynn Shurr

"Shurr is a wonderful story teller."

~The Romance Studio

~*~

"I can attest to the fact that Lynn Shurr knows her subject matter. Her grasp of Crescent City customs, particularly the social swirl surrounding Mardi Gras, is top-notch…Colorfully written, engaging and often poignant, 'Queen' doesn't let up until Roz gets things settled to her satisfaction."

~Ashton Lee, author of
The Cherry Cola Book Club

~*~

"Very easy reads, well written, combined with conflict, believable plots and secondary characters that make the story come alive."

~Jane Lange, Romances, Reads and Reviews

~*~

"Lynn Shurr stories have that distinctive Louisiana flavor…and make you eager for another taste."

~Jeff Salter, author

Dedication

For my mother, Joan Shurr,
who shared with me her stories of growing up
in the 1920s

Chapter One

New Orleans, 1925

"Reigning as queen was simultaneously a rite of passage, an act of submission, and a mark of honor. Participation in the Carnival courts was the outward and visible sign that a daughter was conforming to the demands that "society" placed upon her…A woman became Carnival queen when she was a girl; queenhood ended her childhood. After she was queen she might go on to become a woman, a wife, a mother."
~Reid Mitchell, *All on a Mardi Gras Day*

A stiff wind ripped across the Mississippi picking up moisture as it came. Chilly and damp, it crossed over the levee and descended into Jackson Square, driving the vagrants from the park benches and into the doorways of the Pontalba Apartments. Burke Boylan and Artemus Delamare, having walked most of the length of Bourbon Street looking for action, were now revising their plans under a street lamp on the corner of the old parade grounds.

"Who would have thought bawdyhouses close early on Christmas Eve?" Boylan said in a frustrated voice. He drew a silver hip flask engraved with the Greek letters of his fraternity from a pocket, unscrewed the cap, and took a warming sip.

Artie held out his hand. "I suppose even whores have families and enjoy an evening off."

He received the silver flask and took a swig after wiping the mouthpiece on the sleeve of his raccoon coat. "Great hooch! Where did you get it?"

"I had them fill it up at the Holland House, best booze in town. The stuff they make here in the Quarter is all rotgut."

Artie passed the mouth of the flask over his coat sleeve again and returned it to his buddy who plucked two hairs from the opening before replacing the cap.

"I prefer my liquor without added ingredients, Delamare. By the way, you look ridiculous in that coat."

"Ridiculous but warm. Besides, it's the cat's meow right now. Where to next, my friend?"

"Plenty of automobiles parked around here tonight," Boylan observed.

"Midnight Mass. All the good, or rather the *best* people, are packed into old St. Louis Cathedral having their souls attended to. They should let out in a half hour and scurry off to a *reveillon* to stuff their faces before sleeping in Christmas morning."

Boylan looked up at the ancient cathedral, its stained glass windows ablaze, as if he had just noticed its existence. "*Reveillon?*"

"You took to the vice around here so easily I keep forgetting you come from Philadelphia. It's an old Creole custom to gorge at home after Christmas Eve Mass."

"Sounds like a party to me. I think my mother mentioned it once, but in Philadelphia we do as Philadelphians do—go to bed early. Can we get invited?"

"If you are willing to spend some time on your knees, Brother Boylan."

"Lead the way, Artie."

Artie fished in his coat pocket and withdrew two peppermints, a bit fuzzy but edible. "Won't do to offend with our breath before we even get started on an invite."

Burke accepted the questionable candy and followed Artie across the slick, damp slates to the church.

Heads turned at the rear of the congregation as the cathedral doors thumped open and shut. More than a few worshipers grumbled when the two young men pushed into an already crowded pew with Artie and his coat taking up twice the space he should have. At the far end of the church, the priest raised the chalice and glorified the blood of Christ in Latin. Most people were on their knees. Burke and Artie joined them. As the first rows moved sluggishly toward the communion rail, Burke surveyed the crowd and sharpened his wit on a few of them.

"Would you look at that grande dame, her chest pushed out like a pouter pigeon. Doesn't she know corsets are out of style? But the next woman—ooh-la-la—a Madonna, meek and mild, in a black lace shawl, the golden hair, the pure white skin, the rosy cheeks, the bee-stung lips."

The people just in front of the young men shushed. Artie whispered directly into Burke's ear. "Rosamond St. Rochelle, daughter of the pouter pigeon, very old Creole family, but I've heard she's a wild child, not a Madonna."

"Do the St. Rochelles have a *reveillon?*"

"One of the best in town. They live over on Esplanade in one of the old French mansions."

"Then, that's where we will be going."

"I'll do my best."

The two young men slipped from their pew just before the recessional and took up a post by the side of the cathedral doors. As Rosamond's family exited, Artie stepped forward, hand extended toward a prosperous and substantial older man wearing a black topcoat and a banker's homburg hat. His wife, her chest made even larger by the huge fur collar of her wrap, paused by his side as the two men shook.

"I'm Artemus Delamare. I believe you are acquainted with my father, Cornelius Delamare, from the Boston Club. This is my fellow Tulane law student and fraternity brother, Burke Boylan of Philadelphia. He is unable to be with his family this holy season, and I was hoping to introduce him to one of our charming local customs, the *reveillon.*"

While the husband digested this speech, his wife took charge. "Why, we would be delighted to have two future attorneys join us, wouldn't we, Rosamond?"

She drew her daughter forward. Rosamond had allowed the black lace shawl to slip to her shoulders as she left the cathedral. Her wrap was so large it draped over most of her pearl gray dress with its de rigueur dropped waistline. Still, Burke caught a glimpse of fine silk undergarments beneath the filmy, almost transparent fabric ornamented by a large pink rose on one hip. Rosamond's baby blue eyes crinkled merrily at her mother's obvious ploy to introduce her to yet another eligible young man.

4

"My daughter, Rosamond Grace St. Rochelle. Rosamond is studying the fine arts at Newcomb College."

Rosamond tilted her lovely head with its marcelled waves of blonde hair extending to the bun at the nape of her neck. She extended her hand elegantly. Boylan seized it. "Charmed to meet you," he claimed.

A rustling noise sounded behind Rosamond, then the impatient stamp of patent leather shoes. A girl of about twelve pushed forward. She wore a shawl like her sister, but it was white and covered her from head to toe. "May we go now? I'm getting cold."

"My younger daughter, Roxanne Marie, who is lacking in manners this evening." Madame St. Rochelle gave the child a frown.

Artie removed one of the child's hands from the tangle of the shawl and gave it a light shake. "Looks like it's you and me, baby," he said in a joking undertone.

Roxie's dark eyes lit. She let the shawl drop seductively to her shoulders in imitation of her sister and revealed that she still wore her hair in long, brown pigtails tied at the ends with white ribbons. "I like you. You're funny, and so is your coat."

"So I've been told. Tell me, Miss Roxie, would you have room in your flivver for two equally chilled Tulane men?"

"We don't have a flivver. We have an Auburn Touring Car," the girl answered seriously. "Please, Papa, may they ride with us?"

"I suppose I wouldn't leave a dog out on a night like this. Of course, you gentlemen are welcome to ride with us."

As the St. Rochelles and their company waited for their chauffeur to inch the Auburn through the post-Mass traffic to where they stood, two men wearing dark fedoras and black suits passed nearby. The taller had the same build as Rosamond's father, but less paunch, the same blond hair going gray at the sides, the same light eyes. A family member, then, Boylan calculated.

The other much younger man was slim of body, olive-complected with high cheekbones sharp enough to cut diamonds, and large, dark eyes. A rival for the attention of the fair Rosamond, Boylan assessed, since the fella's eyes skipped over the rest of the family and went right to her pretty face.

Mr. St. Rochelle called out, "Gilbert, my brother, you are coming to the *reveillon*?"

"But of course, Laurence. I have no desire to be alone tonight. First, I must take my colleague back to his digs. It's too nasty a night for walking."

"Bring him along by all means. Any friend of yours is welcome."

Mrs. St. Rochelle viewed her newest guest with hawk-like brown eyes disguised by the fleshiness of her face. She intended to reel in another suitor for her daughter, Burke could tell.

"Pierre Landry, M.D. I would be honored to attend," the young doctor said in some sort of Frenchy accent.

Mrs. St. Rochelle's eyes narrowed. She disliked something about Landry. Boylan felt triumphant. The touring car arrived at that moment. The chauffeur jumped out to open the doors and pack the family and their guests into the auto.

The ride was brief. A servant stood waiting at the

door to take their coats and hats. More servants waited in the large formal dining room, all dark mahogany, white linen, and shining silver. Black faces above red bow ties and white dinner jackets smiled in welcome.

As the house filled with other guests, the servants lifted lids of silver chafing dishes, releasing gusts of steam and the scent of well-spiced meats and fresh seafood. They spooned out generous portions onto china plates.

"Oyster chowder, suh?" The first Negro held up his ladle and a small soup cup.

"I don't care for oysters. Slimy devils." Burke moved along the line.

"Grits and grillades, suh? Rabbit salmis? Crab cakes?"

Burke eyed the snowy grits and meaty gravy, the meat pies and browned patties. "No. I'll just have a slice of that ham, a serving of the eggs, some fried potatoes, a piece of that French bread."

Behind Boylan in the line, Pierre Landry accepted small portions of all offered to him. His own mother had no patience with people who picked over their food. Having enough to eat was God's blessing, and what was served made no never mind. One gave thanks and ate fast before the rest of the children grabbed what was placed on the table. But then, Boylan, a privileged bounder, had looked at the St. Rochelle's golden daughter as if she were a piece of decorated cake that only a wealthy man could partake of.

Hot cocoa and rich, black coffee laced with chicory stood available in urns on the sideboard. Enough small French pastries to stock a bakery were arranged in tiers around the beverages. Boylan popped a bite-sized éclair into his mouth and searched the room for Rosamond. Not seeing her, he wandered into the hallway where guests still arrived. Beyond the dining room, a dark carved mahogany door opened and closed. The aroma of fine cigars and brandy wafted over him, the smell of affluence and power. Burke drifted in that direction until he heard Madame St. Rochelle admonishing her daughters who had perched themselves on the central staircase to eat their feast.

"Rosamond, you have eaten enough. Please go into the parlor and entertain our guests at the piano. Roxanne, finish your plate, then go up to bed."

"Yes, Mama," the girls answered in unison.

Rosamond set aside a plate still piled with grits and grillades and took a small sip of her cocoa. She rolled her eyes at Burke as soon as her mama turned her back. Roxanne held a finger to her lips, then slid down the steps and disappeared into the crowded parlor. Rosamond followed, drawing Burke after her.

He passed Dr. Landry who held a plate piled high with a dab of all the food offerings. Boylan thought the man ate like one who seldom had access to good, rich food. The doctor savored every bite—and looked at Rosamond with hungry eyes.

Seating herself at a well-tuned Playel upright, Rosamond picked out the notes of *Silent Night* and sang softly in a pleasant, but not superior voice. The younger set separated from their parents and gathered round to join in the song. Burke shoved through the group to claim the honor of turning the pages of music for the pianist.

But damn, that annoying doctor had put down his plate and followed. In the excellent electric light of the parlor chandelier, Boylan had to concede that his competition was darkly handsome. Black hair slicked straight back with oil, dusky eyes fixed on the St. Rochelle's oldest daughter, Landry leaned with casual grace against the side of the piano. Artie, much smaller without his coat, bent over and murmured a request in Rosamond's ear.

The dark carved door in the hallway opened again. Laurence St. Rochelle emerged, his coffee cup reeking of brandy. His brother, Dr. Gilbert St. Rochelle, fragrant Cuban cigar still in-hand, accompanied him to the doorway of the parlor.

"That lad who came with you has Valentino eyes, Gil, and they are looking at my daughter. What can you tell me about him?"

"That is my erstwhile understudy, Pierre Boniface Landry of Chapelle, Louisiana."

"A Cajun? I didn't know they could read and write, let alone study medicine."

Gilbert took another puff of his cigar. "Oh, he claims all his brothers and sisters have finished the sixth grade. It seems his family has a great respect for education. As the seventh son of a seventh son, he was supposed to be apprenticed to the local herb healer and *traiteur* at the age of thirteen, but old Doc Spivey up in Chapelle stepped in and claimed the boy as his protégé. Got him all the way through high school by paying Pierre to do work around the clinic so the family wouldn't want for income."

"I suppose the backwaters are in need of doctors, and only locals would consider living there."

"Yes, you see before you a young man sent through college and medical school on the proceeds of cake walks and gumbo dinners. I feed him whenever I can and don't want to know where he lives."

"I don't care for his look or his background."

"Oh yes, our Pierre is quite the sheik. I know he picks up extra cash examining Madam Josie's girls once a month. The word is he always gets a free poke as well. He has a way with women. I've told him more than once he could get rich with an exclusive gynecology practice here in the city."

"You will warn him away from Rosamond. I won't have him creeping into her tent, so to speak."

"That won't be a problem. He is due to finish his studies and return to the bayou to take over from Spivey. Cajuns are loyal to their own, just as we are. I know a few nurses who would follow Pierre there gladly, but I'm sure his family will want him to marry a nice Catholic country girl with no plans other than having babies and keeping house. It's a pity, you know, that Rosamond was not permitted to pursue her interest in nursing."

"No daughter of mine is going to spend her life emptying bed pans and taking orders from arrogant physicians like you. The nuns at Mt. Carmel Academy may have straightened her out, but they also filled her head with nonsense about serving humanity. Rosamond will marry well and take her place in society. There are plenty of charities that will welcome her efforts. We expect the Krewe's selection committee to call tomorrow."

"Ah, so you have managed to make Rosamond a Mardi Gras queen despite her past lapses."

"It took enormous effort on my part, but her mother would have it no other way."

"Naturally, having been the queen of two balls, Emmaline would want the same for her daughter. What about the burly page-turner with the blond hair that looks like he had it marcelled at a beauty salon, another beau for Rosamond?"

As if he had overheard the conversation, Burke Boylan turned toward the men and nodded. The carol finished, Rosamond searched through some music and started a new selection. She banged out the opening chords of *If You Knew Susie.*

"Burke Boylan of Philadelphia, a law student and friend of the Delamares. He says his mother is Genevieve Renard. Do you remember Gen?"

"Indeed I do. Coldest pale blue eyes in the hot South. I see the son has inherited that look. So, he does have a connection to the city."

"His father attended Tulane law and took Genevieve back to Philadelphia with him."

"That was quite the coup, carrying off a queen of Rex."

"Yes, well, I expect cunning in a lawyer is a good thing. I won't have Rosamond carried off to a foreign place. If Boylan wants to court her, he had better plan on practicing in New Orleans."

"And you call me arrogant." Gilbert St. Rochelle shook his head. "Try not to take away all of Rosamond's choices, Laurence. Sending her away to the Academy may have given your daughter the veneer of a lady, but beneath it all, I suspect she is still a rebel."

In a space cleared around the piano, Artie Delamare jazzed it up to the tune of *Susie*—rolling his eyes, kicking up his heels, and flashing his hands. Right beside him, Roxanne St. Rochelle, long braids flying, mimicked Artie as Rosamond beat out the tune. Madame St. Rochelle saw and, scandalized, rushed past her husband and brother-in-law.

"No, no, no. This will not do. This is a holy evening. Rosamond, you will play something more appropriate. Roxanne, you will excuse yourself from the party."

"Yes, Mama," the daughters answered.

Roxanne executed a pert curtsy holding out her white pleated shirt. "*Adieu, adieu, adieu*," she said as she backed out of the room. As soon as her mother turned toward Rosamond, the little flirt blew Artie a kiss. A small round of applause broke out and was silenced by one look from Madame St. Rochelle. Rosamond began playing *Hark the Herald Angels Sing* a bit more stridently than written, and other voices joined in.

Guests departed slowly over the next two hours. At last, Dr. St. Rochelle summoned his intern and gave his sister-in-law a peck on the cheek in farewell. Pierre Landry took the hand of his hostess. In that slightly accented voice betraying the fact that the Cajun patois had been his only language before entering elementary school, he said, "*Merci beaucoup* for having me at your *reveillon*. I passed a very pleasant evening."

Pierre's warm hand, his dark eyes gazing so sincerely into hers, made Madame St. Rochelle draw back a step. As she suspected, he was precisely the kind of inappropriate young man she would have found attractive in her youth, but she had accepted Laurence as her parents wished, and it had been a good marriage. Rosamond must keep that in mind.

"Any guests Gilbert brings are welcome of course." She withdrew her hand, making it clear Dr. Landry would not be welcome otherwise, and turned toward the next departing guest.

Pierre Landry stepped aside. He had been allowed to bask in the glow of the lovely Rosamond all evening, but would never be accepted as Boylan was. A pity. He recognized Boylan as a swine who saw only the pretty package and not the spark or determination of the woman to be something other than another society deb. If, as Dr. Landry, he set up a practice in the city, he would have an abundance of upper class matrons to attend. Some might take him as a lover, but none would give up their cushy lives to marry him. As for any of them going to live on the bayou as the wife of a country doctor—what a laughable idea. No, Rosamond St. Rochelle was not for him no matter how much he might desire her.

Madame St. Rochelle concentrated on Burke Boylan and her daughter.

"I'm so glad we met this evening, Miss St. Rochelle."

"Please, call me Roz."

"And you must call me Buster. All my frat brothers do. But, Roz, that's too harsh a name for a lovely lady. I shall call you Rosie."

Rosamond wrinkled her nose. She had spent the last two years ridding herself of that childish nickname. She saw her mother watching. "How delightful," she answered.

Young Dr. Landry still lurked in the doorway. "Shouldn't you be on your way? Gilbert left several minutes ago," Madame St. Rochelle prompted.

"He is bringing the auto. Mr. Boylan and Mr. Delamare are riding with us, Madame."

"I see. Here comes Gilbert now. Mr. Boylan, your ride has arrived."

Burke strolled, chatting with Rosamond, to the door. Artie wiggled his fingers at the base of the staircase, then hurried after them. To her mother's dismay, Rosamond took Dr. Landry's hand and looked into his dangerous eyes. "So glad you could come, Dr. Landry. Please visit again."

"That would be a pleasure if my schedule should allow it. I will remember to call you Roz." He bent over Rosamond's hand, his breath heating her flesh, his lips not quite touching her skin.

"Gilbert is waiting," Madame prompted again and waved the young men out the door with Artie Delamare still shrugging into his hideous raccoon coat. As the door closed behind them, Madame St. Rochelle took a deep breath. The evening had gone very well with only that small lapse instigated by the Delamare boy. As for Burke Boylan, what a triumph it would be to have haughty Genevieve Renard Boylan's son at Rosamond's feet.

"Rosamond, it's time to retire. You will need your rest. We expect special guests tomorrow, and you must be at your best." Madame St. Rochelle clapped her hands.

"I suppose." Her daughter sighed and ascended the staircase to her bedroom.

From the shadow of a massive pier table in the upper hallway, Roxanne whispered, "May I come to your room, Roz?"

"Sure, kiddo. Don't let Mama see you out here in

your nightie and bare feet."

In the safety of her sister's bedroom, Roxie stretched out on the feather-filled gold satin comforter and watched Rosamond undress. "Did you see Artie wave to me? I think he's the butterfly's boots."

"Artie Delamare is a silly boy. I doubt if he will ever pass the bar exam. Now, Dr. Landry, you can see compassion and dedication in his eyes. Unbutton me, will you? I don't want to call a maid at this hour."

Roxanne fiddled with the tiny pearl buttons down the back of her sister's dress. "Dr. Landry has eyes like the sheik of Araby, and Burke Boylan's eyes are like an icy blue sea. I don't know which one gives me the most frissons."

Rosamond hung her dress on a padded hanger scented with potpourri. "You're twelve years old, Roxie. You shouldn't be having frissons over men."

She loosened the heavy mass of blonde hair gathered at the base of her neck and flipped the pins into a china dish on the dressing table. "I wish Mama would let me bob my hair like all the other girls."

"Me, too." Roxie twisted her braids. "But long hair is a woman's crowning glory."

"How many times have I heard that?" Rosamond pulled the silk underslip over her head and shrugged out of her camisole. Wearing only a breast band and step-ins, she rolled down her stockings and draped them over a chair. Flinging on a white cotton nightgown, she wiggled out of the rest of her undergarments and let them drop.

"Doesn't it hurt to bind yourself that way?" Roxie asked.

"Only when I'm near my monthlies. My biggest

fear is that I'll end up as huge as Mama. Even now they come near to ruining the line of my clothes." She gave her sister a quick glance. "Has Mama told you about your monthlies?"

"If you mean The Curse, yes. I think it must be horrible to have that and a big bosom, too."

"Not so horrible. It's a simple biological function that permits women to have children, and we have breasts for the same reason. I told Mama if she didn't speak to you, I would. My first time, I thought I was dying. If I'd been allowed to become a nurse, I could have given instruction to young girls like you." Rosamond ran a brush through her hair, then turned to her dressing table and removed the light makeup her mother allowed with cold cream and a cotton pad.

Bored with the topic of her impending womanhood, Roxie flopped back on to the bed. "So do you think the Mardi Gras committee will come tomorrow with a proclamation to make you queen of Papa's krewe?"

"I suppose. Mama should be pleased. I kept my part of the deal."

"When I was being seen but not heard, Mama told one of her lady friends that she sent you to Europe last summer before you could shred your reputation any further."

"That's not exactly true. I wanted to tour with Tante Harriet and said I didn't give a care about my reputation if I couldn't go. We agreed that when I came back I would play the perfect ingenue from then until Mardi Gras."

"It's true you haven't been much fun since you came home, but I love the shawl you brought me."

"Spanish dancers wear them. Mama still thinks they're mantillas. And Spanish men—hot, hot, hot."

"Like Dr. Landry?"

"Exactly. Move over, kiddo. You can spend the night, but no more talking. All this proper behavior has worn me out."

****

With headlamps barely showing the way, Dr. St. Rochelle drove down one of the narrow streets of the Vieux Carre, intersected broad Canal Street with its neutral ground and headed toward Tulane with his burden of young men. Concentrating on peering through a miserable drizzle, he barely paid attention to Artie Delamare's chatter. Burke Boylan interrupted his buddy. "Your niece, Rosamond, is an absolutely charming young woman, Dr. St. Rochelle."

"I suppose so. She was a hellion not too long ago. I remember Mardi Gras, the year she turned fourteen. Rosamond was supposed to dress as a medieval princess and view the parades from the safety of a family friend's balcony. Instead, she crept out Mardi Gras morning, put on blackface, rags, and a wig and spent the day disguised as a pickaninny. Of course, she hadn't filled out back then, and people took her for a boy. She returned home well after dark with a burlap sack full of trinkets. My sister-in-law had taken to her bed by then with the megrims, but when she arose, she shipped Roz off to the Academy in Rainbow to be reformed by the nuns. Evidently, there isn't much trouble a young lady can get into at a girl's school in the middle of nowhere."

Pierre Landry laughed out loud. "You can get into plenty of mischief in the country."

"She certainly seems reformed now," Burke persisted.

"I don't know about that. The nuns allowed her to come home for a Mardi Gras holiday last year, and she brought several young ladies from the Academy with her. While my brother and I were having a smoke at the Boston Club, a hired truck with a five piece band pulled up in front, and six lissome cancan girls tumbled out—red wigs, masks, black stockings, petticoats, and ruffled panties—of which the men crowding the balcony saw plenty. They finished their dance and drove away to thunderous applause, but I know my brother saw the same thing I did. The lead dancer's wig had slipped and a long blonde braid hung down her back. Now, how many girls do you know who haven't bobbed their hair yet?"

"Roz, she has a bold spirit," Landry said.

"Surely, it wasn't her. Probably just some ladies of the evening showing off," answered Boylan.

"Most of the men at the club would agree with you, Boylan, but others had their suspicions. Still, Roz graduated with honors last spring and shocked her family again by announcing that she wanted to go into nursing."

"A noble profession," Landry agreed.

"St. Rochelle women do not work, Pierre. They marry and do good deeds through their husbands' charitable trusts. Roz went off to Europe with her aunt and returned to enroll in Newcomb as a fine arts major. Since then, she has been quite subdued. I rather miss the old, unpredictable Rosamond. She reminds me of my late wife in her heyday."

"She's just grown up as she must. There's nothing

sad about that when you have wealth and beauty, too," Burke pointed out.

"Let me out at the corner, doctor. I'll walk the rest of the way. *Joyeux Noel, mes amis,*" Landry said.

Glad to be gone from the present company, Pierre Landry got down from the car and walked toward the mouth of an alley where two bedraggled hookers sharing a cigarette under a torn awning greeted him by name. He stopped and gave each one a gold-banded Cuban cigar acquired at the St. Rochelle house, to smoke or to sell as they wished. "*Joyeux Noel,*" he said again. Even whores should have a gift for Christmas.

"Well, you can take the boy from the bayou, but you can't wash out the low-life. His family probably trapped the furs for your coat, Artie." Boylan fingered his own stash of cigars pocketed on the inside of his coat.

"Actually, Landry is one the most apt pupils I've had in years. He is well ahead of his class and will probably be setting up his practice in Chapelle before next Christmas. Unlike lawyers, he won't be getting rich as a country doctor off his clients' misery. Where can I let you out?" Dr. St. Rochelle asked, thoroughly tired of snobbery for the evening.

"At our fraternity house. It's just another mile or so. We certainly wish Dr. Landry Godspeed in his career, don't we, Artie?"

"Sure, God bless us, everyone."

Chapter Two

"Get up, Rosamond! Your father has been hinting for the last half hour that our special guests are on their way. Roxanne, go to your own room and dress right this minute. Have Odile brush out your hair. Rosamond, put on the red and green plaid dress with the demure white collar. Wear your hair down, too. You'll look like a young Mary Pickford, so innocent. I'll send Odette to assist you," Madame St. Rochelle ordered.

Roxie scampered out the door, but Roz merely stretched and yawned. "What time is it?"

"Time to get up if you want to be queen of Mardi Gras."

"I think I'd rather sleep." Despite the comment, Roz slid to the edge of the bed, put on a dressing gown, and took a seat before the mirrored table. While she cleansed her face with cold cream, no drying soap and water for the fair-skinned St. Rochelle women, her mother ranted on.

"No smart or sarcastic remarks to the men of the committee, Rosamond. Young women should not be known for their wit."

"Oh Mama, we got the vote in 1920 for Pete's sake. You know, if you let me bob and lighten my hair and use a tiny bit more eye makeup, I could look like the starlet, Carol Lombard, instead of Mary Pickford."

"No, no, and no. Someday, when the right man

comes along, he will glory in your hair, and you will thank me. Here's Odette to help you dress. *Mon Dieu*, I think I heard the door chime." Madame St Rochelle hustled out of the room only to poke her head back through the doorway. "It's your Uncle Gilbert. We still have time."

"Is Dr. Landry with him?"

"Of course not. This is a day only for family."

"And the Mardi Gras committee."

"I warn you, Rosamond, no shenanigans. I must check on the refreshments. Odette, carry on."

The middle-aged black maid smiled pleasantly. "Yes, ma'am. Let me comb out your beautiful hair, Miss Rosamond."

"If it were short, I could take care of it myself."

"Enough!" Madame St. Rochelle went to badger the cook.

****

Having stopped for some illicit Christmas cheer away from their wives, the committee members were tardy. By the time they arrived with their archaic scroll in hand, Rosamond sat by the fireplace with her hands folded in her lap and her feet crossed at the ankles. Her hair, secured with a childish red bow and shining deep gold in the firelight, hung down her back nearly to her waist. At least, Odette had arranged some spit curls across her forehead and beside her cheeks. Roz kept her eyes downcast as the merry and well-lit gentlemen of the committee read their proclamation.

"Know ye all men: This document attests to the fact that Miss Rosamond St. Rochelle shall serve as Queen of the Carnival so her beauty, modesty, and virtue may be displayed before all on the glorious date of Mardi Gras in the year 1926. The King himself hath so commanded. This decree is presented and witnessed to by the Committee of Fifty."

Rosamond, keeping her bargain, nodded and replied, "I am so very honored."

Her mother hurried to offer the best of last night's leftover pastries and cups of eggnog. Her father came around with a bottle and topped off all but Rosamond's glass with a mighty fine rum from the locked cabinet in his smoking room. Toasts were made, congratulations offered, hands shaken, and the committee went on its way.

Uncle Gilbert sat next to Rosamond who had barely moved through the whole ordeal and still clutched the scroll she had been given. "It won't be so bad, Rosie. Even your dear Tante Harriet served as queen of one ball, and it didn't cramp her style a bit."

"I miss her so much. We had such a marvelous time in Europe. She knew all the best cafés and most interesting places to go. When she began feeling ill on the cruise home, I didn't stay by her bedside. She kept saying, 'Go have fun, Roz. Dance. Meet young men,' and I did. I think I am bound to be a disappointment to my family all my life."

"Not today, surely, and never to your Aunt Harriet. You couldn't know she had a fast moving leukemia of the blood. No matter how hard I tried, she died by October. It's good to know someone else misses her as much as I do."

"The holidays won't be the same without her. Did Dr. Landry go home to celebrate?"

"No, he's covering any calls that might come in today. He said some of his family is involved with grinding the sugar cane, and they'll have a party and exchange gifts on Twelfth Night when the harvest is over."

"Oh, I hoped—"

The door chimes rang again. Odette announced that Mr. Delamare and Mr. Boylan had come to call. Rosamond heard her mother greet them in a rather pleased voice with, "Back so soon, gentlemen?"

"Here's some young company for you. Artemus informed us all last night that he wanted to go on the stage, but his father forbade him. I suspect that's why he is always entertaining. Enjoy." Rosamond's uncle squeezed her hand and went off to cloud his lungs with cigars and his mind with bootleg liquor in the smoking room.

The new arrivals took seats on either side of Roz. "So you got your scroll, Rosamond. Good for you, but where is the other princess of the family? There she is, sitting in the corner. Dear child, I've brought sheet music. Let's go cut a rug."

"May I, Mama?" Roxie asked, her cheeks already red with expectation.

"I suppose." Her wish was granted.

"Great curls, kiddo." Artie ruffled her long brown hair.

"Usually it's straight as a board and not very pretty, but if I sleep in braids, it turns out this way."

"Another feminine mystery revealed. You know Boylan there sleeps in a hair net to keep his waves in place."

"No fooling?"

"Why don't you go play a rag or something, Artie, while I talk to Rosie?" Burke suggested none too subtly. After all, Artie was supposed to keep the kid sister occupied while he made his moves. His friend took the hint and removed himself from the sitting room to the parlor.

"These are for you, Rosie, winter roses." Burke offered a cluster of blood red camellias. "I got them off a little Negro boy sitting outside the French Market on our way over here. Their color reminded me of your lips."

"Why, Buster, how gallant." Of course, two similar bushes full of the things bloomed by the dependency where the wash was done in the backyard, and these flowers would be dead by tomorrow, but how could a Yankee know, Roz thought.

Madame St. Rochelle cleared her throat. "Eggnog, Mr. Boylan?"

"Please, call me Buster. I prefer it to Burke."

"Buster—like the shoes they sell at Holmes?"

"No, I fought on the boxing team at Princeton and did quite well. Buster, like this." Burke made a fist and slammed it into his open palm. "I took some medals in my time there."

Rosamond looked at Burke with new interest, and Boylan recognized it. He was much thicker through the chest and shoulders than that slim, sloe-eyed Pierre Landry. Women liked muscle on men who knew how to use it.

Laurence St. Rochelle entered, still smoking his cigar. His wife waved a hand before her nose, but he ignored the hint. This was his house. He'd smoke where he wanted. "Good to hear some young men still take an interest in fisticuffs and haven't all turned into degenerates."

"I can assure you that if Rosamond is with me, sir, she will be perfectly safe even in the French Quarter."

"They should tear the place down and put up some decent buildings. The Quarter is nothing but a den of vice," Laurence St. Rochelle intoned.

"It is part of our French heritage, Laurence." Mrs. St. Rochelle turned to Boylan, ready to enlist another in her cause. "My husband is a banker. His only thought is how much revenue new skyscraper buildings will bring. I, on the other hand, am working on the committee to restore the Vieux Carre. When Rosamond takes her place in society, I am sure she will work right beside me."

"Oh, I love the French Quarter just as it is, Mrs. St. Rochelle, and go there often," Burke agreed.

The sound of the Charleston being banged out on the piano drowned the conversation and drew the family toward the parlor. Roxie twirled the long rope of knotted pearls she had begged her mother to let her wear on Christmas day and did the steps Artie had just taught her.

"Oh, my!" said Madame St. Rochelle.

"Degenerate," mumbled her husband under his breath as he headed toward the piano. "Young man, I don't suppose you've ever won any boxing medals."

"No, sir, but I won a dance marathon once. That takes stamina, you know." Artie stopped playing when he saw the look on old man St. Rochelle's face.

"Thank you for visiting," Madame St. Rochelle said.

****

"And thank you, Artie, for getting us tossed out of the St. Rochelle mansion just when I was making time with Rosie and her parents," Boylan griped as they returned to his rooms. He took a swig from his hip flask and ignored Artie's outstretched hand.

"I have to go home for Christmas dinner now, so I'm being punished enough, don't you think?" Artie beckoned for the flask. "Besides, I kept the baby sister occupied. They can be real pests, you know."

"The St. Rochelles won't be adding me to their guest list for the Mardi Gras ball now, all because of you."

"Not a problem, Brother Buster. I'll get Pops to put you on our list. The theme this year is Masterpieces of Art, and if he expects me to dress in some ridiculous costume for the tableaux, he can do me a favor, too. Last year, the theme was Atlantis, and I spent the whole evening waddling around in a fish costume." Artie fluffed his raccoon coat and checked the center part in his hair in Boylan's mirror to make sure the two dark wings still swooped in place above his ears.

"I thought the plans were all hush-hush."

"They are. The Krewe of Hercules is so exclusive they don't parade, and the balls are a bore—some elaborate tableaux, a parade by the court, and then call out dances for the debs. Everyone else watches. You won't get a dance with Rosamond. The middle-aged king will whisk her off to a late dinner. We'd have more fun dancing at the Holland House."

"But you can get me in?" Buster passed the flask at last.

"Sure. I can get you Christmas dinner, too. At least, the food will be better than anything they're serving in Philly. You don't miss your family?"

"They don't miss me, but that is about to change.

When I marry Rosamond St. Rochelle, a woman with a background like my dear mother, all will be forgiven. She will be my ticket back into the loving arms of the Boylan clan. Rosamond and my law degree will pay any debts I owe the family."

"I say, shouldn't you feel something for the girl before you marry her?"

"I do feel something—right down here between my legs—for my own pure, virgin debutante. Except for the southern manners, Rosamond is exactly like the debs back in the City of Brotherly Love. They all want to marry wealth and live in style. Who doesn't matter very much. We'll have the required child or two, then live out our lives separately in perfect civility. What's for Christmas dinner?"

"Goose, I think, with oyster dressing."

"How appropriate. You have any sisters, Artie?" Boylan settled a dark fedora carefully over the waves in his blond hair and buttoned his topcoat.

"No, and I wouldn't introduce you if I did."

Chapter Three

New Year's Eve at the Southern Yacht Club should have been the berries, but by eleven-thirty, Rosamond St. Rochelle prayed for some excitement. She pushed herself up from the cream-colored wicker chair in the ladies' lounge where she had been resting her feet and checked her makeup in a mirror. Mama had made her wear virginal white again, but the addition of a crystal brow band and white plume in her hair did add some style.

The band struck up another waltz, and Roz supposed she should return to her parents' table and make herself available. She didn't lack for partners, but she suspected the musicians had been instructed to play only waltzes, foxtrots and two-steps, just as she had been instructed not to let any of the young men standing in line for a dance hold her too close. There would be no Charleston, Shimmy, or Black Bottom done tonight when all the dues-paying old fogeys attended.

Roz had managed to get the waiter to bring her a Pink Lady so sweet it covered the taste of the gin, but her mother immediately confiscated that and ordered another soft drink for her daughter. She might be able to cadge a cigarette from one of her partners, but then she would have to find a dark corner somewhere to smoke it. Well worth a try. Willard Morrison always had good smokes. Roz chose him for the next foxtrot.

Cigarette palmed, Rosamond headed for the lobby and the shrubbery beyond. By the light of her borrowed match, she noticed two late arrivals, her uncle and the dreamy Dr. Landry wearing obviously borrowed evening clothes. Holding her cigarette in a sophisticated pose between two fingers, she crept from the bushes and managed to intercept them on the path.

"Where have you been? You're so late! I just stepped out for a smoke." Roz took a drag and blew the smoke out into the night air.

"We had a complicated delivery. It was necessary to do a Cesarean section. Pierre assisted. Since when do you smoke, Rosamond?"

"Oh, I've been smoking forever," she answered her uncle airily. He frowned. "All right, since my trip to Europe, but I haven't had much practice with Mama watching everything I do."

"You know, those things will kill you," Pierre Landry told her. "Have you ever seen a smoker's lung? Black as sin, they are."

"Really? You don't smoke then?" Hastily, she dropped the cigarette and ground out the spark of red under her Cuban heel. Roz cocked her head and looked closely at Pierre in the flood of light pouring from the club windows. "Are you growing a mustache, Dr. Landry? That's very good progress for only one week."

The dark hair on his upper lip looked silky, unlike most men's rough bristles. It defined his upper lip, drew attention to an already sensual mouth, and took it away from his somewhat hawkish nose. He smiled, and the darkness of the mustache made his teeth seem even whiter and slightly feral.

"I thought I would get more respect from my

patients if I looked older."

"Nonsense," said Dr. St. Rochelle. "You get far too much attention from your patients already, though tonight you put it to good use convincing Mrs. O'Leary that neither she nor the baby had to die. Throwing in that bit about the scar not being repulsive to her husband added a nice touch. Who would have thought a woman in such travail would still be vain?"

"Not vain, just worried that she would lose her husband's love," answered Pierre.

"I can see why female patients adore you, but we're missing the party. It's nearly midnight, and I need a dance partner." Rosamond drew the new arrivals inside, but veered off to the dance floor with Pierre before her mother could see them.

He led her smoothly into a waltz. Peeking over his shoulder, Roz watched her parents greet Uncle Gilbert and saw her mother searching the crowd. She ducked down against Pierre's chest, dancing close, really close. A heavy hand jerked them to a stop on their circuit around the room.

"I'm cutting in, Landry," Burke Boylan declared, swaying a little on his boxer's feet.

"I'm sure Roz will save the next dance for you, Boylan."

"When did you get here, Buster?"

"Just now. I've been a few other places more fun than here, but I wanted to give my Rosie a kiss at midnight."

"I'm not your Rosie, Buster. Let go of Dr. Landry's arm."

"It's no matter, Roz. Have a dance with Boylan. I need fresh air." Pierre relinquished his partner to Burke and walked toward the balcony overlooking the lake.

Rosamond stumbled around the floor with Burke until he confessed the need to take a quick piss, pardon his language, and staggered off. Midnight approached. Any minute now, the band would play *Auld Lang Syne*, and cool glasses of champagne served because no policeman might dare raid the Southern Yacht Club on New Year's Eve. Roz slipped two drinks from a tray and went after Pierre where he stood alone among nuzzling couples on the balcony.

In the semi-darkness, he accepted the wine. "Thank you for thinking of me, Roz."

"I think of you all the time. I like the new mustache." She drew a finger across his upper lip, first one side, then the other. "It's as soft as it looks."

The crowd inside counted down to midnight. The band struck up the traditional tune, and noisemakers, confetti, and silly hats filled the air as if it were Carnival already. Out in the night, Roz rose on her toes and kissed the lips of Pierre Landry. She thought he shivered.

"Cold?" she asked.

"Hot." He bent over her, returning the kiss with warmth and gentleness and a subtlety that made her want more. Roz leaned in, and he nibbled the edge of her lips, persuading them to open for his tongue.

This time, the heavy hand descended on Rosamond's shoulder. "You're kissing my girl, Landry," Boylan said.

"I believe it's an old custom on New Year's Eve, Boylan, even in Philadelphia."

"Get your stinkin' Cajun hands off of her."

Burke tore Rosamond away and, bending her over

his arm, smashed a bourbon-flavored kiss on her lips. Roz struggled. Pierre jerked the bigger man off her. Boylan looked for his target and drew back for a roundhouse punch that would have broken the jaw of the slighter man if he had still been standing there to receive it. Pierre Landry stepped aside. The drunken momentum carried Buster over the railing. Other couples on the balcony gasped. Someone shouted, "Call a doctor!"

Pierre Landry threw back his head and laughed. "He fell into the bushes. Drunks always find a soft landing."

One of the fine young sheiks with his arm around his sheba leaned over the railing. "Look, he's up and ready to fight. Yowzah! He punched Artie Delamare and knocked down the flapper he was necking with in the shrubbery, too. Nice work, Boylan!"

Roz tugged his sleeve. "Please leave, Pierre. Somehow, they'll blame you because you're not one of us. Go before Mama sees."

"If that's what you want, Roz." He seemed disappointed in her, but he straightened his borrowed jacket and moved out into the crowded ballroom.

Roz counted to ten, then slipped back inside. Immediately, her mother beckoned from across the dance floor. "Come Rosamond, we must leave immediately. There's been a brawl. Some rowdy tossed Burke Boylan off the balcony. Your uncle has gone to attend to him, but we mustn't be associated with this incident. Quickly now, claim your wrap. Papa has called for the car."

Fortunately, Clement drove this evening. Mama had insisted. New Year's Eve was the one night her conservative husband was likely to overindulge. Laurence St. Rochelle settled into the backseat without an argument. Roz climbed in after him.

Her mother's broad bottom barely touched the leather when the lecture began. "Rosamond, do not try to deny that you were involved in that fracas on the balcony. I saw you sneak out after Dr. Landry, liquor in-hand. It's no wonder Burke tried to defend your honor."

"Buster was drunk, Mama, and he did not get thrown off the balcony. He fell. He got upset when I told him I wasn't his girl. It's absurd. We met only a week ago."

"Many a girl has fallen in love in less time. I suppose a young man could become smitten in a week. You might give Burke some encouragement. I did know his mother rather well, and his father's law firm is nationally known, but you must not incite any more brawls."

"This was just a scrape between young bucks, Emmaline. Most natural thing in the world. If our boys had lived, they would have had some scrapes. Yes, they would, but we lost them." A tear from his bleary blue eyes trickled down Laurence St. Rochelle's face.

"Laurence, you promised. No more of this. You still have two lovely daughters who will marry well and bring fine sons-in-law into the business. Someday, you will have grandsons. We must look ahead, not behind. By this time next year, our Rosie could be married and expecting."

"Damned Spanish influenza!" Laurence wiped his face with a clean white linen handkerchief. "I like Boylan. He's a man's man like Pete Herman or Pal

Moran. And, everyone overindulges a little on New Year's Eve. But, I wouldn't want Rosie to encourage that Cajun lad even if he is a doctor. None of my girls should marry down. Why, he'd carry you off to that backwater, Chapelle, and we'd never see you again."

"That's absurd, Papa. Your cousin André and his wife live there, and they visit quite often. Philadelphia is much farther away." Roz snuggled into her white fur wrap, warding off the night's damp chill.

"Yes, that's true. What did André do to get sentenced to a life in Chapelle?" Laurence rummaged through his bag of hazy memories. "Oh yes, he married a girl from there. A guest at one of the Mardi Gras balls, Loretta was. Love at first sight, André claimed. She didn't want to leave her mama, so the family opened a branch out there to give André a living. Poor sap."

The touring car passed Pierre Landry walking toward the streetcar stop. Rosamond looked back, but neither of her parents instructed Clement to offer a ride.

****

The hothouse roses, vermilion against the gray sky, arrived on January second. The note written by Burke Boylan read, "My Dearest Rosie, I am nursing a big head and a broken heart. Please forgive me for my boorish behavior at the Yacht Club. Jealousy drove me to it. With all my love, Buster."

The out-of-season flowers had cost Boylan a big chunk of the miserly Christmas check his old man sent. He watched from across the street as a maid accepted the bouquet. The lavish flowers ought to be effective in getting him back into Rosamond's good graces. All the girls he knew went for jazz like that. As for Pierre

Landry, he would get what was coming to him some day, too—though Artie warned all those Cajuns carried knives. Burke had been lucky to end up in the bushes with a few scrapes and bruises instead of a cut throat or broken neck. For now, Burke Boylan had to let Pierre Landry go, but not forever.

Chapter Four

Twelfth Night came and the revels of Mardi Gras began somewhat marred by rainy weather. The year 1926 seemed determined to be as wet and dreary as 1925, but the festivities in the City that Care Forgot went unhindered. The parades marched on even if the flambeaux that lit the night events were difficult to ignite, and the mules that pulled the floats occasionally slipped in flooded streets. Even the death of Mayor Behrman did not stop the revels, and the mayor would have wanted it so, Roz observed.

Rosamond collected enough silver charms from the King Cakes served at the numerous teas she attended to fill a bracelet. They promised her wealth and a husband, children and luck, but none guaranteed happiness. There were luncheons, of course, and balls. Many young men followed in her wake, though as the season progressed, these dwindled to Buster Boylan, Artie Delamare, and a few of their fraternity brothers who always seemed to cut out the others.

As for Pierre Landry, Rosamond had seen him only once as she rode the streetcar to her college. Pierre had been riding a car passing the other way. She waved frantically, and he lifted a hand and smiled. They watched each other out of sight, but the whole incident possessed more the feel of a farewell than a greeting as they moved farther and farther apart.

Roz continued to take a light schedule of classes at Newcomb. These resulted in the creation of one ugly pot and a knotted weaving. She knew more about Renaissance and Baroque artists than she ever wanted to know. The mystery, Rosamond felt, was how she could be so busy and so bored at the same time.

Of course, she had no objections to the new dresses filling her room, and though the fittings bordered on tedium, Leda Hincks Plauché, the renowned costume designer, was creating her queen's gown. Mama insisted the dress be white. When her daughter objected, saying rumor had it that the Queen of Rex would appear in gold lamé, Madame Plauché winked at Roz and promised that her cape would be covered in silver leaf and edged with ermine, every bit as fine and much more tasteful than anything Rex could offer. The crown would fit low over her head like a cloche hat and pearls dotted her dress. Her father intended to provide a diamond choker and two matching bracelets. Her outfit would be beyond compare.

The never-ending argument cropped up again. "My crown would fit better if my hair were bobbed. Wouldn't it look stunning if I could lighten the color just a little, Madame Plauché?"

This time the grande dame of costume shook her head. "If the arrangement of your hair is a problem, you could always wear it down, Rosamond. That would be charming."

Win some, lose some. Roz conceded the battle.

With the passing days, Rosamond felt herself becoming more and more the daughter her parents wanted and less and less Roz, the woman she wanted to be. The devil-may-care, caution-to-the-wind flapper sat on the sofa holding hands with Burke Boylan while he and her father talked about the latest boxing matches at the Holland House.

In rare moments unchaperoned, she submitted to Buster's crushing, unpracticed kisses and roving hands while wondering if she would feel less indifferent to Dr. Landry's caresses. Her Aunt Harriet had considered some sexual experience essential to Rosamond's education, providing the girl did not go all the way, and so Roz knew that the men of France, Spain and Italy could bring a woman to climax with their hands and tongues alone. Buster wanted to wring a response from her with bear hugs and rough squeezes.

When she questioned her uncle about where Pierre Landry was and what he did, the answers were always "at the hospital" or "very busy." Finally exasperated, Gilbert said, "You must know, Rosie, your parents do not want me to bring him here. Pierre knows his place in society, and you should assume yours." Judging by her vanishing entourage, society assumed Rosamond St. Rochelle had become Boylan's girl.

As the frenzy of Mardi Gras day approached, the parades rolled day and night, and the elite danced at their *bal masques* late into the evening. On Saturday so as not to conflict with the balls of Comus and Rex, the Krewe of Hercules held its grand event at the Orpheum. Rosamond and her court sat in a box adjacent to the stage to view the carefully constructed tableaux of Great Masterpieces of Art.

Slim young men in marbled tights, their faces and hair a stark grayish white, stood on columns and struck the poses of famous classical statues. Each was wheeled forward by attendant Greek slaves to be viewed by the audience. They were followed by the entire company of the Rembrandt's *Night Watch,* who could walk off under their own power after striking the scene.

A picture by Hieronymus Bosch full of grotesques and tiny devils drew the most laughter and applause until the *pièce de résistance*, *Leda and the Swan*. Full-feathered and wide of wing, the magnificent swan glided onto the stage to settle himself between the legs of a very voluptuous and Rubenesque Leda on her ornate couch. The rolls of white flesh, the prominent breasts in their gold halter, wild, tangled hair and twisted draperies must be disguising only one person— Willard Morrison—and the swan—who else but Artie Delamare? Rosamond applauded wildly as the swan, exhausted from impregnating Leda, rested his long neck on her alabaster thigh.

The lights dimmed. A large golden egg rolled onto the stage. It cracked and expelled a dainty Helen and a gorgeous Pollux. Each carried away their half of the egg, and King Hercule, as the French called him, was revealed in all his glory: the paunchy middle-aged businessman well concealed beneath padded tights and a real lion skin, the head of which formed a mask over his eyes. A gilded beard hung down on the king's chest concealing any lack of muscles. Behind him, small pages held up a purple cloak embroidered in gold with the Twelve Labors of Hercules. In one hand, the king held a scepter and in the other, a jeweled cup. He approached Rosamond, his Queen Hebe, on golden sandals and offered a toast. King Hercule beckoned his consort from her box.

Rosamond, her attendants carrying her cape of silver leaf, crystal, and pearl edged in ermine, joined the king on the stage for the final procession. The magnificence of the cape far eclipsed her white dress with its handkerchief hem of lace and droplets of pearl and crystal, but the diamonds her daddy provided caught the light and threw it back at the audience. Burke Boylan and Rosamond's proud family rose and applauded with the rest as the court left the theater for a midnight dinner at one of the finest restaurants in the city. Rosamond had done as she was asked, and the rest of Mardi Gras belonged to her alone.

Chapter Five

Roz slept past noon as expected. She was finally rousted and convinced to dress by Roxanne who said Artie and Buster had arrived to take them walking in City Park and for an ice cream float if only her sister would get up and put on some clothes. Once more, Roz did something to please a member of her family.

The sun had come out and coaxed the bedraggled mounds of azaleas to open their pink and purple blooms. Wearing tilted straw boaters, Buster and Roz, Artie and Roxanne relished the soft spring air as they walked arm-in-arm along the paths. They reached the Holland House and went inside by way of the ladies entrance. The promised sodas were ordered and served. Roz felt kindly toward Buster and Artie and relaxed in a way she hadn't been for weeks. Her reign as Queen Hebe was over. She could be herself again. She hinted to Buster that she would rather have a Manhattan from the discreetly placed bar, but he kidded her out of it by saying, "Not in front of the children." Both Roxanne and Artie made faces at them.

Claiming she wanted nothing more than to sleep away Monday, Roz got them back to the mansion on Esplanade early. Roxie could call her a killjoy all she wanted; Rosamond St. Rochelle had other plans for the rest of Mardi Gras.

Early on Lundi Gras, the Monday before the big

celebration, she asked Clement to take her to visit her Uncle Gilbert. After all, he must be missing Aunt Harriet dreadfully. Harri had so loved Mardi Gras. Her attic was filled with trunks of costumes from years past, and in one corner stood her own queen's gown on a dress form and covered with a muslin sheet. As a child, Roz had played for hours with the clothes in the attic, never particularly wanting to be the queen so much as a pirate or a soldier of the Great War. When she outgrew her tomboy days, her favorite disguise became the Spanish gypsy with its skirt of orange and yellow flounces and bright red blouse. If she deserved any divine reward for her good behavior the last six weeks, the costume would be right on top in the second trunk on the left.

Her uncle, as she had figured, was attending to patients in plentiful supply after the pre-Mardi Gras weekend. Servants who had known Rosamond from early childhood saw nothing wrong in letting her rummage through the trunks in her Aunt Harriet's attic and helping herself to some old stuff she put in a worn pillowcase to carry. Harriet St. Rochelle would never deny her favorite niece anything.

Roz hid the sack in the dependency near the washtubs and across from the old privy the servants used. The house would be lightly staffed on Mardi Gras day since the family went out to dine elsewhere. What a snap to slip into her costume and be on the streets before the parade of Rex rolled if her mother accepted her excuse for staying home.

Mardi Gras morning, Roz joined her family for a breakfast of early strawberries, fresh orange juice, dark coffee diluted with steamed milk, and hot beignets smothered in powdered sugar. Today, she could have devoured a dozen of the pillowy doughnuts and eaten ripe strawberries until the juice ran down her chin, but that would belie her story. She nibbled, sipped her coffee, and winced.

After Papa left the table, Roz lowered her voice and told her mother, "Cramps. I'm afraid my monthly may be starting. If I spend the afternoon lying down, I might be able to attend the ball this evening."

"But, Rosamond, we have seats in the stands by the Boston Club. Don't you want to see the queen of Rex in her gold lamé?"

"I'll see her at the ball. If Odette would bring a hot water bottle to my room, I'll be fine. Have a good time without me."

When the front door closed behind her family, Roz tossed the hot water bottle aside and tiptoed quietly down the stairs, across the yard, and out to the dependency. She wore dark sheer stockings under her nightgown, shoes fit for dancing on her feet, and the Spanish shawl over her shoulders. In the cover of the old building, she traded her nightie for the gypsy's red silk blouse. Without vest or binding, her breasts felt large and loose. She'd forgotten about the daringly low cut bodice of the costume.

The tiered ruffles of the skirt that dragged on the floor when she was a child now hung barely below her knees. She wrapped a long orange scarf around her waist and knotted it over a hip. The silly yellow bloomers that went under the skirt, she pushed up all the way on her thighs.

Wrapping her braids tightly around her head and pinning them in place, Roz settled a wig of real human hair over her own. The wig was dark, lustrous, and curly. Her aunt never scrimped on Mardi Gras accessories, and some Italian girl had probably been paid well to part with her tresses. Over the wig, Roz tied a bright bandana gypsy style.

The bottom of the sack yielded a pile of cheap jewelry. Roz fished out a coin necklace, hoop earrings, and enough bangles to put four on each arm. Using a hand mirror, she painted her lips a deep carmine, and rouged her cheeks like a hootchy-kootchy dancer. She darkened her brows and eyelashes, and for the finishing touch slid on the black half mask. Swinging her Spanish shawl over her shoulders, Rosamond St. Rochelle stepped out into the alley where deliveries were made and the rag-and-bone man drove his horse and cart to pick up discards and began her Mardi Gras celebration. Oh, the freedom!

She joined the crowds on Chartres Street, accepted a drink from a sailor's bottle, but twirled away when he tried to grab her waist. She jumped aside when a car full of prostitutes dressed in tuxedos and smoking cigars barreled down the narrow street. They swigged from their own bottle and called to passing women, "Hey, hot Mama!" doing a fairly good imitation of their customers. From a balcony, a fat man tossed her a necklace of tawdry glass jewels. Roz hung it around her neck.

On a cross street, she intercepted the two palmetto-covered floats of the Zulu Parade with its Negro men dressed in blackface, their eyes and lips ringed in white, making a daring loop into the French Quarter. Their mules pulled up in front of an Italian eatery.

"I say, I say, King Zulu gots a big thirst, a mighty

thirst. Who can slake this thirst of mine!" King Zulu, with his crown of gold paper and mantle of purple velvet, pointed his scepter, a large zucchini, at the good natured proprietor who looked both ways before handing up a raffia-covered jug of cheap red wine. King Zulu drank deeply, then passed the jug around the float. "Witch doctor, give that man one o' my special signed coconuts, then get these mules headed back to niggah town. King Zulu gots places to be."

The witch doctor in his grass skirt and horned headdress flipped the man a coconut. Looking directly at Roz, he held up a coconut carved like a hideous monkey. "Show me yo' coconuts, I throw you mine, hot Mama!" he challenged boldly, probably taking her for a whore trolling alone for business. Instead, Roz turned her back, flipped up her skirt showing off her absurd ruffled panties and the rolled tops of her stockings.

"Good 'nuf. Here it come."

Roz caught it two-handed and swung along the street holding the coconut by its fibers like a trophy taken by a headhunter. On any other day, the exchange would never have happened, but this was Mardi Gras, and the black man could be a Zulu warrior, and Rosamond St. Rochelle could be anyone she wanted to be.

Ravenous after her small breakfast, she bought a nickel hot dog from a vendor and wolfed it down. She broke out of the Quarter onto Canal Street and moved among the revelers until she came to an old Negro strumming a battered guitar for change.

"I'll trade you this coconut for a Spanish tune, good sir," she offered.

"Well," he scratched his head, "I'm guessin' I

could crack it and eat it. Sho', a Spanish tune, lez see."

The song he plucked from the old guitar was no fandango, but it had enough rhythm to pass for a dance tune. Rosamond twirled in her ruffled skirts and swung her Spanish shawl out behind her. Her breasts bobbed loose beneath the red silk blouse, and passersby, mostly male, threw nickles and pennies in the old man's case.

"You sho' good for business, honey. Keep it up."

Roz caught more necklaces tossed her way and draped them around her neck. She danced until she was breathless and dizzy, staggering with joy, not liquor.

Then, she saw him on the edge of the crowd watching her performance. He was dressed as Zorro in tight black trousers and a loose black shirt unbuttoned far enough to show a patch of dark chest hair. He wore the required cape and sword, and a black cloth mask pulled over his hair and half his face. His mustache was real, thicker now and longer at the sides than Roz remembered, but just as silky. She twirled his way, the crowd parting before her, until she collapsed against his chest.

"Buy a poor gypsy girl a drink, *Senor* Zorro?"

If he hadn't recognized her before, he knew her voice. He hadn't forgotten that or the softness of her lips, the boldness of their one kiss. "Certainly, *Senorita*. I know a place."

Arm around her waist, he drew her back into the Quarter. They entered a gumbo shop where customers sat before steaming bowls and side orders of potato salad and drank hot coffee or lemonade. Masks hung temporarily on the back of chairs as the people ate.

"Lemonade wasn't what I had in mind, *Senor*."

"Me neither, *Senorita*."

He scratched on a dingy door in the dim back of the shop. A peephole opened and then the door. A blast of music and the smell of gin and whiskey spilled out as the revelers slipped inside. They took seats at a corner table and tried to talk over the noise of a three-piece band with a trumpeter, a bass player, and a clarinetist blasting out a hot jazz tune. On the tiny dance floor, a lone flapper did the Black Bottom to the applause from a table of drunken seamen.

Weaving her way between the closely packed tables, a waitress in a black leotard and pink tutu came to take their orders. She drew a pencil from her red hair drawn up on top of her head in a dancer's bun and said, "What you drinkin'?"

"Oh, I'd like a Manhattan, please," Roz answered. Zorro grinned.

"We got gin. The whiskey ran out about an hour ago. You want it on the rocks, with tonic or straight?"

"Lovely *Senorita*, I don't suppose you would have a bottle of fine wine anywhere on the premises?" Zorro asked.

The waitress scratched her head with the tip of the pencil. "Might have a bottle of Granny's cherry bounce under the counter."

"*Excelente.* Bring that and two clean glasses."

"Your poison." The waitress shrugged and gyrated among the tables to get their order.

"It is unwise to drink the gin in this cantina, gypsy lady, though the whiskey would have been safe," the bandit shouted over the racket of the band. In the heat of the small, crowded room, he removed his cape and hung his sword on the back of the chair, but did not unmask.

47

As it turned out, Granny's cherry bounce, served in a dark bottle with a cork stuck in its top, provided a very nice buzz by the time they reached its bottom. Roz motioned to a rear door that was being opened and closed often enough to let in bursts of sunlight and let out some of the smoke. "What's in the back?"

"Ah, a courtyard, some rooms, a necessary, and a way out if the place is raided."

"Well, I could use some fresh air and the necessary."

He held her chair in gentlemanly fashion and broke a way through the crowded tables to the rear door. They exited into a surprisingly pleasant courtyard with a small fountain in its center and clumps of banana trees sprouting in its corners. A rear gate leading to an alley, rows of small numbered rooms on either side, and a privy off to the right surrounded by lush foliage ringed the space. Roz floated in the direction of the outhouse. "I won't be long, *caballero*. Don't leave."

When she returned, greatly relieved, her Spanish gentleman was talking to a mulatto woman who held a bundle of dirty laundry in her hands. As Roz crossed the courtyard, a costumed couple, still giggling with drink, emerged from one of the rooms and went back into the speakeasy.

"Doing a good business today, Anna-Marie?" she heard her masked man ask.

"No rest for the wicked, Doctor Pierre. Eh, you want a room? I won't tell JoJo. He don't count the sheets I wash. Lucky number seven, she's all made up and ready to go. I got the key right here. Some lagnaippe for taking care of my girl when she got the clap." The yellow woman tossed her load of soiled linens into a basket and took a set of fresh sheets from a pile stacked on one of the bar's bentwood chairs. Draping her burden over one arm, she fished in her apron for the key and dangled it before him.

"Not today, *Senora*, but you have my thanks."

"Yes," said Roz as she came up behind him. "Yes, we want the key."

She stroked the dark hair at the nape of his neck and recognized the same small shiver she had gotten out of him on the balcony of the Yacht Club.

"Ah, you should take the room. It's Mardi Gras, and who knows when you will have another chance with the gypsy lady, eh?" Anna-Marie said, still dangling temptation.

"You're sure? You must be sure," he said to Roz so seriously, his breath hot against her cheek.

She took the key for him and led the way to number seven. In the small, dim room, the only light came through the open transom over the door. The floor was cool linoleum, and someone had thrust a stalk of narcissus with a scent as strong as sex into the neck of a green bottle centered on a small table. He pulled a cord, and a naked lightbulb burned overhead. A single chair stood handy to hold discarded clothes. The sheets on the double bed smelled clean and were crisp to the touch.

Roz reached up to untie his mask, but he stopped her hand. "No. If we unmask, I must take you home, as I should."

"The girl you know is at home with a hot water bottle on her belly. Forget her, and be with me, *Senor*."

He placed his lips on hers and drew the red silk blouse down low on her white arms. He kissed her neck and moved across the top of her breasts with his lips, the feel of his moustache on her skin arousing. Urgently, Roz struggled free of the sleeves of the blouse. He pulled the silk to her waist and suckled each of her nipples in turn. With his hands, he rubbed them lightly until her knees buckled against the edge of the bed with its ironed sheets.

Roz reached up to open the black shirt and move her hands over the dark hair covering his chest and ran in a line down his taut belly. It felt as smooth and soft as his mustache. She unbuttoned the top of his pants.

"Not yet." He stopped her. Tossing her ruffled skirt to her waist, he raised her hips and removed the silly pantaloons. Bending, he kissed her inner thighs above the rolls of her dark stockings. His mustache tickled as he drew closer to her center and kissed her there. He used his tongue to turn the heat gathering low in her body into flame. Roz tossed and arched.

He came up to meet her mouth, and she could taste herself on his lips and the hair of his mustache. He said against her cheek once more, "Are you sure?"

"Yes. Please. Just don't leave me with a baby."

He nodded against her shoulder. Roz fumbled with the rest of his buttons, and when he sprang free, she shoved up with her hips and urged him inside her with both hands on his buttocks. He entered partway and teased her with small, shallow thrusts until she raked his back with the long nails she had lacquered red the night before.

He pulled back and surged forward until she was full and in discomfort, until he moved again, faster and without stopping. The fire roared inside her and burst into a shower of sparks she felt all the way to the tips of her toes and fingers. He moved even faster, and the sparks flew until suddenly, he left her and turned aside. Against her hip, the sheets became warm and wet with his seed. He rested with his head between her breasts.

"Pierre, I—"

"Only El Zorro is here. He robs from the rich." Roz heard his bitter laugh against her chest. "You must understand, *mi corazon*, at midnight we repent and wear our ashes. There is no future for a bandit and his gypsy girl."

She wouldn't cry. He had given her exactly what she wanted, but nothing more. Roz drew up her blouse, and when he rose, she lowered her ruffled skirt and found her pantaloons on the floor. She patted her head and found the wig and mask still in place. Shaking a little, she picked up the Spanish shawl that had fallen to the floor, wrapped herself tightly, and moved toward the door.

"Let me take you back to Esplanade," he said.

"No. I'll go alone."

Roz left by the alley, following it until she reached a major street. When she glanced back, she saw El Zorro had retrieved his cape and sword and stalked not far behind. She merged with the revelers and walked toward home, her Mardi Gras over well before midnight. When she passed into the alley behind her parents' mansion and slipped through the gate into the dependency, he remained behind her, seeing her safely home.

She changed back into her nightgown, and back into Rosamond St. Rochelle, Queen of the Krewe of Hercules. When her family returned, she was freshly washed and dressing for the *bal masque* of Rex.

Chapter Six

The Lenten season had begun in the St. Rochelle mansion. To the cook, it meant shopping the stalls for a glorious variety of seafood fresh from the Gulf, rather than purchasing the roast of beef or thick chops of pork. To Roxie, Lent meant no sweet rolls for breakfast or candy treats. To her mother's mah-jongg club, it meant that refreshments would consist of thin-sliced cucumber sandwiches or fat dumplings from one of the Chinese restaurants in town, not tiny petits four cakes, to go with their green tea. For Laurence St. Rochelle, Lent meant drinking much more discreetly, and for his child, Rosamond, it meant accepting the inevitable course her life would take.

Rosamond confessed to an indiscretion on Mardi Gras, had been given absolution, and wore her ashes all of Wednesday. The days ahead looked just as gray as the smudge on her forehead. As if she possessed the gift of self-prophecy, Roz had real cramps and her monthlies by Thursday. She stayed in bed until Sunday when her mother demanded she recover enough for Mass and dinner because Mr. Boylan would be joining them.

During the open dancing at the Rex ball, Roz had let Buster monopolize every set. A glare from Burke discouraged cutting in from any of the other boys, who went to dance with young women not yet taken. Of course, Mr. Boylan was coming for Sunday dinner. He and Rosamond were accepted as a couple now. Papa would thump Burke's back in greeting and take him to the smoking room for a cigar and a nip after dining. She was glad she'd made Papa so happy if not herself.

Uncle Gilbert joined them for the meal. Roz asked if he had been able to enjoy Mardi Gras. "No," he replied. He could not face his dear Harriet's favorite day without her. He had stayed at the hospital and given the day off to young Landry.

"And did Dr. Landry have a good carnival celebration?"

"I should say so. He asked me to dress some rather deep scratches on his back when he returned, and I don't believe he got them in a fight. He's a fine doctor, but you understand, Rosamond, he's not our kind. Your parents want the best for you, the very best."

"Oh, I'm full to the brim with understanding, Uncle."

"Don't look so glum. Your nineteenth birthday is only a week away, and I believe there will be cake and a party, Lent or no Lent. I know your father and Burke are concocting some sort of surprise. I believe it might involve something on the racy side. You'd like that, wouldn't you?"

"Racy, sure. I can tell you I am sick to death of being Goody Two-Shoes."

Uncle Gilbert looked around to make sure her mama was elsewhere. "Next Friday night, Burke is going to fight an exhibition match at Holland House against one of the Italian lightweight contenders. We've arranged for you to view the match from a discreet spot on the balcony. If you want, I'll even place a bet for you in the back room. Don't pretend you aren't interested. I can see a light in your eyes. Don't let on I've told you."

"Oh, Uncle Gil, I'm the best at keeping secrets."

****

When Friday night arrived, Laurence and Gilbert announced they were taking the birthday girl for dinner at the Holland House, but no one else was invited. Burke would meet them. He and Roz could dance to the band afterwards.

"As if I would intrude. They have those dreadful boxing matches on Friday nights. You will keep Rosamond apart from that crowd, Laurence," her mother said, her dark eyes full of disapproval.

"Absolutely, my dear," her husband replied, and the two men, snickering like small boys, put Roz in the touring car and tooled off to the environs of City Park.

A mass of men already swarmed about the temporary ring. A handful of women in gaudy dresses hung on to the arms of big bettors, and small boys ran their selections to Beansy Fauria in the back room. As an amateur and unknown, Burke "Buster" Boylan would fight first against Kid Pesci, the Italian boy from the French Market. Pesci was a lightweight and known to be lightning quick. Bets were on him for the most part, except for the desperate hoping for a long shot and a big payoff.

Roz sat behind the louvered section of the balcony. She wasn't alone. Some respectable wives sat with her, keeping an eye on their spouses below. A rowdy group of heavily painted females, possibly prostitutes, sat out in the open area. Both groups ignored the others as if a physical wall stood between them.

Buster and the Kid entered the ring from opposite corners. Clearly, Buster was no lightweight. Slipping out of his robe, he flexed the heavy muscles of his biceps and stretched on the ropes. Every wave of his blond hair sat in place, and his chest was as naked as if he had shaved it. Across from him, the Italian kid jogged and jabbed, warming his muscles.

One of the whores leaned over the balcony and called out to Burke. "Oh pretty boy, you send up a note to Flora if you want your boo-boos kissed afterwards."

Burke looked her way and grinned.

"Oooh, he's got killer eyes," Flora told her companions. "Let's see what you can do with those great big muscles, Killer."

The referee announced the rules. The bell rang. The Kid came out fast pummeling Buster with light punches. Burke absorbed the blows as if they were nothing and kept his guard up. Then, he swung wide and hard, and the Kid got in a quick hit to the face that split a lip. Buster roared and put in a punch just below the belt, hiding it from the referee with the bulk of his body. A few men on the far side of the ring booed, but no one seemed too disturbed. Round One ended.

In Burke's corner, Artie Delamare offered a water bottle and a cloth to blot Buster's lip. The second round went much the same with the Kid dancing and jabbing, and Buster going for the big knockout. He glanced a blow off the side of the Kid's face and sent a trickle of blood dribbling from Pesci's nose. By the end of Round Two, the heavier man was clearly tiring while the Kid still looked fresh.

Round Three began. The air stank with the odor of sweat and blood that reminded Roz of the bullfights she and Aunt Harriet had seen in Madrid. She found herself up off her chair and rooting for Buster. The whores, all except Flora, cheered for the Kid. "Hit him, hit him. Knock 'im out."

The fighters went into a clinch. Buster whispered something to his opponent, a reminder that the wop had been paid well to take a dive in the third. This was only an exhibition match. Who cared, really, with the payoff bigger than the prize? Still, the Kid danced and jabbed. Buster's face grew red with anger and exertion while the Kid grinned and led him around the ring like a bear with a ring in his nose. Then, a feint, a slip on the sweat-soaked canvas, and the Kid's arms opened wide. Buster drew back and smashed a gloved fist into the wop's jaw. The Kid flopped on the mat like a freshly caught mackerel and lay still. Buster drew back a foot as if he were about to kick Pesci in the ribs, but the referee pulled him to the center of the ring, grabbed Burke's arms and raised them over his head in the traditional pose of victory.

Bettors groaned over their losses and put down more money on the next bout. Artie Delamare went to stuff his winnings in his pants pocket. Rosamond St. Rochelle raced down the staircase and found Buster, still gloved and wearing a robe over his shoulders, in the hallway. She rose on her toes and kissed him on the lips, taking in the salty taste of sweat and blood. Burke engulfed her with both arms, smashing Rosamond tight against his slick chest.

This could work out, she thought. Buster was dangerous and unpredictable, not as dull and stuffy as most men of her class. He could be taught to be more subtle in making love, less bearish and clumsy. If she had to marry as her parents wished, might as well be Burke. Papa would be so pleased.

"Now, now, your mother would say you are creating a scene, Rosamond. Let the man clean up and dress. Burke, I'd be pleased to buy you the biggest steak they've got and a shrimp cocktail for starters. I won enough on you to pay for the meal." Laurence clapped Buster on the shoulder and led Rosamond away.

Burke heard her saying, "I'd like a Manhattan, Papa." Sure, tonight she could have one. In the years ahead, he would cure Rosamond of sluttish habits so her behavior matched her Madonna-like beauty. Her old man had been right. Show Rosie the goods she'd be getting, and all her indifference would fade. College girls liked a display of the manly arts. So did whores.

****

Saturday afternoon was a different matter. Pastel streamers hung from the dining room chandelier and a big frosted cake with pink sugar roses cascading down its sides sat on the table. Madame St. Rochelle had invited the girls of Rosamond's court to attend the party as well as some of her bluestocking friends from Newcomb. Burke and Artie brought their fraternity brothers from Tulane, and of course, all the family was invited to celebrate Rosamond's nineteenth birthday soiree.

Madame St. Rochelle rejoiced that she had engaged the snowball man to set up in front of the house. For the last week in March, the weather had turned unseasonably hot. Waiting for the old colored man to shave the ice from his block and pour on the flavoring of choice kept the smaller children outside with their sticky treats. Inside, the ice melted in the bowls of chilled shrimp and had to be replenished. She fretted that the chicken salad sandwiches might turn, but everyone seemed to be having a lovely time.

Odette and Odile continually refilled glasses with lemonade and cold, sweet tea. The men took their drinks into the smoking room and came out looking happier. There was an instance when Madame spied Hazel DuLac, one of the maids of the court, taking a small flask from her garter and spiking the beverages of all the girls sitting with her on the front gallery, Rosamond included. She would have to speak to Hazel's mother, but for the moment, all the guests appeared very gay and lively.

Emmaline St. Rochelle called to her daughter to come cut the cake and begin opening a small mountain of presents. Rosamond, looking rosy in a many layered pink silk crepe frock and a long string of pearls, exclaimed over the scarves and artificial flowers her friends gave her to accessorize her dresses. The girls from Newcomb had gone in together for a large box of art supplies. Papa got a kiss for the new wristwatch and Mama a hug for the diamond bar pin to be used to keep her bodice closed.

Of course, one tasteless joker slipped in a silver flask engraved with "Roz." Madame suspected that dreadful Artie Delamare, and she wasn't pleased when her daughter turned her back, slipped the flask in her garter, and asked if anyone could tell she wore it. Buster, who stood very nearby, frowned. Emmaline St. Rochelle said a silent prayer that nothing would make the young man change his mind at the last minute. But no, Burke Boylan called for everyone's attention. He had one last gift to present.

Taking Rosamond's hand and flipping open a ring box with his other, he asked, "Dearest Rosie, will you be my wife?"

For a moment, Roz looked stunned, then stared desperately over the gathering of friends to the doorway as if she expected a dark, caped stranger to come rushing in to carry her away. Artie said later when he razzed Buster about giving up his freedom that his intended had been looking for an escape route. The comment earned him a cuff on the jaw that left a bruise.

Roz stared down at the ring. "It's lovely," she said. A large diamond shone in the center of a most fashionable art deco setting. Smaller stones were channeled along the band and around the geometric design. Her girlfriends chanted, "Answer him, answer him!" She could see her father bursting with approval and her mother gloating over her snagging Genevieve Renard Boylan's son.

Finally, Roz looked at Buster. "I suppose I must marry you, Burke Boylan. Everyone thinks it's the thing to do."

She gave him a small smile, and he returned it with one of his big, smothering kisses. On cue, Artie went into the parlor and struck up the *Wedding March* on the piano. The newly engaged couple was pushed apart by the surge of young women who wanted to see the ring up close. Burke went to hulk by the piano where Roz's little sister languished over his friend who had sworn to play only love ballads for the rest of the afternoon.

"That's over with. For a minute there, I thought she was actually going to turn me down after I went to all the trouble to humble myself before Father to get the money for that ring. Now, I just have to get the St. Rochelles to set a date fairly soon, and I'll be living in clover."

"You'll be an old married man with a wife you probably can't handle," Artie joked.

"There's no one I can't handle." Burke gave Artie a shove from the piano bench that landed him on the floor in mid-stanza.

Roxie glared at her sister's fiancé. "I don't like you, Buster."

"Then, it's a good thing you're not the one I'm marrying, brat." Burke yanked her pigtails hard enough to smart and took himself off to the smoking room.

****

When the guests had gone and only family remained, the engaged couple sat with the bride's parents to discuss the wedding date. Burke pushed for June when he would most likely have passed his bar exams and be ready to set up a practice.

"As I promised you, sir, I'm staying right here in the Crescent City. I won't be carrying your daughter off to Philly," Buster swore.

"There's a lot of work the bank can send your way, son. With business booming, mortgage closures alone could make you rich. I'll see to it."

Emmaline, however, objected to a date only two months off. "People will think, well, they will think you had to marry in haste. That won't do. July and August are much too hot for festivities, and the best people will be at their summer homes. Perhaps, October at the earliest. The weather is usually very pleasant then, but that gives us only six months to plan."

"The first week in September. I won't wait any

longer to make Rosie my bride. The way I feel, accidents could happen. We might even have to elope."

Madame St. Rochelle seemed horrified. Her husband assured her, "He's joking, my dear, but I don't see why they shouldn't marry in September. We could have the reception at the Jung. It's air-conditioned, you know, and very elegant."

"Yes, the Jung might do. If I engage Madame Plauché immediately to design the wedding dress, we might have enough time. Wouldn't it be fine to use your queen's cape as an altar cloth, Rosamond? I must speak to the priest at the cathedral tomorrow about reserving a date."

"Whatever you think would be right, Mama." Rosamond put her hand in Burke's, and he gave it a crushing squeeze.

Chapter Seven

If the engagement was any proof, then marriage to Buster Boylan would be one long party. At first, he visited his intended mostly on weekends, always being there for Sunday dinner. With Burke cramming for the bar exam and Rosamond completing her year of college, this might be expected. Everyone agreed Roz had no need to take classes in the fall. She would be setting up a household and, God willing, starting a family.

When Buster passed the bar, they held the celebration at the mansion on Esplanade where Artie Delamare rejoiced almost as hard at having failed the test. If Burke drank too much and got a little rowdy, so did most young men. When Madame St. Rochelle caught him pressing Rosamond against a wall while he ran his hand up her dress and fondled her bosom, she turned aside and pretended not to see. They were an engaged couple after all. Times had changed, perhaps too much, since the days of her courtship. Petting—she thought they called it petting.

Roz allowed Buster to run his thick fingers over her thighs and squeeze her breasts when alone or at least secluded. Other men had touched her in the same places. If American men were ham-handed, so be it. Wishing for a lighter touch would do no good. She was going to marry Buster.

Her father saw to it that Burke attained a position in one of the finest law firms in the Crescent City and sent a steady stream of bank business his way. This work did not fill Buster's days or impede his pleasures. Any afternoon, he might show up at the Esplanade house in the roaring white Mercedes Model K with its nickel-plated exhaust pipes and 6.2-liter engine with supercharger that he purchased with the monetary gift his father sent when his son became an attorney-at-law. Snaring Rosamond St. Rochelle and becoming a lawyer like the old man opened the Philadelphia moneybags wide.

He came to collect Rosamond and stuff Artie and sometimes, Roxie, if she begged hard enough, into the rear seat, and they'd be off to the beach and amusement park at Spanish Fort. The ladies much admired Buster in his trunks and sleeveless striped tank top that spanned across his chest even though he burned a lobster red.

"You got a real Johnny Weissmuller there, dearie. Ain't you lucky?" remarked a young woman with her bob covered by a bathing cap and her tiny waist accented by her belted bathing outfit. Kicking her shapely gams over the edge of the swimming pier, the flirt fluttered her eyelashes at Buster.

Buster enjoyed being compared to the five-time Olympic medal winner and famous swimmer. He yanked the sisters under water by their long single braids, and pushed Artie down until he turned blue in the face while his admirer giggled. Roxanne, however, surfaced angry and launched herself on to Boylan's red shoulders.

"Let Artie up! You're hurting him."

Burke flopped backwards pushing Roxie toward the lake bottom with the weight of his body, but Artie surfaced spluttering and gasping for air. Roz ducked under and came up hugging her sister while Buster stood examining the white marks Roxie made in his sunburn.

"See if I ever bring you to the beach again, you vicious brat," he told the child.

Artie gave Roxanne a hug. "Well, you may be a vicious brat to Buster, but you're a heroine to me, kid. Roz, I tell you, you don't have to marry this lug. There are plenty of other men on the beach." When he noticed Burke's glare, Artie flexed his own puny muscles into a strongman's pose. "Like me," making the bathing party and the flirt on the pier laugh.

"Honey," the floozy said, "if you're in over your head, I'll take the big one off your hands." Burke preened.

Because Buster enjoyed playing games of strength in the arcade and winning an armload of Kewpie dolls, Teddy bears, and cheap, beaded lamps for Rosamond by ringing a bell with a sledgehammer or knocking over wooden bottles with a hard-thrown ball, they spent hours at such amusements along with the rides offered at the park. A small bribe to the operator was good for getting the couple stuck at the top of the Ferris Wheel for a few minutes of necking while Roxie and Artie waited impatiently below to move on to the next ride.

They played tennis in the early morning before the temperatures became unbearable on the courts at Audubon Park. Once the sun went down, they took trips to the flickers to be scared by the likes of Dracula or the Phantom of the Opera from the safety of a theater seat.

Buster would punch the air afterwards and tell his Rosie that is what he would do to any monsters that tried to molest her. When Roz asked if he never felt pity for the creatures of the dark, Burke put back his head and laughed at her.

On an evening cruise on Lake Ponchartrain aboard the Camellia while the great King Oliver jazz band played, Artie turned his date over to Burke for a dance. He asked Roz if she wanted to shake a leg, but she said she'd rather get some air out on the deck. Artie followed her.

"Roz, I've been wanting to say something. You know, I wasn't joking that day at Spanish Fort. Buster has a mean streak, and I got the bruises to prove it. I kind of regret introducing you two on Christmas Eve. We'd been drinking, you see."

"Do tell, Artie Delamare."

"No, really. I'm not kidding now either. Something happened back in Philly. I don't know what, but it got Boylan sent down here to his mama's people for law school. I know they told him to straighten up and settle down if he wanted to get back in his family's good graces. Of course, he moved right into the frat house, but the Renards keep an eye on him and report back. So I'm saying, maybe you should find out what happened up north, and get yourself another man to marry."

"Why, are you proposing, Artie?" Roz teased.

"No joke, Roz. I worry about you."

"Thanks, Artie, but this girl can take care of herself. I've gone too far to back out now. Mama would die if I broke it off. Probably, Papa, too."

Artie looked over his shoulder, as he did frequently when around Boylan, and saw Buster coming their way.

"Okay, my conscience is clear. Be careful, Roz. Burke, old buddy, are you ready to trade back?"

"Yeah, mine's prettier. That dog you brought is back at the table. She says I tread on her feet. Come on Rosie." Buster reclaimed his fiancée by jerking her into his arms and laying on one of his rough kisses.

The amusing pastimes continued with day sails across the water to Mandeville and Milneburg to visit friends at their summer cottages. Meanwhile, Madame St. Rochelle complained endlessly about having to stay in the sweltering heat of the city during the summer in order to bring off a wedding the first week in September when she would so much rather be taking in the Gulf breezes at the Pass or Biloxi. Playing the martyr, Madame continued to bend florists, caterers, and hotel managers to her will in order to create an event that would leave Genevieve Renard Boylan speechless.

A polio scare closed the beaches and chased them from the water in late August. With the wedding only two weeks off, Roz felt oppressed by the relentless heat and humidity that sent her to her room to change two or three times a day. She spent hours laying in her skivvies beneath the ceiling fan in her darkened room trying not to think about the wedding approaching as inevitably as autumn. That's where she hid from her future on the afternoon when giggles and commotion filled the house. She didn't have the energy to rise and see what went on until Odette came to tell her guests had arrived.

"Tell them I have a sick headache. Tell them I have my monthlies. Tell them to go away, would you, Odette?"

"Can't do that, Miss. Let me help you put on a

party dress and fix yo' hair up nice. They's waitin'."

"Oh, no! A surprise shower. Why won't Mama simply leave me alone? It's not enough that I have to be dragged to final fittings for the trousseau all week, now this."

"It yo' time of the month, honey? Still, you got to get up and go. Peoples is waitin', and you been raised with better manners than that."

Two more weeks of this, and she'd be a married woman who could do as she pleased. At least, something good would come of all this fuss. She put on her best smile and her lightest cotton frock and descended the staircase into the flurry of guests, declaring herself totally caught unawares.

Knowing full well that no St. Rochelle would need a set of pots and pans, her friends gifted Roz with fine linens, some naughty black lace lingerie from Hazel DuLac—known to be a little fast—and a pair of the best vases the Newcomb kilns had turned out that week presented by her old college friends. The most beautiful object of all, a perfume bottle in a Tiffany box, came all the way from Philadelphia sent by her future mother-in-law. Of weighty Favrile Glass, its sides appeared to be adorned with iridescent peacock feathers. Of all the gifts, this was her favorite.

The company of women settled around the parlor with refreshments of tiny rolls filled with shaved ham, pastel bonbons, and cups of fruit punch made slushy with shaved ice. Several of the girls had gotten engaged since Mardi Gras, and the talk was all of wedding preparations and honeymoon plans that went on and on until Roz thought her head would split with the agony of listening.

Burke arrived brandishing steamer tickets as the party ended. "We take the train to Philly with my family, then the liner to Paris, two weeks in Gay Paree, then home the same way."

Several of the girls squealed with envy, but Rosamond's lack of appreciation rubbed him the wrong way. Buster squeezed her shoulder beneath the sheer fabric of her dress hard enough to cause some pain. "What's the matter with you, Rosie? I thought you'd be excited about a month long honeymoon, just you and me."

"I am, Buster. My head hurts, and," she said in a whisper, "it might be that time of the month. I think I need a week to myself."

Buster dropped his hand. "Okay. We won't have to worry about that mess on our wedding night. I hope you show a little more enthusiasm then."

He went to find Laurence in the smoking room. Women were good for only two things, sex and babies. Otherwise, they were just too much work.

Chapter Eight

By seven p.m. on the first Friday in September, the wedding guests sat in the echoing vastness of St. Louis Cathedral. The sun had yet to sink below the levee, and the air remained as stifling as if it were still August. The humidity hovered at ninety-eight percent, just shy of a full rainfall. Sweat trickled between Rosamond St. Rochelle's shoulder blades as her bridesmaids fussed, arranging the lace panels of her train and a tulle veil of equal length just so. The lace brow band holding the veil in place seemed to be pressing into her forehead, aggravating the headache that none of Uncle Gilbert's powders could cure. The bouquet of three-dozen ivory roses, accented with fern and trailing ivy arranged in a cascade covering her from waist to pointed hemline just below the knees, hung heavy in her hands.

One by one, her maids, every one of whom had served in her Mardi Gras court, walked down the aisle until only Roxie and her father remained. Roxanne kissed her sister's pale cheek. "Good luck, Sis. When I marry Artie, I want you to be in my wedding."

That made Roz smile. She watched her feisty sister, who had fought with Mama for the privilege of being in the wedding party, practically skip toward the altar.

Papa took her arm. "Steady now," he said when she faltered. "This will all be over soon, and we can go enjoy the wonderful reception your mother has planned at the Jung Hotel."

They made their way toward the priest standing before the altar covered with her silver queen's cape. Buster stood to one side, massive in his evening clothes, and grinning like a victor in the decathlon. On the end of the line of groomsmen, Artie Delamare twitched nervously. As Roz passed the front row where the Boylans sat, she felt Genevieve Renard Boylan, once queen of Rex and still handsome of form and cold of eye, measuring her every step.

Because her mother would have nothing less, the priest began a full nuptial mass that would end in a communion for three-hundred people if they wished to partake. With the long periods of standing and kneeling, Roz went faint twice, but Buster refused to let her fall. He pinched the tender skin under her arm each time he pulled her upright to make sure his bride stayed alert. She repeated her vows by rote, and when she failed to say the "I do" promptly, got an elbow in the ribs from her groom. As for Burke, he bellowed out his promises and sealed them with one of his signature rough kisses. He gained applause for his manly eagerness.

Papa was right, of course. Once she left the cathedral and went on her way to the fabulous new Jung Hotel with its travertine walls and indoor fountain, the bride revived. Her rise in spirits might have had something to do with the flask Hazel DuLac produced from its place in her garter and passed around generously, declaring she'd never been so dry for so long. Good old Hazel, ever the life of the party. Most of the guests brought their own additives to perk up the reception punch.

If the band chosen by her mother played tepidly, the menu at least displayed excellence, from the chilled vichyssoise to the Lady Baltimore cake. The wedding party partook of the feast after the official photographs culminating with the bride and groom formally posed between two large potted palms.

With the lace train detached from her dress and flowing veil removed from her headband, Roz was free to dance, beginning with her heavy-footed husband, then with other men who crowded in for a spin around the ballroom with the bride. Buster had no objections tonight. He used his time slipping out of the ballroom and stumbling back in ever more red-faced and clumsy.

Gilbert St. Rochelle took his favorite niece in his arms and waltzed her to the far side of the ballroom. "Little Rosie, a married woman. I wish your Aunt Harriet could see you now."

"What would she say?"

"Probably that you should have finished college and seen more of the world first. Before I forget, Pierre Landry sent a gift, good of him since he wasn't invited to the wedding."

They paused on the edge of the dance floor by the potted palms. Gilbert took a small, oblong box from his jacket pocket and weighed it in his hand. "My guess is a silver cigarette box. He said to open it when you are alone. I gather you aren't to share it with Buster. Perhaps, he had it engraved with some lovelorn phrase."

"Pierre is against smoking, and the last time I saw him, he gave the impression he could live without me. Here." Roz turned her back and secured the box to her leg with one of her two new blue garters. "If anyone notices, they'll think it's a flask. I do hope it's not more silver. Mama has scads of it on display at the house already."

"You'll have servants to polish it, never fear. If you had taken up with Pierre that might not be the case."

"Yeah." Burke came swaying up behind them. "If you had married Pierre, his family would be sending iron gumbo pots." Buster laughed heartily at his own joke. "It's time to go up to the suite, Rosie-posey, and make sure you never ever think of Pierre Landry again."

"We have to say good-bye to our families and our guests, Buster. I think there is supposed to be some throwing of rose petals at midnight."

"Now. We are leaving now." Dragging Rosamond along, Buster staggered toward the bandstand and heaved himself up beside the leader. "A drum roll please, my good man."

"Atten-shun! My new wife can't wait for the honeymoon to begin. She's hot to trot. So we're going up there," Burke pointed his thumb toward the bridal suite, "and get started. All of you, stay, enjoy the party."

He tripped coming down off the bandstand, but caught himself on Rosamond's shoulder. She buckled slightly under his weight. Nearby, she saw the shock on her mother's face and the distaste with which Genevieve Boylan regarded her son.

Recovering quickly, Emmaline St. Rochelle gestured to the guests to form two lines down the dance floor. Roxanne and the bridesmaids darted down the rows handing out small net bags of dried rose petals.

Behind them, Buster Boylan dragged his wife

along with an iron grip on her wrist that he didn't release until they stood before the door to the suite. He fumbled with the key, finally turning it in the lock, and shouldering open the door, banging it shut with his heel. Immediately, he pawed at the wedding dress.

"Buster, please. Let's slow down. It will be better for both of us."

"How would you know, my pure queen of the Mardi Gras, my virgin bride? Did you sleep with other men when you went traveling in Europe?" he asked, suspiciously.

"No, of course I didn't sleep with them. Buster, I have a surprise for you. Hazel DuLac gave me the most naughty negligee at my shower. It's all laid out in the bathroom. If you'll only let me go, I'll put it on for you. Black lace, Buster…it's black lace."

"Yeah, I can wait for that. Not too long though."

As soon as his fingers released their grip, Roz ran to the bathroom and locked herself inside. She could take her time and let Burke get some of the alcohol out of his system. She struggled from her dress and took the pins from her hair, rubbing her neck to ease the tension. Standing there in her straight slip with its wide lace straps, she felt the pressure of the box she'd stuck in her garter. Thank heaven Buster hadn't groped her legs. Anything regarding Pierre Landry was bound to set him off.

Roz took the plain white box—held shut with only a single blue ribbon—from her garter. The object inside did gleam silver, but it wasn't made of precious metal. Resting in a purple satin holster with a strap to wear around a thigh lay a small two shot pistol. No antique derringer purchased from a shop on Royal Street, the gun and the slightly soiled holster looked as if the gift had been redeemed at a pawnshop or won in a poker game. It came with a box of bullets no bigger than one joint of her little finger and a simple pasteboard card that read, *Roz, Take Care, Pierre.*

Aunt Harriet had worn a similar weapon on their jaunt across Europe. She called it a "discourager," not big enough to kill a man unless you got in a lucky shot, but certainly dangerous enough to be discouraging. Aunt Harri hadn't used the little pistol. European men tended to be charming.

A fist hit the bathroom door. "Hurry up in there!"

Roz tucked the strange gift into the bottom of her makeup case, tore the card in tiny pieces and flushed the bits down the commode. Pierre persisted in being as melodramatic as he had been on Mardi Gras by insisting they not unmask during their tryst. If he cared for her all that much, why hadn't he said to hell with the conventions of society instead of leaving her to Buster?

Her new husband paced outside the door, his breathing loud and his footsteps heavy. Roz remained under no illusions that Buster loved her despite his jealousy, but he did want to possess her, and as a prized acquisition, he would do her no harm. She finished her toilette, brushing out her long hair down the back of the negligee. The gown came only to mid-thigh and was largely transparent except for the bodice and a deep black lace trim that started several inches below her navel, a far cry from a silly pair of yellow pantaloons and a red silk blouse that would probably be wasted on Buster.

"Do I have to knock down this door?" he roared.

"I'm ready. I'm coming out, Buster." She posed in the doorway to appease him.

He jumped her like a feral dog on a purebred bitch in heat. Pulling her head back by her hair, he forced her mouth to take his tongue, ran his other hand over her breasts, squeezing tightly the way he always did. On the bed, he held her down with one knee while he divested himself of his evening clothes. His penis throbbed hard and thick against her leg.

"Buster, shouldn't we be taking precautions?"

"Precautions? What do you know about precautions? Aren't you a good Catholic girl, Rosie?"

"I thought we might wait a while for children. Travel, have some fun, get to know each other better. There's plenty of time for kids."

"Your old man gave me one piece of advice, Rosie. He said give my daughter a baby the first year. That will settle her down. I can't disappoint your papa, now can I? My brother was born nine months to the day after my parents' wedding. Got to keep up the old traditions. You're fighting me."

"No, no, I'm not," she said, aware for the first time that she did push against his chest with both hands. "I only need more time."

"Time is up. Been waiting eight damn months, and don't tell me I couldn't have had you sooner. Let's get it over with quick. Quick and hard, that's how the girls in the Quarter like it."

He forced her legs apart and thrust himself inside in one brutal stroke. He went as fast as he promised, but unready, she cried out in pain. He pounded away mindlessly toward his release which came in one great heave. Burke collapsed over his bride, not bothering to shift the weight of his body for her comfort. At last, he rolled aside and searched his clothes for a pack of cigarettes. He took casual notice of the tears rolling down Rosamond's cheeks.

"Hurt, huh? A little blood on the sheets. So you were a virgin. I have to tell you, Rosie, I had my doubts. Cigarette?"

"No. I gave up smoking."

"Good. Burke Boylan's wife should never be seen smoking in public. I feel like a million dollars. I think I'll take a shower."

When Buster returned to the bed, Roz lay huddled beneath the covers pretending to sleep. He soon snored beside her, a heavy sleeper who wouldn't wake until morning.

Chapter Nine

Rosamond still huddled on the far side of the bed when morning came, and she felt the weight of Buster lift from the mattress. She feigned sleep while he shaved, perfected his hair, and dressed. When the door closed behind him, she got up to bathe and scrub herself clean of her husband. She covered her bruised body in a thick robe provided by the hotel and let the black negligee lay in a heap in a corner of the bath. When a respectful knock came at the door, she hesitated to answer, but then, Burke would have the key, wouldn't he?

A waiter wheeled in a breakfast cart holding flaky croissants, a covered dish of eggs Benedict, the makings for café au lait, and a single red rose in a silver bud vase. Roz read a message from her husband as the waiter made a show of blending the rich coffee and steamed milk into an oversized cup.

My Dearest Rosie—Sorry about last night. I was hot for you. Maybe I was too rough. Let me tell you, I got a lecture about it this morning. Tonight will be better. I promise. Your loving husband, Buster.

Dear God, he'd bragged to someone—his older brother, his father or hers—about their wedding night. Roz shook as she searched the pockets of Burke's evening clothes, still in heaps around the room, for a tip.

"No need, Madame. Your husband has taken care of it. If I can be of service in any other way?"

"Thank you, no. It all looks so wonderful."

After the door shut, she forced herself to eat a croissant and finished the coffee. The two poached eggs riding on a muffin and the slice of ham in a puddle of yellow sauce, she covered with a linen napkin, unable to bear the sight of them. Still, she had a very long journey ahead and must prepare for the trip. Roz picked up the second croissant and pulled it into tiny, bite-sized pieces.

****

The newlyweds were to travel on the sleeper train with the Boylans to Philadelphia and endure a second reception for friends who had not made the trip to New Orleans. Afterward, the bride and groom would embark on a liner for France. All had been planned out for them. In the narrow bed provided by the railroad, Buster stayed swift and silent in his sexual demands and soon snored. In his parents' house, he bothered Roz not at all.

Once in the stateroom of the liner as the couple steamed toward France, Rosamond learned what she had to know about her husband in order to survive. If she encouraged him like a two dollar whore saying, "Oh, Buster, you're so strong. This is the way I like it, hard and fast," he finished quickly, the only difference being she wasn't paid and no other customers waited.

If Burke drank until his nearly colorless eyes glazed—and she encouraged him to do so—her husband would be asleep before she came out of the bath. On nights when she gauged his condition poorly, intercourse became hell. He'd be brutal. She would struggle. In the morning, bruises ringed her wrists where he'd held them over her head, marked her breasts and thighs. Once, he'd wrapped her long hair around her neck and pulled until she'd seen purple.

The many diversions of Paris worked their magic on Burke. While he had no interest in the museums, the artists of Montmartre, or the cathedral of Notre Dame, Buster took full advantage of a city where Prohibition was nonexistent and even ridiculed. Once he discovered the pleasures of the Folies Bergere and Josephine Baker doing her notorious banana dance, Rosamond's evenings became easier. While watching the topless Baker stomp and gyrate in her skirt of rubber bananas increased Buster's desire, his drinking decreased his abilities. He bought his wife a souvenir doll of the dancer in her suggestive skirt, then bought more for his friends. Roz wondered if she should offer the doll bits of food and drink out of thankfulness, the way practitioners of voodoo did to their statues.

On a side trip into Spain, Buster gloried in the gore of the bullfights, but they lacked the soporific effect of Baker and French spirits. In a dusty cantina near the bullring, he jerked his wife by the hair into a back room holding casks of wine and pottery jars of oil and punished her sexually for an imaginary flirtation with a slim, olive-skinned man, mustachioed and dark of eye, who sat at the next table. As Burke pounded against her body pinned to the whitewashed wall by his hands, it slowly dawned on Roz that the man who had paid a compliment to her beauty in Spanish resembled Pierre Landry. She had given the stranger only a small, polite smile, but now she closed her eyes and imagined another man's face as Buster reached his climax.

When Buster finished, he pulled up her drawers and yanked her, wobbly-legged back into the bar room. The two other women in the place turned their eyes away from the white smudges on the back of her navy blue dress and her straggling yellow hair from which all the pins had been ripped. A group of men made obscene comments in their own language. Burke smirked, enjoying what he thought they said about his manhood.

Paris was better. While Roz shopped she could count on Buster to find his own amusements. Certainly, he sampled the goods of French courtesans just as she selected silk scarves, exotic perfumes, and strange pieces of art portraying women that looked as if they had been taken apart and put together again wrongly. In Paris, his appetite for her blunted, but the long sea voyage home loomed ahead.

The seas turned choppy on the return trip. Roz suffered terribly from *mal de mer*, though by evening she could usually keep down the light foods the ship's physician recommended. Still, the illness put off Buster who worked out his frustration in the gymnasium, slamming his fists into punching bags and lifting weights to maintain the physique that French foods had increased by several pounds. At her most miserable, Roz cheered herself with the thought that if she were always sick, Buster might take his interests elsewhere.

****

Back in Philadelphia, Mother Boylan, as she wished to be called, observed that her daughter-in-law seemed even paler and punier than before the trip while Buster obviously thrived on marriage. She watched Roz shed the gray wool coat with the silver fox fur collar and its matching cloche hat and hand them to the maid before Burke could assist her.

"How stylishly thin you've become, Rosamond. That is a very elegant outfit, I must say. Let's have tea, just the two of us, in my rooms and let the men to their brandy and cigars," the former Genevieve Renard said, looking at Rosamond from head to toe, her pale blue eyes assessing and finding fault as they had done since their first meeting a little over a month ago.

They went to her mother-in-law's personal sitting room in her private wing of the monstrous brownstone paid for years ago with Renard money. The room had windows enhanced with Tiffany side panels and a wonderful view of anyone coming and going in Genevieve's household. Surrounded by antique Chippendale, the silver tea service sat on a piecrust table centered on an oriental rug. The red velvet draperies could be pulled if privacy was desired, but today, Mother Boylan preferred to allow the clear October light to pour in. As Roz unbuttoned her gray kid gloves, the lace on her long sleeves falling back, Gen Boylan noted the yellowish bruises around both wrists.

Mother Boylan poured the scalding tea into two cups. "You will take cream and sugar. You need building up, my dear."

"I suffered from seasickness on the return voyage. My stomach is still unsettled. Thank you for your concern." Roz picked up a piece of Melba toast spread with cream cheese and a small garnish of red caviar and ate it while waiting for her tea to cool. The sweets presented on small silver plates did not appeal to her.

"I am concerned. Of course, you realize by now

that my son is a vainglorious bully just like his father at his age. Oh, Baxter Boylan was big and blond and domineering in a way no southern man could match. He exuded power, which I found very attractive. Like many young women, I made a foolish choice."

Genevieve Boylan sat regally in her chair as if still enthroned next to the king of Rex. Her hair retained its pale blonde color thanks to a skillful beautician, but she wore it atop her head in a thoroughly dated fashion. Her face showed no wrinkles, perhaps because she never smiled. She sipped the steaming tea prepared with one slice of lemon, no sugar, as if it were a chilled beverage.

"He hit me only once while we made the rounds of family visits after our marriage. I was already expecting my first son—as you might be."

Rosamond shook her head. "It's just the aftereffects of the sea voyage. That's all."

"Time will tell. I had the sense to insulate myself with old family servants and the power to demand a suite of my own when I agreed to come to Philadelphia. I let Baxter Boylan know that if he ever touched me again, I would return to New Orleans with his child and never grant him a divorce. As for mistresses, I didn't care how many he took. Shocked, poor child? No wonder when you grew up with that pussycat of a father, Laurence St. Rochelle, all bluster and no bite, and Emmaline Fabre who had four children and two miscarriages before she figured out where babies came from. And dear Gilbert, marrying that raging suffragette who probably remained childless by choice. How handy being married to a doctor must have been. I had to resort to locking my bedroom door."

"But you had a second son," Rosamond rushed to point out, wanting to defend the St. Rochelles.

"The result of a terrible lapse on my part. Burke was a mistake. He has always been favored by his father. They have the same looks, the same brutish nature. He has been encouraged from childhood to use his fists and his power over others. If he failed to win, Baxter disciplined him in the same way. My first, Roland, is cool-natured like myself, an exemplary young man. You will note Rolly is in no hurry to marry. Burke, on the other hand, we sent south with an ultimatum to curb his temper and settle down. The incident with the maid was the last straw, so to speak." Mother Boylan selected a cherry cordial from a dish of chocolates, sucked out the center and popped the rest into her mouth.

"The maid?" Rosamond questioned.

"Well, you're family now, and really should be told for your own sake. We've paid out a great deal of money over the years to people Buster has damaged—his several nannies, a boy at boarding school, the young man at Princeton he nearly killed in the boxing ring—but the maid was the worst. Deirdre, such a sweet Irish lass, became pregnant. She claimed Burke raped her." Gen Boylan fluttered a long-fingered hand.

"The Irish, you know how they lie. Burke is an attractive man used to getting his own way. We had already arranged for a discreet delivery and an adoption into a good middle-class family when Buster came home from Princeton for a visit. He beat the poor girl senseless, not because she had gotten herself pregnant, but because she'd cried rape, a blow to his vanity, I suppose." Mother Boylan observed her daughter-in-law's face taking on a faint green tinge.

"What became of Deirdre?"

"Oh, she lived, but ruptured her womb. She won't be troubled by childbearing in the future. The small fortune we gave her along with a ticket back to Ireland should buy her a husband no matter what condition her face is in."

Rosamond glanced frantically around the sitting room with its three exit doors, not knowing which one would be closest to a bathroom.

"Here, my dear child." Mother Boylan held out the silver waste bucket from the tea tray.

What little she had in her stomach came up immediately, but the dry heaves continued for some time afterwards. She could feel Genevieve Boylan patting her back in a way that did not comfort.

"There, there. I fear you are too weak to be Buster's wife, Rosamond. He will probably kill you."

Chapter Ten

As it had been before under the constant scrutiny of Genevieve Boylan, Buster barely touched his bride while under the parental roof. On the return trip to New Orleans, he was again swift and quiet in their private compartment. The couple would be staying with the St. Rochelles until a proper house could be found. Burke must be on his best behavior under Laurence St. Rochelle's eye. Rosamond counted on that. She planned to extend their stay as long as possible and consult her Mama about her misery.

The whole family awaited them with the touring car at the station. Arrangements were made with a porter to bring the trunks, but the St. Rochelles did not go directly home. Honking his horn to encourage a mule-drawn wagon to move aside, Laurence turned on to Prytania Street and parked before a narrow house in the middle of the block. Insisting that all the passengers get out, he cleared his throat.

"Earlier this year, the Widow LaHaye passed on to a better world. Her only kin live in Texas of all places, and they were eager to convert her house into cash after the will passed through probate. They've taken what they wanted of the furnishings, and what remains belongs to Mr. and Mrs. Burke Boylan." He flourished the house keys.

"It's small, of course, only three bedrooms, a fairly

modern bath, an attached kitchen with a gas stove, a good-sized parlor and dining room, all a young couple really needs until those bedrooms fill with children. Here, take a look."

He passed the keys to his daughter who dropped them on the walkway, her fingers feeling suddenly numb and clumsy. Burke picked them up. "You are too good to us, Laurence."

"I couldn't let a bargain like this get away while you were off enjoying your honeymoon. Wait until you see the interior. Emmaline has had the servants polishing for a week."

"I've arranged all the crystal and fine china you received in the sideboard. Widow LaHaye's cousins left most of the kitchenware, and her houseboy and cook are willing to stay on. You might want to add a maid. The Texans took the fourposter bed and armoire that must have been made before the war, but we've moved your bedroom furnishings here until you can shop for something more suitable." Madame St. Rochelle paused for breath.

"Thank you, Mama," her daughter said woodenly.

"Now, let's go in," her mother urged, much more excited than Rosamond, who felt cold and ill despite the balmy October day.

As they entered through the iron gate and walked to the raised porch, the front door opened. A light-skinned Negro man with gray in his wiry hair smiled broadly above a red bow tie and a white jacket.

"This is Wilbert, your houseboy."

Wilbert stepped aside. People thronged from the dining room and parlor. "Surprise, Rosamond! Surprise, Buster!" Artie Delamare cranked up a borrowed

Victrola to add to the commotion.

"Wait until you see the spread Oralee has prepared." Emmaline gestured down the hall to where a dark woman of bulk and presence filled the kitchen door. The cook wore a white uniform and an old-fashioned red calico tignon on her head. She nodded tersely over a pair of brawny folded arms and moved back into her domain.

"She's a gem really, Rosamond, but a bit temperamental. Try not to aggravate her."

"I'm overwhelmed, Mama. Truly overwhelmed."

****

After the company left, Rosamond finally got a chance to see her house. The mahogany and horsehair settees from another century had been covered with young women in bright dresses up until an hour ago. The dining table, so big it filled the room leaving space only for its carved matching sideboard and the massive chairs placed back along the walls, had not looked so forbidding covered in the Irish linen tablecloth that had been among her wedding gifts and anchored by the coconut and chocolate layer cakes, the platters of ham biscuits, dishes of olives and pickles, and a silver punch bowl with their wedding date engraved upon it.

Dark wainscoting decorated the halls, the side of the staircase, the parlor, bedrooms, and dining area. Two windows faced the street downstairs. Upstairs, four more windows, two in the master bedroom, one each in the smaller rooms, pierced the walls. None of them seemed to let in a great deal of light. Crammed in mid-block as the residence was, Roz held no hope of trying to add any more glass to the house.

The LaHaye relatives had stripped all the bedrooms

bare, leaving only the furnishings below too massive or outdated to bother with. Every room except the kitchen bore walls covered in a large floral pattern, faded except for dark spots here and there where family portraits or works of art had been removed.

Rosamond wandered into the kitchen while Buster went outside to help in loading the Victrola in Artie's borrowed auto. Oralee, having cleared the leftovers and snatched the cloth from the table, prepared to leave.

"Ham biscuits is in the ice box. Cake under the dome there. Rest of the punch is in this here pitcher. You want something else tonight tell Wilbert go get it for you. He live over the ole carriage house." The cook jerked her head with its several chins toward a low range of windows over the sink. At the back of a small yard, Buster's white Mercedes lurked like a stalking beast in the dark recess of what had once been a one horse stable. Rickety stairs on one side led up to a room for a servant.

"In the mornin', hot biscuits and coffee be on the sideboard. I makes eggs any way you likes 'em, ham and bacon, too. You call Wilbert if you wants breakfast in bed 'cause I don't do no stairs. You let me know way head o' time 'bout lunch and dinner. If I gots to go to the market in the heat, I likes to go early. This my kitchen, and I don't care to let nobody else in it." Oralee laid a fat, affectionate hand on a fancy gas stove that filled most of the space along a side wall.

"Now, Miz LaHaye, she di'nt eat much. Jus' wanted fancies for her ole lady friends when they come to call. That man o' yours look like a big eater, so I'm gonna need a raise in pay. And you, Miz Boylan, you looks sickly. I ain't no nurse."

"I'm fine. I suffered from motion sickness on the train and on the boat before that. It's nothing. I can take care of myself." Remembering her mother's advice to never let servants get the upper hand, Roz pulled herself up straight and looked Oralee right in the eye.

Oralee cocked her big head again, this time toward Roz. "How long you been married, honey?"

"Just over a month. We've been traveling. I'm quite tired, so you may go for the evening."

Oralee nodded. "You breedin'." It wasn't a question, but a positive statement.

"No, oh no! I'm ill from traveling, that's all."

"Whatever you say, Miz Boylan." Oralee picked up a large cloth purse bulging at the sides, probably with ham biscuits and cake. She looked over Rosamond's shoulder. Roz felt Buster's hands descend on her.

"There's my bride. Oralee, I expect coffee and breakfast by eight. I like three eggs scrambled, hot toast, and a side meat. Don't ever give me grits. I won't be home for luncheon, but will expect my dinner at seven. Do you understand me?"

"Yassah." Oralee turned away, making a small sign to ward off the evil eye. "I be goin' now."

"Fine. My wife and I have had a long day and will be retiring early. Tell Wilbert that on your way out."

"Yassah."

Burke led his wife down the narrow, dark hallway and up the stairs. There hadn't been enough hooch at the party to make Buster either belligerent or fall-down drunk. Tonight, she would have to tell her husband what a great lover he was over and over and over again.

****

Strange how in her parents' house, her double bed

had always seemed roomy and luxurious with its gold duvet and curvaceous white headboard. Now, the bed appeared cramped and soiled with Buster taking up three-quarters of the mattress. As usual, Roz pretended to sleep when her husband rose and went down the hall to the bathroom. She lay still, holding back her rising nausea, while he dressed.

Once Burke had gone down to breakfast, she tiptoed to the large closet that had been added when the bath was put in and vomited into an antique chamber pot with Yankee General Beast Butler's likeness on the bottom, left behind in a dusty corner by the Texas relatives. Roz watched her husband from the rear window as he crossed the barren yard and backed his roadster into the alley. He was gone for the day. She exhaled and went to the bath to clean General Butler's face.

In a light wrapper and slippers, Roz made her way down the staircase. On the landing, she noticed the wallpaper with its monstrous pink flowers was peeling just above the wainscoting. Rosamond picked at it with her fingernail. A large strip tore off. She worked her fingers under another section, and the paper peeled off easily. Dusting her hands, Roz continued down the stairs where she handed a startled Wilbert the wad of paper.

"Dispose of this, Wilbert. After I breakfast, we shall take down the rest."

The formidable cook appeared in the doorway to the kitchen.

"Oralee, I'd like a pot of hot tea with mint to go with my toast." Feeling much better, she went to sit alone at the dining room table. Out in the hallway, she overhead the servants talking.

"She breedin', Wilbert. It make some women crazy, don't you know."

****

With Wilbert's help and kettles of steaming hot water to treat the stubborn places, most of the wallpaper in the halls vanished by the time Buster returned home. He frowned as Wilbert took his hat. "Where is my wife?"

"Nappin', suh. She done wore herself out pulling down paper today."

"I see." He pounded up the staircase. Rosie, in an unflattering housedress, slept on top of the duvet. Her long hair was undressed and held back by a thin black ribbon. Burke gave it a yank to wake her.

"A man doesn't want to come home to chaos, Rosie."

"I'm redecorating, Buster. I want light and room and air, the latest styles and colors."

"Your old man better be paying for it, Rosie. I can't eat a decent meal with all this dust around. I'm going over to the Boston Club."

"Suit yourself. Tomorrow, Wilbert is bringing some boys to tear out the wainscoting."

Alone again, Rosamond came downstairs and happily surveyed the wreckage of the day. She poked her head into the kitchen and asked Oralee what she'd cooked for dinner.

"A nice stewed chicken. It what you need."

"Wonderful." Roz seated herself in the dining room. Tomorrow, she'd call an auctioneer and have this table and sideboard hauled out of here. She dined alone on the stewed chicken, vegetables in broth, a crusty

French roll, and bowl of soothing rice pudding full of raisins for dessert. By the time Buster returned, she would be asleep.

Chapter Eleven

By the end of October, everything dark or overbearing that could be removed from the house on Prytania had been, including the crystal chandeliers in the two front rooms and the mahogany wainscoting. The legs were removed from the dining room table, and the parts carried to the auctioneer's van where two dray horses waited patiently to take it away. Six large Negroes hauled the sideboard down the front steps and out the iron gate. Even the heavily carved banister to the second floor had been removed, causing the new maid to complain of the danger of falling while hauling fresh linens to the bedroom. Each item was to be sold, and the profits put into the remodeling.

Buster dined out often and came home late smelling of liquor and other women. Back on the turf he knew, he seemed to be taking his brutal interests elsewhere. Rosamond managed to be always in an exhausted sleep when he returned. Unless he shook his wife awake, she barely noticed his comings and goings. When he did demand her attention, she stared up at the ceiling and waited for him to finish.

On the second floor, she saw no reason to redecorate. Upstairs, nothing had changed. Two of the three bedrooms remained empty; no need to hurry there. Why order a new bed when she could lie in the one she'd made for herself?

Ah, but downstairs where her friends and family visited, the floors had been stripped and stained a light oak, the walls replastered and painted a pale peach. A sleek steel railing in an interlocking diamond pattern was on order for the stairwell. The new dining table, glass-topped and metal-rimmed, sat only eight. Above it, a six-bulb lighting fixture with frosted globes shaped like giant lilies lit the surface. Her wedding silver and crystal glittered behind geometrically patterned glass panels in a breakfront of warm oak.

In the parlor where horsehair had been ousted, the new divans and chairs were covered in peach silk and sunk in fluffy white area rugs. Mama St. Rochelle tutted over the impracticality of it all. Children, even well-behaved little girls, would make a ruin of it. Rosamond laughed as she directed two men in hanging a large mirror over the fireplace where a still life of a dead rabbit surrounded by the makings for its stew had previously been on display. Mama might have to wait for grandchildren.

Occasionally, Rosamond caught a glimpse in that mirror of a thin, hollow-eyed young woman who hadn't bothered to put up her hair in weeks. She wore old cotton frocks from the back of the closet with a slip and step-ins, breast bands and stockings abandoned. Though the dresses hung on her loosely, any pretense they had to style was ruined by the bumps of her sore and swollen breasts. She wanted to howl whenever Buster grabbed them, but wouldn't give him the satisfaction. Mostly, he left this haggard woman alone.

While the builders tore the dining room apart, Roz had taken to eating breakfast in the kitchen, to the discomfort of the servants who offered to bring her breakfast in bed. She enjoyed sitting at the scarred wooden table sipping her second café au lait because black coffee made her stomach churn. All she wanted to eat was toast, no trouble for Oralee, so why should the cook be grumpy?

Roz looked out the low windows over the sink at the two narrow strips of clipped yellowing lawn and the walk to the carriage house. She dreamed of planting banana trees, putting in clumps of bird-of-paradise, some hibiscus the same peach shade as the parlor walls, not red, and a small fountain or at least, a birdbath. Right now, the only flowers in the house were the yellow daises with the black, cone-shaped centers that some people called nigger-tits sitting on the kitchen table in an old brown jug and probably picked in the alley by Oralee on her way to work. She daydreamed of another courtyard ringed with banana trees until a large, dark shadow blocked her view.

Oralee stood over her, a fragile porcelain egg cup clutched in one mighty fist. "Miz Boylan, you gonna eat this nice soft-boiled egg I done made for you this mawnin'."

"Oh, give it to Wilbert, or eat it yourself. I have no appetite."

"Honey, you expectin', and you gotta eat for two now."

"Whatever gave you that idea? How dare you speak to me that way!" Roz drew herself up in her tatty dress and patted her snarled hair.

"That new girl yo' mama sent over, she say she ain't washed no rags for you yet, and it bin a month." Oralee jerked her head toward Lucille, the maid, and Wilbert who stood over by the stove in the hottest part of the kitchen.

"You know, I could be dying. Aunt Harriet was tired all the time and had no appetite before she died." Rosamond smiled, almost happy with the idea.

"You ain't dyin'. You gonna have a chile. Now you eat this nice egg."

"I'm mistress here, and you can't tell me what to do!" Roz said with some fire.

"No, ma'am, but I can walk out this door and go work for Miz Rochon like she been beggin' me to do 'cause I don't gots to work for no crazy woman."

"Am I crazy?" Before Roz could stop herself, her eyes filled with water.

"It the baby makin' you nuts, honey. It gonna get better."

The tears overflowed and rolled down Rosamond's cheeks. She covered her face with her hands. Do not cry in front of the servants, another of Mama's rules. The words came out regardless. "I don't want Buster's baby."

Oralee exchanged a look with Lucille. Any black woman in the city could tell this sickly white girl how to bring off a baby, but it wasn't their place. "Sometimes, the chile worth more than the man. You think 'bout that, okay?"

"I gots a side chile, Miss Ros'mond, and he worth more than me fo' sure," Wilbert added since Oralee glared at him as the only man in the room. He saw he'd gotten a wobbly smile from Miss Roz, and that was good enough. As the one who had to wait up for Mister Boylan and sometimes help him to bed, Wilbert tended to agree about the low-down nature of men, himself included.

"Maybe you should see a doctor?" Lucille suggested. She had been educated by the black nuns of New Orleans and still ended up as a maid for a crazy white lady her expression said.

"No, let's wait a few more weeks," Roz said softly.

She could hardly run to Pierre because she carried Buster's baby. What did she expect him to do—perform an abortion? He was as Catholic as she was. Dump his medical career and run off with her, play father to another man's child? Maybe the child *was* the answer. She could raise a son to be a better man than Burke Boylan or a daughter who would never have to be queen of Mardi Gras if she didn't want to be.

"I'll eat that egg now," she said.

Chapter Twelve

Lucille held up a navy blue dress with brass buttons down the front and an adorable sailor collar while she waited for her mistress to finish the breakfast on the bed tray. Miss Rosamond looked better now after two weeks of getting more rest and eating more food. Her hollow cheeks and the dark smudges under her eyes were gradually disappearing. She'd let the maid wash her hair with lemon-water and put it up for daytimes.

"You have so many nice clothes, Miss Roz. Auntie Odette told me you liked to dress up. This one would be so nice for a walk in the park since the weather's holding fine for November after all that rain we been having. You won't be showing for maybe another month, and the way this one is made—oh, no, there's white marks down the back. Must have gotten up against some of the painting going on around here. What a shame."

Roz's knees bucked under the tray, spilling café au lait across its surface. "Please put that dress away, Lucille," she snapped. "Come get this tray."

The maid rushed over and mopped up the coffee with the linen napkin that had covered Mrs. Boylan's lap. "Sorry if I upset you, Miss Roz, but you have other pretty things. I bet if we dressed you real nice, Mr. Boylan might stay home in the evenings or take you out to the Yacht Club for dancing now that you feel better. You could tell him about the baby, and I bet he'd be real proud."

Roz gestured for the china chamber pot she kept under the bed. Lucille got it to her mouth just in time as her mistress lost all her breakfast. The maid hurried off and returned with a wet cloth by the time Roz finished heaving over the picture of the hated Beast Butler in its bottom.

"I think I'll stay in bed today. No need to fuss over me." Rosamond rolled to her side and curled her knees up around her belly.

Lucille backed out of the room with the bed tray and chamber pot and made her way carefully down the stairs, which still lacked a railing. Miss Roz swore it would be put up in the next two weeks. "Sure, before someone like me breaks their neck," muttered the maid.

She set her load down on the kitchen table. Oralee raised the lid of the chamber pot. "What my good breakfast doin' in here? You take that back upstairs and flush it down the commode, you hear? Ain't my job. I jus' cooks. She spittin' up again?"

"I do suppose. All I said was she might dress up nice for Mr. Boylan, and here it comes. She could have give me that blue dress with the stains on it if she didn't like it no more, but no, she too busy puking to make the offer."

"Girl, two weeks ago, she don't even want his baby. I'm guessin' once it come, she gonna keep that bedroom door locked for good. Mr. Boylan, he a scary man. Wilbert say he come home some nights with blood on his clothes. That poor chile done make a big mistake when she marry him."

"Mr. Boylan seems big and handsome to me. Rich, too. Look at that car he drives. Guess he's no worse than any other man."

"He gots *des yeux goueres*, evil eyes."

"No such thing as the evil eye."

"Sho' is. Ain't that so, Wilbert?"

Wilbert, who had just walked into kitchen, looked from Lucille to Oralee. "Well, if there was such a thing as the evil eye, Mistah Boylan would have it. Give here, Lucille, I empty that pot fo' you." Taking the chamber pot, he got out of the room. As he started up the stairs, the doorbell rang. Wilbert set the pot on the edge of the open staircase, straightened his white jacket, and went to do his duty. "Good day, Mistah Laurence."

"Is my daughter up and about, Wilbert?"

"No suh, she feelin' poorly this mornin'."

"Hmmm, well, I brought Roxie for a visit. I thought Rosamond might like some company this fine Saturday morning, first without rain in a long time."

"That so, suh."

"They could get out, go shopping. Perhaps, Mr. Boylan would take them to Audubon Park if Rosie feels better after lunch. My wife always felt better later in the day."

"He lef' early, suh, for his boxing club befo' Miz Boylan got up. Didn't say when he be back."

"They can have a girls' day out, then." Mr. St. Rochelle beckoned to Roxanne who sat in the car. As full of energy as her sister had once been, Roxie bounded up the walk.

"Nothing strenuous, now. Your sister might want to just sit and talk, but if she feels well enough to go out, I've given you enough money to treat her to lunch at Holmes Department Store. Give her a kiss for me and say I hope she will feel better."

"You got it, Pops."

Laurence St. Rochelle grimaced at his daughter's language. He returned to his car, concerned for one daughter and upset by the cheeky young woman the other was becoming.

Without waiting for Wilbert to announce her presence, Roxie, totally unconcerned about the missing railing, dashed up the stairs to her sister's room. Rosamond sat at her dressing table with its skirt of tulle and its array of perfume bottles where Buster sometimes squatted to put on his shoes. She wasn't primping, merely staring into the mirror, running her fingers through her long hair, when Roxie burst in.

"Hey, Sis. Pops gave me shopping money. I'm supposed to take you to lunch at Holmes."

"That would be nice, but my stomach is very upset today. When did you start calling our father Pops?"

"Oh, a few months ago while you were gone. That's what Artie calls his father. I sort of missed you, so Mama allowed Artie to come visit. We had to sit on the porch or in the parlor, but sometimes Mama let him play funny songs on the piano. Are you going to have a baby?"

"Why do you ask that?"

"Mama says she suspects that's why you're sick and moody, but not to say anything about it. You'll tell us in your own good time."

"But you're asking?"

"Yes. I started my monthlies while you were gone. I need to know how you can tell if you are going to have a baby now that I'm a woman. Mama won't say.

Odette says your monthlies stop coming."

"Odette told the truth. But honey, Artie hasn't touched you in a way he shouldn't, has he?"

"No," Roxie said sadly. "He won't even kiss me on the lips. I get these little pecks on the cheek, or he pats my head."

Rosamond exhaled. In her own misery, she had given no thought to her baby sister. She could see now how small breasts budded under the flat-fronted dress the girl wore, that Roxie's childish roundness had fallen away as her waist slimmed and her hips flared. And, she had her first crush—on Artie Delamare of all hopeless people.

"Artie is a twenty-four-year-old man who still lives off his parents and never wants to finish college. Even if he weren't too old for you, Papa would not be pleased about your interest."

"I know." Roxie exhaled a world-weary sigh. "Mama and Papa don't understand Artie. He wants to be an actor, you see. He says talkies are the future of motion pictures, and it won't be long before someone makes a flicker with its own sound, but his family won't let him go to Hollywood. About this baby…"

"Okay, I'm telling you and only you. I am expecting, I guess. I haven't been to a doctor yet."

"So I'll be an aunt. You wouldn't want to tell me how you got to be expecting, would you?" Roxie opened the perfume bottles and sniffed the contents, lily and gardenia. She dabbed a sophisticated fragrance purchased in Paris from the peacock bottle behind her ears while watching herself in the mirror.

Roz gave an exasperated sigh. "No, I wouldn't care to tell you. Let's say, keep your knees together, and don't let any guy in your drawers, and leave it at that."

"Well, that's more than Mama would tell me. Please, don't you want to go shopping? You haven't been out in ever so long and never come to visit us."

Roz put her blonde head against Roxie's dark hair and looked at them both in the mirror. "You know what, we need a change. We need to do something for ourselves. Let me get dressed. We're going to the beauty parlor, then out to lunch. By the time we're finished, people will think we're movie stars."

****

"You look just like Carol Lombard. I swear you do," Roxie said in awe of her older sister. "Who do I look like?"

Roxie had chosen an Eton crop, so short and shingled and plastered to her head she could have passed for a boy if she hadn't been wearing a dress. Again, Roz thought, a young and willful woman was emerging from that round, childish face.

"You look like a total stranger. Remember, you tell Mama I'm to blame so you don't get in trouble."

"Will you get in trouble with Burke for cutting your hair, Roz? But how could you when you look so glamorous?"

Roz smiled. Her hair had been lightened to a striking platinum blonde and marcelled in waves close to her head. The beautician carefully crafted one spit curl in the center of her forehead. A makeup girl made her pallor and shadows disappear with light rouge and an artful smudging of eye shadow both above and below her baby blues. With a daring red lipstick, she looked quite the vamp. The stylist handed the sisters two little round boxes with silk cords.

"Your braids. If you should like to wear them for a special occasion, I can attach them for you, though yours, Mrs.Boylan would have to be bleached to the same shade."

"I don't believe I will ever want to wear long hair again, even temporarily. I feel so much lighter now, so free." She tipped the woman generously.

"Let's go buy red cloche hats, Roxie. For once they'll fit properly. But lunch is on you."

****

"My, oh my!" exclaimed Emmaline St. Rochelle, her double chin wobbling, when her daughters finished modeling their new hats and lifted them from their shorn heads. "What will Papa say! All your beautiful hair, gone."

Roxie twirled her hat with is perky upturned brim and cluster of artificial cherries on one finger. "May I invite Artie to dinner? I want to show him my new hairdo."

"As if Mr. Delamare hasn't eaten enough of our food in the last month."

"Please, please, please."

"Very well, call him. A few more morsels won't make any difference."

As soon as Roxie left the room for the telephone in the hallway, Mrs. St. Rochelle turned to her other daughter, who regarded a more simple hat ornamented with only a wide black grosgrain ribbon resting in her lap.

"Won't Buster be upset? He was taken with your hair from the very first."

"He's rarely home, Mama, and probably won't notice for days. As for me, I haven't felt so good in ages."

Madame St. Rochelle glanced toward the hallway where Roxie could be heard chattering to Artie Delamare. "No, it's *not* Greta Garbo, silly."

"One always feels better in the fourth month," Emmaline said to her elder daughter in a low-pitched voice.

"Mama, no!"

"My darling girl, I know young women are not as chaste as they were in my day, and Buster was very—ardent. Even those old biddies who count the months from the marriage to the birth won't be able to quibble about a week or two. It's going to be all right. Have you discussed names yet? Buster will want a junior, I suppose."

"If there is a child, a boy, I want to call him Laurence Gilbert after Papa and Uncle. Maybe Emma Roxanne if I have a daughter."

"But won't the Boylans feel slighted?" Emmaline asked even as she exuded pleasure over the choices.

"I don't believe I was put on this earth to please the Boylans, Mama. Am I invited to dinner, too?"

"Of course. Oh, Rosamond, it's so good to have you home and feeling better."

While Roz called her house to tell Oralee and Lucille that they could leave for the day, Artie Delamare showed up in his father's car. Her new hat pulled hastily over her haircut, Roxie ran to greet him at the door,

"Do you like my new hat, Artie?" She twirled so he could see the chapeau from all angles.

"Sure do, kiddo. It's da berries." He flicked the artificial cherries with a fingertip.

"And my new hairdo?" Roxie carefully raised the hat so as not to muss the styling.

"Say, everyone will think you're my kid brother," Artie joked until he noticed the girl's crestfallen expression. "No, I didn't mean that. It's the latest thing, and you look great. Give me a smile, now." He chucked her under the chin, and Roxie turned and ran halfway down the hall. She crossed her arms under her small chest and pouted.

"I'm not a baby any more, Artie."

"Yes sir, that's my baby. No sir, I don't mean maybe. Yes sir, that's my baby nooow!" Artie slid across the waxed boards of the hallway on his knees, his hat across his heart, stopping at Roxie's feet.

Roz put down the telephone and applauded as Roxie giggled and blushed. Madame St. Rochelle snorted and said, "Please get up off the floor, Mr. Delamare. Dinner will be served momentarily."

At dinner, Artie continued his banter, offering to take Rosamond dancing because she looked so different no one would know he was with another man's wife.

"Yes, she's blooming now. Our Rosie is blooming," Laurence St. Rochelle said with a catch in his voice. "It's too bad Buster couldn't join us."

"Oh, Buster rarely comes home this early."

"He leaves you home alone in the evenings? No wonder you've been distraught."

"I don't mind, Papa, truly. Don't say anything to him, please."

"Look, I'll drive her home this evening since Pops let me have the car," Artie offered. "But first, we will dance."

They did, but in the parlor where Roxie could join

in taking turns on the piano. Even the older St. Rochelles did a stately waltz around the room when Roz played *Three O'Clock in the Morning* for them. Artie followed after, holding Roxanne at a proper arm's length while she held up a corner of her pleated skirt in one hand in gentle mockery of old-fashioned ways. When Roz suffered a dizzy spell after demonstrating a vigorous Black Bottom dance step, the evening was declared over.

As Artie helped Roz to the car, her parents stood in the doorway. They waved cheerily. Their words wafted to their daughter's ears as her escort helped her into the borrowed vehicle.

"I always thought I wanted Rosamond to settle down, but I've missed her spirit, Emmaline. I thought things had gone badly wrong on the honeymoon, she was so subdued."

"Nothing is wrong at all, Laurence. We're going to be grandparents. Things couldn't be more right."

In the darkness of the car, Roz asked Artie why he wasn't out carousing with Buster.

"Oh, I kind of enjoyed hanging around with the kid while you were gone. It's nice to have one person who admires you and doesn't laugh at your dreams. You know, Roz, Burke always had the best hooch, the best cigars, and the best girl, but going around with him can be hazardous to a man's health. I'd like to live to see thirty. Again, so sorry I ever introduced you to him."

"The fault is all mine, Artie. I got myself into this marriage. I'll have to get myself out."

Chapter Thirteen

Feeling newly reborn from the ashes of her honeymoon, Roz sat at her dressing table debating whether she should put on the hairnet the beautician suggested to keep her waves in place. She drew the stopper out of the peacock glass bottle and let the seductive Parisian fragrance wash over her. Her senses seemed more acute these days, she suspected because of the baby, her baby, not Burke's child.

She heard him come in, mumble something to Wilbert, and tread heavily up the stairs, tripping and cursing to the top. When he entered their bedroom, Roz continued to fidget with the objects on her dressing table, the silver-backed brush and comb with the matching and monogrammed hand mirror to check the back of her hair, gifts Buster had given her for a wedding present, items she would hardly need any more. His hulking shadow fell across the looking glass.

"What have you done to yourself, Rosie?"

"I cut my hair. I had my face done. For the first time in a long while, I like what I see in the mirror."

"I don't." Burke snatched up the round box and cloche hat sitting on the dainty French empire chair where he usually threw his clothes. He dumped out the long, honey-blonde braid and twisted it around his fist.

"When you leave the house, Rosamond, you will pin this at the back of your neck and wear your hat pulled down over the rest of your hair until it grows out. Mrs. Burke Boylan does not go about looking like a cheap whore, or smelling like one either." Buster knocked over the peacock bottle. Expensive perfume soaked the tabletop and filled the air with its exotic essence.

"That's true Buster, because Mrs. Burke Boylan doesn't go out at all, does she? She doesn't get paid to say, 'Oh Buster, you're so big, you're so strong' like the prostitutes who endure your abuse."

Buster gripped her shoulders and spun her around to face him on the dressing table stool. He moved one hand as if to seize her hair and pull her head back, but his fingers fumbled in the shingled ends where her bun used to rest.

Roz laughed in his face. "I'm leaving you, Buster."

Burke drew back his right fist still entangled in the severed braid and lashed out. Roz turned her face aside, but he clipped the top of her cheekbone, the edge of her eye. Groping for a way to defend herself, she fell back against the dressing table. Her hand closed over the peacock bottle. She smashed it against the bridge of Buster's nose. Blood spurted over both of them.

Rosamond struggled past the stool and the bulk of her husband who covered his nose with both hands. She nearly made it to the door. Then, he fell upon her, turning her with his grip, smashing a fist into her stomach, hitting her again lower as she crumbled to the floor and curled around her belly. He drew back his foot and kicked his wife hard, twice in the ribs, as he'd wanted to kick Kid Pesci when the wop made a fool of him in the ring.

He wanted to work over her pretty face until no

man would look at her again, but Wilbert called from the kitchen, "Everything all right up there, Mistah Boylan? You done had an accident? I gets the broom and the dustpan."

An accident, of course, this was an accident. At the least, he'd get the house and sympathy if his wife did not survive. The best idea would be to get rid of the bitch entirely. Burke picked up Roz as if she were no more than a piece of trash to be taken out to the alley. She gasped but did not become fully conscious. He carried her to the head of the unguarded stairs and flung her over the edge. She should have hit hard, maybe hard enough to kill her, but that old fool darkie came along down the hall with his cleaning supplies.

Wilbert dropped the broom and held out his arms. Miss Roz fell right on top of him, and they both went down on the hardwood floor.

"Lordy, Mistah Boylan. I think I done broke my arm, and Miss Roz, she bleedin' down below. Gots to call the doctor right now."

Burke Boylan clambered down the rest of the stairs. Wilbert's eyes went wide as he took in the man's swollen nose and blood soaked shirt. "Yeah, I'll go for a doctor all right."

Buster stormed out the door. Minutes passed, too many minutes. Miss Roz bled more and more from between the legs. Wilbert, who had been holding her head up with his good arm, laid her gently on the floor. He struggled with the telephone and dialed Gilbert St. Rochelle from the number in the book.

"Doctor, you gots to come quick. Miss Ros'mond. I think she dyin'."

Chapter Fourteen

The walls were white and the bed narrow and covered with sheets that smelled strongly of bleach. Someone had tucked a gray blanket tightly over her chest. Every breath Rosamond St. Rochelle took hurt. Beyond the half-open door, masculine voices, speaking low, said her name. She turned the side of her face that didn't ache in their direction.

"Pierre, would you talk to Rosamond? I'm too close to this case, much too close, and you have a way with distraught women." She recognized Uncle Gilbert, his voice sounding as choked and strained as it had the night Aunt Harriet died. Perhaps, she would die, too. The idea did not upset her all that much. Then, Pierre Landry came into the room and drew a chair to her bedside.

"Have I died and gone to heaven, Pierre? But no, girls like me don't go directly there. They have to spend a long, long time in purgatory first, and the powers that be probably wouldn't allow us to be in the same room together. Maybe being married to Buster will count against my sins as serving time in hell on earth." She tried to laugh, but her face throbbed, and she gave up the effort.

Pierre took her hand from under the blanket. She could hardly bear the deep sympathy showing in the darkness of his eyes, but sick as she was, Rosamond felt the same surge of warmth that always flowed through her at his touch.

"Roz, you will recover from this. The broken ribs will mend, and this," he touched a finger gently to the swollen side of her face. "This will heal without a scar."

"The baby?"

"Lost."

"My fault. I didn't want Burke's baby, and now it's gone. Funny, I'd just begun to think of the child as mine, one I could raise alone after I left Buster."

"Not funny and not your fault. Wilbert, your colored man, says you fell off the open staircase, a terrible accident. You miscarried, but you will be able to have more children."

"Not like the other woman, then, not like her."

"Other woman? Do you want to tell me about this?"

"Buster beat a maid until she lost her baby back in Philadelphia. The family paid her off, sent her back to Ireland. She is barren now. I wonder what they'll do with me?"

"Roz." Pierre leaned closer to her ear. "Why didn't you use the gift I sent you? I knew about Burke from some of the women I sewed up in the Quarter. He enjoys hurting people, especially when he drinks. You must not go back to him. Next time, and there will be a next time, he may kill you."

"I know. We argued about my hair. Isn't that ridiculous? I said I was leaving, and he hit me in the stomach—more than once. After that, I don't remember anything."

"I always wanted to run my fingers through your long hair, but you should be free to do as you want with it."

Tenderly, Pierre drew a finger around the bedraggled curl in the center of her forehead. Rosamond raised her hand and lightly brushed her fingers across his mustache and down the side of his face.

Dr. St. Rochelle watched from the half-open door and understood what he saw. About this time last year, he'd been sitting with his wife in her last hours. They had touched in the same ways, the bittersweet farewell of lovers. He heard his brother approaching with his gruff voice comforting the sobbing Emmaline, and stood in the doorway blocking the view of the brief kiss Pierre gave to Rosamond's lips.

"Oh, Gilbert, will she live? Will she be able to have other children?" Emmaline sobbed. "Such a dreadful accident. I knew that open staircase was a danger."

The taller Laurence looked over his brother's shoulder. "What's that Cajun voodoo doctor doing in my daughter's room? Where's Burke—didn't he bring her in?"

"No. Wilbert called me. We set his broken arm, but he's still in the colored waiting room, I believe. He said he didn't want to leave until he was sure Rosamond would be all right."

"A good boy, that Wilbert. May we see her now?"

"Of course. Dr. Landry broke the news about the baby. She'll want her mother now. Pierre, the St. Rochelles are here."

Pierre stood, letting Roz's hand slip slowly from his. "I'll be going then. I want to speak to Wilbert. I'll let him know he can leave now."

113

As the St. Rochelles moved to their daughter's bedside, Pierre Landry left the room and took the staircase to the hospital lobby. The colored waiting room sat unadorned and crowded with long benches that looked as if they had come from a train station. At this early hour of the morning, only Wilbert and two women waiting for their men to be sewed up after a brawl occupied the dreary space.

"Wilbert. I'm sorry, I don't know your last name."

"Johnson, but jus' Wilbert is fine."

"I wanted to thank you for saving Mrs. Boylan's life, both in the fall and afterwards. If you hadn't called, she might have bled to death. She's going to be fine thanks to you."

"Well, at first, I was waitin' for Mr. Boylan to come back wit' a doctor, but he didn't come. He was bleedin' hisself so maybe he passed out somewheres. Don't know. Glad to help."

"Did you see Mrs. Boylan fall off the staircase?"

"No, suh. Jus' saw her comin' down, but she didn't scream or wave her arms like people do when they fall, more like she passed out. I tried to catch her. Broke my arm."

"How did Mrs. Boylan land?"

"Right on top of me."

"Not on her face or side or stomach?"

"No, suh. Guess I must be like a big ole cushion."

"Before that, did you hear any sounds of fighting, a struggle?"

Wilbert paused, squirmed on the uncomfortable bench. "Well, something got broke upstairs. I heard that, went to get the dustpan."

"Did you hear what was said?"

"No, suh. I was getting ready to go out the back to my room, but I heard the crash, some thumps. Thass all."

"Thank you. Thank you again, Mr. Johnson. I'd offer you a ride, but I don't have a car."

"That be okay. Here come Mr. Boylan now. Maybe he give me a lift."

Pierre noticed Burke Boylan staring into the waiting room but not entering. He sported a swollen nose with a line of dark sutures across the bridge. Dr. Landry went to face the man who had beaten Rosamond St. Rochelle and nearly caused her death.

"I see she fought back, Boylan. Good for Roz."

"She went crazy when I said I didn't like her hairdo. Hit me with a perfume bottle, then tried to run down the staircase, missed her footing. It was her own fault."

"You know, she lost your baby when you hit her in the stomach," the doctor said quietly, but his tone implied something more lethal.

"I don't know anything about a baby. Rosamond never said a word. She's a lunatic, Landry. Be glad you aren't the one stuck with her."

Pierre Landry came very close to the larger man, the man who had broken a lovely, spirited woman to pieces as he would a discarded liquor bottle. He stared into the pale, cold eyes of Burke Boylan until the man dropped his gaze.

"Roz did not get those injuries falling on an old colored man. I'll file a report with the police testifying to that. She can use that statement to be rid of you."

"You think our easily paid-off officers of the law won't lose that paperwork? Who in this city is going to take the word of some over-educated Cajun whose family only crawled out of the swamps a generation ago?" Buster sneered.

"If I were you, Boylan, I wouldn't be taking any trips outside the city. My kin are everywhere, and they know what to do with vermin when it crosses their path."

Pierre fixed his black eyes on Buster again, then turned his back and walked away so noiselessly that Boylan had a brief feeling of having been stalked by a panther in the dead of night. He dealt with that moment of fear with his usual bluster.

"Are you threatening me, Landry? I'll have your job! Do you hear me?"

Chapter Fifteen

They had her surrounded like a wildcat beleaguered by baying hounds. Papa on one side of the bed, Mama on the other, Uncle Gilbert at its foot as if she might try to escape. Father Darby in his black garments loomed over them all.

"I'm not going back to Buster, Papa. I want a divorce," Roz asserted for the second time. "I tell you he hit me first and punched me in the stomach. I may have fallen off the stairs trying to get away from him, but I know what happened before that."

"Now, sweetie, Buster says you were upset that he objected to your hairdo, and you slapped him. He has fighter's reflexes, honey, and says he did cuff you, though he pulled his punch. You hit him in the face with the perfume bottle and rushed out. Your injuries were caused by the fall. We know you don't want to believe you caused the death of the baby, but it wasn't intentional. Father Darby says he can certainly give absolution in a case like this." Laurence St. Rochelle patted her hand.

"You've only been married three months, Rosamond. Think of what people will say," her mother pleaded. "Perhaps, you would consider a short separation until you feel better. No one would question your wanting to be in your mother's care under the circumstances, or maybe you'd prefer a nice rest at a

117

sanatorium."

"I've had a stern talk with Buster. He understands that he must curb his natural temper when dealing with you or suffer the consequences," her uncle added.

"You, too, Uncle Gilbert?" Tears gathered in his favorite niece's eyes.

Gilbert St. Rochelle had to turn his head away. Full of anger and passion, Pierre Landry had come to him with the houseboy's story. He was so sure Roz had been beaten before the fall, so ready to believe the worst of Boylan. Clearly, the young doctor loved his niece. He'd had to ask a favor of his old friend from medical school, Leonard Spivey, who lived in Chapelle, to remove the lad from this awkward situation before Pierre ruined his career and his life by getting between a married couple.

Dr. St. Rochelle saw his niece's eyes turn toward a simple cobalt blue vase holding two white calla lilies pure in color and form. One for her and one for the baby, Pierre said when he brought them. Roz cried on his shoulder, and young Dr. Landry held her as if the child had been his own. As embarrassed as he'd been to witness the scene, Gilbert did not feel he could leave them alone together. So far, Rosamond refused to see Buster.

A nurse interrupted the family meeting. "Mrs. Boylan, your husband sent these. Aren't they gorgeous?" She held out an arrangement of two-dozen red roses that looked like splashes of blood against her white uniform.

"Take them away. Give them to the nurses or the elderly. I don't care."

"Now, now, child. It is a sin not to forgive," Father

Darby said. "Let me speak with Rosamond alone for a few moments."

Closing the door behind them, the family members went out to hover in the hall while the priest had his say. "I've known you for several years now, and you have done little to curb your tendencies toward impulsive, even immoral behavior. Your husband tells me that as soon as you moved into the house on Prytania, you began tearing the place up to his discomfort, depriving him of a quiet home to rest after a hard day's work, spending all his money on decorations. He says you were too tired to fulfill your conjugal duties, and that drove him to seek relief elsewhere. The duty of a good wife is to provide these comforts for her husband."

"And what is the husband's duty?" Roz questioned, staring the priest straight in the eye.

"Why to love, honor, and support his wife, as it is yours to obey. If he preferred your hair long and your face unpainted, was it so much to ask, Rosamond? That you struck out at him when he mildly chastised you is a sin on your part, not his."

"Father, Burke has brutalized me since the day we married."

"Did you give him cause, child? Your own temper brought about the loss of your baby, God's punishment for your willfulness. His mercy is that you can conceive again. Submit to your husband. Try to be a dutiful wife, and you will be rewarded with more children."

"I never want Buster to touch me again."

"Understand, my child, if you divorce your husband, you will be cut off from the sacraments of the Church and endanger your immortal soul. I will pray that you won't go down the road to perdition."

"Please, leave me alone. Please."

"For now. We will talk again when you are feeling better." Though Roz turned her head away, the priest blessed her.

"Very hard-headed, your daughter," he told the family as he went on his way.

"I want to rest now. Please go, all of you, except Uncle Gilbert," Roz called.

As soon as the others left, Roz turned to her uncle. "I want to see Pierre. Where is he?"

"He was called home last night. Doctor Spivey suffered a mild heart seizure and needed his help immediately. I signed off on his training. Since you were asleep, I asked him not to disturb you."

"He didn't leave a message?"

"No. He had to leave on the midnight train." The note Pierre had given him for his niece burned in his pocket like a coal from Hell. Just as he had blocked Burke from seeing Roz, he'd told the switchboard she wasn't to be disturbed by telephone calls either. Unable to endure the despair washing over Rosamond's face, he made his excuses.

"I have patients to see, dear girl. Pierre might inquire about you later once he is settled in his practice—as any friend would."

Safely out of the sight of those tragic blue eyes, Gilbert whispered, "Forgive me, Harriet. This is for the good of the family. You would understand if you were here. No, no, you wouldn't. You'd probably give those two enough money to run off together."

****

Rosamond St. Rochelle held out alone for three

more weeks. If Buster came to speak with her father, she locked herself in the guest bedroom at her parents' home where she slept. She made do with old clothes she'd left behind before the wedding because no one seemed inclined to help her bring her belongings from the house on Prytania. Still feeling physically weak, she rested a great deal and took the medicine prescribed by her uncle to help her sleep in the evenings, untroubled by dreams of Burke driving his fists into her stomach.

Was it pride or the fear Pierre Landry felt only pity for her that kept her from sending a letter addressed to him in care of general delivery, Chapelle, Louisiana? In a town so small, everyone would know the village doctor. Instead, Roz waited for a call or a letter to give her hope for a new life away from Burke Boylan.

When the telephone rang in the evening, Emmaline St. Rochelle quickly answered it before the bell could wake Rosamond. Thank heaven, the young doctor stayed busy with patients most of the day. At first, she politely assured him that Rosamond was recovering her strength and thanked him for calling, shutting him out with fine manners. In the end, she resorted to lying about her daughter reconciling with her husband. Dr. Landry didn't have to concern himself with her welfare anymore. At last, the calls stopped coming.

Still, the man didn't give up. She barely intercepted a telegram before the maid carried it to Rosamond. The words were bland enough. "Are you well? Stop. Do you need help of any kind? Stop. I am at your service, Pierre."

Emmaline St. Rochelle crumpled the yellow tissue containing the message and using the large table lighter, incinerated it in one of the smoking room's ashtrays.

She knew exactly the kind of help and service the doctor offered her daughter. For the good of Rosamond's social standing and also her immortal soul, her daughter could not be allowed to accept it.

****

Emmaline made special plans for Thanksgiving. The St. Rochelles were to be honored by the presence of Father Darby who would offer a prayer for the family over the oyster-stuffed turkey. After that announcement, Roz found the energy the day before the event to go out and have her hair retouched and trimmed. If Burke appeared at the dinner table, she hoped the sight would infuriate him.

Her estranged husband arrived as the family seated themselves to celebrate the feast. He took the empty chair across from Rosamond after making a great show of presenting his mother-in-law with a bouquet of golden mums and greenery. Before Roz could rise to leave the table, Father Darby stood at his place and offered a blessing. All heads bowed under the weight of his authority.

"Dear Father in Heaven, we thank thee for this bounteous feast, for the love of the family gathered here, for hospitality toward guests who come to this door. Do not let anyone at this table lack in appreciation for a fine home, a good provider, and all the blessings of prosperity. Let there be forgiveness for past sins and misunderstandings, especially between the fine young couple seated here today. Let the spirit of reconciliation fill them this day and remind them of the vows they spoke before the altar of the Holy Catholic Church not so long ago. Reward them with renewed love and the blessings of married life in the name of the Father, the

Son and the Holy Ghost. Amen."

As the family crossed themselves, Father Darby took his seat, and Buster sprang up and extended his arm across the table in a gesture looking as if it had been rehearsed a dozen times in front of a mirror. "Rosie, I want you to come home with me tonight. I swear before this man of God I will never raise a hand to you again—if you will swear your obedience to me and be the loving wife you vowed to be."

Roz sat frozen, staring at his large, extended hand. With a pink scar and a bump across the bridge of his nose, Buster looked more like a thug who would beat someone's brains out than ever. She thought she might be sick again.

Beside her, Roxie whispered an almost inaudible plea, "Don't do it, Roz. Don't do it."

Buster turned his pale eyes toward the girl. Roxie ducked her head as if he might take a swing at her. That flinch released the words from her sister's lips. "I don't trust the words of a bully and a drunk," Roz said.

Madame St. Rochelle gasped. "Darling, won't you take Buster's hand? Forgive and forget since you were both at fault."

"I'm certainly not perfect, Mama, far from it, but I no longer regard myself as Burke Boylan's wife." Roz stood. "I've lost my appetite and will excuse myself from the table."

As she left the room, she hoped Buster would rage or break the dinnerware, showing his true colors to the St. Rochelles. His face had turned red enough when she'd had her say. Instead, she heard her father commend Burke for trying, and her mother apologize for raising such a stubborn, willful daughter. Father

Darby gave Burke a sympathetic pat on the back. She heard nothing from her Uncle Gilbert or Roxie as she locked herself in the guest room.

Chapter Sixteen

Roz guessed Buster would take a long holiday after Thanksgiving and return to work on Monday. She bided her time for three days. When Papa left for work and Mama had gone to her mah-jongg club, she summoned Clement and asked him to drive her to Prytania Street.

Roz rang the bell at her own home, which brought Wilbert running from the kitchen to answer. "Is Mr. Boylan home, Wilbert?"

"No, ma'am. He at the office."

"Good. I want to pack my belongings. Would you ask Lucille to come upstairs and help me?"

"You ain't comin' back, Miss Roz?"

"Never." Roz stood in the small foyer and admired the newly installed banister, sleek and silver. She'd thought she might hang the pictures of the strangely fragmented women along the staircase. How those paintings would have shocked visitors. Burke told her often how much he hated the two Picassos and single Bonnard when she'd brought them back to their hotel in Paris. She need not worry about Buster's opinion anymore. She supposed she'd take the paintings with her. They might be worth a great deal some day. One never knew about art.

Oralee filled the kitchen doorway. "Come let me fix something for you, Miss Roz. You need feedin' up, I can see. Lucille, you get yo'self upstairs and pack her trunks if that what she want."

Roz looked at the three servants and wondered if Burke would keep them on since she did not intend to come back. "Is Mr. Boylan treating all of you well?"

"He never gave me any trouble," Lucille said resentfully as she brushed past to go up to the bedroom.

"High and mighty girl, that one," Oralee said loud enough for the maid to hear. "Come on in the kitchen, sit down, and let her do the work. Wilbert, you go on about your business."

Roz followed Oralee for a last visit with the cook. Oralee opened the icebox and took out a half a cooked beef roast. "Red meat, that's what you need to build you up again."

She sharpened a carving knife on a strop attached to the kitchen wall. "Wilbert say you two had a bad fight. He figured Mr. Boylan was beatin' on you, so he pretended like he come upstairs to clean up a mess, maybe stop him that way. Then, here you come flying through the air like you been dropped from the landin'. Honey, I had a man who hit me once. I took off his ear with a razor, and no man ever messed wit' me again."

Oralee sliced off three cuts of beef, then turned the knife on the fresh loaf of French bread she'd gotten at the bakery that morning. "How you want this po-boy dressed, Miss Roz? I gots fresh lettuce, mustard, onions, and pickles."

"No onions. Oralee, will you stay on here if I don't come back?"

"No, ma'am. I was jus' waitin' to see if you was comin' back and needed Oralee's help. Good cook gots lots of places to go, and I ain't stayin' here wit' the evil eye on me all the time."

"Before I met Burke, I would have said there was no such thing as the evil eye. How wrong can a girl be?"

Wilbert came in to join them. "That uppity girl was out there talkin' away on the telephone. I say to move her behind upstairs and pack yo' trunk. 'Fraid I gots to stay here. Old man like me might not find another job."

"I wish I could take both of you with me, but Mama doesn't need more help, and frankly, I don't know exactly what I'm going to do. Perhaps, I can persuade Papa to let me attend nursing school now, but he's so attached to Buster that he may not let me do anything to gain my independence."

Oralee set a doorstopper of a sandwich in front of Roz and poured a cold tea Roz finished half and offered the rest to Wilbert. "I need to get upstairs and see that Lucille packs everything I want. Thank you both for watching over me when I was so alone."

"God bless, Miss Roz."

She'd miss them, well-meaning Wilbert and the formidable Oralee. Lucille, she wouldn't miss at all. In the bedroom, the maid held a party dress up against herself and gazed into the dressing table mirror.

"Lucille, please put that in the trunk. Let me get something from under the dressing table."

Roz found her makeup case sitting behind the tulle skirt exactly where she had left it. Dust covered the top. Evidently, her maid hadn't bothered to clean under the skirting. The top of the table no longer sat in disarray. The peacock bottle had disappeared, but other perfume containers were arranged around the comb and brush set. When she lifted the stoppers, most of the scent seemed to have evaporated. She glanced up when the bedroom door closed behind Lucille and a key turned in the lock.

"Lucille! What are you doing?"

"I work for Mr. Boylan. He's the one who pays me, not you. You're a crazy woman."

Roz recognized the footsteps pounding up the stairs before Buster said a word. "Welcome home, Rosie. Glad to see you'll be staying."

****

The November light faded early from the window. Roz wondered if a jump from the second story would kill her, but she was denied the chance to find out. Nails had been driven into the frames to prevent the sashes from being raised. She had other ways out if it came to that. She opened the makeup case, lifted the top tray, and took out the soiled purple holster and the tiny gun. Carefully, she fitted two of the small bullets into the chambers and slipped the weapon under the bed pillows. She could use it on Buster—or on herself if the situation became unbearable.

The house stayed strangely still. She'd worn herself out pounding on the door and calling for Wilbert and Oralee to come help her. She heard Burke's presence in the creak of the floorboards as he moved around the rooms.

Several times, Lucille laughed as if she and Buster were having a party to which Rosamond had not been invited. Glasses clattered in the dining room and the aroma of a late meal made its way under the door. No one brought her food and water. She was forced to put the chamber pot under the bed to its original use. Then, she slept.

With the light of dawn, Rosamond got up. In her

first act to gain her freedom, she took a red lipstick from the makeup case and wrote "Help Me!" on the window facing the street. As automobiles and wagons offering fresh vegetables passed, and maids and cooks went on daily errands, the doorbell rang several times. Burke answered inquiries in a low, sad voice. She pressed her face against the glass and mouthed the words, but even the mailman shook his head and stared at her with pity.

Around noon, the telephone rang. Lucille answered promptly and summoned Roz's husband. Burke's voice boomed out loud for Rosamond's benefit. "Yes, Laurence. As I told Clement, Rosamond came to her senses and returned home. She's very ashamed of herself for that scene on Thanksgiving. Lucille is taking good care of her. Yes, she's eating well and resting. I'm taking a few days off from work to be with her. Let's just say you caught us in an act of reconciliation."

Buster's manly chuckle turned Roz's stomach, and she thought how wonderful she had nothing to upchuck.

"Yes, of course we'll be over for Sunday dinner. By that time, you'll see an entirely new Rosamond. Always good to talk to you, Laurence."

During the passage of the long afternoon, the bedroom grew warm and stuffy. Roz slept some more, her hand resting on the pistol beneath the pillow. She woke with a headache and a dry tongue that cleaved to the roof of her mouth. Sitting up made her dizzy and weak-kneed. What had she heard to disturb her? Someone rapped on the door again.

"Don't play possum, Rosie. I know you aren't dead yet. I'll bet you'd like some bread and water, maybe a little of that cold roast beef you left on your plate yesterday."

Despite herself, some saliva spurted into her dry mouth at the thought of the half-eaten po-boy. Cautiously, she answered Burke. "Yes, I would."

"First though, we have to get a few things clear, dear wife of mine. You will never leave me. You will never lock your door against me. Get the upper hand, that's what my father taught me, and never let it drop unless there is a fist on the end of it. In a few minutes, we will start on a new family. Forget trying to keep this one a secret because Lucille will let me know if you are on the rag or not. Wilbert and Oralee are gone, fired, and they'll keep their big darkie mouths shut if they know what's good for them. You are completely mine."

Roz wanted to tell him to go to hell, but that wouldn't do. She had to get him into the room and close enough for the small pistol to do its work. Still, if she were too pliant, Buster would be suspicious.

"Burke, the doctor said we shouldn't have relations for another two weeks at least. Can't we wait? I'll be good. I'll be very good by then."

"I can't wait Rosie-posey. I'm no longer welcome at some of the better whorehouses in town, and I feel the urge. The best thing for you will be to have another child to replace the one you lost through your own fault. Anyway, I've had to tell the neighbors how the loss and the guilt seriously unhinged you, but we are trying so hard to keep you at home until you are better. The sanatorium will be the last resort."

"I do feel much better, Buster. Please, don't send me away." Roz put a small quaver in her voice. Oh, how he loved to be the bully.

"Then, you have to understand, Rosie, you are Mrs.

Burke Boylan. Mrs. Burke Boylan is all you will ever be. Do you understand, Rosamond?"

"Yes, Burke, I understand."

"I'm coming in now, and you will be very happy to see me and will do whatever I ask."

"Yes, Burke, but please don't hurt me again. I'm so weak I might not be able to please you."

Roz cocked the dual hammers of the little gun. "Come in. I'm ready and waiting for you." Knowing he would assume she was lying on the bed, she took three shaky steps toward the door.

Full-chested and confident, Buster entered the room like an emperor coming to visit his concubine. Aiming point blank at his heart, Roz pulled the trigger. The little gun bucked more than she expected. A small rosette of blood blossomed in his starched white shirt just to the right of his red braces.

Buster looked surprised, then furious. That little bullet stopped him no more than a mosquito bite would bring down an ill-tempered bull. One lunge forward and he seized her wrist, bending it back to make her drop the pistol. Roz discharged the pistol again. The bullet angled upward carving a course through Burke's scalp. A veil of blood welled from the wound, curtaining his cold, blue eyes and forcing him to raise his hands to his face to clear his vision.

Roz ran. She kicked over the dressing table stool in her flight, tangling her legs, nearly going down. Buster lumbered after her, fell over the upturned stool and crashed to the floor. He lay still. Roz kept moving out into the hall, down the staircase, the new metal railing cool under her sweating palms. Lucille waited at the bottom, perhaps to stop her. Roz waved the empty pistol.

"Run, Lucille, if you don't want to die like Buster."

The maid took her advice and clattered down the hall in what seemed to be a pair of Rosamond's best T-strap dress shoes. She left the kitchen door wide open behind her and headed for the alley.

Calmly, Roz picked up the telephone receiver and dialed. "Papa, I think I've killed my husband."

Chapter Seventeen

Not feeling she had to say any more, Roz replaced the receiver and went into the kitchen. She took a drinking glass from the cupboard, removed the pick from the cutting board and went to the icebox to chip some shards from the big block it housed. Without Oralee to take care of it, the drip pan was nearly full to overflowing. Roz had the urge to remove the pan and soak her face in the cold water, but instead, she turned and held her glass to the tap.

A shadow blocked the sunlight from the open kitchen door. Clutching the ice pick, Roz spun around. Oralee filled the doorway with her bulk.

"You okay, honey? A friend come in the place where I was waitin' and said she seen Lucille high-tailin' her high-yaller behind down the alley. I done left two messages for yo' uncle that you in trouble. He come get you out?"

"No, Oralee. I had to take care of the situation myself. I shot Buster. He may be dead," Roz said matter-of-factly as she sipped on her ice water. Upstairs, she thought she heard a bump, a groan. "Maybe not."

Roz took a seat at the worn kitchen table and kept the ice pick in easy reach. Oralee eyed her uneasily. "You want I could make you a nice egg sandwich."

"Thank you, I'd like that. I don't expect I'll be

living here much longer, and I'll miss your good cooking. Will you be all right, Oralee? And Wilbert?"

"Sho' thing, Miss Roz. I told Miz Rochon I come and work for her soon as I know you safe. Don't know where Wilbert hidin'. Mr. Boylan scared him bad."

The cook took eggs and a quart bottle of milk from the icebox. She broke the eggs into a small bowl and whipped them with fury, adding a little milk. While the iron frying pan heated a dollop of butter to sizzling over the gas flame, Oralee chopped a little onion and bell pepper to add to the mix along with a pinch of salt. She opened the breadbox and sliced off two pieces from the loaf. The bread had gone a little stale, but would be fine toasted. This was the last little help she could give the girl.

When Laurence St. Rochelle and his brother arrived, they found Rosamond calmly eating that egg sandwich. The ice pick lay near her right hand and a small pistol near her left. Her bobbed blonde hair formed a sweaty cap around her face, and her blue eyes seemed unnaturally large in her pale face. She wore yesterday's clothes, rumpled and stained with a few dark splotches.

"Where is Buster, Rosie?" her uncle asked quietly as if she might turn the gun on him.

"Upstairs, and please don't call me Rosie any more."

Before taking his black bag to the bedroom, Dr. St. Rochelle thanked Oralee for her help. "I was in surgery when you called. The nurse disregarded the messages. She said it sounded like some crazy colored woman calling from a bar."

"Don't mean it ain't true," Oralee answered,

crossing her arms.

"Indeed. Laurence, I'll see how bad the situation is. Stay with—Roz."

The three in the kitchen listened to the noises from above and the tick of the clock mounted on the wall over the table. Footsteps left the bedroom. Water ran in the bath. Someone cursed loud and long. Roz shivered but kept sipping on her ice water.

Gilbert returned. "Well, Burke is alive. He dragged himself to the bed, but as the worst of his injuries is a bad concussion, he probably couldn't stand well enough to get down the stairs. He lost a lot of blood from the scalp wound. As for this," the doctor rolled a small, bloody bullet on to the table. "It lodged in his shoulder muscle. I've cleaned and stitched up both injuries. None are likely to be fatal, but we do have a problem. He wants Rosamond committed to an asylum in return for his silence about the matter."

Laurence St. Rochelle turned red-faced. "We'll see about that! My attorney will be taking statements from Oralee and Wilbert—and that Dr. Landry if we can find him. We'll see who gets put away!"

"All I want is a divorce, Papa. I don't care who is blamed. I need to be free."

"I'd suggest you do go away, Roz, until this mess is straightened out."

Seeing the fear on his niece's face, Dr. St. Rochelle held up a hand. "Not to an asylum or sanatorium. Cousin André and his wife over in Chapelle might enjoy your company. I think your spending some time in the country might be exactly what is needed to fix this situation."

****

Oralee Biggs had some tale to tell that evening in the speakeasy over the colored funeral home. "And I tole 'em, I ain't stayin' and takin' care of that evil-eye man, so they gots a private nurse fo' him. Maid come over from the Esplanade place to finish packin' Miz Roz's belongings and clean up the bedroom. Blood everywhere, she say. That fancy gold bedspread ain't good for nuttin' but rags now. Then, they taken Miss Roz somewhere I can't say. Tomorrow, I makes my statement to a lawyer."

"Law ain't gonna believe no colored cook." Bessie Clarke had stopped in for a nip on her way to deliver a load of fresh laundry to Miss Josie's establishment and should be getting gone. The girls would be wanting their ironed finery about now, not to mention clean sheets.

"Police don't know. If they do get wind, I 'spects the St. Rochelles pay 'em off. This jus' to keep Mr. Boylan in line. Gonna be a divorce."

Having squeezed all the details she could, Bessie went on her way. She traded the story for a good dinner in Miss Josie's kitchen. Some of the working girls still sat finishing their meal, and one in particular enjoyed the tale.

Lulubelle Blanco, whose face had been considerably devalued by Buster Boylan's fist before he was banned from the house, called to the barman to put a bottle of real French champagne on her tab.

"A toast," she cried. "To Rosamond Boylan, Queen of the Mardi Gras Ball. May she never hang for her sins!"

****

Not everyone rejoiced in the news. Roxie St.

Rochelle sat on the porch swing and cried as the servants loaded her sister's trunks to be taken to the docks. The old paddlewheeler that still hauled goods from New Orleans up and down the bayous would leave at dawn. Her parents thought it prudent that Rosamond spend the night in one of the ship's cabins for safety in case Burke was not as indisposed as he seemed and came after her. The train might have been faster, but the elders agreed Roz needed some time to gather herself and Cousin André's wife would need to make preparations for the unexpected guest.

Roz put her arm around her baby sister. "Don't cry, Roxie. I'll call. I'll write. In the summer, you can visit me."

Roxie shoved her sister's arm away. "I'm not crying for you. Mama says there will be a big scandal when the divorce papers are filed, and I must be protected from the gossip. They're sending me to Mt. Carmel Academy all the way out in Rainbow right after Christmas when the nuns can take me. I'll never see Artie again, and it's all your fault!"

"Oh, Sis, Artie will still be living with and off of his parents when you graduate. By then, you'll see he's no great catch."

"Oh, certainly not as great as Burke Boylan. I wish you'd killed him and gone to jail. Instead, they're sending you straight to Dr. Landry because now you're damaged goods, and no one else will marry you."

"Who said that?"

"One of Mama's friends. Mama was crying to her because you wanted a divorce. You always get everything you want. I might as well be dead myself!" Roxie bolted from the swing and ran to her room.

For the first time since shooting Burke, Roz began to tremble. She sobbed, but not for Buster. Being sent in disgrace to Chapelle, Louisiana, she doubted if she would be welcomed with open arms by her cousins or by Dr. Pierre Landry, a man who had held her, comforted her, and then left her without a word one month ago.

Chapter Eighteen

The journey to Chapelle passed slowly, some would have said tediously, as the vessel docked at each village along the way. The first night aboard, Roz slept poorly, but the farther from New Orleans they sailed, the more she was able to rest in the small, private cabin equipped with a moss-stuffed mattress on the bed frame and a mosquito bar over it. Insects weren't a problem as the weather turned cool and rainy.

She watched the scenery pass from the windows of the tiny first-class lounge—the cypress trees tinged a rusty autumn orange, the wild pecans, basswoods and swamp maples bare, the live oaks and magnolias a glossy evergreen. In the larger second-class area, two Cajun families laughed and joked and chattered in their own patois. Listening and translating what she could with her private academy French, Roz gathered they had been to a wedding. Some of the comments were bawdy and made her smile to herself as she paged through a magazine or read a newspaper purchased at one of the stops. One of the men brought a squeezebox along and sang wailing Cajun songs to pass the time, or picked up the tune and encouraged the others to dance as he tapped a rhythm with his foot.

While she ate her solitary meals of plain but hearty food heavy on the biscuits and gravy, the Cajuns shared from baskets they brought aboard. They handed around a sack of oranges and a bunch of bananas purchased in the city to their children like candy. At stops, the men went ashore and returned with tinned sardines, crackers, cold boudin sausages, big dill pickles, and long French loaves if the town had a bakery.

As Roz walked the decks for exercise, black-eyed, dark-haired children raced past her playing tag and taunting each other in two languages. On the second to last day of her journey, as she sat outside wearing her gray Parisian coat against the damp and chill, one of the boys stopped their game and asked, "What kind of animal make dat fur?"

"Guess," Roz told them, hungry for their company.

"Not beaver, not muskrat, not otter, nedder," the oldest boy said, studying her collar with a trapper's experienced eye.

The smallest girl shyly ran a finger over the lush, silvery pelt and guessed, "Bunny rabbit?"

"*Stupide*, Mimi," her brother said. "Maybe wolf, no?"

"Fox, silver fox all the way from Russia," she told them.

"*C'est vrai?*" the children exclaimed with amazement.

"Yes, it's true. I bought the coat in Paris, France. Do you know where that is?"

The little girl shook her head, but the eldest boy shrugged. "You learn dat in da six grade. Next year, I don't to go school no more, me. I trap and fish wit' my papa."

"Oh, but you should finish school!"

Roz received another Gallic shrug. "I can read, write, figure, speak da English. Dat's all I need, Papa says. *C'est finis.*" The boy wiped out his American education with a wave of his hands.

"But you could grow up to be a doctor. Like Dr. Landry, do you know him? He lives in Chapelle."

No, they shook their heads. They don't live by Chapelle. At the next town, the families disembarked and piled into a wagon drawn by two mules named Clotilde and Alphonse and driven by Mimi's *parrain*, as the little girl told Roz when she came to say good-bye. Roz pressed a shiny dime into her hand. "For a treat for you and your brothers and sister. Remember to share."

She saw the father frown, his mouth half-hidden under a wide, bushy mustache, as Mimi displayed her gift. Though her own French roots in Louisiana were probably older than his Acadian origins, Roz knew he considered her a blonde, blue-eyed *Americaine* dressed in smart city clothes. She called out in her questionable French, "*Un petit present pour mes amis,*" and waved them an airy good-bye with her kid-gloved hand.

The father nodded curtly. "*Merci,*" he said. "Mimi?"

"*Merci beaucoup, belle Dame,*" Mimi replied, showing her manners.

Her papa lifted her into the wagon, and they started on their way home, mud from the wheels splattering up from the road. Whether her attempt to use French or her emphasis of the smallness of the gift convinced the man that she wasn't offering charity, she would never know. Rosamond St. Rochelle was traveling deep into the country where Pierre Landry had been raised, and she never felt more out of place, not in Rome, Madrid, or Paris. Had he felt the same among the Creoles of New

Orleans?

The boat whistle sounded, and the crew of Negro men who had carried a few crates ashore came aboard, pulled up the plank joining the paddlewheeler to the bank, and cast off the mooring ropes. That night, the only music came from their quarters among the cargo boxes, a lonely tune played on a harmonica and the moan of the blues. The next morning, the ship docked in Chapelle.

****

Roz wore her red hat for courage and her fine coat for style. She'd applied her makeup with care in order to make a good impression on Cousin André and his wife and whomever else she might meet that day. Above all, she didn't want to appear beaten, bedraggled, or crazy the way Pierre Landry had last seen her.

Her hosts waited inside their auto by the dock, keeping themselves dry from the persistent drizzle that resurrected the ferns in the live oaks and dripped from the swags of gray Spanish moss festooning the trees. The bayou ran high and cloudy under the gangplank as Roz crossed. His gray felt hat pulled low over his eyes, Cousin André came running with an umbrella. He tipped a porter to bring her trunks along in a wooden handcart and hustled his guest to the automobile.

Cousin André, not really her cousin but her father's, had a few years on Laurence. Both men stood tall and had a sort of portly presence that spoke of money and power, but Cousin André possessed a much larger bald spot in his fair, thinning hair and rarely went about without a hat to cover it. His wife, Loretta, short, plump, and olive-complected, allowed gray to streak in her thick, dark hair without resorting to dye as Emmaline did. Roz had to exercise her imagination to see them as a smitten Romeo and Juliet sort of couple who had married for love and settled far away from the disapproval of the St. Rochelles.

Loretta offered a hand across the seat as Roz slid into the back of the car. "Did you have a restful voyage, dear?"

"Yes, very restful."

"With the last of my girls away at the Academy in Rainbow and the older ones married, we have plenty of room. Of course, our youngest is still at home, and eight-year-old boys like Henri can be a handful."

"I'm sure Henri and I will get along fine, Cousin Loretta." She knew well that the couple kept trying until they had a son, though Cousin André always spoke of his six lovely daughters with pride. Two of their female brood had studied at the Academy during Roz's stay. Neither had been in her class, however.

"Feel free to stay as long as it takes—as long as you want," Loretta said delicately.

"I believe the standard waiting time for a divorce is one year, but I wouldn't dream of imposing so long."

There, that got the scandal out in the open and effectively killed the conversation as they traveled two blocks up from dock and four blocks to the right on Main Street to stop before a low, gracious home of white siding and deep green shutters. The house sat on a corner lot and was wrapped on two sides by a deep porch scattered with wicker furniture and draped by hanging baskets of Boston ferns that hadn't yet been taken in for the winter. A boy peered through an opening in the railing and popped up to his full height when the grown-ups climbed the three steps to the porch.

"Ain't she a looker, Daddy?" Cousin Henri said to his mother's embarrassment.

André St. Rochelle cleared his throat in a way that made Roz miss her own father. "Henri, this is your Cousin Rosamond, and yes, she is certainly an attractive young lady, but it's not your place to say so."

"Hi, I'm Roz." She held out her gloved hand, and Henri gave it a quick shake.

The boy had the dark eyes and hair of his mother, curly lashes that Roxie would have envied, and a sprinkling of cinnamon freckles across his nose. He possessed the assured smile and outgoing nature of a child who had rarely been reprimanded in any serious way.

"You're supposed to have Janelle's old room. She's married away, so it's free. It's way down the hall from mine 'cause Mama says you need your privacy, but we can visit. I'll show you where it is." Henri raced to open the front door and sprint up the staircase.

Roz followed him to a comfortable bedroom at the end of the hall. It wasn't far from the modern bathroom and offered a pleasant view of the backyard, which still had an outhouse with a sweet olive planted by the door in its far corner. The flowerbeds had been put to rest for the winter, but large azalea bushes screened the yard from the side street.

A double bed with a white iron headboard and an old-fashioned armoire took up most of the space, but a night table with a reading lamp had been squeezed in along with two ladder-backed chairs on either side of a window curtained in frills that matched the bedspread.

Dainty posies patterned the wallpaper, a maiden's room—how kind of them.

"Why don't you have a rest until dinner? We'll send up your trunks, and you can arrange things as you want them, but if you need help, call for the maid. Then, tomorrow we will all go to early Mass. It's a pleasant walk if the rain lets up."

"We used to make quite a procession when all the girls were home." Cousin André gazed fondly at his wife. "Won't it be nice to have a young woman with us again?"

Loretta didn't respond to that question. "You'll want to meet Father Grainger and some of our friends after Mass. Afterwards we treat ourselves to hot beignets at Pommier's Bakery right on the square."

"No, thank you. I'd prefer to sleep in."

Loretta gave her husband an "oh my!" glance. "Yes, I can understand how the journey must have tired you. Perhaps, next Sunday."

"No, I don't think so. If I am going to be cut off from the sacraments as a divorced woman, I believe I should get used to doing without the Holy Catholic Church."

Loretta was too shocked to reply, but Henri piped up, "Can I stay home, too?"

Cousin André came to the rescue. "No, you may not, son. Besides, you don't want to miss out on those beignets, do you?"

"Guess not."

"You may feel differently after you've been here a while. Most of the social life, such as there is, revolves around the Church, and you aren't a divorced woman yet so—"

145

Loretta cut him off. "Let's simply allow Cousin Roz to rest."

"Thank you. I'm sorry if I've been rude. I do appreciate your taking me in, truly. I'll try not to be a bother. Let me unpack and rest until dinner." Finally, they left her alone.

Roz put her clothes away, some folded in the armoire, some hung in the closet, a few items left in the trunk at the foot of the bed. Whatever possessed Odette to pack both her wedding gown and her Mardi Gras ball dress in tissue at its bottom? Perhaps, the maid couldn't bear to leave the costly garments behind on Prytania Street. Whatever, they could stay there in the dark of the trunk, unused and unwanted.

Roz tried to relax but found herself pacing the small room as she had the deck of the ship. She did not want to rest. She wanted to prowl the streets of Chapelle until she came face to face with Pierre Landry.

Chapter Nineteen

Cousin Roz was a bother. She stayed in bed until the family left for Mass and didn't take any breakfast when she rose. Instead, she dressed and went out, who knew where, meeting them at the bakery after Mass where she declared the beignets to be as good as any in New Orleans. That may have won her approval from Baker Pommier, but dressed in that fancy coat and red hat, how could anyone not know she hadn't attended Mass? Without telling her friends the whole sordid story, how could Loretta explain Rosamond St. Rochelle?

Roz, herself, seemed unbothered by this quandary. "I went for a long walk. That's all. After being on the boat, I needed the exercise."

She'd set out after being quite sure Mass had begun. As she passed the old frame and stucco church of Ste. Jeanne d'Arc with its statue of the martyred saint—another woman no one understood—on its manicured lawn, she wondered if Pierre worshiped inside. Did he come here to pray? Did he attend with his family? Did he go for beignets after Mass? She kept walking.

A block from the Catholic church stood the substantial red brick First Methodist. By the rousing sound of the organ, the service was in full swing. The signboard claimed, "The Methodist Church Welcomes

You!" and announced the sermon for today as "Come Unto Me." Roz never believed in omens but seemed to have come face to face with the real thing. She slipped quietly inside and sat in the very last row to escape notice. Of course, a minister always notices who sits in the last row, especially if they wear a red hat.

When the time came to greet visitors, he urged her to stand and receive the welcome of the congregants beside her and in the row just ahead. She gave her name, indicated she visited relatives, and politely turned down an invitation for coffee, cake, and fellowship following the service.

Roz sat again and marveled at the plain walls free of the Stations of the Cross or statues of saints. She regarded the naked cross above the altar that seemed to say Christ had finished suffering and gone to be with his Father. Though the tall stained glass windows sparkled and the high ceiling of wooden vaults free of gilding were beautiful, she enjoyed the simplicity of the service the most—few rote replies, no mystical Latin phrases, and at least this week, no communion and no need to confess personal sins. Roz swore that even in the last row, she could smell the light scent of burning candles and the fragrance of the altar flowers unobscured by the heaviness of incense.

Reverend Grant took her hand as she left after the service and invited her to worship for the duration of her stay. If he'd known about the mess she'd made of her life, Roz doubted he would be so cordial. He'd probably suggest she give the Baptists a try. Still, she felt lighter than she had in a long time and hungrier, hungry for hot beignets at the bakery across from the Catholic church.

She found Loretta, André, and Henri standing in a long line waiting to purchase a brown paper sack of the square little doughnuts fresh from the vat of boiling lard. Henri dashed from the line to greet her and on the way back to his parents introduced her to his friends.

"These're my buddies, Teodore Broussard, but we call him Tubbs, and Aldus Thibodeaux. You can call him Boozoo."

Roz could see how Teodore became Tubbs. The chubby boy steadily made his way through a personal bag of beignets, the powdered sugar drifting down the front of his shirt. Boozoo Thibodeaux was as thin as his friend was fat and looked almost like a cranky old man until he smiled and elbowed Tubbs to share his doughnuts before they all disappeared down his friend's throat. Henri tugged on her coat until Roz bent so he could whisper in her ear.

"Tubbs' grandpa runs the biggest and best speakeasy in Ste. Jeanne Parish. He gives us free root beer when we deliver his hooch to customers. Don't tell Ma."

"Henri, come here! It will soon be our turn. Roz, glad you decided to join us," Loretta called out, but she didn't seem all that happy.

Roz stood with the family as the line inched forward. The baker's wife handed another bag to yet another customer. "*Bon appetit*, Madame Landry."

Roz stepped from her place. "Excuse me, but are you related to Dr. Pierre Landry?"

"Dere's lotsa Landrys in Ste. Jeanne Parish. We all related. What you want wit' him?" the stocky woman in the plain brown dress asked suspiciously.

"We knew each other in New Orleans. He cared for

me once."

"Dat's our Pierre. He been carin' for women since Susu Theriot in da eight grade," replied a lean man wearing his dark Sunday suit and fresh, ironed white shirt. His best hat sat tipped back on a head of iron gray hair the same color as his drooping mustache. Tanned and lined, his face portrayed a life of outdoor work. This was the visage Pierre Landry would wear when he passed fifty.

"You must be his father or a very close relative," Roz said.

"I'm guilty of dat, *oui*. Simon Landry, his papa." Pierre's father shook her hand and offered Roz a beignet from one of the two large sacks he carried.

Knowing the grease would stain her kid gloves she reached in and took one anyway. The powdered sugar snowed over her coat and caught in the silvery fur collar when she took a bite.

"*Bon*, no?"

"As good as any in New Orleans."

Behind her cash register, Madame Pommier beamed, but directly in front of Roz, Pierre's mother gave the city woman a hot, angry glare. She said something to her husband in a rush of Cajun French. The only word Roz caught was "trouble."

"Don't mind Alida. She still mad she can't drag Pierre to church by da ear no more. He ain't much for religion."

"Too much school, dat's what," Alida Landry snapped. "Too much in da city."

"Please tell Pierre I asked after him. I'm staying with the André St. Rochelle family if he has the time to call."

"Sure t'ing." Simon Landry nodded pleasantly as he steered his wife toward the door.

Alida let out another burst of French. Roz understood none of the words, but they had the tone of "not a chance in Hell."

From her place in line, Loretta St. Rochelle watched and thought, Oh, yes. Rosamond would be quite a bother.

Chapter Twenty

Pierre didn't come to call. Rosamond took up a place on the front porch and spent hours reading there on the wicker lounge with a quilt over her legs and a heavy sweater covering her dress. Loretta suggested she might be more private on the side porch, but Roz replied she liked to watch the cars and wagons go by. All the vehicles in Chapelle seemed to be the reliable Ford Model T in its standard black color. One of them slowed as it passed, and she stood up letting her book drop and the quilt slide to the damp porch floor, but the car moved on. She couldn't be sure Pierre Landry had been behind the wheel.

When she grew too chilled, she took her book inside and sat in the warmth of the kitchen where Ethel, the cook, tempted her with pralines right off the marble slab, and slices of pecan pie cooled just enough to eat.

"Gon' put some meat on yo' bones," Ethel promised.

"You remind me of Oralee, my cook in the city."

"Doan know nobody in Naw Or'lins. Dis here weather makin' my pralines all sticky. Never seen so much rain." The cook looked out the back window. "You gon' cotch a cold you keep sittin' outside. You be too puny to fight it off."

"If I stay here long enough, I'll get fat on your cooking."

"Not de way you walkin' all over town." Ethel watched the rain come down and shook her head. "Miz Roz, dey talkin' 'bout you. Had it from Verna Harkrider's girl. Dey sayin' you shot yo' husband and gon' get divorced 'cause of it."

Roz stared into the black pool of coffee in her cup. She had a bitter taste in her mouth from the last bite of the pie, a bad pecan maybe.

"He beat me, Ethel. He beat me, and I lost the child I was carrying. Truth to tell, I wish I had killed him— that he wasn't waiting there in New Orleans for me to come back. I guess that makes me unrepentant."

"Had a man who beat me, had my boys by him. I was raised Cat'lic. My mama was so strict she wouldn't let us never eat nuttin' befo' Mass. Always fish on Fridays. When I divorce dat man, she say I damned to Hell. Know what? I gots myself a new church, the AME. I may never go to Cat'lic heaven, but I be singing wit' de AME choir in paradise. Dat's how I figure."

Loretta bustled into the kitchen. "Are the pralines ready for the Garden Club meeting, Ethel? Pie before dinner, Rosamond? You'll lose your lovely figure. Heaven knows I lost mine to having children." She put her fingers up to her plump cheeks. "Oh, I'm so sorry I said that."

"Here be your pralines, all packed up for de meetin'," Ethel said a trifle sullenly.

"I suppose you let Henri run off with some of them," Loretta went on, trying to act normally.

"My pies and pralines don't hurt nobody."

"Of course not. They are divine, as I tell all my friends. Roz, won't you come with me? Afterwards, some of us are going to decorate the church with greenery. You've been here two weeks, and it's time you met some people in Chapelle."

"But, do they want to meet me?"

"I don't know why you would say that."

"If I could borrow an umbrella, I think I'll walk to the library and get a new book."

"Certainly you may borrow an umbrella. There are several in the hat stand by the front door. Louisiana weather, you know. Come, I'll show you."

Roz followed her down the hall and selected an umbrella as Loretta pulled a stylish dark green hat with the tiniest spray of quail feathers on the side over her thick bobbed hair and buttoned up a brown wool coat trimmed in beaver.

"Sammy is bringing the car around. Why don't we take you to the library? It's on the way to my meeting. Emmaline will never forgive me if you catch your death of cold while you're visiting."

"Thank you. I'll get my wrap."

Sammy ran up the walk and held two black umbrellas over the ladies' heads as they made their way through the downpour to the automobile. He opened the back door, keeping them dry all the while.

"You know, Rosamond," Loretta began as soon as they were seated, "you shouldn't spend so much time in the kitchen talking with the servants. I know your mother would not approve."

"Oh, my mother doesn't approve of much that I do."

"She has your best interests at heart, dear. If you live with us quietly until the divorce goes through, you know that afterwards, you may seek an annulment and be free to marry again within the church. Under the circumstances, I am sure an annulment won't be any problem, and of course, the St. Rochelles have the money to pay for it."

"I'm aware of that. The last time I did as my parents wanted, I married Burke Boylan. Now, they want to buy back my maidenhood," Roz said, that bitter taste in her mouth again.

"I know a year seems like a long time at your age, but if the divorce is granted on separation rather than on, well, violent acts on both sides, it will be so much better for your reputation. You can go on with your life as if none of this ever happened. Oh, and I wouldn't make any more inquiries about Dr. Landry. You know how people will talk, a St. Rochelle running after one of the Landrys."

"Yes, I know what you mean. The St. Rochelle reputation must be protected at all costs. Frankly, I'm surprised at you, Cousin Loretta. I thought that you and André had defied the family by marrying because a Chapelle girl wasn't good enough for the St. Rochelles. The city cousins say the only reason Chapelle has a bank is because they had to give André a way to make a living here."

Loretta colored all the way to the rim of the hat pulled down nearly to her eyes. "The Duchene family is descended from French royalty driven out during the Terror and forced to make lives in Louisiana."

"Yes, it seems that everyone in Chapelle is descended from French royalty except the Cajuns. At least they don't lie about their origins."

"I'll have you know my daddy owned the biggest mercantile in town. The dress I wore to the *bal masque* of Rex came all the way from Paris. All my girls have been or will be debs. None of them have ever made a misstep and the three oldest married very well. That's why I was asked to look after you, to keep you in the arms of the Church until you are free to take your place in society again. The St. Rochelles asked a favor of me, Loretta Duchene, who was never good enough, no matter how hard I tried."

Roz thought at first the rain had blown in through a crack in the window and landed on Loretta's cheek, but those were tears, genuine tears, rolling down her keeper's soft-chinned face.

"I'm sorry. What I said was cruel and ungrateful. I'm having trouble with gratitude right now. I keep thinking of women who can't afford an annulment, who stay with brutal men because the Church tells them they must. My heart says this isn't right."

"There I sat in my beautiful gown at the Rex ball after all the debs had danced, and no one came to call for me. Daddy had begged the invitation from a business associate in the city, and nobody knew who I was or cared. Then, I looked up, and there stood André, so tall and handsome. He asked why the loveliest girl at the dance looked so sad. I said no one had asked me to dance. If that was all it took to make a pretty woman smile, he said, then it was totally within his power to make me happy," Loretta went on, entirely caught in the past.

"Cousin André said that?" Roz would have sworn portly, balding Cousin André's greatest love was squeezing big profits out of his tiny bank.

"He found excuses to come to Chapelle, said the town was growing, needed a bank, and he wanted to look for a good location. One night after Daddy had gone to bed we snuck out to Broussard's Barn and got married. The St. Rochelles tried to have it annulled at once, but we told them we'd made a baby, a lie we worked hard to make true. We had our union blessed by the Church, of course. And then my girls started coming one after another. André looked at each one and said, 'Another beautiful daughter, I'll bet she'll be queen of the Mardi Gras one day.' By the time Henri made his appearance, my dragon of a mother-in-law was dead and gone. She called my lovely girls the country bumpkins."

"Yes, I remember Great-aunt Mildred. She slapped me across the stomach if I slouched, but Uncle Bert slipped me quarters for treats. Were any of your girls Mardi Gras queens?"

"Oh, yes, each in their turn, but just here in town. André is a pillar of the community and a very successful businessman. That matters even more than 'who's your daddy' in Chapelle."

How gladly she would have given her crown to one of Loretta's girls. Roz opened her handbag and handed Loretta a compact mirror. "Here, fix your face before you go to your meeting. Don't let those garden club ladies see you crying."

Loretta glanced around, suddenly aware that the car was parked by the Methodist church hall, which housed the town's tiny one room library. She blotted her face with the powder puff and used her embroidered hankie to erase the dark rings under her eyes.

Handing the engraved silver compact back to Roz, she said, "Thank you. Take an umbrella with you. It's sure to rain again, Rosamond. Sammy, I'll be late. Step on it.""

The rain had ended, and Roz dodged the deep puddles left behind right up to the door of the hall. She entered and headed for the room where ladies of Chapelle had set up a small lending library stocked mainly with their donations. The gray-haired volunteer sitting at the old oak desk told Roz the previous week that as a visitor, she would be allowed to take out only one book. When that was returned, she could have another. Roz planned to trade Agatha Christie's *Murder on the Links* for the *Mysterious Affair at Styles*. The waiting list for the single copy of *The Murder of Roger Ackroyd* was dreadfully long, she had been informed.

Roz smiled at today's volunteer, a black-haired, sharp-eyed woman who watched her every move as if Roz planned to smuggle *Peter Pan* out under her coat. She ducked behind the single stack where she couldn't be seen just to irritate the woman who had to get up out of her chair and stretch to see around the corner. Roz waved her fingers at the vigilant volunteer and withdrew a volume of short stories from the shelf.

She thumbed through *In Our Time* by Ernest Hemingway, which seemed to be a collection of depressing stories about the Great War. She reached the back of the book and was about to close it when she noted the name signed half way down on the book card in its manila pocket. Pierre Landry had held this book in his hands not more than a week ago. She couldn't seem to put the volume back on the shelf. No doubt he read short stories because he had no time for longer works, for phone calls, or personal visits. Despite her flare of anger, Roz hugged the book to her chest for just a moment. The librarian of the day gave her a very peculiar look.

"Please put the book back on the shelf where you found it, Miss, if you aren't going to check it out."

Rosamond St. Rochelle, book molester, whatever would people say? "I may want this one, but let me look at the Christies again. No chance I could take home two, I don't suppose?"

"That would be against the rules, Miss, unless you are a resident of Chapelle, and I haven't seen you around before."

"Sadly, just a visitor. I'm a guest of André and Loretta St. Rochelle."

Roz drifted up the alphabet to the C's, intentionally keeping the Hemingway tucked under one arm. The door to the library opened, and another patron entered, shook out her umbrella in the hall, and then propped it next to Rosamond's against the wall. The ersatz librarian was forced to return to the desk to serve the next customer.

"Slow today, Verna?" the newcomer asked.

"The rain keeps people away. I have time on my hands, I'm afraid, Rena."

"Well, you can always read!" The two ladies shared a laugh.

Roz stayed behind the stack, but watched Verna beckon silently to the other woman through a break in the books. Quietly, Roz came as close to the desk as she could without being seen.

"That's her back there, Rosamond St. Rochelle. The newspaper said she was visiting André and Loretta for a long stay," Verna whispered.

"Poor young thing. Loretta said the girl miscarried her first child and is having difficulty getting over it,"

Rena answered softly, the wattles of her aged neck wobbling.

"Not what I heard from my Aunt Gertie in New Orleans. Truth is she shot her husband and threw herself down the stairs to get rid of the baby. You know these flapper girls. They want to sleep around and not ruin their figures with children. The high and mighty St. Rochelles are trying to cover it all up, but the word is out. She might even be a little...you know, loony." Verna spun a finger around her ear.

Roz popped out from behind the stack. She laid the Hemingway on the desk. Looking Verna in the eye, she pointed to a shelf holding a dozen books marked on their spines with a red letter A, which appeared to have been painted on with nail lacquer.

"Give me *The Scarlet Letter* by Hawthorne. The nuns at Mt. Carmel Academy wouldn't allow it in their library, but I think it might be exactly the book for me."

Verna lowered her eyes as she stamped a due date on a slip of paper and had Roz sign the book card. "Since you're staying with the St. Rochelles, you could have two books if you want. Everyone knows André and Loretta."

"This is all I want, thank you." Roz seized *The Scarlet Letter* and marched over to get her umbrella.

"Think she heard me?" Verna asked in an undertone.

"Oh, yes," replied Rena, gazing at Roz with sympathetic eyes. "So young."

Don't let them see you cry. Don't let them see you cry. Roz started out of the church hall but a gentle hand on her arm waylaid her. She spun around. Reverend Grant held out a Bible.

"I know the St. Rochelles are affiliated with the Catholic church, but I couldn't help but notice you've been attending services with us the last two weeks. I thought, perhaps, you'd like to have a Bible. I know reading the Scriptures isn't encouraged by the Papists, but the good word does bring comfort in time of need. Ah, I see you're reading *The Scarlet Letter*. We've come a long way since those days."

"Do you really believe that, Reverend?"

"I do. I hope to see you again this Sunday, Mrs. Boylan."

"Perhaps. Good afternoon, Reverend."

Roz walked out into a new shower. Despite the umbrella, the wind blew the rain against her face. She was free to cry all the way down Main Street without anyone noticing at all as she clutched the two volumes close to keep them from getting wet.

Chapter Twenty-One

Roz stopped displaying herself on the front porch and tried to stay out of the warmth of the kitchen for Loretta's sake. She avoided Pommier's Bakery, and instead accepted a slice of lemon pound cake and some very good coffee from the Methodists after service. The aged woman named Rena made a point of speaking to her, and Mrs. Grant introduced Roz to others in the congregation. Methodist fellowship didn't last nearly as long as the line at Pommier's, and Roz found herself back at the house before her hosts. She had nothing to do but sit and read in the parlor.

The Scarlet Letter, as it turned out, wasn't nearly as spicy as its banning at Mt. Carmel implied. In fact, Roz found it rather a drag despite her sympathy for the outcast Hester cooped up with her slightly creepy child, Pearl. The Bible, now, turned out to be much juicier than expected. From the very beginning, the Bible abounded with murder, incest, betrayal, and adultery taken to its highest levels by good King David. As for the *Song of Solomon*—no way that psalm talked about the Church. Roz suspected the poem to be simply too beautiful and passionate for even the fathers of the church to excise.

Bearing a grease-stained bag, Henri raced into the room with his offering for Roz. "I brought you some beignets, Cousin Roz. Whatcha reading?"

"The Bible."

"Any good?"

"They should probably put a red A on the spine. Let's go back in the kitchen, and we can eat these with a glass of milk. No, on second thought, ask Ethel to bring a couple of glasses of milk in here."

Ethel brought two glasses of milk on a tray and set it down with a thunk on a marble-topped table next to Roz. She stood there for a minute, her big bosom heaving over the beverages. "Just so's you know, I gots Sunday dinner to finish up. Den I go to my own church rest o' the day."

Roz noted Ethel's polka-dotted dress covered by a large white apron splotched with whipped potatoes. Ethel had her best hat secured to her head with a pin large enough to spit a chicken and driven through her small steel-wool topknot.

"If we want more milk, I'll pour it. Enjoy your church service."

"Nuthin' I enjoy more dan praisin' de Lawd, Miss Roz." Ethel stomped back to the kitchen.

"That was a close one," Roz said to Henri. "She could have killed us both with that hat pin."

"Aw, Ethel's okay, just kinda touchy. She lets me have cookies between meals. Don't tell Mama."

"I wouldn't dream of it. Say, is there a Sunday matinee at the theater here in town?"

"Naw, people are supposed to go to church on Sundays, and old Mr. Elmer who owns the place is a hard-shell Baptist. There's a Charlie Chaplin flicker showing next Saturday," Henri informed her hopefully.

"It's a date, then. You, me, Tubbs and Boozoo. How about that?"

"Well, we'll have to meet Tubbs and Boozoo at the Palace. Ma says they're guttersnipes, but they're lots more fun than the boys at St. Jeanne's Parochial. Boo lives in that little white house behind his daddy's gas station. I'll ask Ethel's Willie to get a message to Tubbs." Henri thought for a minute. "We could take Willie with us, too, but he'd have to sit in the balcony."

"I always thought sitting in the balcony might be fun."

"Guess so, but only niggers are allowed up there, same as in church."

"We don't call them that, Henri. You should say colored or Negroes."

"Yeah, that's what Mama says, too."

"Well, Willie is invited. My treat."

****

Roz kept herself busy in acceptable ways leading up to her big date with four very young men on Saturday. She supposed Verna Harkrider would blow that up into an orgy involving three white men, a black, and the mad divorcée. Nothing Roz could do to stop the gossip other than to go about her business trying to adhere to Loretta's wishes.

She took some of the generous allowance her father banked with Cousin André and attempted to do some Christmas shopping in the small stores that lined Main Street. At the only jewelry shop where watches were repaired and engraving done, Roz found a slim, silver ladies' fountain pen among the heavy barreled masculine writing implements. She asked them to engrave it with Roxie's name.

At the Chapelle Mercantile Emporium, she managed to buy a box of good writing paper that gathered dust among the school supplies. That would take care of Roxie whom Roz hoped would write when she got over being angry. She found a large sack of glass marbles there for Henri. He seemed to lose his on a regular basis to Tubbs and Boozoo who sometimes returned enough to Henri to allow the games to continue. Roz passed over a clasp knife the boy might have preferred, knowing his mother would object to any dangerous object.

La Petite Dress Shoppe, named for the size of the establishment and not for the large, sack-like dresses in last year's styles that made up the merchandise, yielded nothing for her mother or Loretta. Still, she had the silk scarves bought in Paris and given to no one in the turmoil that followed her return to New Orleans. Mama could wear the red one with the oriental motif as a sash for her kimono when she went to her Mah-jongg club, and the dark blue with golden stripes scarf, once intended for her chilling mother-in-law, would look lovely on Loretta.

Fortunately, the tobacco shop and newstand carried a good grade of Cubans for special customers, and Roz made a friend of the owner by purchasing two entire fragrant wooden boxes of the cigars, one for her papa and one for André. The array of cigarettes tempted her. She had days when she would have walked a mile for a Camel, but Loretta permitted no smoking in her home, and her husband took his cigars out on the porch or enjoyed them in his office at the bank. Just as well. Smoking might soothe her problems but wouldn't solve them.

Catching Mrs. Elmo at the ticket window of Palace Theater, Roz bought a dozen moving-picture passes for

Ben-Hur which the proprietors were showing again this year during the holidays. Evidently, no one in Chapelle ever tired of Ramon Novarro in the title role, Francis X. Bushman as the evil Messala, the thrilling chariot race, or the Christian message of the film. The passes would serve as small gifts for anyone she might have overlooked, and any leftover could be given to Henri and his friends.

On another fair day, Roz returned *The Scarlet Letter* to its place on the adult shelf at the library, still wondering how anyone could not suspect Arthur Dimmesdale right from the beginning. But then, men, apparently, could get away with anything until God caught up with them, an opinion she expressed to the library volunteer of the day. Miss Rena gave her a warm smile and nodded a head covered with short, frizzy salt-and-pepper hair. "That's the Lord's truth," she agreed and encouraged the visitor to take out two books, *The Sun Also Rises* as well as *The Great Gatsby*.

The following day, Roz stopped by the only beauty salon in town and entered cautiously. All gossip stopped at the shampoo bowls and barber chairs as Roz asked for an appointment. Miss Irma, the proprietor of Irma's Kuts and Kurls who had two girls performing their tasks under her, figured she could work Roz in if all she wanted was to have her roots retouched. It was. After looking at some of Irma's frizzy handiwork, Roz made an instant decision to let her hair grow out into softer, looser waves.

Roz flipped through old copies of *Good Housekeeping* while she waited. Conversation resumed—women complaining about husbands and children, exchanging recipes, talking about their

Christmas preparations, women with normal lives getting away from it all for an hour or two. No one spoke to her or to the redhead occupying the third chair.

Roz reached the bottom of the stack of magazines where an old copy of the *Daily Mirror* tabloid yellowed, still flashing its lurid headlines about the Hall-Mills murder case in which a wife arranged for the killing of her unfaithful husband and his paramour. Feeling queasy with the thought that she might have ended up as fodder for the press if the St. Rochelles had less influence, Roz wanted to get up and go silently back out into the drizzle that had begun to fall. She imagined the headline, "Queen of the Mardi Gras Ball Shoots Husband."

As Roz stood, Miss Irma, sensing the loss of a client, whipped the drape from the neck of a customer, declared the fat, graying woman, gorgeous, absolutely gorgeous, and hustled her out of the chair. "Miz Boylan, you're next."

Irma did her best, talking about the weather and asking where Roz came from as if she really didn't know. As the hairdresser waited for the timer to ding, she confided to Roz that the woman who had gotten the henna rinse and gone on her way after giving a big tip was one of Wally Broussard's girls. When Roz looked blank, Irma leaned closer and said, "You know, a lady of the evening from out at the Barn."

Overhearing, the young woman in the next chair who was having her black hair shingled and her brows waxed to a thin dark line, remarked, "I don't know why you accept their business, Irma. Some of us would rather not mingle with Chapelle's soiled doves, you know."

"Well, Miz DeVille, I guess they got to get their hair done like anyone else. Wasn't that one the Elmo's youngest girl who got herself in trouble but never had the baby? You're about the same age, aren't you?"

"Yes, we knew each other slightly. She used to sell tickets at the theater. Her name was Marian then, but she goes by Eloise now, so as not to shame her family any further. They won't have anything to do with her. If I keep running into trash here," Mrs. Deville declared, "I might have to take my custom to Lafayette." She looked pointedly at Roz.

The narrow-hipped young matron, showing a belly with the gentle curve of the mid-point of pregnancy, rose from her chair as the assistant named Nancy fussed over her, brushing off her client's shoulder to remove snips of hair. The woman fished in her alligator handbag for a quarter and handed it to Nan along with the fee for the cut. She fluttered her fingers to the other ladies in the shop, making the diamonds of her wedding and engagement rings flash under the lights, and walked out beneath the awning where her driver and a large black auto waited by the curb.

"Last year's Mardi Gras queen, can't y'all just tell," Nancy commented. "She'll never have to work for a living since she snagged Mayor DeVille's oldest boy right out of college this past spring. Eloise gave Betsy a whole dollar."

When Roz left the shop, she carefully tipped fifty cents.

****

Saturday came at last as eagerly anticipated by Roz as by the boys. Henri ran ahead when he spied Boozoo and Tubbs waiting under the red and green marquee of

168

the Palace, its rows and rows of light bulbs shining through the gray of the day. Ethel's Willie, immaculately dressed in a clean white shirt and brown knickers that were probably Henri's outgrown clothes, trailed behind.

She saw Henri tip his big, floppy cap over his eyes in imitation of his friends as if he were trying to make up for the fact that his mother had forced him to wear an argyle sweater vest over his shirt to keep off the damp. Roz doubted Henri even owned denim overalls like his friends wore over their cotton shirts.

Catching up with the group, she was about to purchase the twenty-five cent tickets when the boys protested. They wanted to sit in the pit right up close to the screen, so instead, Roz doled out fifty cents for all of them. Inside, she purchased each boy a popcorn, a soda pop, and some licorice whips, and sent Willie off to the balcony with an order to meet them again in the lobby after the film.

The inside of the theater hardly lived up to its name. The walls were green with a red border and a sagging, moth-eaten velvet curtain covered the screen. Despite the cleanliness of the aisles, a faint odor of mildew rose from the upholstered seats. Under the shadow of the balcony, a few young couples necked, not heeding the admonitions of the nuns at Ste. Jeanne's that if the upper deck collapsed they would die in a state of sin.

Henri and his gang led Roz to the second row in the very front of the theater, the first row filled already with squirming boys. Before long, Mrs. Elmo positioned herself at the upright piano, stretched her fingers, and launched into a short recital to quiet the customers. Slowly the curtain opened, and the newsreel began to run. The young boys hooted at pictures of Mrs. Calvin Coolidge and her son in a sissy suit decorating Christmas trees in the Blue Room of the White House. Mrs. Elmo, who played appropriately festive holiday songs, removed her fingers from the keys, spun on her stool and told them all to hush or the usher would eject them from the theater, no refunds given.

After the shorts, Charlie Chaplin at last made his appearance, twirling his cane and doing his funny walk as he endured mishap after mishap. Mrs. Elmo punctuated every pratfall by pounding on the keyboard, then resumed a merry tune as the Little Tramp went on his way to the next disaster. Although Roz had seen the film before at the magnificent Loew's State Theater in the city, she laughed along with the boys. One never got tired of Chaplin.

The lights came up, the smoochers in the back rows unclenched, and Roz followed the boys into the lobby. Beyond its glass doors, the sky had clouded over again. As they walked back toward Thibodeaux's Canal Station, Boozoo wet the end of a licorice whip, smeared black under his nose and did a creditable imitation of the Chaplin walk, twirling an imaginary umbrella they soon wished was real. He and Tubbs peeled off at the gas station and ran for the cover of the Thibodeaux house. Roz, Henri, and Willie bolted for home but arrived soaked to the skin and laughing.

Loretta was not so amused. She hurried Henri upstairs to soak in a tub of hot water while she brought him dry clothes. Roz, glad she had worn the cloth coat with the wide lapels instead of the fur and a hat that shed some of the rain, stripped out of her wet garments and wrapped up in a housecoat and slippers. She made her way to the kitchen for a cup of the scalding coffee always on the stove and heard Willie regaling his grandmother with his adventure.

"Charlie, he threw down a banana peel and dat cop went bottoms up, he sho' did."

Willie's shoes were already stuffed with newspaper and drying in the oven. His shirt hung over a chair back near the stove while the boy himself, wrapped in a quilt, drank coffee milk from a tin cup.

"What you say to Miss Roz for takin' you?" Ethel prompted.

"I 'preciate it, Miss Roz. Thank you kindly."

The cook gave the boy a stage plank ginger cookie frosted in pink. "You want I should bring coffee to your room, Miz Roz?"

"No, no, I think I'd like to sit here near the stove and listen to Willie talk about the movie. It was the nicest time I've had since I came to Chapelle."

After a while, Ethel's husband arrived to collect the boy. The cook looked on both of them fondly as they left. "Dat's my man, Andy. He do yards 'round town. Met him at the AME. Helped me raise my boys and now Willie, too, since his ma run off. I done told Jackson, my oldest, she was no good, but men, dey doan listen."

Roz nodded her agreement. "Say, Ethel, do you know anyone who could dye a dress for me?"

"Sho'. De laundry woman come on Monday. She do it fo' you."

"Great. Let me run upstairs and get it. I want it dyed red, bright red."

Roz went to her room and rummaged through her

171

trunk filled with the white, virginal clothing she'd worn all year. At the bottom lay her wedding gown wrapped in tissue and probably placed there by her mother as a reminder of the sanctity of marriage. If Emmaline expected her to burst into tears over it, she had another thing coming. The white plume she'd worn New Year's Eve at the Yacht Club lay nearby. Roz seized that, too.

Roz returned to the kitchen with the dress draped over her arm. "Do you have a sewing shears handy, Ethel?"

Ethel found a pair in a drawer and watched wide-eyed as Roz snipped the bottom band of lace from the dress. She held it up against herself. The gown now hung satisfyingly above the knee.

"Oh, Miz Roz, dat's a weddin' dress. You shouldn't be messin' wit' it."

"Do you think the feather would take the dye, too? I can use the extra lace for a brow band. I am so sick to death of white. I want a red dress, a red dress for this New Year's Eve."

"I give it to Florence on Monday if you wants, but Miss Roz, you crazy to ruin a nice dress like dis, jus' crazy."

Chapter Twenty-Two

By Sunday night, Henri complained of a sore throat, and by Monday morning, he had a rising fever. Over a bowl of cool water, Loretta wrung out a rag and placed it on the boy's forehead. She pulled his bed covers up to his chin.

"He caught pneumonia from being out in that rain, I just know it. Or it could be scarlet fever. I heard that was going around. Should I call the nuns at Mt. Carmel and tell them to keep the girls there for the holidays in case we get quarantined?" she asked Roz.

"I think you should call the doctor and see what he says before you cancel any visits."

Loretta looked across the bed at her guest. "You'd like that, wouldn't you? Your mama told me—"

"I'd like Henri to get well. I'll stay in my room during his visit if you want."

"That's not necessary. I'm simply overwrought. Let me see if Dr. Landry will put us on his list of house calls for this afternoon. Please stay with Henri and keep the cool rags on his forehead." Loretta rushed from the room.

"How are you feeling, kiddo?"

"Sore throat," Henri croaked. "Think I can have some ice cream?" He pushed down his covers.

"I'll go get it for you if your mama will allow it. What flavor do you want?"

173

"Chocolate—with sprinkles."

"That may be pushing your luck, but I'll see about it."

Loretta returned and took over soothing her boy's fevered brow. "Dr. Landry will be here shortly as soon as he finishes office hours. All his other calls are farther out in the country, so we are first on his list."

"Henri would like some ice cream. I'll go get it for him if you think it will be all right."

"Well, he isn't throwing up, so I suppose it would be okay. Just plain vanilla though."

"Aw, Ma!" Henri motioned to Roz to come close. "Sprinkles," he whispered in her ear.

"I'll do my best to please."

Roz ran her errand of mercy and returned to the house bearing a hand-packed pint of vanilla ice cream in a paper carton and a packet of chocolate sprinkles. For once, she was grateful for the cool weather. The ice cream hadn't started to ooze from the seams of its container yet.

In the kitchen where Ethel stewed up a hen to make soup, Roz put two scoops into a glass dish, added a pinch of sprinkles and a spoon, and stashed the rest of the treat in the coldest compartment of the icebox. She was starting up the stairs when a solid knock sounded on the front door.

"I'll get it, Ethel," she called and opened the door.

There he was, Dr. Pierre Boniface Landry, looking very professional with his black hat, tie, topcoat and medical bag. Despite this, she wanted to brush away the tired lines from around his dark, luminous eyes and run her finger down the silky slope of his mustache.

"Pierre, it's good to see you again."

"Roz, you've been well?" He looked at her hands, her ringless white hands holding a green glass bowl of vanilla ice cream.

"I'm getting better. And how are you?"

"Busy, very busy."

"Yes, my uncle said you'd been called home to replace a doctor who had a heart attack."

"You didn't get my note?"

"No note, no calls, no letters." She refused to take her eyes off his. She would not glance down even though her cheeks burned.

"I called. I sent a telegram, but your mother informed me that you and Buster had reconciled."

"No reconciliation."

Pierre looked at her hands again. "Your ice cream is melting."

If her hands were as hot as her face, she supposed it was. Loretta called from the top of the stairs, "Ethel, is that the doctor?"

The worried mother moved down a few steps. "Roz, don't keep Dr. Landry waiting on the porch."

Roz stood aside and let the doctor pass. She followed him up the stairs and waited just inside Henri's bedroom.

"What seems to be the trouble, young man?" he asked in a manner adopted from old Doc Spivey.

"Sore throat," Henri said hoarsely.

"Any nausea or vomiting?"

"Naw, no upchuck. Can I have my ice cream now?" Henri's eyes swerved to the dish in Roz's hands.

"In a few minutes. We have to check some things first. It won't hurt." Pierre opened his black bag, took out his stethoscope and listened to Henri's heart and lungs. He asked the usual, "Say Ahhh," as he checked the boy's throat, then his ears. Shaking down a mercury thermometer, the doctor attempted to insert it in Henri's mouth. The boy's hand came up.

"My ice cream is melting."

"For heaven's sake, Henri, listen to the doctor! I'm going to put this back in the icebox until he's finished with you." Loretta seized the bowl from Roz and marched down the stairs. The telephone rang in the hallway. They heard Loretta pick up and explain that she was staying home with a sick child this afternoon and would have to miss bridge club.

Pierre inserted the thermometer under Henri's tongue. Roz positioned herself on the other side of the sick bed. She might as well say it. "I shot Buster when he tried to keep me locked up. That's why I'm here— waiting for the scandal to die down. We'll file for separation in January. I'll be free next year."

Henri's eyes went wide and his mouth around the thermometer formed a tight little O. His head swung from his Cousin Roz to the doctor and back again.

"Since you still have to go through the legal steps, I assume Buster is alive, no?"

"Yes."

Dr. Landry took the thermometer from the boy's mouth. The words, "You shot a man, Cousin Roz?" came out along with it. Pierre deftly inserted a red lollipop.

"Suck on that for a while, son."

Loretta rushed to the bedside, and Roz stepped back. "Is it pneumonia or scarlet fever?"

"No, Mrs. St. Rochelle. His lungs are clear, and there's no rash, but those tonsils will have to come out.

Let's say seven tomorrow morning at the clinic before I start office hours. Henri can spend a few days in the hospital, miss a tee-tiny bit of school, and be up and running for Christmas."

"Tonsils, only tonsils. I'm so relieved."

"When he comes home, feed him soft food for a while—and all the ice cream, junket, and Jell-O he cares to eat, but nothing after eight this evening before the surgery."

Henri appeared supremely happy. No school, tons of dessert, and a cousin who was a gun moll, what more could a boy want? Wait until he ran into Tubbs and Boozoo again.

"See, Ma, it wasn't because I ran in the rain with Cousin Roz," he felt compelled to say around the lollipop.

"Oh, so you went running in the rain with Roz. Lucky boy." The doctor closed his bag and prepared to leave. He smiled at Rosamond across the room.

"I hear we're due for more rain, much more rain," Roz answered, never taking her gaze from his mouth.

They only talked about the weather, and still Loretta hadn't felt such frissons since, well, since she and André were courting. Her own girls had been properly chaperoned and courted in a seemly manner. They had, in turn, married a lawyer, the son of the owner of the largest department store in Lafayette, and a promising assistant at André's bank. Perhaps, she had been too strict with them. Flushing at the thought of what her daughters might have missed, Loretta said, "Let me show you out, Doctor. I appreciate your coming so quickly."

"I'll show him out. I know you want to be with

Henri." Roz moved to the bedroom door, but they didn't say a word as they passed down the staircase and out the front door.

"I know you have other patients to visit, but could you stay and talk for just a few moments—on the side porch?" Roz added. A Model T splashed by on the wet roadway.

Pierre nodded. They walked toward the more secluded area. He took a seat in one of the rattan chairs and picked up the two library books Roz had carelessly left out in the damp that morning.

"*The Great Gatsby* and *The Sun Also Rises*. Are you enjoying them?" he asked.

"Not very much. Daisy is so vain and self-centered. She'll destroy Gatsby," she answered—as if she really wanted to discuss literature.

"A silly, city flapper with more dollars than sense."

"That sounds like a quote."

"From my mother, only she said it in French."

"Oh." Roz looked down at the books in his hands.

"Are people being unkind to you, Roz? Chapelle is a small town with gossip as a major form of recreation. It's easier to hide in a city."

"I'm not in hiding. It's more as if I'm in voluntary exile—like Hemingway. I'm not worried if folks think I'm like Daisy. What bothers me is that I might become Lady Brett, empty and unable to fill myself with what I really desire."

"Give yourself some time. Let people get to know you."

"Sure. But you look tired." She reached out a hand to touch his cheek, and he drew back.

"Don't. Don't give them more to talk about.

You're still married to Buster, and I won't make an adulteress of you. He could have spies watching you to get more evidence for the divorce, to get more money from your family."

"I don't give a care!"

"Well, I do. For your sake, I do. Doc Spivey spent two days going over his cases with me when I arrived. Then, he hopped a train for Phoenix saying he was going to bask in the sun with the tuberculosis patients. He'll be coming back after he recuperates, but in the meantime, there is enough work for three doctors. I live in an apartment on the third floor of the clinic where Doc used to stay when he had patients in the ward on the second floor. I barely have time to eat or sleep, and that's how I've gotten through not knowing what became of you. Did you recover? Did you really go back to that bastard? And now, here you are, well and as beautiful as ever."

"Yes, here I am. What are you going to do about it?"

"Nothing. Absolutely nothing. Because now you are in my hometown where I'll make my living for the rest of my life."

"And a divorced woman would ruin that for you? Do you truly want to stay here for the rest of your life? You could practice medicine in the city."

"Roz, this is what I trained for. The city has a hundred doctors. Here, there is only me. If I hadn't been here last week, Arno Bourque would have died of a burst appendix. Mrs. Tauriac and her baby would be dead because I wasn't here to do an emergency section, and the Babin brothers would still be spreading TB up and down the bayou instead of getting treatment at the state sanatorium. This is where I belong, but I'm not sure the fun-loving, city girl I knew in New Orleans could tolerate Chapelle for very long."

"I don't think that girl exists anymore, Pierre."

"Going from Buster to me isn't going to mend what's broken inside you, Roz. That's something I can't fix. You must heal yourself, but I will help in any way I can. I must go now."

"Do, then." She stood up very straight. Even though she ached where her ribs had knitted and felt the emptiness of her womb and wondered why her heart didn't stop beating right this moment, Roz offered him her hand very briefly. He barely touched her fingertips.

"*Au revoir*, Dr. Landry. *Au revoir*."

Chapter Twenty-Three

By Christmas Eve, Loretta's home overflowed with
people. Her three youngest girls came home on holiday
from the Academy, and her married daughters returned
to the nest with their prosperous husbands and six
assorted grandchildren for the celebration. Henri was,
as promised, up and running. All but the youngest
noticed that Cousin Roz slipped out quietly for the
Methodist service and hymn sing at eight and remained
at the house during midnight Mass.

A few family members raised eyebrows when Roz
wore her newly dyed crimson dress at Christmas
dinner, but on the whole everyone remained pleasant
and convivial with the exception of two cranky babies
whom Roz took a turn at rocking. She gave pairs of
movie passes to the younger sisters, doled out four
more to the grandchildren old enough to attend a
flicker, and gave the last two to Ethel and Willie. In
return, she received the last minute gifts of the
unexpected guest—cruciform lace bookmarks tatted by
the nuns at the Academy, a box of good but plain
stationary, and from Loretta's eldest daughter, a
beautifully and sometimes gruesomely illustrated *Lives
of the Saints* because she'd heard Roz liked to read.

After a filling meal, Cousin André took his box of
cigars and his sons-in-law out to the porch. Loretta
thanked Roz again and again for the lovely scarf,

running it through her fingers, and saying "all the way from Paris" as if it were that long ago ball gown she'd worn to Mardi Gras. Henri was happy with his marbles but hinted that a knife to play mumbletypeg with would have been even more welcome, and he did have a birthday coming up at the end of January. The boy rose up on his tiptoes and pecked his cousin on the cheek.

"Why, thank you, Henri."

He pulled Roz's head down near his mouth and whispered, "When I asked him what you'd like Dr. Landry said you needed a kiss for Christmas. It don't cost nothing, but would mean a lot. I think he's sweet on you. Oh, and I'm sorry that Whitman's Sampler I got you had some of the chocolates missing. See, I met Tubbs and Boozoo on my way home, and you know how it goes. You can't stiff your pals." Henri kissed her cheek again.

Roz went smiling up to her room to get two packages from New Orleans still wrapped in their brown paper and string. Roxie hadn't sent a gift, but somehow, having Henri around made up for that. Had that small kiss really been sent by Pierre to soften his harsh words, or was she making of it what she wanted? Still clinging to that little sign of affection, Roz heard the voices coming from the bedroom next to hers and recognized the sharp, cultured tone of Loretta's eldest, Janelle.

"How could you give her my room, Mama!"

"Dearest, you've been married and living in Lafayette for six years. You're the mother of two. It really isn't your room anymore."

"Everyone knows Cousin Roz is as scarlet as that dress she has on, and I don't like her sleeping in my old bed or being around Henri and your grandchildren."

"Janelle, who is everyone?"

"I heard some of the women gossiping after Mass. You know she's gone over to the Methodists, too."

"Well, shame on women who gossip after Mass. The girl reads, mopes some, and plays with Henri. She could be more formal with the servants and less interested in—never mind all that. Except for taking Henri out in the rain without an umbrella, she's been good company for him."

"Mama, women who are getting divorced are always on the lookout for another husband. What if she goes after mine or Lois' husband or even Daddy because he has some money?"

"Believe me, Roz is not interested in your father or any of your husbands. She—Oh, here she is, out in the hallway. Roz, dear, I have a special favor to ask of you. The Harkriders are having a New Year's Eve party, and I wondered if you would mind staying home with Henri. You're so good with him, and I really do trust you with his care."

"Sorry, Loretta. I believe I'll be out looking for my next husband. After all, if a girl already has a certain kind of reputation, she might as well enjoy it. Oh, and I'll try to find another place to stay after the holidays."

Roz turned on her heel, went into Janelle's old room, and shut the door. Did Pierre think that, too—that she was so weak and helpless she needed another man to take care of her? She buried her face in her hands.

"See what you've done! I promised Emmaline I'd watch out for her, and now things will be worse than ever," Loretta moaned in a voice that could be heard clear through the keyhole.

****

Roz stayed in her room, or rather Janelle's room, for most of the week between Christmas and New Year's Eve. She worked the large tablet of crossword puzzles her mother had sent to pass the time, using the little wrist dictionary that came with them to look up clues she couldn't solve. She returned the Hemingway and Fitzgerald and checked out more murder mysteries that suited her mood. She ate chocolates using the guide on the lid to avoid flavors she didn't like and shared them with Henri when he was sent to coax her downstairs.

"Know what, Cousin Roz?" he told her on the last day of the year 1926. "I'm going out to Tubbs' grandma's place to spend the night. We'll be able to hear the music from the Barn and watch the fireworks old man Broussard is going to set off at midnight in his field. Well, it probably won't be him setting them off 'cause he's so fat, but some of Tubbs' uncles will do it. Ma didn't want to let me go, but when I told her Leroy Mouton was going, she couldn't say no. His daddy is on the Police Jury. We call Leroy "Lamb" because Mouton means 'pretty lamb,' and he hates that. Boozoo is coming, too, but don't tell Mama. She always wants me to play with Mayor DeVille's kids, and they're no fun. Where are you going tonight?"

Henri knuckled some marbles across the hardwood floor of the bedroom and managed to hit two others and knock them under the bed where he had to wriggle to get them back. Setting her makeup case on the night table, Roz sat applying a little more rouge to her cheeks than usual. She checked to see that her red lacquered nails matched her lips and the scarlet wedding dress laid out on the bed. Slipping on the brow band, she turned the vermilion plume downward to frame one side of her face. After all, why not look the part of the scarlet woman?

"What's the hottest place in town, Henri? That's where I'll be."

"Broussard's Barn. Like I said, there will be fireworks and a really hot jazz band. Mama says Mr. Broussard puts all his ill-gotten gains in Daddy's bank, so we have to be nice to him. She still doesn't like when I go over there."

"Thanks for the information, pal. Maybe I'll see you there."

"Naw, I can't go in 'cause there's hooch and bad women. You aren't a bad woman are you, Cousin Roz?"

"Time will tell, Henri."

Loretta came looking for her son. "There you are, Henri Phillipe St. Rochelle. Get your overnight bag and toothbrush. Sammy will drop you off first at Mrs. Broussard's place before he takes your father and me to the Harkriders."

"I don't need a bag or a toothbrush, Ma. We're going to stay up all night and eat wieners we cook outside for breakfast."

"Go get your bag and toothbrush, or you stay home, Henri."

The boy gathered up his marbles and went dragging his feet to his room. Frowning at the red dress, Loretta sat on the edge of the bed. "I still can't believe you dyed this lovely gown that awful color. Well, that's neither here nor there. Roz, please stay home tonight. Making a scene in public won't help matters. Just ignore what Janelle said. I'm afraid I've raised her to be somewhat of a snob."

"How about sanctimonious and judgmental, too? I'm a married woman, and my husband is not around to tell me what to do, thank heaven. I'm not your responsibility. As I said, I'll be moving out as soon as I can find a place. Right this moment, I want to have some fun before I go mad."

Loretta rose and put her hands on Roz's shoulders. She placed a gentle kiss on her forehead just below the platinum blonde spit curl. "Take care, dear child. Take care."

****

Loretta hadn't left her any transportation, but Roz didn't worry about that. She sat on the front porch steps, her sheer-hosed legs stretched out before her, the streetlight glimmering off her patent leather shoes. Roz threw the black Spanish shawl over her shoulders to keep off the damp of the misty evening and took another drink from the silver hip flask with her name engraved on the side. Filled with Cousin André's secret stash of brandy, the flask was just another way of shaking off the cold. The house faced the main drag of Chapelle, and she'd watched the restless youth of the small town troll it in their jalopies every weekend she'd been here. Someone would come along. If Pierre did not want her, some fella would.

Not ten minutes passed before a red convertible ornamented with raccoon tails and overstuffed with young men pulled up in front of her. "Hey, pretty lady, all dressed up and nowhere to go?"

Roz capped her flask, raised her skirt to the sound of wolf whistles, and replaced it in her garter. "I'm Roz, and I'm going where you're going."

"I'm Dennison DeVille. Call me Denny. Home from Yale for the holidays. Bobby, you get up on the back and make room for Miss Roz here. We're going to Broussard's Barn where the liquor flows, the band is hot, and all the women are fast."

Chapter Twenty-Four

Walet Broussard sat behind the counter of the country store his daddy built way back in the last century. The good part of owning a store was you never went hungry. The bad part was it didn't make you rich. When his daddy had gotten out of farming, the barn behind the store sat empty for a while until a much younger Walet had come up with the idea of holding dances there on Friday and Saturday nights featuring cheap local chank-a-chank bands. The dances made modest money with the ladies sipping soft drinks inside, and the gentlemen stepping outside to take a sip of Wally Broussard's fine White Mule. Yes sir, it had quite a kick.

Then, Prohibition came along, and Wally's White Mule manufacturing went from a hobby to an industry. He had so much money coming in that he'd expanded his enterprises to include a row of cribs behind the barn where hookers, white and high yeller, could ply their trade for a cut of the profits. They'd tie off a man's arm and give him a little taste of heroin or mellow out the band members with the marijuana Wally provided for a price. His three grown sons pimped, bounced, and tended bar.

The legitimate businesses did well, too—the post office franchise for that end of the parish and the justice of the peace services. Why, Wally Broussard could deliver your mail or marry runaway couples of opposing religions, slipping them a forged health certificate and selling them a cheap ring besides. He'd marry the high and the drunk, and brag that his record of happy unions scored better than that of the Church.

Hell, Wally Broussard owned more than half the politicians on the Police Jury and all of the law enforcement in the parish, which was damn good for business because he could guarantee there wouldn't be any raids on Broussard's Barn tonight. Someday, the Walet Broussard family would run the entire parish. Meanwhile, he sat behind the counter of the old general store like the fat Buddha of happiness doling out earthly pleasures, and here came some more pleasure seekers now.

Looked like one of the DeVille boys coming in, the one home from Yale. Let's see, he had a taste for fast cars, a little Mary Jane, the tawny bourbon kept under the counter for high-paying customers, and loose women of all colors. Denny brought a bimbo with him now, all dressed in red and toting her own flask flashing silver when her skirt rode up as she got out of the convertible.

What were women coming to now that they had the vote? He, Walet Broussard, was grateful for his fat, placid wife who kept a clean home, cooked a good meal, and went to Mass twice a week to pray for his soul. Right now, she watched one of the grandkids and his friends, giving them a little party with chocolate cake and ice cream, as they waited for the fireworks at midnight on the other side of the big field that separated Wally's private and public lives.

****

Henri St. Rochelle got tired of waiting. He'd had all the chocolate cake and ice cream he could hold. Then, he'd run around the yard chasing his friends with the sparklers Tubbs' granny let him light with a punk. They'd set off a long string of firecrackers, and for the grand finale, blown up a tin can with a cherry bomb, all activities his mother forbade because he might lose a finger or even a hand. Still, the wait for midnight seemed endless.

Old Miz Broussard had fallen asleep in her porch rocker after the noise died down. With a shawl wrapped around her big bosoms, the old lady snored into the folds of her many chins. Off in the distance, the boys could hear the sound of the Negro band Tubbs said his granddaddy brought all the way from New Orleans for tonight. Whenever the music stopped, the high laughter of women floated over the field where a low fog had risen above the grass.

Tubbs could tell some of the boys were going to doze off and put an end to the party if he didn't do something soon. "Tell you guys what, let's sneak over to da Barn. I know a place we can hide and watch what goes on. Might even be nekkid women dancing in dere. Sometimes my daddy brings 'em in from da city for stag nights."

"What's naked women got to do with hunting?" Henri asked innocently.

"Hey, Bebé, a stag night means only for guys like we got tonight right here."

Henri hated when they called him "baby" even if he was the youngest of the group. "Well, Lamb didn't know that neither."

"Did, too," claimed Lamb Mouton. "I want to see

nekkid ladies, Tubbs."

"Okay. Come on den. Don't wake Granny, or we'll get it. I'm not supposed to go over dere Friday, Saturday nights."

The boys crept across the yard until they came to the edge of the unplowed field. Lamb Mouton giggled nervously and was shushed by the others. Once in the field, they beat it as fast as they could across the acre of mud and brown weeds until they stood at the edge of the light thrown from the strings of big, yellow bulbs nailed around the barn door. They streaked into the shadow of the building and grouped together in a dark corner. Tubbs took out his pocketknife and carefully removed a knot from one of the wall planks. It came out easily because he'd removed it so many times before. He pressed his pudgy cheek against the wall and his eye to the hole.

"You see any dem nekkid womens?" Boozoo Thibodeaux asked hopefully.

"Nope, but I'm getting an eyeful of your coozan Roz, Bebé."

"Lemme see!"

"You get to see her all da time. Lamb, go first."

"Gaw, she's dancin' on a table. You can see her garters and everything."

The walls of the old barn pulsed with the music. The voice of a colored woman belted out, "Runnin' wild, lost control. Runnin' wild, mighty bold," over the microphone. Henri felt a little sick.

"Now, Boozoo, you get a look."

"Dat's Miss Roz for sure. All dem men sayin' 'get hot, Rozzie, get hot.' You can hear 'em all da way over here if you put your ear to da hole."

"My turn, my turn," Henri insisted, but the music had stopped by the time Tubbs let him take a peek through the hole. All he saw was Roz taking a long drink from a silver flask and swaying a little on the wobbly tabletop. One of the guys surrounding her— Henri thought he recognized Ernie DeVille's older brother—snaked a hand up her skirt, but she kicked his arm away with the toe of her T-strapped shoe and took another drink.

The band struck up an Argentine tango. Perplexed Cajuns kept their seats, but a few sophisticated couples ventured out on the floor to do the dance of love. On her tabletop, Roz bent over, giving her companions quite a view, and plucked her Spanish shawl from the back of a chair. She wrapped it tightly around her body, then holding one end high, slowly unwound the shawl as she gyrated to the music. Her eyes were closed and her red mouth partly open. Henri stepped aside. Lamb pushed forward.

"Yowzah! Your cousin's runnin' that shawl all over her bubbies and between her legs." Lamb put his big ear to the hole. "Ernie's brother is sayin' 'Let's get a room.'"

The door to one of the little cabins in the rear opened, casting light over the cluster of boys. They flattened themselves against the barn wall, all but Lamb who couldn't take his eyes off Roz doing her fandango.

"*Merci beaucoup* for comin' out here, Doc. I know you was at some swell party, but dat *fils de garce* cut up Delia pretty bad. Couldn't wait for mornin', no."

"*N'importe*, Gaston. I didn't mind coming. It was mostly older folks at the Harkriders. They wanted me to meet their daughters, I think."

"All da *bonne filles*, dey want to marry a doctor." Gaston laughed from deep in his squat, muscular bulk that hadn't yet turned to fat.

"A doctor, yes. Me, no."

"Take dis, den go on in and tell Bubba at da bar, best in da house for *Monsieur le docteur*." Gaston peeled off several bills from a roll.

"That's three times my normal fee, Gaston."

Gaston shrugged. "*Bonne annee*."

Some movement caught the bouncer's eye. "You, you boys, you. Go on home to *Memere* before I whup your derrieres."

Three small forms sprinted for the wide field. The smallest of the group ran in another direction and grabbed the doctor by the arm as he was about to enter the rear door of the barn.

"Doctor Pierre, you got to help Cousin Roz. She's in there with bad men. Please," Henri begged.

"*Allons!*" shouted the burly Gaston. "Come back when you twenty-one."

Henri bolted after his friends, and Pierre Landry opened the barn door.

He couldn't help but see her immediately through the haze of cigarette smoke. She dressed in scarlet and swayed on top of a table to the heavy beat of the tango. Four young men sat looking up her skirt and more had gathered to watch her dance. Roz drew the black Spanish shawl across her ruby lips. Her eyes were wide and blue in their rings of dusky makeup just above the lace. She rolled her hips as she turned away from him.

Dropping his black bag on the bar where Bubba was already pouring his drink, Pierre pushed through the crowd to the table's edge over the objections of the onlookers. "Hey, buddy, get your own Sheba! This one's ours."

"Get out of my way. I'm a doctor. This woman is in my care."

"Yeah, I guess, a doctor. That's a good one. She looks pretty healthy to me. Well, I'm the mayor's son, so why don't you just go cook a radish, Mr. M.D." The dapper young man in a blue blazer and baggy pants put up his dukes.

Pierre opened his arms in a friendly gesture and put a relaxed arm around Denny DeVille's shoulder. Suddenly, he had a strong grip on the college boy's neck. "You know Mr. Mayor's Son, if pressure is applied to the carotid artery for just a few seconds, you can kill a man. They teach us that in medical school."

Denny stood very still. Several of the young men in the crowd looked as if they wanted to jump the man who interferred with their pleasure, but weren't so sure how to go about it.

Roz peered down with unfocused eyes from her perch on the table. "Pierre, *c'est tu, mon amour*?" she said and threw herself into the air.

Pierre released the college boy and caught Roz against his chest just as her legs folded. He took her in his arms, and she nestled against his chest.

"I'm taking her to the clinic if anyone needs to know."

"Yeah, fella, I really believe that, too," Denny DeVille snarled, rubbing his neck.

As Pierre slid his bag from the top of the bar on his way out, Bubba Broussard asked, "Need any help dere, doc?"

"No, we're fine. *Merci*."

Bubba opened the back door for him and watched the doctor carry the lady in red to his serviceable Model T. The bartender shrugged and returned to his duties, carefully pouring the expensive shot of whiskey back into the bottle because his daddy would have his hide otherwise.

"Hey you, Eloise, you go entertain dose college boys before dey tear up da place," he said to the redheaded whore who was drinking an expensively priced glass of flat Coca-Cola some john had bought for her. Eloise gazed at the back door with hot green eyes.

"Yeah, yeah, you ain't gonna get your turn wit' da doctor. Look like amateur night to me, *cher*. Go see if dey got any money on 'em, dose college kids."

Bubba gestured toward a teenaged colored girl, her pregnancy just starting to show, who washed glasses behind the bar. "And take Kitty here along wit' you. Denny, he liked her good enough last summer."

Chapter Twenty-Five

Roz woke when the elevator jolted into action. She lost her balance and fell back against the heat of a man's chest. "Where am I? Is it you, Pierre?"

"We're at the clinic, Roz, and this is the only elevator in Chapelle. It's just big enough for a wheelchair. The house belonged to the Spivey family, but Doc donated it for a hospital when his wife wanted a more modern place. Here we are, second floor. Everyone out."

Roz regarded the grand staircase on her right wide enough for two southern belles in hoop skirts to pass each other. "I wish you had carried me up." She flung her arms wide and toppled back against Pierre again.

"I did carry you from the car, up six steps and through the front door, and that doesn't include hauling you out of Broussard's Barn. Sorry you missed it, but the time has come to be practical. I can give you a bed in the ward to sleep off your drunk, or take you upstairs and fill you with coffee until you're sober. Which will it be?"

Roz turned toward him and fitted her body to his. "I want you to make hot, passh-nate love to me." She drew her scarlet brow band down over her eyes and peeped through the lace. "Let's pretend it is Mardi Gras."

Roz shrugged out of the shawl Pierre had draped

around her, put it over his head, and drew it across his lips. "You be the Sheik of Araby, and I'll belong to you."

A grandfather clock in the lower hallway began to chime. "Nope, nope, not Mardi Gras. Nine, ten, 'leven, twelve! Happy New Year, Pierre!" Roz uncovered his mouth and planted smeary, red kisses across his lips and cheeks.

A door at the end of the hall opened. "Is that you, Dr. Landry?" a robust, gray-haired nurse asked. "I wondered about the racket. You woke Tommy Avery."

"Yes, sorry, Nurse Melancon. I brought in a case of possible alcohol poisoning. I'll tend to her. You stay with the Avery boy and call me if there is any change in Mrs. Murphy's condition tonight. We'll be—I'll be upstairs if you need me."

"Alcohol poisoning, you say? Hmph, I guess we'll be seeing plenty of that before the night is through. If you need to strap her down, let me know. How was the Harkrider party?"

"Dull. I didn't mind leaving when you called about the emergency at the Barn. I had to put in twenty-three stitches to close the wound."

"Wunnerful Dr. Pierre." Roz kissed the side of his face as yet unmarked with lipstick.

"Ah, carry-on, Nurse Melancon. *Bonne annee!*"

"Same to you, Doctor." Throwing Dr. Landry a skeptical look, Nurse Melancon returned to the small ward and her two patients.

"We have to get up the stairs, Roz, if you don't want to sleep down here." Pierre peeled her off his chest and put his arm under her shoulders to provide some support.

"I want to sleep with you, Pierre." Roz poked him with a finger in case he didn't get the point.

"Up the stairs. Here we go."

They ascended a steep, narrow staircase hidden behind a hall door. Pierre fumbled for his key as they stood on the small landing and finally got them inside the room at the head of the stairs. He dumped Roz into a comfortable chair sitting before a cold marble-manteled fireplace and turned on a floor lamp with its globe supported by a long, bronze serpent whose forked tongue flicked against the yellow glass.

"Hiya, snakey!" Roz pulled off her headband and plume and hung it on the snake's lower jaw.

"A gift from Doc Spivey. He saw some connection between that and the snakes on the medical caduceus. Strange taste in furniture if you ask me."

"Nice snakey." Roz ran her hands up and down cool bronze scales of the lamp stand.

"I'll make coffee. Doc used to stay up here if he couldn't get home. I think this space used to be a guest room when the family occupied the house. They probably couldn't get that piece back down the stairs."

Pierre gestured to a massive armoire squatting on claw and ball feet across from a gabled window that let light into the area. The colored balls of a Roman candle someone shot off down by the bayou arced past the glass, and firecrackers popped in the distance.

"Happy New Year!" Roz said again as she struggled to her feet and tottered toward the small kitchen area. She put her arms around Pierre's waist as he tried to transfer the coffee from the grinder and into a French drip pot with Roz hanging on him. He turned on the hot plate sitting on a sturdy but gouged table and started boiling the water in a saucepan.

Gently removing her hands from his body, Pierre led Roz to a plain hospital-style bed covered with a brown and white striped cotton coverlet. The four-poster that once filled the space was long gone, but Doc Spivey had added a fine old desk and worn leather chair in the corner. Roz tripped over a stack of medical journals as Pierre guided her to the bed.

"Lie down, Roz, until the coffee is made."

"Lie with me, Pierre. Lie with me." She sank onto the bed.

He crossed to the other side of the mattress, lay down, and spooned against her back. She wiggled her hips against his groin. "I know you want me, Pierre. I can tell you want me."

"Ah, Roz, I've wanted you since I first saw you at the *Reveillon* last year. So golden, so unattainable."

"You attained me. You know you did, mask or no mask."

"Rest, Roz."

"When I was with Buster, sometimes I had to pretend he was you. You know, to get through it. I had to say things to him to make him go faster, to make it end."

"I understand."

"You don't, or you'd make love to me now, Pierre. You would." Her shoulders shook. As she cried into his pillow, he kissed the nape of her neck and breathed in the scent of her hair, smoky from the Barn but underlaid with the sweetness of lilies. He held her long after the water in the saucepan boiled and evaporated into thin air.

****

The sound of Nurse Melancon's sturdy shoes on the stairs woke Pierre. The knock came. "Doctor Landry, two patients downstairs needing stitches. Car and buggy accident on Main Street. Lucky they aren't dead, but the horse is."

Straightening his rumpled suit, Pierre opened the door.

"What's that scorching smell?" Nurse Melancon asked, taking in the sleeping girl on the bed and the plume dangling from the serpent's mouth with one sweep of her eyes.

Pierre turned off the hot plate. "I dozed off—in the chair over there—while I was making coffee," he claimed, though they both clearly saw the dent in the mattress next to the woman in red. At least, she had her clothes on.

"You need to be more careful, Doctor. Much more careful," Nurse Melancon warned.

"You're right, of course. I'm coming down immediately."

****

Roz woke to the noise of rain pounding against the gable window. Each gust sounded like a cannonball exploding next to her head. She wobbled to her feet. Oh, how she needed the toilet. Where was it? Where was she?

She tried the door on the other side of the bed and prayed she wouldn't find a closet because she couldn't hold it in much longer. Success! A long, narrow bathroom complete with tub, sink, commode, and long chain dangling from the light fixture on the ceiling was revealed. She lunged for the light chain and kicked the door shut behind her.

Having emptied herself, Roz downed two cups of water to unstick her tongue from the roof of her mouth and wash away the fuzzies. She took a good look at herself in the mirror and turned away from the face with red lipstick smeared on its chin and eyes as ringed as a raccoon's. She found a washrag hanging on a rack and cleaned off her spoiled makeup, had some more water.

All the while, she thought, "Where am I?" Had she come to this place with Denny DeVille? Already a tad tipsy at the time, she remembered getting in his convertible. She recalled dancing—on a table. Thank heaven, she still had her clothes on, but any college girl knew how easily a fella could get into a girl's panties these days without taking off her dress. Still, she didn't feel damp or sticky down there.

Roz returned to the adjoining room. The covers weren't even turned down on the bed, but she'd made a mess of what looked like a hand-woven brown cotton coverlet, now spotted with lipstick, eye shadow, and small damp splotches. She passed to the kitchen area with its crude table, small sink, and hot plate. Raising the lid of the coffeepot, she saw someone had filled the top with fresh grounds. The least she could do was complete the process, and oh, how she needed the coffee.

When the water in the saucepan boiled, she dripped a little of it over the grounds and waited for the coffee to drain slowly into the bottom of the pot, then added some more. Pouring, listening to the drops fill the pot, pouring again, gave her some time to think. Pierre had come to her rescue, certainly, but then, she often dreamed he would save her. Had she resorted to her old survival habit of imagining another man to be Pierre?

She served the coffee, strong and dark, in a blue speckled enamel cup that matched the pot and sweetened it with a lump of brown sugar she found in a small crock on the table. Her hands shook as she raised it to her lips, but inhaling the aroma of fresh coffee cleared her brain.

Footsteps sounded outside the door. Roz tensed and set her coffee down before she spilled it. The apartment door swung open, and there stood Pierre, no dream at all, but stubbled and disheveled and dead on his feet.

"*Merci bon Dieu!* Coffee," were the first words out of his mouth. "Thank you for making it."

"I only boiled the water. I really don't know how to cook."

"Black, black, hot, hot, and sweet, sweet as my papa would say. Just the way I like it." Pierre stirred two lumps of the brown sugar into his brimming cup. "Sorry there's no milk. I don't have an icebox up here."

"I don't think I could stomach milk right now." Roz kept her eyes on her cup.

"How are you feeling?"

"Hung over." Shame kept her from looking at him.

Pierre moved aside a short curtain that covered shelves full of canned goods and a few five-and-dime store glasses and plates. He took down a can, a small red bottle and a tiny, brown sack. Punching open the can with a penknife, he poured tomato juice into a glass, added a dash of hot sauce, a pinch of herbs, and set the concoction down in front of Roz.

"Drink this. It might help. The local *traiteur* tells me this will cure a sore head, and he does sell a lot of this stuff. Modern medicine has nothing better, but I'll prescribe the usual two aspirins to go along with it."

"Thank you," she said in a small, embarrassed voice. Roz took a large gulp from the glass, gasping as the hot sauce penetrated her sinuses. "A little heavy on the red pepper."

"It's a hangover cure, not a breakfast. Drink it all. Then, I'll see about getting us some food."

Roz looked up quickly and saw the humor in his eyes. She glanced away. "I was upset about being snubbed by the Harkriders. I know it was childish, but I wanted to dance and drink and forget about my troubles for a while. I guess I threw myself at you."

"In more ways than one."

"I should go. Loretta has no idea where I am, and she's good enough to worry. You look worn out and shouldn't have to put up with me either."

"I had a busy night. After I sewed up one of the girls at the Barn and brought you here, there were two accident victims needing stitches and broken limbs set, a Negro with a stab wound from a bar fight, three children with fireworks injuries—one lost his little finger—and a drunk who fell in the bayou and nearly drowned. Comparatively, you could call the Harkrider party downright dull, but I did take the time to call Loretta this morning and tell her you were safe at the clinic."

"What did she say?"

"Thank you, of course, but I believe she was suspicious of my good deed. What are you going to do next, *Rose du Monde*?"

"I don't feel like the rose of the world, more like the last rose of summer. I wish I knew. I'm a burden and an embarrassment to André and Loretta. I can't go back to the city yet, according to my parents. I just don't know. Mama's friend called me damaged goods." Roz sank her head into the cup of her hands and closed her eyes.

Pierre lifted her chin. "Roz, when a bone is broken, it forms a callus, a knot that makes it stronger than before. You have survived. You will heal and be stronger."

"You think?" She held out her arms. "Last night I had a sale on damaged goods, but you didn't take me up on the offer?"

"No, I didn't, but I had the urge. You are still very young. I must wonder what Rosamond St. Rochelle will be when she grows up entirely."

"A drunk?" She crossed her eyes and made a face.

"I think not." He considered her clean-washed face. "Gilbert mentioned once that you wanted to go into nursing."

"Yes, I burned to care for the sick when I came home from the Academy. I was surprisingly good at my science classes, and I'm not at all squeamish, but my parents felt I should study art until a suitable husband came along. The funny thing is, I can't draw or paint worth a damn so I had to take art history as a major."

Pierre thought for a moment as Roz choked down more of the hangover remedy. "If you are sincerely interested in medicine, Katherine Emory is starting a class for midwives next week. It's a three-month course that will end with certification if she has her way, and as a public health nurse coming from one of the most influential families in the area, she usually gets it. The class would give you a step in the right direction. In the fall, you might consider nursing school at SLI and St.

John's Hospital in Lafayette."

"Papa would never pay my tuition. I'm supposed to wait here until my divorce goes through, get an annulment from the church, and then go home and find a better husband, one who will take me such as I am." She plucked at her scarlet dress.

"Midwives do get paid, though it may be with a bushel of sweet potatoes or a ham. If you were successful at it, a scholarship in nursing might come your way. Nurse Emory has enormous influence she can bring to bear if she likes what you do. I can put in a word for you, too."

"I'd like to give it a try." Smiling brightly, Roz stood up, then sat again abruptly. She rubbed her temples with her fingertips. "I guess that hangover remedy hasn't kicked in yet."

"Let me go find us something to eat."

"What time is it? Heck, what day is it?"

"Nearly noon, January first, year of our Lord, 1927."

"Oh God! I'll bet Loretta's entire family is dining at her house as we speak. I'll only make things worse if I don't go back there right now. Pierre, thank you for taking care of me again. That's all you did, take care of me?"

"Nothing else, *cher* heart. Sorry."

"What a pity. You know, Pierre Boniface Landry, you may be eight years older than me, a doctor, and much more mature, but you aren't my Papa, my uncle, or even a brother."

Roz took his face in her hands and laid her lips over his. She swept her tongue along the edge of his mustache until he opened his mouth, and she could taste the sweet brown sugar and the strong Cajun coffee he'd been drinking. He kept his arms by his sides, but he didn't pull away as he should have if he didn't desire her. Oh, yes, he had answered her kiss. When she finished with him, Roz plucked her crimson plume from the mouth of the snake lamp, put it on and went to the door.

"I'm going to show you and everyone else that I'm a grown woman and can take care of myself, Pierre."

"Still, if you ever need me, I will come, Roz."

"Not necessary," she said airily and stepped out on the landing. She misjudged its small size, the steepness of the stairs, the steadiness of her legs, and rode to the bottom on her backside. Standing up, she rubbed her fanny. Pierre ran half way down the stairs, fear for her showing on his face, but she waved him away. Roz struck a pose and patted her rear. "Guess I can do the Black and Blue Bottom now. It will be the newest dance craze. I'll be fine."

"*Mais, oui*. I see that you will be, *Rose du Monde*."

Walking awkwardly, Rosamond found her way out of the clinic and went to face the St. Rochelle music.

****

As usual in this small, country town, the front door of the St. Rochelle home stayed unlocked. Roz attempted to scoot quietly by the dining room where the family assembled for another abundant feast. The youngsters at the children's table caught sight of her red dress and pointed, but she held a finger to her lips and shook her head.

Just as she thought she'd gone unobserved by the adults, Cousin André's voice sounded from the head of the table. "Roz, please join us. We've just finished our prayers for a safe and prosperous new year. There's a seat at the end of the table."

Rosamond cringed. Being careful to keep her rumpled dress out of sight, she poked her head into the dining room doorway. "I'm so sorry if you waited for me. I'm not feeling well. I went over to the clinic, and now I think I'll just lie down in my—in Janelle's room. Please go ahead without me."

"I'll have Ethel bring you a tray, dear, with some of the lighter foods," Loretta said with concern.

"Then, after dinner we will have a nice, private talk, Rosamond," Cousin André added.

"I suppose we must. *Bon appetit, bonne annee*, everyone."

Roz hadn't gotten to the staircase when Janelle's sharp voice cut in. "Five will get you ten, she got drunk last night and was probably with a man."

She heard Loretta gasp, "Such language! I taught you to be better than that."

The youngest girl giggled. "You sound exactly like the nuns at the Academy when we use bad words, Mama, but they slap our fingers with the ruler."

"I can think of someone who ought to have another part of her anatomy slapped with a ruler," said Janelle's stuffy husband.

"Who wants ham? Please pass your plates to Grandpapa," Loretta interjected.

The clatter of dishes drowned out more commentary on the error of Rosamond's ways. She slinked up the steps and collapsed on Janelle's childhood bed.

The rattle of a tray being set on the nightstand woke her. Ethel loomed over the bed. "Mistah André be comin' up soon as the men finish wit' ci-gars out on the po'ch. Best you eat some—and me, I'd change out dat red dress, I was you. Like wavin' a flag in front of a bull."

"Thanks for the warning, Ethel. And for all your kindness."

"Sounds like you sayin' good-bye."

"I believe that I am."

The Cajun hangover remedy seemed to be working. Roz drank down the cup of turkey noodle soup and ate one of the ham biscuits. She was cutting into custard pie when André and Loretta arrived. Loretta sat on one of the ladder-back chairs while André remained standing with his hands behind his back, looking for all the world like Washington about to address the troops.

"Rosamond, you are welcome to stay in this house as long as you wish, but I do feel I must discuss some rules of behavior. As a young married woman, I expected you would have some sense of decorum, but Loretta keeps reminding me you are only nineteen and have suffered some terrible blows in your short life."

"You've got that right," Roz said with bravado.

"Please, no sass! If you live under my roof, I will expect you to behave as my daughters were raised to behave. That is, no drinking, no swearing, no immodest dress, no staying out all night, no running with young men," said André as he paced. "No dancing on tables at Broussard's Barn or anywhere else!"

"Oh!" said Roz.

"Yes, Mayor DeVille had the courtesy to call when his son came home complaining that Doctor Landry had carried you off, drunk as a skunk. At least, we knew where you were before Pierre called this morning. You will go to confession, wipe the slate clean, and attend church with the family each and every Sunday."

"I have been attending church."

"As a baptized and confirmed Catholic, you know that attending a Methodist service doesn't count."

"Cousin André, I am changing my religion, and I want to change my life." Roz looked him in the eye instead of hanging her head. "I know my papa has been sending you money for my board and my allowance. I'd like you to give that money to me. I intend to get a room in town."

"So you can run wild and continue to embarrass the family?"

"No, so I'll learn to make my own way and cease embarrassing Loretta who has been nothing but well-meaning. I want to attend a school for midwives. Classes start next week."

"Rosamond, you've led a very privileged life. Most women would be grateful for a nice home, regular meals they don't have to cook, clean sheets they don't have to wash, menfolk who take care of them."

"And midwifery is so-so—messy," Loretta, mother of seven, said for lack of a better word.

"I promise you, if I don't succeed at this, I'll come back and live by your rules."

André frowned. "Let me discuss this scheme of yours with Laurence. Then, we shall see."

****

Roz explained her plan to her father over the telephone. She held the receiver away from her ear as he shouted his objections, then turned it over to André.

"No, Laurence. We are happy to help, but your

daughter is, well, quite a handful. I can't see any harm in letting her try a new path in life. Many women work nowadays. We'll be right here if she needs us. She should be able to find lodging on the stipend. Chapelle isn't New Orleans, of course." André heaved a large sigh. "Very well, if that's the way you want it."

"What did he say?"

"He said you may try to live on your own, but I'm not to give you any more money than I pay the domestics."

"I see what he's trying to do, but I won't turn back."

In life, Rosamond St. Rochelle had received more than her fair share—wealth, beauty, education, and opportunities for rich experiences. She knew that very well and suspected she was about to learn life is not very fair at all.

Chapter Twenty-Six

Widow Purdue's boarding house sat a block from the village square. With a pleasant gingerbread exterior and a fanciful onion-shaped tower on one end where the chemistry teacher at the local high school roomed, the widow's establishment catered to academics and traveling salesmen. The front porch was broad and full of rockers, but the side porch had been enclosed to make another room for rent. This room tended to be cold and damp in winter, hot and humid in summer. Although the cheapest of Mrs. Purdue's accommodations, it did come with a change of sheets once a week, use of the bathroom on the second floor, and a hot evening meal. The newest boarder moved into the space on the third day of the New Year.

White-haired and ample-bosomed, Widow Purdue, who had dressed in black since the demise of her mister nearly thirty years ago, and whose only son had grown up and married away, took Roz's deposit with reluctant fingertips.

"No men in the room, Mrs. Boylan, or you'll be out on your ear. No drinking on the premises. That's illegal, you know, though one can hardly tell. Smoking is allowed only in the parlor where you may entertain guests until nine p.m. Can't have my livelihood burn down about my ears. Can't be as choosy as I'd like about my boarders, either, a poor widow lady like me.

I'll be keeping an eye on you."

In other words, the terms of her lease weren't much different from Cousin André's rules. Roz nodded and said, "Yes, ma'am."

Even though Roz suspected that Cousin André had given her Ethel's salary rather than that of the maid or laundry woman, she had very little cash left over once she paid the rent in advance. With Loretta's permission, Ethel put together a crate full of useful if shabby items culled from the kitchen and attic. Roz now owned a rusty can opener, an old bowl and pitcher set with a hairline crack, some chipped dinnerware and dented tin cups, a small cast iron skillet and saucepan, and a table lamp with a Tiffany shade missing one panel thanks to Henri's throwing a ball in the house.

Roz purchased a hot plate, a coffeepot, and an extra blanket to ward off what was predicted to be one of the wettest and chilliest years on record. As she regarded the leftover change, she thought she might be starved into submission before the end of March. She shivered from the cold in the room and the memory of Buster.

Widow Purdue's place did have some advantages. The boarders were allowed to share the parlor, bang away on the upright piano, and engage in games or conversation until nine each evening. Two young teachers recently out of normal school and near to Roz's own age shared one of the larger rooms on the second floor. Skinny Faye with her frizzy ginger hair and freckles, and plump Edna, who wore her straight black locks pinned to the back of her head because teachers weren't permitted to have a bob, proved to be fonts of information on stretching small salaries.

The widow, who kept a few chickens and a cow

out back, could be persuaded to part with eggs and new milk for pennies. If one got to Pommier's Bakery first thing in the morning, day old French loaves could be had for cheap, but the competition was fierce with the cooks around town who wanted the bread for their puddings. Roz offered to take on this task in exchange for a loaf since the teachers had to be in the classroom before eight when the bakery opened. Lusting after delicate petite fours and fat sugar cookies, she stood in line among dark domestics and Cajun housewives at least twice a week.

Faye and Edna showed her how to make *pain perdu* with eggs, milk, and old bread in her skillet, and shrimp wiggle—a concoction of canned peas and shrimp in a white sauce served over toast, which they had survived on in college—in her saucepan. They were also very adept at mooching free samples of stockings or cosmetics from itinerant salesmen on a wink and a promise they never kept. So skilled were the teachers at bumming cigarettes they nearly tempted Roz back into a habit she could not afford. Because the two teachers paid their rent on time, the widow kept mum about their smoking, which, if discovered, would put the teachers out of a job and lose her two reliable tenants.

Fortified by her new skills, Roz set out for her first day of midwife training. Putting her best foot forward, she wore the demure plaid dress, white gloves, a peekaboo hat, and clutched her newest leather purse. She inquired at the reception desk at the clinic where the class might be meeting. Though the nurse on duty gave her a peculiar look, she did say, "Meeting room is around back in the old pantry."

Roz trod daintily in her shiny pumps across the sodden grass to the rear of the old house and found a plain wooden door. By the sound of an authoritative voice speaking on the other side, she assumed she'd arrived late. Cautiously opening the door and hoping to slip into a rear seat, Roz found herself instead facing three solid benches full of colored women of every shape, size, and shade. They all stared at her with their large brown eyes.

"Are you lost? The clinic is in the front of the building," the nurse with the stern voice said. She dazzled in pure white from the tips of her shoes to the large, starched cap covering most of her short, dark hair shot through with a little gray.

"I'm looking for the midwives' class Dr. Landry said started today. I'd like to register."

The dark women chuckled. Some outright threw back their heads and laughed. They dressed in long white skirts and sturdy shoes, loose blouses, and spotless aprons. All of them had heads wrapped in tignons, covered with makeshift veils of muslin, or capped with sunbonnets. Here and there, a gold tooth glittered as they smiled.

"Order!" The nurse in charge clapped her hands. The laughter subsided. "You were misinformed. This is a class for experienced Negro midwives. Our goal is to improve and certify their skills and lower infant and childbirth mortality in the parish. Isn't that correct, ladies?"

"Yas'm," a few of the students murmured without enthusiasm.

"For poor colored women living in rural areas, the midwife may provide the only pre- and postnatal care she will receive, whether it is due to lack of money or the reluctance to be examined by a white doctor."

"Uh-huh," several members of the class agreed as if they responded to the gospel at the Baptist church.

Roz stood her ground. "I see. Well, there must be poor, rural white women in the same situation. I'd like to learn to attend to them."

"Doan look like she even married, let alone birthed a baby herself," said one of the students who was as black as a stovepipe and as broad as an oven.

"I am married, and I miscarried my first child. I think it would be a fine thing to prevent that from happening to other women."

A few in the group murmured sympathetically, but the blackest of the women spoke up again. "Dis class ain't for yo' kind, little white lady."

"I decide who attends, Mrs. Senegal. You may sit in, Mrs…" Nurse Emory gathered her authority about her and stared down her class with a steely gray glance.

"Mrs. Boylan, Rosamond Boylan. Roz would be fine."

"In this class, we will address each other by our proper surnames. If you should succeed in completing the course," Nurse Emory paused as if that possibility were doubtful, "you will be known as Midwife Boylan. Ladies, please make room on one of the benches for Mrs. Boylan."

None of the dozen students moved. Nurse Emory stared at the first row, and a general shifting of wide-hipped women occurred. Roz perched on the end of the bench, and broad Mrs. Senegal bumped the midwife next to herself harder to put even more space between her and the white lady. Roz opened her purse and took out a leather-bound notebook and a small pencil. The members of the group snickered.

"Order!" shouted Nurse Emory, who got what she wanted. "We will begin with cleanliness and the proper washing of hands for the prevention of infection. Orderly, fill the basins!"

A colored man, who had been standing by in an adjoining room, entered with a steaming kettle and filled three basins set on the long table. Nurse Emory beckoned to the back row. "They who are last shall be first."

The midwives immersed their brawny arms in the steaming water to the elbows and scrubbed with antiseptic soap. Nurse Emory monitored their technique and checked their nails. Roz came last in line. She removed her gloves, dipped her hands, then pulled them back.

"Do you have a problem with using the same water as a colored woman, Mrs. Boylan?"

"Oh, no! It's just that the water is still very hot."

"As it should be. In to the elbows. Scrub under the nails."

Roz did as she was told though her arms turned red, her fingers wrinkled, and her manicure deteriorated. She held out her hands for inspection, as had the others.

"Those long nails will have to go, Mrs. Boylan. They harbor germs and are difficult to keep clean, not to mention the danger of punctures. Get rid of the red polish as well. If you come back tomorrow, you will have your head appropriately veiled. This is not a Sunday church service. Also, you will need an apron and practical shoes." Nurse Emory stared at Roz's patent leather pumps.

Roz took her seat among the women who did their own laundry, scrubbed their own floors, and worked their own gardens. Their competent hands with thick, clipped, and yellowed nails hadn't hesitated a second to plunge into the steaming water. Once again, she was in over her head, but by damn, she would be here tomorrow!

****

Roz searched through her trunk for a suitable dress and found one of gray so out of style its hem still reached mid-calf. She snipped off the broad lace collar and cuffs. Then, taking a deep breath, she cut her long nails one by one. This action caused her more pangs than mutilating the dress. Lace in hand, she went to find Widow Perdue.

The widow was finishing up dinner on a boarding house-sized range. Roz could tell the boarders would be eating rice and gravy again tonight, cabbage boiled with salt meat, a platter of thinly sliced ham, and bread and butter. There was a *tarte a la bouie* for dessert. Since the widow never lacked for milk and eggs, she specialized in custards and puddings.

"Excuse me, Mrs. Perdue, but I wondered if I might trade this lace for one of your white aprons and perhaps, a pillowcase."

"Whatever for?" the widow said as she dished the cabbage into a bowl with a slotted spoon.

"I'm training to be a midwife and need an apron and a veil. My funds are rather short at the moment, and I thought—"

"I have no need for lace, none at all, being widowed these thirty years, but I do understand why a woman might have to make her way in the world alone. You're welcome to take one of the mended aprons and an old pillowcase, too. I approve of women learning a trade. Wish I knew more than cooking and cleaning, yes, I do."

"Thank you. Could I help take the dishes to the table?"

"Why, that would be very helpful. You're not as bad as they say, after all."

As Roz backed through the kitchen door with the platter of ham, she caught sight of a pair of pictures on the whatnot shelf. "Your grandchildren, Mrs. Purdue?"

She nodded with her head over the paper-thin slices of meat. "My son as a toddler and my new grandbaby," the landlady answered with pride.

"I think you could make something very nice with the lace for your grandchild in exchange for a discount on next month's rent."

"It's a deal, then. Be a dear and go back for the bread and gravy."

The schoolteachers, already seated, raised their eyebrows and whispered to Roz as she set down the breadbasket and took her seat next to them. "Wowie, from being a bad woman to a dear in only one week. I need to know your secret, Roz. My principal suspects I smoke, and he cautioned me about setting a poor example for the children, yesterday. I told her she smelled the aroma from the drummer's cigars," Edna commented.

Faye looked at Roz's hands as she passed the gravy boat. "Have you been doing your own laundry, city gal? You know the washerwoman comes by on Thursday and doesn't charge much, though I wouldn't give her any silk undies."

Roz viewed her ravaged hands. "A hazard of becoming a midwife, I guess, but we were informed this is a suitable career for married women, even women with children. That's a good thing since everyone in the class is married already."

Edna sighed. "If we marry, our contracts aren't renewed. Not that we're likely to meet anyone in Chapelle, and if we go out to the Barn to have a little fun, Principal Gates is sure to hear about it."

"The whole town will know the very next day," Roz guaranteed.

Bernard Toomey, the chemistry teacher, sat across from the women. He had lived with his mother until her death when the rest of the family sold the house out from under him. He twisted the ends of his small, waxed moustache and adjusted his tweed coat and bow tie. "Ahem, as teachers we must set a moral standard in the community. Please pass the rice."

"Oh, go fly a kite, Bernie!" Edna told him.

"I'm free tonight if you ladies want to go dancing," offered a traveling salesman in a checkered suit. He stayed in one of the attic rooms when he passed through town.

"Sorry, papers to grade, but we could have a smoke in the parlor after dinner and check out your wares." Faye vamped with a flutter of eyelashes.

"Finest hair care products in the U.S. of A, Miss Faye," the salesman claimed.

"See you after dinner, then, big boy," Edna answered with just a hint of Mae West in her voice.

Bernard Toomey took a large swallow of his glass of milk, dabbed his moustache, and refused to talk to anyone except the landlady for the rest of the meal.

****

Feeling incredibly self-conscious with a pillowcase folded and knotted behind her head, Roz took her seat on the end of the bench at the next day's class. Nurse Emory entered from the small kitchen where meals were prepared for patients and coffee was always on for the doctor and nurses. A whiff of dark-roasted brew made Roz salivate. She had wasted a great deal of time trying to make the pillowcase veil attractive, and failing in that, simply getting it to stay on her head. Breakfast had been a heel of a stale loaf filled with cane syrup and washed down with water. At least, she remembered to bring a lunch in a paper sack today.

"Still with us then, Mrs. Boylan? Let me see your hands. Better, much better. Head covered, more practical garments. Good. You will be sorry if you continue to wear high-heeled shoes, however," Nurse Emory warned.

"Yes, ma'am. I'll be getting other footwear as soon as I can. Would tennis shoes do? I have a pair of those."

"She gots shoes jus' to play tennis wit'. Look like we be going to school wit' Miss Helen Wills," quipped one of the midwives sitting behind Roz. Beulah Senegal expelled a single deep laugh.

"Tennis shoes are quite acceptable," Nurse Emory said in a quelling voice. The class came to order.

"Childbirth is a natural function of a woman's body. It is your duty to interfere with that function as little as possible or great harm can occur. To gain a better understanding of parturition, that is childbirth, we will study today the anatomy of the genital organs and the changes that occur in the female body during pregnancy."

With the snap of a wrist, Nurse Emory pulled down a wall chart showing the insides of a naked woman. Beside it, she tacked a smaller picture with a gynecologist's view of the business end of a female. A few eyes widened. They'd seen what was on the smaller chart dozens of times, but actual insides remained a mystery.

"Pay attention, class. After the lunch break, we will have a short test on the terms. Repeat after me— ovaries." The instructor stabbed the body part with her pointer.

Although Roz dutifully repeated with the rest of the class, this part went easy. The nuns had taught female anatomy as well as abstinence in hygiene class at the Academy. They had also checked for clean fingernails. She was beginning to feel right at home.

The lunch break came, and the midwives turned on their benches to form small groups as they opened their tin pails. Nurse Emory disappeared through the door to the food preparation area. Roz opened her paper sack and took out the three peanut butter and marshmallow fluff crackers she'd made that morning and a small, greenish orange Henri had brought her from his mother's yard.

Beulah Senegal looked over toward where Roz sat alone. She bit into a fried chicken leg and watched Roz daintily eat her crackers. "I had me a two chicken delivery las' night. Didn't waste no time ringing dose necks and frying 'em up in a pan. What? You ain't gonna run over to the St. Rochelle place an' have a fine, hot lunch like you did yesterday, gal?"

"Yesterday, I ran to my boarding house and ate

pretty much what I'm eating today. I no longer live with the St. Rochelles."

"Dat so? Be a frozen day in Lou-siana 'fore I live on crackers and mashed nuts."

"Oh, it's supposed to be very nutritious. Did you know a colored man named Dr. George Washington Carver invented three-hundred uses for the peanut? He had great faith in them," Roz replied brightly. Black, bulky Beulah Senegal scared her, but she wasn't about to show it.

"Do tell. Here you be, pecking away at cracker crumbs like some little, yaller chick. I think you too puny to bring babies into the world, Peep."

"And I think I'm tired of people telling me I'm too weak to be worthwhile. I can keep up with you, you'll see." Say it often enough and it might come true, Roz hoped.

"Ha!" Beulah turned back to her group of friends and left Roz to peel and eat the orange that tasted sour after a lunch of marshmallow fluff and peanut butter.

In short order, the midwives packed up the remnants of ham sandwiches, chicken bones, and the casings of cold boudin sausages. The only student who had a more humble lunch than Roz was a nearly toothless granny who had gummed down cornbread and syrup. The women filed out across the soggy lawn toward the outhouses near the bank of the bayou.

The little granny paused by Roz and said kindly, "I 'spects you can use da white people's toilet up on second flo', honey. Cut through da kitchen and it take you out in da hall."

"Won't Nurse Emory be angry if I do that?"

"Oh, she ain't so tough. I was da one brought her

into dis world out on the Island more'n thirty years ago. She like her grandmama, wantin' to do good."

"Thank you, Mrs.?"

"Miz Savage, but you call me Granny Sue like all da rest." The smallest and oldest of the midwives tottered after her associates across the back lawn to the colored facilities.

Roz walked into the kitchen area, startling two workers who were doing up dishes and wiping down trays. A table where the staff could sit and relax stood empty. Roz scooted out into the hall. Through the glass doors at the front of the clinic, she observed Nurse Emory leaning against one of the porch pillars and drawing on a cigarette. Not waiting to get caught, Roz darted up the stairs and into the clearly marked ladies room.

After relieving herself, she checked her appearance in the mirror over the sink. Fluffy blonde curls escaped around the edge of the makeshift veil. No wonder Beulah Senegal called her Peep. She pushed them back only to have them spring out again. Finally, she pulled the pillowcase low over her forehead. She hadn't bothered with makeup or hair cream and did look pale and puny, she decided, but no help for it. Oh, the time! She checked her wristwatch and bolted from the room.

Pierre Landry caught her by the elbows just before she smashed into him. "Running upsets the patients, nurse," he said with a wry smile. "They think someone is dying when you rush." He took a closer look. "Is that you under there, Roz?"

Roz looked up knowing she turned red. She hid her chapped, stubby-nailed hands behind her back, remembering all too well the feel of his lips, the brush of his moustache against her cheek. "Yes, it's me. I'm attending the midwives' class—which you neglected to tell me was for colored women."

"Sorry, I didn't know. Nurse Emory asked me to speak to the class toward the end of March about the complications of pregnancy and childbirth. She didn't mention any restrictions on who could attend. Still, she allowed you into the class. Is it going well for you?"

"Easy so far."

Below the couple at the base of the staircase, Nurse Emory called out, "Mrs. Boylan, back to class. Don't take up Dr. Landry's valuable time."

Roz fled down the stairs without saying good-bye. Nurse Emory followed behind her, back to the classroom. The tests were handed out, and when it became clear that some of the women could neither read nor write, she asked those students to form a line for oral quizzing. Roz finished well before the rest of the class and took her paper up to the teacher.

"One hundred percent, Mrs. Boylan. Very good. Take your seat."

That left plenty of time for Roz to speculate that Nurse Emory was probably a better match for Pierre than she, even if the woman had passed thirty a while ago. When a pounding began on the outer door, the nurse gave her the nod to answer it.

A young colored man, barefoot and wearing only denim overalls, asked in a panic, "Miz Senegal in dere? I needs a midwife. Baby's comin'! My mules and wagon's out front."

"Dat you, Roscoe?" Beulah Senegal heaved to her feet. "You come out wit' no shoes nor hat, boy, Maisie's gonna be a widder to pneumonia 'fore dis baby comes. She a first-timer," Beulah explained to the class in general.

"Primipara. Repeat," ordered Nurse Emory.

The class followed her lead, all except Beulah who headed for the door. Roz shot to her feet. "May I go with you, please? I've never seen a birth. I'll do whatever you need me to do."

"Most likely what I needs you to do is stay out my way."

"I think it would be beneficial for Mrs. Boylan to see the birth, Midwife Senegal. She might want to change her mind about midwifery as a career if she hasn't the stomach for it," Nurse Emory suggested, though it seemed more like an order.

"Oh, sho'. Come on wit' Roscoe and me, Peep. See if you gots what it takes. Roscoe, we needs to stop by my house and pick up my bag."

"But Maisie…"

"She still on her feet, Roscoe? Her water broke yet?"

"Yas'm, and no'm."

"We in no hurry, den. Be hours yet by my guess." Beulah lumbered out the door followed by Roz and Roscoe.

After Roscoe pushed Beulah Senegal on to the front seat of his farm wagon where she took up most of the space, the young man scratched his close-cropped head. "Doan know rightly where to put you, Miss."

"I'll ride in the back."

"I can put down some sacks for y'all to sit on."

"That would be fine, Roscoe."

"We in a hurry or not, boy!" Beulah grumbled, but the first-time father spread the sacks and helped Roz up into the wagon bed.

As they headed to the edge of town where the Negroes had their shanties, heads turned in their direction. One of those heads belonged to Verna Harkrider. Roz gave her a merry wave. She wondered if the vicious gossip recognized her and how Verna would translate the wagon ride into something scandalous.

Stopping before a small house painted a bright yellow across the front but just as gray and weathered on the sides as the surrounding homes, Roscoe hopped down to help Beulah from her seat. She waddled to the gate in the low fence and let herself into the yard where a plaster hen, rooster, and chicks shared the space with a few real chickens. Minutes later, Beulah was back on her small porch and heading toward the wagon with a large, white linen sack slung from her shoulder. She handed the bag to Roz.

"Don't get no dirt on it, Peep. Dis my birthin' bag."

They were off into the countryside where they passed newly planted sugarcane—acres and acres of it—rising above water-filled ditches. A stately but abandoned house sat among live oaks in a break in the fields, then, a white mansion surrounded by towering old camellia bushes and enormous azaleas. A gray-haired yardman raking fallen blossoms raised a hand as they passed.

"My grandpappy," Roscoe said as he slapped the mules with the reins to get more speed. "Soon he gonna be a great-grandpappy. Geddup, Blackie 'n Buck."

They passed another mile of cane. The team turned off the paved road into a muddy lane lined on both sides with gray shacks. Pickaninnies ran barefoot in the puddles, and a few dark women with babes in arms came out on their porches to watch the midwife pass.

"Midwife comin'," shouted one child. The word went from mouth to mouth down the quarters and arrived at Roscoe's place before the mules. A hugely pregnant young woman clutching her stomach came to the door of the cottage. Not more than seventeen, Roz was sure, maybe younger, the girl wore a muslin dress printed with purple flowers and probably put together from flour sacks. The garment rode tight across her breasts and belly. Her feet were bare, and she was free of underwear, Roz noticed, the dress being so thin. They climbed the two steps to the small porch.

"How often the pains comin', Maisie? Yo' water broke yet?" Beulah asked the scared girl.

"Don't got no watch, ma'am. Pretty often, I guess. Doan guess da water broke yet, but dere was some blood in my panties so I tuk 'em off."

"Where they at, child?"

"In da basin."

Beulah examined the panties. "See here, Peep, dat called bloody show. Means labor gonna start soon." Roz took a look at the mess of blood and mucus, proud of herself that she didn't gag.

"Roscoe, get de water boilin'. Maisie, you gots clean sheets like I tole you?"

"Yas'm."

"Peep, soon as we gots hot water, you wash and make up de bed. Put this under de linens." Midwife Senegal took a rubber sheet from her sack. "Maisie, it good to walk so long as you can. Helps bring de baby. First ones, dey don't come fast mos' times."

Once the bed was made, there wasn't much to do but watch Maisie pace the small room. Roz and

Midwife Senegal sat in straight-backed chairs while Roscoe fretted out on the front porch. From time to time, Beulah got up and measured contractions with what looked like a railroad conductor's big watch. Once, she used some of the water boiling on the wood stove to make coffee for herself and the others, but not Maisie.

"No eatin', no drinkin' once it start, Peep, 'cause it all jus' come up or out, and dey be mo' mess to clean up."

When Maisie doubled over with the intensity of the pain, the midwife helped her to the bed. Beulah scrubbed in the hot water. "Let's see what we gots here." She inserted her fingers into the girl's bulging vagina. "Five fingers. Dat be half way, Peep. Now you wash her good all around dis area, and keep an eye on her. Maybe wipe her face, rub her belly. Girl, you want to scream, you do it, or bite down on a rag. Head starts to show, you come get me quick, Peep. You don't do nothing yo'self, hear? Me, I'll be gettin' some shuteye in the front room."

"Yes, ma'am," both the young women answered.

Roz followed Beulah into the front room. "Wouldn't she feel better if her mother was here? I could go find her."

"Her mama dead, Peep. Roscoe was raised by his grandpappy 'cause his own mama run off and his daddy dead in de Great War. We all she got, but de women in the quarters, dey come in the mornin' to see to her."

As the hours passed, Roz wiped the girl's face with a cool cloth and ran a rag dampened with water Roscoe hauled from the pump halfway down the quarters over Maisie's dry lips. She rubbed the big belly in a circular motion she hoped soothed, and let the mother-to-be cling to her hands when the pains came. Roz had been around colored people all her life, the maids, her childhood mammy who'd gone on to nurse other St. Rochelle children, but she'd never once been in their homes or done them an intimate service. When it came to childbirth, that didn't seem to matter. All women sat in the same boat riding up and down those waves of pain.

"Can't stand it no more! Dis baby comin' out," Maisie screamed.

Roz checked between the girl's bent legs. A small circle of dark curls had appeared at the mouth of the vagina.

"Don't push, Maisie. Let me wake Beulah!" Roz dashed to the front room and shook the midwife. "It's time."

Beulah stretched and washed up quickly. "Okay, Maisie chile, you bear down 'til I tells you stop. Stop! See here, Peep, we deliver de head. Now, we turns de baby so de shoulders can come out. We got a fine big head, here, Maisie, big ears. Gonna be a great big boy, my guess."

"Don't want no great big baby! He gonna kill me."

"No such thing. Here come de shoulders. Not too hard now, Maisie. We don't want no tearing."

Maisie whimpered. Roz watched raptly as the newborn slipped into Beulah Senegal's big hands once the shoulders were delivered. The midwife held up the child by his heels and administered one sharp slap to his backside. Fluid drained from the baby's mouth and nostrils. He trembled, and his mouth opened wide with a big, lung-clearing cry. Beulah rested the baby on his mother's hip and tied off the umbilical cord in two places. She waited a few beats, then cut the cord with what seemed to be nothing more than a pair of scissors. Roz flinched.

"See here, Peep, you waits 'til the cord stop pulsin'. Then you cuts quick an' clean. You take dis fine little man and wipe him off. No, don't put him in de water, not 'til his cord come off. You hear dat, too, Maisie. Yes, he a big boy. Now, give him to his mama and hand me dat granite basin. We ain't done yet."

Roz watched the midwife press on the girl's belly until the afterbirth plopped out into the pan. "No tears or patches missin'. Look like it should." Beulah waved the pan under Roz's nose, but the white girl didn't back away. She forced herself to observe what lay in the pan like a strange cut of meat.

"Okay. Maisie, you want to save dis, or should I bury it?"

"Bury it out by da fig tree."

"Okay, what's our time here, Peep?"

"Four-thirty-five a.m."

"Okay, you remember dat. Diaper little man and swaddle him up. Maisie gots clothes an' blankets laid out on de dresser. I'm gonna clean up Mama, here, change de sheets. When you done, take him out to meet his daddy. What you gonna call him, Maisie?"

"Rudy, after poor, dead Mistah Valentino, and Roscoe for his daddy."

"Dat a fine name, Rudy Roscoe Sampy. I give you his birth paper 'fore I leave."

As Roz struggled to pin the diaper onto the still squalling child and get him into a small, handmade shirt, she couldn't help but admire how easily Beulah raised the mother, stripped the sheets and remade the bed. Roz tried twice to get a knitted blanket around the kicking child, but he kept throwing it off.

"Here, here," Mrs. Senegal said. "You gots to tuck de end in first, wrap de sides tight. He'll settle down once he feel like he in de womb again. Bet you never dressed a black baby befo', have you, Peep?"

"I've never dressed any baby besides my dolls, Midwife Senegal. All I know from showers and such is that you must support their heads."

"Like dis." Beulah adjusted little Rudy Roscoe in Roz's arms. "See how he settlin' down."

The baby nuzzled against Roz's breast. She felt a tingle not unlike sexual excitement and let out a soft, "Oh!"

"He want his mama's tit, but first you take him out to see his daddy."

Roz carried her burden to the porch where Roscoe had been joined by his grandfather and bolstered during the long hours with coffee and nips from the bottle provided by a few other men who waited with him. The young father wasn't drunk, though. His hands trembled as he took the child, and his eyes went wide with awe.

"Lookit da size of him. You done give me a fine great-grandson, boy."

"Maisie?" asked Roscoe as if he were terrified he might have to raise the baby alone.

"She's doing so well. You may go inside if you want."

Rudy Roscoe vigorously searched the front of his daddy's overalls. "He want his mama bad." Roscoe tried to hand the baby back to Roz, but she shook her head.

"Carry him in to Maisie. Tell her what a good job she did."

The boy nodded and carried the baby gingerly into his house where Maisie waited in a clean white nightgown half unbuttoned down the front. She put the baby to her breast.

"Oooh! Dat hurt. He a strong sucker."

The young couple laughed. Roz felt a pang of envy as she watched the new family forming. A crude but lovingly made cradle sat in a corner of the room. Who knew how many babies it had held or would hold in the years to come?

In the front room, Midwife Senegal labored over her papers, which seemed more difficult for her hands than the delivery. She filled in the names of the parents and baby, date and time of birth, the sex of the child. In a cloth-bound notebook, she wrote her own record of the birth. Finally rising, she took one set of papers to the couple. Roscoe followed her into the front room.

"I gots a bushel of sweet 'taters set aside for you, and a ham I been savin'. I put 'em in de wagon for you. Divide it how you wants."

"Be fine. Let's get us back to town." Midwife Senegal heaved herself on to the wagon where the patient mules waited.

They rolled off into the dark of a January morning. Women came from down the quarters with pots of food for the family and small, humble gifts for the baby.

"It a boy," Roscoe shouted to them. "A fine, big boy."

"Yeah, we heard him cry all the way down de row," one neighbor answered.

A faint line of gray lightened the horizon as they

turned on to the paved road and approached the gateway to the big house. A car careened from the drive, startling the mules that balked to a stop. The vehicle blocked the road and stalled as a uniformed black man, his jacket half undone, tore out of the driver's seat.

"Roscoe, they need the midwives up at the house quick. Your grandpappy saw them come, and I was praying they was still in the quarters. I'm going for the doctor, but Miz LeBlanc, she delivering early and bleeding heavy. Might be too late for Doc."

With Roz clutching the midwife's bag and jolting in the wagon bed along with the ham and sweet potatoes, Roscoe turned the mules into the driveway and whipped them down the lane.

Chapter Twenty-Seven

The big house sat amidst its dark bushes lit up as if a ball were in progress. A maid, disheveled and harried, answered the door after Beulah pounded stoutly on it.

"Thank God Almighty, Vernon done caught you on the road, Miz Beulah. It real bad upstairs. Who you got wit' you?"

As they moved toward the staircase, the midwife looked behind her at Roz carrying the birthing bag. "Guess you could say she my 'prentice, Netta."

In the upper hallway, they followed a trail of dark red splotches across a small rug and along the waxed floorboards to a large bedroom. In a canopied four-poster so massive it made the occupant seem doll-like, a petite brunette woman, eyes wide with fear, lay panting. Under the covers, a small child about five years of age snuggled in at her side. He raised his curly head when the strangers entered.

"Come on now, Bobby. Let me carry you back to Mammy. These ladies are here to take good care of your mama." Netta lifted the boy from the bed and took him out of the room despite his tears and struggles to get back to his mother. Thinking of the distress his cries would cause the woman in the bed, Roz shut the door.

"It was so silly of me. I 'eard Bobby crying for me and put on stupid shoes to go to him. I trip on a rug and fall 'ard against a big table. Now my baby comes early, and I bleed."

The woman spoke with the hard accent of the Parisian French, not the soft tones of the Cajuns. She gestured toward a pair of high-heeled pink mules edged with soft white marabou feathers. Dark stains dotted the slippers. "I am vain to wear them when I am so far along, no?"

"Don't matter now. Let's see what we got down here, Miz LeBlanc."

Beulah raised the covers. The woman's small hips rested on a thick cotton pad soaking up the blood and birth waters. Her delicate pink silk nightgown had been pushed up over her blue-veined belly to her breasts, but was already soiled. Roz knew she'd gone pale, but the midwife's black face remained impassive.

"Where can we wash up, Miz LeBlanc?"

The woman gestured to an adjoining door.

"Come on, Peep. We need to work quick."

They put on clean aprons and scrubbed up with gardenia-scented soap in an elegant basin shaped like a shell. All the hot water they could want splashed from the tap. They dried their hands on fresh linen embroidered hand towels. In the privacy of the bathroom, Midwife Senegal spoke quietly but firmly to Roz.

"We don't get the baby out quick, it gonna die. Mama could bleed to death, too. A doctor would cut it out, but we ain't allowed to do dat no more. We real lucky this ain't her first, and comin' early, it small. My hands is too big to get in dere and pull dat baby down, so you gon' do it, Peep."

"Me?" Roz said faintly.

"You jus' do what I tells you." Beulah rummaged

in the linen sack. "Here some stuff to make yo' hands slicky. Hold 'em out. Don't touch nothing when we go in the room."

Beulah opened the bathroom door with the hand towel wrapped around the knob and returned to the bedside. Roz followed, greasy hands held out in front of her.

"Yes, ma'am. It be all right, Miz LeBlanc. Put yo' knees up and spread wide for us, honey. Now you, Peep, slide both hands up de vagina. Keep goin 'til you feels de baby's head. Good now. Cup dat head and bring it down slow. It comin' easy?"

"I think so." Roz said, alarmed by the screams of the mother and the warm flow of blood seeping over her arm.

"We praise de Lawd for dat. Least it not breach. Good, we gots de head out. Now turn it to deliver de shoulders like you seen me do wit' Maisie. Shouldn't be no trouble, it so small."

Roz carefully did the rotation. The baby, pale and bluish, bald and tiny, slid from the womb. Beulah inverted the small body and gave it a gentle tap. The little girl mewed like a newborn kitten blindly seeking its mother. The midwife quickly tied off the cord and cut it. The mother, watery-eyed and weak, eyed her daughter with concern.

"See here, Peep. I boiled dese up at Roscoe's 'cause you never know how soon you gots to use 'em again. Keep dat in mind," the midwife said, setting the scissors aside.

Someone knocked softly on the bedroom door. "May I come in? It's Mr. LeBlanc. The doctor is on his way. Vernon called me from the clinic."

"No, suh. You jus' wait a bit. You gots a daughter, and she breathin' good, but I needs to see to yo' wife." Beulah delivered the placenta into a fancy blue and white china bowl from the dresser set as she spoke.

"Rub her stomach, Peep. We needs to stop the bleedin' See here how de afterbirth torn. Bad sign."

Roz rubbed the now flaccid belly as Beulah cleaned the baby and wrapped it warmly in a towel from the bathroom. She tucked the child in against the mother's chest.

"You let her suck a bit. It help to stop de bleedin' and give her some comfort. How far along was you, ma'am?"

"Eight months, but I did not intend to feed her myself. Granny Sue, she delivered my son and got 'im a wet nurse last time. No time to get her now?"

"Let's see if yo' baby girl strong enough to feed. Doc can tell you how to stop de milk later, but it good for you now, too."

Reluctantly, the mother exposed one of the small breasts covered in pink silk. "Ooooh-la-la, she pinches."

"Good sign. Means she strong. You jus' let her go 'til she tires. Won't be long, she so small. Why we could put her in a shoebox to sleep. Peep, you done good wit' yo' white lily hands."

"Lilliane, a pretty name," the new mother said drowsily. "What are you called, you who pulled my baby out?"

"Uh, my name's Rosamond Boylan. I'm afraid the midwives call me Peep," Roz said, still rubbing the woman's belly.

"Peep, so funny, but no. Rose is better. Lilliane

Rose, my daughter." Mrs. LeBlanc closed her eyes. "I believe I have enough of the children now."

"Let me check fo' bleedin', Peep. No, I should call you Midwife Boylan now you done delivered a chile."

"You know, I'm getting to like Peep. Call me whatever you want."

Beulah drew the light blanket up over the mother's legs. Both she and the baby had fallen asleep. "No sense in changing her clothes 'til de doctor done checked her out. Tell Papa he can come in, but to be quiet."

Roz was surprised to see a tall, stooped man with iron gray hair and wire-rimmed glasses enter. He could easily have been the baby's grandfather. A.A. LeBlanc studied his frail new daughter with her lashless eyes and barely formed fingernails. He placed a kiss on the cheek of his wife who had lost her usual vivid coloring.

"Will they live, Miz Beulah?" he asked in a whisper.

"I thinks so. Eight mont' babies is stronger dan they looks, and your wife was thrivin' up 'til now. We stays 'til the doctor get here."

"Let me pay you. Is twenty dollars enough?' He took two bills from the money clip in his pants pocket and handed one to each woman.

"I heard you delivered a fine baby boy to Roscoe and Maisie as well. Roscoe's granddaddy is my yardman. I gave them that cabin when I heard the girl was expecting. It's not much, but they had nothing. If they owe you, I'd be happy to pay your fee."

"This plenty, suh. I 'preciates it."

It astonished Roz to see Midwife Senegal obviously shaken by this largesse. As for herself, she wanted to go right out and buy a big rare steak. Visions of the placenta resting in the china bowl crossed her mind. Well, maybe a nice roasted chicken would be better, but she wanted to eat the whole thing herself. Many hours had passed with nothing but coffee since the peanut butter crackers at lunch. Still, she felt exhilarated.

The front door slammed, and footsteps sounded rapidly up the stairs and down the hall. Pierre Landry appeared in the doorway to the birth room.

"I'm too late, I see. It looks like the midwives have taken care of the matter, but let me examine mother and baby as a precaution. Mr. LeBlanc, if you'd step out for a moment. Ladies, please stay."

"Afterbirth in dat bowl. It gots a tear."

"I see. I'll check to make sure we've got it all," the doctor said as he worked beneath the blanket. "Bleeding has stopped. Very good work."

Dr. Landry lifted the sleeping baby from the arms of the mother who barely stirred. So gently the child didn't wake, he listened to her heart and lungs and checked the reflexes of her feet and hands.

"Small but strong. Ladies, I'm going to speak to the father out in the hall if you would finish cleaning up in here. *Merci*."

"Ain't dat always the way," grumbled Beulah. "But Doc Landry ain't so bad. He know where he come from."

The bedroom door opened again to make way for Netta who pushed an elaborate cradle hung on a graceful wheeled stand to the bedside. The maid placed the infant on lacy sheets and pulled a veil of netting close around. Though the open door, the women could hear the doctor giving instructions to Mr. LeBlanc.

"I'd prefer not to do a transfusion at this point. Let your wife rest. See that she gets plenty of fluids—beef bouillon would be good—and anything she wants to eat to rebuild her blood. I'll come back late this afternoon to see how she's doing, but unless she suffers a fever or lethargy, I'd rather not move her to the clinic. I can see she'll have the best of care here and will probably be more comfortable in her own bed."

"Thank you so much." The grateful father pressed another twenty-dollar bill into the doctor's hands.

"This is much more than my usual fee, Mr. LeBlanc. Really, all I did was check the work of the midwives."

"My wife is priceless to me." Seeing the midwives about to leave, he called out, "Cook is up. She will make y'all a breakfast. Miz Beulah, just go on down to the kitchen. I'll have Netta set a place for the lady and Dr. Landry in the dining room."

"I need to get back to the clinic for early rounds, but thank you. Roz, I mean Midwife Boylan, would you like a ride back into town?"

"No, thank you, Dr. Landry. I do believe I would like some breakfast. Don't set a special place for me, Mr. LeBlanc. The kitchen will be fine." With that, Roz followed Beulah's broad backside down the stairs to the rear of the house.

The cook appeared to know the midwife, and the two talked the whole time she prepared the breakfast, though she seemed a little uneasy about the white lady waiting for food. Beulah recounted the story of the birth, giving Roz credit where it was due, and telling the cook what foods the new mother should have for building the blood and nursing if she wanted.

"Cook all her meals in iron pots, you hear. She need red meat. No strong greens, no onions or garlic. It give de baby colic."

The cook fried up ham slices and forked them on to thick yellow plates. She stirred the redeye gravy and poured it out over the heap of grits next to the meat. Two fried eggs with the yolks done perfectly for mixing with the grits followed. Even as the women ate, the spread kept increasing with fluffy biscuits, crisp toast, fig preserves and orange marmalade. Slices of pound cake were added just in case they didn't have enough to fill them.

"Mr. LeBlanc was a surprise. He could be the French woman's father. There must be a story about them," Roz said as she tucked into her eggs, breaking the yolks and blending them with the grits and gravy.

"Sho' is. People still talkin' about how old A.A. went off to be a soldier in de Great War when he near forty and still not married. He come home wit' dat bit o' French fluff, and peoples still doan know what to make of her. Maybe she jus' wanted to get out of Paris. But LeBlancs, dey always marry out of the parish." Beulah lowered her voice even more. "They gots black blood in de family, and everybody in town know it."

"Mr. LeBlanc certainly doesn't look it."

"It from way back. One old granny midwife told me so. Some long ago LeBlanc took a quadroon chile for his own. Dis family tainted, white folks say."

"People do like to talk whether they know the truth or not. I don't believe it." Roz cut off a chunk of ham and chewed.

"Whoa, Peep. For a little thang, you sure can eat,"

Beulah observed.

"To be honest, I haven't had a meal this good since I left the St. Rochelles." Roz crammed a biscuit dripping with butter and preserves into her mouth. "I'm always late getting up for class and mostly have just bread and syrup in the mornings."

"Well, midwifin' do raise the appetite. Say, Peep, why you don't go back to de clinic wit' Doc Landry? Every single white lady in town want a ride in his car, know what I mean?" Beulah gave her a wink.

"I am still a married woman, as the doctor reminded me a short time ago, Midwife Senegal. And, my Mama always said, 'You come home from the dance with the one who brought you'."

Roz looked down at her shoes splattered with blood and birth fluids and sighed. "One more thing, I'll never wear these pumps to a soiree again."

Chapter Twenty-Eight

By the second week of classes all the midwives could predict that if one of them was fetched for a delivery, Rosamond Boylan would jump to her feet and ask to come along. An undertone of black voices would murmur, "Peep, Peep, Peep," quickly quelled by a stern look from Nurse Emory.

"I'm allowing Mrs. Boylan to accompany you because you have a wealth of practical experience to share. I might add she is well ahead of the class in book knowledge. There is no playing favorites here."

"It okay." Beulah Senegal spread her big bottom in the space Roz left behind. "She didn't faint nor nuttin' when she went wit' me. Even knows how to swaddle a baby now, and dose little hands of hers come in handy."

"Very well then. Class we shall discuss determining pregnancy and due dates today."

"Seems babies come when dey wants," said a thick-bodied yellow woman in the second row.

"True, only three percent of births actually occur on the due date, but a date gives the mother a comforting goal, and the midwife the knowledge that a baby may be long overdue and in need of induction. What is induction?"

"Bringing da baby on," said a woman wearing a white sunbonnet.

"Rupturing the membrane surgically," shouted Roz

as she followed Granny Sue out the door. A chorus of Peeps followed her, but she took it good-naturedly. After all, she was going to assist with another delivery.

****

Twelfth night came. In New Orleans, Roz would have been attending parties where the names of the new queens of Mardi Gras were announced. Instead, she jumped out of the back of a rickety truck that held a sack with two laying hens. She'd already turned down the offer of a live chicken in exchange for any eggs it might produce in the future.

The delivery, the tenth for the woman concerned, had gone swiftly and easily, and Roz arrived back at the boarding house in time for dinner. A large cardboard box across his knees, Henri waited on the doorstep.

"Mama said I should bring this to you. It came in on the mail boat. She said your mama thought it might be stolen if it was left at the boarding house. What do you think it is?"

"I have no idea. I wasn't expecting anything this big, just some papers."

"Oh, this came, too." Henri pulled a large legal envelope out of his sweater. "Ain't you gonna open the box?"

Instead, Roz ripped off the top of the envelope containing her separation papers from Buster. They had been filed the second day of January. By this time next year, she would be free of Burke Boylan forever. She gave Henri a dazzling smile.

"So, what's in the box?" the boy persisted.

Roz tugged on the strings tied around the cardboard. When they failed to budge, Henri took out a dull pocketknife and sawed away until the wrappings split.

"Finally got your knife, Henri?"

"I won it from Tubbs on a bet. He said I was too chicken to climb to the top of the live oak in his yard and jump, but I did. Don't tell Mama."

"Oh, Henri, you are so like me. Doesn't your mama ever say 'If your friends jumped off a bridge, would you do it, too?'"

"All the time. It's a cake " the boy shouted as Roz parted some tissue and a layer of waxed paper.

A ring of King Cake dressed in all its gaudy green, purple, and gold sugar glory sat in the box. Roz lifted it out on its flat of cardboard and set it between them. "Cut yourself a piece, Henri, and one for me, too. After you finish ruining your dinner, you'd better go home. Your mother will worry if you stay too long."

"She worries about you, too."

"I know."

Loretta and Ethel constantly sent over odds and ends for her room and small offerings of food. Cousin André, whether still angry over the New Year's Eve debacle, or embarrassed about the niggardly allowance he doled out to her, usually greeted Roz aloofly on the street and hurried away.

Henri licked the last of the frosting from his fingers and raced off. "Thanks for the cake, Cousin Roz."

Roz carried the rest of the treat inside and gave it to Widow Perdue for the night's dessert. She anticipated a good meal. The widow had Roz's share of the sweet potatoes being candied in a cast iron pan. Turnips greens with chunks of the vegetable enfolded boiled in a neighboring pot. Cornbread cooled off to one side of the stove. The ever-present thin-sliced ham waited on its platter. Roz had parlayed her "fee" from helping with Maisie's delivery into another rent reduction, and she still got to eat it.

Widow Purdue eyed the cake. "I suppose you'll want another dollar off your rent for that?"

"No, I want to share it with the others. We can have a Twelfth Night party just like in the city. It's a little stale, though."

"We'll warm it just a bit, but not enough to melt the frosting. Take out the cornbread and call the others."

As usual, the others didn't need to be called. In January, the roads were bad and the water was high, higher than usual, so drummers were scarce, and none sat at the table tonight. Edna and Faye slipped into their seats, and Mr. Toomey held his utensils at ready.

They plied the widow with compliments on the candied sweet potatoes, and she, flattered, promised she'd make a pie out of the rest of the yams. As Roz cut the King Cake, Miz Purdue surprised everyone by taking her good cordial glasses from the breakfront and pouring portions of her own cherry bounce from a dusty jug that looked like it had been involved in fermentation for a year.

"It's not really liquor, you know," the widow assured them. "Just a little hobby of mine. I make it for medicinal purposes."

"My mama used to make this," Bernard Toomey said nostalgically.

The drink made Roz feel a longing, too, for a speakeasy in the French Quarter. How wild cherries soaked in sugar and illicit whiskey and left to ferment couldn't be liquor, Roz didn't question. Both the cake and the jug went around a second time. Faye bit into her piece of pastry and winced. "There's something in here, a bean or a stone."

She spit the object out into her hand. She held a silver charm shaped like a rose. "Oh, this must be for you, Roz."

"No, no! It means you are Queen for a day, and the rest of us must do as we're told."

"Really?" Faye's gingery eyebrows raised with possibilities. She looked across the table at Bernard Toomey. "Mr. Toomey, loosen your collar and take off your coat."

"In the presence of ladies?" he questioned.

"You are going to be my court jester and amuse me while Roz paints my toenails with some of her fancy polish. Edna, you can do my nails. Miz Purdue, keep the wine coming."

Roz brought not only the nail polish from her room, but her Mardi Gras crown, packed, certainly, to remind her of who she was.

"Is it pure gold?" Faye marveled.

"Plate, I'm positive, but fit for a queen. I crown you Queen Faye, Mistress of Revels."

To everyone's amazement, Bernard Toomey turned out to be a good jester. First, he licked a spoon and hung it off the end of his nose, then recited the inspirational poem, *Invectus*, which suddenly became very funny. He called for vinegar, baking soda, and a basin of water, and made a little boat from a piece of the evening newspaper. When he fueled the paper boat with the vinegar and soda, it puttered around the basin on its own power. The women applauded.

"It's all science, the magic of chemistry," he said

modestly.

As the jug of cherry bounce reached its bottom, Bernard sang a fair but maudlin rendition of *When Irish Eyes Were Shining* and followed it up with an attempt at a jig. Feet tangling, he ended up on the floor next to Queen Faye's cherry-colored nails. He kissed each toe. The cherry color spread over the schoolteacher's entire body, obliterating her freckles as it rose.

"Lovely toesies," Bernard murmured as he finished with the last little piggy.

Roz expected the widow to call the evening at an end, as it seemed to be going in a strange direction, but Miz Purdue slept soundly in the chair where she'd been sitting since she brought out a second jug of wine. Edna dozed face down on the table, and her own head buzzed.

"With your permission, Queen Faye, I think I'll call it a night. I have class in the morning." Roz pushed unsteadily out of her chair and wobbled off to bed. As Twelfth Night parties went, this one had been better than most.

****

Roz, Edna, Faye, and Mr. Toomey had no more parties for the remainder of the Mardi Gras season. They got up the next morning with cherry bounce headaches and went about earning or learning for a living. Edna refought the War Between the States with her history students. Faye taught the Romantic Movement in her English class. Mr. Toomey tightened his tie and tested on the periodic table.

The Kiwanis and Rotary Clubs selected the king of Chapelle's Mardi Gras from amongst their members. King Louis XVI would be portrayed by a prominent sugar planter, the local paper announced with no secrecy about it. The article revealed his Queen Marie Antoinette as the daughter of a local judge. Verna Harkrider told anyone who would listen that the queen should have been her Dorothy, but old Queen Bagasse, the wife of the king, was jealous of her Dottie's beauty.

Even the midwives had a chuckle over the feud. "That girl, Dottie, she jus' plain ugly. They put her in the court so she has to wear a mask."

"Why does Verna keep referring to the judge's wife as Queen Bagasse?" Roz asked.

The women threw back their heads and laughed some more. "Peep, the bagasse is what's left after all the sweet juice done been squeezed out the sugarcane."

"I believe that could apply to Verna as well," she answered. No one disagreed.

Roz gave no more thought to Mardi Gras. She applied herself to learning the stages of pregnancy and fetal development, the progress of labor, and the warning signs of eclampsia, recognition of venereal diseases, and a host of other subjects that would horrify her mother.

She practiced delivery on an anatomical model and marveled at the experienced midwives' ability to turn a badly positioned baby for birth. They showed her their techniques for coaxing along a breach birth and pushing an infant determined to be born butt first back into the womb until the head presented. Nurse Emory hovered all the while, reminding them again and again to call the doctor if complications occurred.

Best of all, the women allowed Roz to accompany them to birthings. They had begun to refer to her as the only chick in a coop full of old hens—Beulah Senegal summed it up.

"Not many wantin' to learn our trade anymore, Peep. Everybody want a doctor now, even po' people. My own daughters, dey wants to be nurses. I keep tellin' 'em, times ain't changed that much. See de colored men come back from de Great War? What dey do over there? Not fight, most of 'em. Dey dug ditches and drove mules same as here. In a hospital, my girls be scrubbing floors and cleanin' bed pans."

"Someday, things will be different. More and more women are working now," Roz told them.

"Negro women have always worked, Peep. It don't make no difference."

"One day it will," Nurse Emory said crisply. "That is why you must be the best at what you do. Class, come to order."

During the lunch break when Nurse Emory had gone for her smoke, the women gossiped about their instructor. She was the granddaughter of an abolitionist lady who had come down after the War to teach black children to read and write. That fine person married into one of the oldest planter families in the area. They owned their own island and all. The do-gooder New England bride passed on her beliefs to her children and grandchildren to the ruination of the Emory family, many of the white folks thought. Nurse Emory might be starchy, but her heart beat in the right place under her spotless white uniform.

Roz soaked up all the information she was given, the most attentive student in class. Though when she heard Pierre's voice in the coffee room, her mind strayed. She was always whipped back to the present by a pointed question from the nurse who missed nothing.

As her skill progressed, Roz found herself called out at night by various midwives. They would rap on the thin siding that enclosed her drafty room. "I'se birthin' twins tonight, Peep. You wants to come?" or "Dose little white hands might come in useful." Gradually, they let her do normal deliveries, then trickier ones.

One damp night as they rode in the back of a wagon from a routine birth, Beulah shared some of the secrets of the midwives' trade. A misty rain fell, making their veils limp and heavy, as they put their heads close together to talk. The father, already daddy to nine youngsters—this made ten—sat half asleep behind the mules who found their own way into town.

"Women wear out birthin' so many. Here in my bag, I gots some seeds from de Queen Anne lace plant. It don't grow so well here, but my cousin sends me jars of 'em from Nort' Carolina. Woman take a spoonful of seeds wit' warm water after she been wit' a man, won't no baby take. And dis here bottle, gots ergot of wheat. It can speed up a birthin' or bring off an unwanted chile. Can kill de mother if you not careful."

"Wouldn't it be better just to recommend rubbers?" Roz whispered, appalled.

"Priests speak against 'em. Men don't like to use 'em. Womens has gots to look out fo' demselves, Peep. Don't you be tellin'no white doctor what I jus' say."

"Never," she swore.

In class, Nurse Emory spoke of spontaneous abortions, their causes, and the treatment of the women who suffered from them. Roz lingered behind after the lecture. "What about women who try to kill their babies in the womb?"

"Technically, this is a crime committed by both the mother and the person who supplied her with a drug or performed the surgery. Mostly, people keep quiet about abortions unless the baby was born alive and killed afterwards. Then, it's murder, of course. You need to assess the situation. If a woman won't hold or nurse her baby, you might want to suggest she give you the infant to take to one of the orphans' homes. A lot of tragedy can be prevented that way."

"Are these cases frequent, then?"

"Not among the Cajuns. They tend to force young couples who got carried away to the altar or raise the bastard within the family. You do see it among the Negroes with too many children to support, and more and more among desperate college girls. The upper crust isn't immune, though they're more likely to send a pregnant daughter on a long visit to an auntie in another state. Six months later, the girl comes back fresh as a daisy to marry as she should."

Nurse Emory, seeing all her students but Roz gone, took a pack of cigarettes from a drawer in the table and offered one. Roz shook her head, but the nurse lit up and took a long drag.

"Bad habit. I picked it up in France while I nursed the war wounded. You know, plenty of incest occurs in the back country and in-breeding that leads to terrible birth defects. It would be better for all concerned if abortion was legal, but I won't live to see the day. There's not a woman in this class except you that can't bring on a miscarriage with some kind of poison she stirs up. You stay away from that shit, or you'll lose your license before you get it. Understand?"

"Understood."

****

The brief month of February seemed to pass by in minutes rather than days. March, usually a time of warmth and blossoms, began cold and wet. Nurse Emory announced a day's recess for the celebration of Mardi Gras and said she didn't want to see any hungover students straggling in on Ash Wednesday. The midwives laughed and adjourned to enjoy their holiday.

Roz had no plans other than to sleep late and study her textbook. The teachers went back to their hometowns for the celebration. Even Mr. Toomey had been invited to the home of one of his sisters for a party. The Widow Perdue might have fallen on hard times when her husband died, but she maintained social connections with the better families in town and received an invitation to the *bal masque* which André and Loretta would, no doubt, attend. While brushing off her best black dress with its jet beading, the widow told Roz she wouldn't be cooking today, but she was sure a pretty girl like Rosamond would have other places to go. Roz shrugged.

"My many invitations must have been mislaid."

"Oh my! Let's watch the parade together from the porch then, before I leave for luncheon with my friends. If you want to mask, I have trunks of old clothes in the attic you are welcome to use."

The attic selection was not inspiring, mostly black dresses outgrown in size over many decades of mourning and small garments that must have belonged to the widow's son as a baby. Roz shook out a bodice of black taffeta. Small buttons ran up the front from the waist to a high collar between rows of ruffles that ended just under the chin. A matching skirt that draped across the front and pulled into a small bustle in the back completed the outfit. She could squeeze into the costume without a corset, thanks to sparse rations and late night midwifery.

In her room, she slicked her hair back with pomade, inserted a tortoise shell comb high on the back of her head, and draped her Spanish shawl over it. Roz hoped the shawl would hide the fact that she hadn't been to the beauty parlor in months. Usually hidden by her headdress, her hair hung in an unfashionably long half platinum and half golden blonde cascade of waves down to her shoulders. She tied it back into a small knot at her nape. For the finishing touch, she clipped a spray of seven sisters roses from the trellis in the yard and tucked it behind her ear. With stark white makeup, red lips, and darkened brows, Roz thought she resembled a ghost from the past century.

Sitting on a rocker waiting for the parade, she drew stares from by-passers and gave them a languid wave. Most of the adults weren't costumed but accompanied children who had dressed up like bunnies or kittens. Henri and his pals came along wearing their version of wild Indian garb—fringed vests made from brown paper bags with crayoned designs of eagles and arrowheads, headdresses of multicolored construction paper feathers, and lots of war paint filched from their sisters' cosmetic cases. One fat, one tall, and one small Indian carrying an umbrella perched on the front steps of the boarding house, keeping company with Roz and the widow.

The parade, when it came, was brief. The king's mule-drawn float approached with the sugar planter, stuffed into white hose, golden knee breeches, brocaded vest, and a powdered wig. He waved his scepter from his throne. Little boy pages in purple velvet doled out glass beads and handfuls of candy to any friends they recognized.

The queen's float followed with the maids settled on pastel pedestals like fancy iced cakes in a bakery window. They, too, flung necklaces sparingly as if the cheap junk were real treasure. Among them, Roz saw Verna Harkrider's big-nosed, black-haired daughter who had been passed over in favor of a young woman bearing a strong resemblance to Clara Bow, the It Girl. Evidently, the queen had "It," while Dottie Harkrider did not.

The last two floats brought the boys to their feet. Tubbs grabbed Henri's umbrella, inverted it, and charged down the sidewalk shouting, "Throw me something, mister!" On these conveyances, the Rotarians vied with the Kiwanis for the generosity of their throws and the spectacle of their costumes carrying out the theme of "Circus of Delight."

A tall, stooped ringmaster in a top hat and crooked handlebar moustache slung a cluster of beads up on to the porch where they skittered to Roz's feet. She draped them around her neck. Beside the ringmaster, an Indian elephant trainer in black face and a bejeweled turban took more throws from his animal hook and tossed them into Tubbs' umbrella. The same man pitched additional fake jewels to the boarding house ladies. Roz squinted. Could it be Cousin André? Both men were too tall to be Pierre.

The floats overflowed with clowns and strongmen in leopard skins and padded tights. A dapper young man dressed as a trapeze artist resembled Denny DeVille, but Roz doubted that Yale gave vacation days for Mardi Gras. He had to be a brother. A Fat Lady with a red wig and polka dot dress leaned over to shower candy on the boys and nearly fell off the float. Wally Brossard, Roz guessed, because most of his bulk was certainly real. His float also seemed well-supplied with beverages of an illegal nature and a surfeit of sweets. If Pierre rode among the maskers, she hadn't discovered his identity.

The parade passed, and the boys ran off in its wake, hoping to catch more throws. The widow excused herself for her luncheon date and left Roz on the porch alone. As she stood to go in and take off her stifling outfit, she glanced across the street, and there he stood, Pierre in a dark suit, white shirt, black tie, and carrying his medical bag. He crossed against tide of people following the floats and dodging mule dung, and met her on the porch.

"A senorita again?" he asked.

"A reformed gypsy." Roz gestured to her long sleeves, high collar, tight-laced bodice, and ankle-covering skirt.

"A pity," he said.

"I'm sorry I can't invite you in. It's against house rules."

"I understand, but I have come to invite you out."

"Moi? A married lady—or perhaps, a merry widow judging by the color of my gown. And who are you to ask me?"

"A well-meaning doctor inviting you to a family fete very well chaperoned." He held up his black bag. "Unless, of course, you are going to the ball tonight."

Roz cocked her head and laughed. "The courier with my invitation must have been waylaid by bandits. Yours as well?"

"No, the Harkriders made sure I got invited, but I declined as none of my family was going to be there. You'll have to change and put your grand airs aside. We'll be eating boiled crawfish with our fingers."

"The best invitation I've had. Let me put on other clothes. Wait here."

Roz rooted through her trunk and found nothing suitable for eating messy foods. Still in a quandary, she washed off her grotesque makeup and reapplied the lightest touches of pink lipstick and rouge. She could do nothing about her hideous hair. She hid what she could beneath a green cloche hat with a rolled brim, but a rim of platinum curls escaped all the way around. Well, she could always claim she masked as Harpo Marx. She'd seen him and his brothers do their act on the vaudeville stage at the Crescent. All she needed was a horn to chase the women. Sighing, Roz put on the hated red and green plaid dress from last Christmas. At least, it wouldn't show stains, and she didn't care if she spilled on it. Her black stockings and pumps would have to do. Pierre awaited.

They talked shop as they drove along. Pierre kept his hands on the wheel and his eyes on the road as they passed cane growing tall and spindly in the wet weather. Roz told him of interesting deliveries. He countered with his latest cases.

When Roz let her mind go astray to last year's Mardi Gras, she wanted to scream for their loss of intimacy and the possibility of love. If Pierre had driven into the cane fields and pulled her into the backseat of his Ford, she would have been just as willing to throw up her skirts as she had been in the French Quarter. Nurse Emory's stern voice lecturing on the need for good moral character among midwives sounded in her mind and ruined the memory.

Pierre saw her eyes stray to the dark lanes among the canes. In his teen years, he had taken more than one loose country girl into the fields for a romp. His Papa boxed his ears and told him to take his needs to a lady of the evening because that's why prostitutes existed— to keep good women pure. He knew what Papa would say if he took up with a married woman of a certain reputation. "Find a nice girl and settle down, Pierre. Den you forget all about her." Not likely. His hands itched to turn up one of the farm lanes, but he forged ahead on the main road.

He kept the conversation formal and professional until they came to a large, unpainted cypress board home set up off the ground on crumbling piles of brick. Behind the house, the bayou spilled over its banks into a grove of cypress trees, but in the front yard, the puddles had been filled with straw to keep down the mud. Black buggies parked beside Model T's, both cars and trucks. The carriage horses turned out into an adjoining pasture hung their heads over the fence hoping for a chunk of turnip or lump of brown sugar from the hands of a dozen small children running wild among the vehicles. Pierre honked the Ford's horn to warn the swarm as he parked on the end of the row.

He stripped off his coat and tie before leaving the auto. Taking her elbow, Pierre steadied Roz as her heels sank in the sodden yard. Three men perched on the outside staircase leading up to the traditional *garconniere* where Pierre had slept with his six brothers, raised their fruit jars of clear liquid and shouted out, "Eh, Pierre! *Quelle est la jolie blonde, ti-frere?*"

"My brothers, Odon, Euclide, and Ursin. Clovis, Minos, and Zenon are probably out back," Pierre told Roz.

"How did you get the ordinary name of Pierre?" she teased.

"Born on his saint's day, but don't forget my middle name is Boniface."

"Close call for you."

Two of the men were older versions of Pierre more poorly dressed and showing the lines of outdoor work in their faces. Ursin, however, was broad and fat, and displayed his hairy arms without modesty.

"I brought a friend from the clinic," Pierre answered in English as they approached the porch. "Roz Boylan."

In rapid Cajun French, the loudest of the three, Ursin, asked if his little brother was sleeping with the pretty woman. Roz answered for him. She hadn't spent hours in Sr. Marie Claire's French class making up salacious phrases out of boredom for nothing.

"No, he isn't." Roz smiled. At least, one man here didn't think she looked like Harpo Marx.

Switching to English, the mouthy brother jibed, "What's da matter wit' you, *ti-frere*? You sick? You got the syphy-lis?"

Like a cannonball shot from the front door, Alida Landry crossed her front porch and thwacked her eldest son on the forearm with a large, wooden cooking spoon. "You don't talk dat way in front of da bebes, no,

Ursin!"

Ursin licked the brown splotch that landed just below his rolled up shirtsleeve. "*Bon roux*, Mama."

"Ha! You don't buy me off wit' dat." Madame Landry came off the porch, took Pierre's face in her hands, and kissed both his cheeks. "*Mon bon fils.*"

She looked over her son's shoulder with hard eyes at Roz and whispered in his ear just loud enough for the girl to hear, "Maybe she da one got syphy-lis, a fast girl like dat."

Roz hadn't blushed when bantering with the brothers, but she did now. She wanted to turn and go back to the car when spare Simon Landry ran out of the house with his arms open. "*Bienvenu! Bienvenu*, Rosamond Boylan."

He kissed her cheek. "I never miss a chance to kiss a pretty girl, me. Clovis, he late wit' da crawfish, but you come inside. We got chicken gumbo and turtle soup on da stove to keep you 'til we eat. Alida, she makin' beignets to use up da fat before Lent."

"I'm afraid I'm one guest too many."

"No, no! We just add more rice to da pot. Come."

Pierre cocked his head at his father. His Papa winked. Maybe he would have given his son different advice from the lecture Pierre had imagined.

Simon Landry took his guest's arm and escorted her to the crowded kitchen built on to the back of the house. Most of the women bustling around appeared to be in some stage of pregnancy, and Roz was hard put to separate Pierre's sisters from his sisters-in-law.

Alida, scowling, had returned to her beignet making, turning over square pillows of dough in an iron pot filled with boiling lard. A bunch of hungry children waited for the batch to be lifted from the oil. As their grandmother drained the doughnuts, small hands reached up and were slapped away with an admonition to wait 'til they cooled. An older girl cranked a large flour sifter full of 10-X sugar over the beignets, and another carried the plate to a long plank table with benches on both sides. The flock followed.

Pierre sat two toddlers on his lap to make a space for himself and Roz at the table.

"Café brulot?" one of the women about six months along offered, holding up the pot. Roz thought it might be his sister, Collette—or was she the one in her fourth month wearing the blue dress?

"Yes, thank you." The sister passed a red enameled cup to her. Roz took a sip of scalding coffee brewed with caramelized sugar water. "*C'est bon!*"

"Here, you try dis." Simon Landry squeezed between the bellies of the women with a small bowl in his hand. "Odon, he caught a big *tortue* in da bayou last week and keep her alive 'til just dis morning, him."

Roz spooned up the rich brown turtle soup. "Wonderful, just like our cook used to make—no, it's better."

Another bowl passed her way before she finished the first. "Try my gumbo," insisted a nursing mother holding her infant up to a swollen breast. That one might be Matilde, Euclide's wife. Roz wasn't sure.

She sipped the soup in its thin Cajun roux, missing the thick okra base of New Orleans style gumbo. The chicken was tender and the andouille sausage spicy. "Very good, but could I have the filé powder? I'm used to it being thicker."

"You make dat slimy okra kind where you come

from?"

Roz started to say she'd never made gumbo, but she was saved from this confession by the arrival of Clovis and the crawfish. People spilled out of the kitchen on to the long back lawn sloping toward the swollen bayou. Adolescent boys tended two metal pots full of boiling water hung over open fires.

"Da water in da Basin, she high. Lost some of my traps, but I t'ink we got enough to stretch dis feast." Clovis set down two enormous burlap sacks that throbbed with live crawfish.

"Now we cookin'." Simon tossed fresh dug and scrubbed red potatoes into each pot and laid on the spices—garlic cloves, and small onions, handfuls of salt, a whole box of cayenne pepper, and lemons split in two with his clasp knife. Testing a spud for doneness, the old man signaled to Clovis who upended the first sack into one of the pots. A few lucky mudbug survivors who fell outside the kettle scrambled for the bayou, but they were scooped up by small boys who used the snapping claws of the crawfish to terrorize their sisters. Mothers shouted in both French and English to their children not to run so close to the fire.

While Simon and Clovis stirred the pots with cypress paddles, the women laid out newspaper across the porch. In minutes, the pots were ready to drain. Boiled crawfish, turned a deep red and upended from the pot, spread out across the papers. People carried piles of them away to any convenient peeling place so long as they remained outdoors, Alida reminded them all.

"Don't want no stink in my house, you hear," she said.

"Save the porch swing." Pierre pushed Roz in that direction. In a moment, he had two paper cones full of steaming crawfish to set between them.

Roz picked up one good-sized crustacean and winced when its red pepper and salt coating pierced the tiny cracks in her chapped hands. Looking up, she felt as if the whole family watched her. It wasn't as if she hadn't eaten crawfish before. She'd savored them in a bisque and seen them used as a garnish. True, no knives were provided to cut off the heads or little silver seafood forks to withdraw the meat, but she knew how to go about it. Roz twisted off the head, pinched the back, and pulled out the succulent tail. She stripped the vein with one of her short fingernails and popped the meat into her mouth.

Big-bellied Ursin prodded a school age boy forward. "You gonna suck da head, Miss Roz?" the boy asked, staring at his bare toes.

"Oh, you gotta suck da head. Dat's where all da fine fat is," Ursin dared her.

Roz looked at the beady eyes and long feelers of the beheaded crawfish, put it up to her mouth and sucked. She gagged down the lump of head fat and forced herself not to chug the glass of lemonade someone handed her.

"She all right. She one of us now, Brudder." Ursin turned to his own pile of crawfish to begin twisting, pinching and pulling.

"Here, you better put dis on before you ruin dat fancy store-bought dress." Alida Landry handed Roz a white apron and again pointing out the guest as an outsider.

Pierre had rolled up his sleeves like his brothers.

"*Merci*, Mama. You have another one for me so I won't have to get my suit pants cleaned?"

"Men don't wear no aprons. You should know better den to come to a crawfish boil wit' fancy t'ings." She stomped off to eat with her husband at a table beneath one of the live oaks that framed the house.

Piles of shells accumulated and got dumped in the bayou to discourage the flies. Rows of sweets were laid out to replace the crawfish. Children grabbed sweet dough pies from a tray, or gobbled more beignets. The men and women helped themselves to slices of sweet potato or blackberry pie, coconut or fig cake to go with their coffee. Some of the older boys, already fishing and trapping with their fathers, got into the stash of white mule and became rowdy. Music was called for to burn off the food and liquor.

Odon and a brother-in-law picked up their fiddles. Ursin rested a small accordion on top of his belly and pumped away. Papa Landry found his wife's washboard and two spoons and kept the rhythm going. Ignoring the mud, couples stepped lively. Ursin's hugely pregnant wife scooped up a toddler and bounced him lightly on top of her big belly in time to the music. Little girls whirled together or chased down a boy cousin to drag into the circle. Awkward adolescent males suddenly found the courage to ask their pubescent female relatives to dance. Roz twirled with Pierre. Better than the Yacht Club dance, the dancing went on until a light mist rose from the saturated earth and the dew dripped from the Spanish moss beneath a cloud-covered moon.

Those with cars and sleepy babies began to depart. Those who came in buggies would stay the night in order to be close to the church to receive their holy ashes in the morning. Alida Landry urged them to finish off the sweets before the strictures of Lent began. Ursin's wife raised another piece of fig cake to her mouth but lowered it before taking a bite.

"I t'ink I ate too much, me," she said. "Or maybe dis baby comin'."

"We got seven already. Don't you know, woman?" Ursin said helpfully.

Pierre stepped forward. "Would you like me to examine you, Mignon, before you go home?"

"Mon beau-frere, mais no!" Mignon said, horrified that her brother-in-law might want to see her private parts.

"I'm in training to be a midwife. I could take a look," Roz offered. "I've delivered several babies. If you should need my services, I'll be licensed at the end of the month."

Alida Landry bore down on the group. "You don't touch my grandbaby, you. We get Mignon a good Cat'lic woman who ain't banned from da Church for her evil ways, you hear. You chase my Pierre when you got a man already back in New Orleans, so my son don't marry nobody else. Go back where you come from!"

"Woman, go in da house!" Simon Landry shouted.

His wife didn't budge. She remained breathing heavily into Roz's face. Roz stood her ground, but she was shaking when Pierre took her hand. He spoke in rapid patois to his mother. Roz knew he had called her husband a wild beast though she did not catch all he said. Of one word shouted by Alida Landry, she was certain—*putaine,* a prostitute.

"Let's go. You can't reason with her. Mignon,

come in to the clinic if your pains continue." Pierre tugged at Rosamond's arm, but she didn't move.

"Mrs. Landry, I left a man who beat me, and I'm trying to make a new life. I'll be a good midwife, and I won't need Pierre or anyone else to support me."

"Won't nobody come to you, a woman who abort her own child and leave her husband. Maybe you deserve beatin'."

Some of the other women murmured, whether in her favor or not, Roz couldn't tell. Ursin let one end of his squeezebox drop. It made a small, hurt noise.

"I'm sorry you believe that of me." Roz shook off Pierre's hand and walked regally toward the parked cars. Behind her the argument raged in Cajun French, several voices joining in. She didn't strain herself to translate.

Roz got into the passenger seat of the Model T and closed the door. She sat in the dark waiting for Pierre. He came along shortly and, grateful for the automatic starter that spared his good right arm, made their exit a quick one.

When they turned onto the road, he apologized. "I'm sorry. This wasn't a good idea."

"Really? Your mother hates me. My family thinks you are some low class opportunist trying to break into the upper crust. We'd make quite a couple."

Pierre ignored her sarcasm. "I'll make it up to you. I think I have a likely candidate for a C-section due to deliver in the next few weeks. We'll do a trial by labor, of course, but I'm fairly sure her pelvis is too narrow for a normal delivery. Would you like to observe?"

"Oh, Pierre, you do know the way to a girl's heart."

When they passed the clock on its post by the bank,

she noticed the hands had passed midnight. Mardi Gras was over. Lent, when all temptations must be put aside, had begun. Roz let herself down from the car and walked into the boarding house without a backward glance.

Chapter Twenty-Nine

Roz had a problem. She hadn't expected to see Dr. Pierre Landry again so soon after the awkward Mardi Gras celebration, but here he stood, not three feet away, lecturing the midwives on the reasons for Caesarean sections and the operation itself. A careful procedure performed by a surgeon in a hospital could preserve the mother's health and fertility he told them. No need these days to choose between the life of the baby and the life of the mother as had been the case in the last century. The midwives should never attempt the operation themselves, but be ready to call for a doctor or get their patient to the clinic as soon as it became apparent normal labor had failed.

Hard as she tried to concentrate, Roz found herself listening to the sound of his voice and watching his lips form words beneath the soft, drooping moustache. She wished she had stayed in his car for a kiss on Mardi Gras Eve instead of flaunting her independence. As his hands, tanned and confident, moved over the model he used to demonstrate the surgical technique, Roz dwelled on how sure and gentle he was with women, with her. Being a modern career woman could be awfully lonely.

At the lunch break, Nurse Emory escorted Dr. Landry from the room, and the midwives pulled out their tins and baskets. The woman who had received the two laying hens for her services tossed Roz a boiled egg to go with her orange and crackers. Beulah sat beside her and took out a fried pork chop with the bone still in it sandwiched between two slabs of bread. She ate a big bite, swallowed, and washed it down with a container of buttermilk.

"My, my, I do have an appetite today. Nothing I likes better than a man wit' a tickly moustache, his hair all slicked back, and nice, clean hands. Fine skinny ass, too."

"Doan let Nurse Emory hear you talkin' like dat about da doctor," Granny Sue warned.

"What? She thinkin' the same, I bet. Jus' listen to her laugh. You ever hear her laugh befo'?"

In the adjoining lunchroom, the midwives could just make out the sound of Pierre's low voice and a husky answering chuckle from Nurse Emory.

"Won't do her no good. Doc looked at Peep dat whole time."

"That's not true," Roz protested.

"Ha! When he was strokin' de uterus and lookin' at you, I could feel it in my woman parts, good as going to one of dose hot moving pictures wit' John Gilbert and Greta Garbo makin' steam."

"Nothing can come of it."

"Peep, here's a few things I knows. You can't keep de rain from fallin', a baby from comin', or a man and woman apart who wants to be together. Bide yo' time, girl. It gonna happen."

Roz sighed with relief when Nurse Emory returned without Pierre and continued the normal course of the class, though he did several more lectures on recognizing and reporting venereal diseases, abnormalities in the newborn, and the normal development of the infant. Roz kept her eyes on her notes, concentrating on moving the pencil clutched between her stubby-nailed fingers across the paper. She didn't raise her hand to answer his questions. She didn't give anyone a reason to gossip.

At the end of March, Roz stood with the other midwives to receive her certificate. Widow Purdue had helped her make a proper white uniform and veil and her midwife's bag from cloth purchased with the carefully hoarded twenty dollars received for the birth of Lilliane LeBlanc. She invested in white nurses' shoes and stockings and had her hair cut for the occasion. Edna and Faye offered to touch up the darker blonde of her roots with a bottle of peroxide, but considering Faye's orange frizz and Edna's homely hairdo, Roz decided on a style as short as a nun's to even out the color.

Nurse Emory told her students she was proud of their accomplishment and desire to improve their skills and gave each one a colored cardboard wheel that made it easy to determine a mother's due date. Dr. Landry did a brief congratulatory speech, shook each hand, and presented the certificate. If he held Roz Boylan's fingers longer than the others and gazed into her eyes while he did it, no one commented.

A photographer paid by Nurse Emory snapped an official picture of the graduates. In years to come, people seeing the photo would assume Rosamond Boylan had been one of the instructors along with Nurse Emory, the only white faces in the group. The truth shocked them, and as Roz continued to display the picture, she was able to enjoy the reactions more and more over the years.

What she did not enjoy was having no family attend the ceremony. André, to keep peace with the St. Rochelles, kept Loretta away. They were not to validate Rosamond's choice of such a shabby career, or offer any encouragement for her to continue on its path. Despite this, Henri snuck in about the time they served punch and cake and delivered a small package containing extra white stockings sent by his mother.

At the boarding house over a chicken killed and cooked for the occasion, Widow Purdue and the others presented Roz with a her own shingle reading "Rosamond Boylan—Certified Midwife." They trooped outside to watch Mr. Toomey nail it beside the front door. All the widow asked was that Roz answer the door if calls came in the middle of the night.

As they admired the sign, Dr. Pierre Landry came to call. Having heard all about Roz's Mardi Gras with the Landry family, Faye and Edna stared at the attractive and forbidden doctor as he walked up the steps. Bernard Toomey stepped manfully and, perhaps, jealously in front of the women to see what the doctor wanted.

"Mrs. DeVille has gone into labor. I promised Roz—Mrs. Boylan—she could observe the delivery."

"In that case," Bernard said protectively, "go ahead, but don't keep her out too late."

"That's up to the baby, I'm afraid, but she'll be safe with me."

"Very well, then," Mr. Toomey said very seriously. "Ladies, I think the rest of us should get out of this cold and damp."

Feeling as giddy as a girl about to elope, Roz went

to get her veil and bag. Imagine observing her first surgery! Being with Pierre was just *lagnaippe*, an extra goodie, as the Cajuns would say.

"I have something for you. It's not new. I used it as a student." Dr. Landry indicated a package lying on the front seat of his car. Roz stripped off the paper and held up the stethoscope.

"I'll be the envy of all the midwives. Thank you, and thanks for remembering to come for me tonight."

"I never forget you, Roz."

She let the words pass by and evaporate in the chilly air. This relationship could go nowhere. She needed to establish good moral credentials as a midwife. Roz repeated that ten times to herself on the way to the clinic. Easier said than done.

They entered the hospital lobby only to be immediately intercepted by Mayor DeVille and his eldest son Hector already smoking cigars in the waiting area. Behind them, a distraught woman cried into a hankie while the mayor's wife comforted her.

"Doctor, is it time?" the mayor's son asked.

"If your wife hasn't progressed since I last examined her, we will have to perform the surgery I mentioned before both she and the baby become too exhausted. Mother and child should come through it well. Please, excuse us. We need to prepare."

The crying woman sobbed harder. The men stared curiously at Roz, but stood aside. As she trailed Pierre to the stairs, the younger DeVille nudged his father.

"You think the doc took a nooky break while my wife is in labor?" he said. "That one is hot to trot."

"Wouldn't mind having a nooky break with her myself right about now, so I can't hold it against him."

The mayor took a long draw on his cigar and reluctantly turned back toward the hysterical female. "For your sake, son, I hope Anaise doesn't take after her mother."

Anaise Olivier DeVille occupied the clinic's only private room. After ten hours of labor, she was hardly the chic and haughty lady who snubbed Roz at the beauty parlor. Sweat plastered her dark hair to her scalp, and her big belly, rippling with hard contractions, dominated her slim body. A nurse wiped the beautiful, suffering face with a cool cloth and murmured words of comfort. "Here's the doctor, dear. It will soon be over."

Roz took a place to one side of the bed as Pierre began his examination. "Let's see how things are going. Mrs. DeVille, the baby's head has not engaged in the pelvis. Your labor is not progressing normally. It is time to perform that surgery we discussed during your last visit."

"No!" Anaise DeVille's dark eyes widened with panic beneath her finely plucked brows. "I can do this. I was cut out of my mother, and the surgery left her sterile. She has a terrible scar and suffers from nervous attacks. She couldn't even bear to stay in the room with me." She gritted her teeth as another contraction began.

"Take a deep breath, let it out slowly, and try to relax the rest of your muscles. It will help with the pain," Roz told her.

"What is she doing here? Tell her to get out!"

"Mrs. Boylan is a certified midwife. I've asked her to stay with you while I prepare for the surgery. I can assure you that surgical techniques have improved since your mother gave birth. It will be possible for you to have one or two more children, and I will do my best to minimize the scar, but we cannot wait any longer.

Nurse, please tell the staff to see that everything is ready. Anaise, there is really no choice."

Pierre left Roz standing by the bed alone with the patient. "Could I rub your back or get you a wet cloth to suck?"

"Keep your nigger-loving, baby-killing, husband-shooting hands off of me!" Anaise DeVille swore.

"Very well." Roz put her hands behind her back. She couldn't help but notice that Mrs. DeVille's manicure remained as perfect as if she had taken the time to do her nails before coming to the hospital.

Another spasm came and went. As Anaise DeVille gulped down air, a sly look crossed her face. "I've heard you and the doctor are lovers. Convince him not to do this to me. I'll be your friend. I'll see you are invited to the best homes in Chapelle and Lafayette."

Roz knew women said all sorts of ugly things in the throes of labor, and she, as a midwife, needed to ignore any insults and soothe the patient. She'd done that a dozen times in humble houses where poor women, black and white, gave birth while their husbands sat on the front steps and listened to their screams. She'd been called whitey, bitch, slave driver, and whore by mothers in transition.

She'd been promised their milk cows, best iron pots, and eternal prayers for her soul that would get her out of purgatory snip-snap if she would make the pain stop. The pain always stopped when the baby came. The promises transformed into crocks of butter, a dozen eggs, or a simple thanks.

Roz took none of this personally. These women didn't know her or judge her. Pain formed their words. Somehow, she doubted this was the case with Anaise

DeVille. This woman thought she knew Roz and what she wanted most. Anaise DeVille was so very wrong.

"You are no longer queen of the Mardi Gras ball, Anaise, but you can be the living mother of a healthy child. It's time to stop worrying about your beauty and your pride, and do what has to be done. If you married a man who loves you less because you got a scar up your belly delivering his baby, then you made as big a mistake as I did with Burke Boylan."

Roz punched out the words, and from the stunned look on the patient's face, they might as well have been physical blows. The face of Anaise DeVille crumpled. Tears ran down her cheeks. Another contraction began, and she arched her back and writhed until it subsided.

"I don't want to be ugly. I don't want to be like my mother."

"Then don't be. Choose to be different. Stop whining. Be brave. Here the orderlies come to take you into surgery. If you see your family, give them your best queen's smile and wave. You'll be given an anesthetic for your pain and when you wake, you'll be a mother. Your recovery will take a much longer time than a regular birth, and you will have some pain. Eventually, you and your baby will go back to a lovely home where you will be waited on hand and foot with never a harsh word spoken. After that, it's up to you how this shapes your life."

"Give me your hand," Anaise said as another spasm began. "Oh, it's rough."

"Yes, it is."

"Will you be here when I wake up?"

"If you want me to be."

"Good. I might need to hear that little speech

again."

As the orderlies moved Anaise from the room, the young woman fixed a smile and gave a regal wave. Roz plastered the same sort of smile on her own face and returned the wave.

"Dear Lord," she prayed. "Let Anaise DeVille be delivered of a healthy child without complications." With that thought in her mind, Roz went to witness the Caesarian section.

****

The doctor carefully lifted the bladder. Pierre Landry made his next incision into the thick wall of the uterus. He worked quickly, scooping up the baby, tying off the cord, removing the placenta, as the surgical nurse sopped up the blood and birth fluids. He announced the time of birth as the baby began to cry and placed the infant in Roz's hands. She carried the big boy aside, cleaned and weighed him as his mother was put back together with the finest stitches Dr. Landry could manage.

Roz cuddled the child as the orderly wheeled the sleeping Anaise back to her room. "He's beautiful. I'd heard C-section babies were, so pink and white, a little sleepy though."

"I worked fast, but he probably got some of the anesthetic. Eight pounds, nine ounces—he's large enough to handle it."

"Was my child a boy? I never asked you."

"Yes."

"Well, then. I think I'm glad I don't live in a century where a midwife would have plunged a knife into a dying woman's belly to save the child or taken the child out in pieces to save the mother. I am impressed by your skill."

"You have the nerves and the hands to learn it if you want, Roz."

"Let's see if I can make it as a midwife first."

****

Roz was holding Anaise DeVille's hand when the woman's eyes opened. "It's over, and you have the most beautiful baby boy Chapelle has ever seen. How do you feel?"

"Headache, bellyache," Anaise croaked. "Water?"

"Right here." She lifted Anaise to drink and laid her gently back on the pillows. "And here's your son waiting to see you along with a whole room full of people out in the hall if you feel up to visitors."

Anaise regarded the sleeping boy wrapped in a blue flannel blanket and placed in the crook of her arm. "He's big."

"And healthy. What are you going to call him?"

"Lionel Olivier DeVille, we decided."

"Will you nurse? You will heal quicker, and it is good for the baby."

"Mother says nursing ruins the breasts. We should use a formula."

"Remember, it's your choice. Don't let anyone bully you, including me. Let me bring in your family now."

"I'll recommend you to my friends, Mrs. Boylan. And I'm sending you a case of the best hand cream money can buy."

"The perfect gift. Thank you."

"Name anything else you need. My husband and father-in-law will get it for you."

"Oh, I think I'll have to get it for myself. You be

well and a good mother to Lionel. I believe I'll be in Chapelle long enough to see how you do."

Chapter Thirty

Roz's midwife business didn't exactly boom. Young women of Anaise DeVille's class wanted a hospital birth with an attractive doctor in attendance. The poorer white women looked at her with distrust as a lapsed Catholic, and the colored stuck to their own race for birthing.

A week into April, Roz worried about paying next month's rent. She had hoped her father would relent and send a check for her twentieth birthday, which passed without notice, or she might be able to convert an expensive gift from her mother into cash. Neither form of help arrived. She allowed herself a brief cry and was still dabbing at her eyes when Faye knocked on her door.

The English teacher's eyes were almost as red as her own. "Must be a really bad day if both of us are crying. May I come in?"

"Certainly. Self-pity should not be indulged, as my mama used to say." Quoting her mother nearly set off her tears again. "I'm moping because no one remembered my birthday."

"That's terrible! I'll tell you what, Bernie, Edna, the widow and I will all chip in for one of those fancy cakes they have over at Pommier's Bakery. We'll have it for dessert after dinner. Maybe we can sneak out to Broussard's Barn and go dancing since it's Friday."

"After our Twelfth Night party, I don't know if any of us can be trusted around alcohol again, even Bernie and the widow." Roz laughed, but Faye's lips trembled.

"What is it?"

"Oh, Roz, I'm pregnant. After the party, all of you were asleep except for Bernie and me. We went up to his room so he could show me more chemistry tricks. Have you ever been up there?"

"I haven't had the pleasure."

"Well, I did." Faye gave a wan smile. "It's like a wizard's tower with a big bed in the middle and all his scientific gadgets set out on tables under the windows. I should have known better. I mean, I've been to college, and this wasn't my first time. I know about rubbers and all, but we were having so much fun. He kissed my toes again, and then, he sucked on them."

Roz held up a hand. "I don't need the details."

"A midwife embarrassed?"

"No, horny. Are you sure about the pregnancy?"

"I've always been regular as clockwork. I've missed my monthlies twice and feel like puking all the time, but I don't let myself. I'll lose my job if anyone finds out. I haven't even told Edna."

"Have you told Bernie?"

"Of course not. Ever since that first time, we've been really careful."

"This is still going on right under all our noses?"

"Not always. Sometimes, we find time at school when we both have a free period. There's this supply closet…"

"I don't need to know. So, are your breasts tender, nipples darker in color? I could examine you down there if you want. There are other signs like the violet color of the cervix, the softening of the uterus."

"I don't want to know! Roz, I have to get rid of it. You must know how."

"I don't—can't—do that, Faye, even for a good friend. Tell Bernie. Give him a chance to do the right thing, and if he won't, go home to Crowley and have your baby."

"I'm the first in my family ever to go to college. If I go home this way, I'll never be able to teach again. Everyone will know about me even if I give the baby away. You must know someone else who will help me."

"Faye, it's dangerous to abort a baby, not to mention that you have to live with the knowledge for the rest of your life."

"You should know. I've heard you threw yourself down a staircase to get rid of yours, but I never believed it until now, you're that cold."

Roz did feel a chill that her new friend could believe it of her. "I'm sorry you think that of me. I believe my husband threw me from the stairs, but since I was beaten unconscious at the time, I don't really know."

"I didn't mean what I said. Roz, please, I'm desperate."

Roz sighed. "You can ask Beulah Senegal. She has the knowledge and the means. I know she helps out colored women with too many children to feed and young black girls in trouble. I don't know if she will give anything to a white woman. She could go to jail for it."

"Where can I find her?"

"She has a place on the edge of town with some

plaster chickens in the yard. It's on the main road. Please, Faye, tell Bernie. Give him a chance."

Faye sat on the edge of the bed, her hands in her lap. "You know Bernie is shorter than me. When we do it standing up, he has to use a stepstool. And he's prissy about how he dresses, sort of old-maidish about a lot of things. I didn't expect him to be so enthusiastic after the first time. With the guys in college, sex was always once and done. I mean most men don't care for tall, freckled women with little breasts. I guess they are bigger now." Faye rubbed a light hand over her chest.

"They want girls like you, petite blue-eyed blondes with nice, clear skin. Bernie never told me he loves me. I guess I'm just convenient for him."

"You don't know that. The fact he hasn't spoken up doesn't mean he doesn't care about you. Look Faye, you're tall, as you said, and fashions are loose right now. I'll bet you could finish out the school term without anyone noticing. I know people in New Orleans who would take you in until the baby comes. Then, if you wanted, you could give the child to the nuns to put up for adoption."

Faye had ceased listening. "If I get the medicine from Mrs. Senegal, will you be here to help me if anything goes wrong?"

Giving up, Roz nodded. "Yes, I'll be here."

****

The cake purchased from Pommier's for her birthday tasted scrumptious, rich and yellow and iced with a thick layer of white buttercream dotted with pink sugar roses. Roz had little appetite for it. The boarders did go dancing, dragging the widow along in her black-beaded gown.

"My, my. I haven't been to Broussard's Barn since the mister and I were young and came out here to do the two-step. They had the chank-a-chank bands back then. It certainly has changed." She settled at a table near the dance floor where a colored band blared out a jazz tune.

"Could I get you something from the bar?" Roz offered, hoping the small change she'd brought along would be enough. She was determined to pay for one round since the others bought the cake.

"A ginger ale, dear. That would be lovely."

"Do you want anything in it?"

"Ice?" the widow said as if asking for too much.

"Sure." Roz went to place their order with Bubba the bartender and watched the dancers as she waited. Faye kicked up her heels in a frenzy as if she could shake the baby lose. When a slow dance started, Bernard Toomey comically rested his head on Faye's shoulder instead of the other way around, but Roz was sure the little man in the tight collar cared for her friend.

"Ginger ale, three gin and tonics, a whiskey and water. You look familiar, honey. I know you?" Bubba set the drinks on a tray.

"I've only been here once before." Roz lowered her face as she handed over her change and the bill Bernard insisted on giving her for good bourbon.

"Must have made some impression, den," Bubba answered, trying to get a better look at her face.

Roz picked up the tray, grateful she had gotten her hair shingled back to its original color and glad she wore the same demure party dress she'd worn last year for her birthday. On her way back to the table, she noticed the widow had been taken for a twirl by an older gentleman. Miz Purdue was flushed, and wisps of her hair had come down from the bun on top of her head as her partner executed a quickstep. Edna had found a partner, too, with patent leather hair and a big, toothy grin. Strange, not to be the center of attention at her own party.

Roz took a seat and sipped her questionable gin and tonic. Silently, she toasted herself, "Here's to the Queen of Hercules. May she no longer reign."

A finger tapped her shoulder, and she turned with a smile, expecting to see a dance partner, hoping to see Pierre. It was Bubba, the bartender. "You da midwife? The Old Man said you was, and you'd be cheaper den callin' da Doc. We got a girl in labor back in da cribs. Eloise says the baby's comin'."

"I don't have my bag with me, but of course, I'll come. I'll need hot water and soap, a basin, string, and something to cut the cord, a clean apron if you have one."

"Got one behind da bar. Don't see what da big deal is. The bebes, dey jus' come. Da Old Man delivered half of us hisself."

She had half a mind to tell the Old Man to deliver this one, but that would be unfair to the woman. Roz got up, collected the clean apron from the bar, and followed Bubba to the row of one-room huts behind the barn. Under the glare of a single light bulb hung from the ceiling, a girl of about eighteen labored in a double bed that took up most of the room. She was mixed race but light-skinned, full-lipped but straight-nosed. Her eyes, squeezed shut, had a slight slant above high cheekbones, and her hair had been straightened and bobbed close to her head. She lay naked under a white sheet. Her belly taut but not overly large indicated a good sign for a small baby.

As a contraction began, the red-haired whore, Eloise, shoved a leather strap between the girl's even white teeth. "Don't you cry out now. You know how Wally hates for the guests to be upset, but he sent you the midwife, so he can't be all bad."

The girl tried to smile at the jest but had to bite down instead.

"Just let me get a look between your legs. Crowning. Miss, would you see if Bubba is coming with the things I need?"

"Good thing it's Lent and business is off, or she would have been in here all alone," Eloise remarked as she slouched out.

"Try not to push for a minute. You're doing so well. The pain will be over shortly."

Bubba banged the door open and sat a sloshing bowl of hot water on the chair Eloise had vacated. He slapped down a bar of yellow soap, scissors and twine beside it. "I ain't no fuckin' orderly, you know. Deliver da kid and take it wit' you. Come by da bar for your pay."

Eloise slinked in behind the bartender and leaned against the wall. One strap of her acid-green satin dress slipped down her shoulder. From her posture, she could have been soliciting on Main Street.

"My baby died. She came early and died. People think I killed her, but she died all on her own, too little to live," the prostitute remarked.

Annoyed, Roz said as she scrubbed. "Don't listen to her. Are you full-term? Nine months?"

The girl nodded while still biting on the strap.

Tears squeezed out of the corners of her slanted eyes.

"Yeah, Denny DeVille got to her last summer. Our Miss Kitty here believed all that hogwash about how he was going to set her up nice in a little house the way they used to do back in the old days. Hell, I believed that traveling salesman who said he'd come back and take me away from my holier-than-thou parents, too. But, everybody in town knows the DeVilles like fooling with the dark ladies. Then, fine Mr. Denny comes roaring in here on New Year's Eve with you, takes one look at her belly when she's behind the bar washing glasses, and he don't know who she is. Funny, ain't it? Mayor DeVille has got himself two grandbabies in the last month. One will probably grow up to be president of the Police Jury, and the other one will end up here, working on her back like her mama before her."

"That's your name—Kitty?" Roz asked, ignoring the spew from Eloise.

"Yes'm. Kitty Brown."

"Okay, Kitty. Bear down, but stop when I tell you. Eloise, hold her up by the shoulders. Help her to push."

"As long as I don't get any of that stuff on my dress. Wally hates big cleaning bills." Eloise lifted the girl and helped her bend forward.

"Stop! The head is out. A sweet, tiny baby with a knot of black curls. Another push now. Here comes the rest, and it's a girl." Roz administered the slap, and the infant gave a sharp cry.

Kitty gazed down on her squalling daughter as Roz tied off and cut the cord.

"I need another little push for the afterbirth. That's great." Roz caught it in the spare basin. "Let me clean you up a bit, then we'll wipe off your beautiful daughter. Eloise, are there any blankets or diapers for the baby?"

"Hell, no! Wally would say this ain't no nursery."

"Find something," Roz commanded.

Eloise sauntered over to an old cabinet with half its varnish worn away. "Wally likes the sheets kept clean. We got to change them every day. There's always towels for the customers to use when they wash up. Naturally, this gal was too big to work by the time she figured out Denny wasn't owning up to being the father. Here we go, a nice, clean pillow slip and a towel." She handed Roz the items but couldn't seem to stop talking.

"You might have ended up the same way, drunk as you were New Year's Eve. Once Denny's friends were through with you, you wouldn't have known who the daddy was. Then, along comes the good doctor to your rescue and carries you away. I've had that dream myself more than once. Don't think Pierre Landry is too good for you just because he's a doctor. He comes from a family don't hardly speak English, but I like his ways. He came out here often enough when he first got back to town, not so much since you showed up. But I guess you ain't so satisfying because he still asks for Eloise."

Roz ignored her and went about washing the baby with a damp cloth. What Pierre Landry did was his own damn business. After all, they weren't married, engaged, or seeing each other. She'd married someone else. He'd gone his own way.

"Jealous, ain't you? Those pretty teeth of yours are going to crack if you grind them any harder." Eloise gave way to a fit of laughter.

"Kitty, would you like to hold your baby?"

"No, ma'am. You take her. She real white lookin' like Denny. Maybe she pass or some good Creole family adopt her. Wally, he don't allow no kids around, and I got to work off my time because he put me up all these months."

"Yeah, that's what I said, and I'm still here, tootsie. No one is coming to carry off Eloise. It's not such a bad life until you lose your looks. Good eats, plenty to drink, drugs if you want them to dull the pain, fancy clothes, and sometimes fancy men. The lucky ones out here are dead before they pass thirty."

"Come with me," Roz told the girl.

"Wally and his boys would slice you up for taking someone who owes him," Eloise said casually.

"It true. Take my baby girl somewhere good. Tell them her name is Innocent."

Roz swaddled the baby in a pillowcase and nestled her in a towel. "Then, you hold her, Eloise, while I finish here."

She dumped the dirty water out back and disposed of the afterbirth in the privy. Gathering up the basins, scissors and string in a bundle of soiled linens, Roz reclaimed the infant, flipping a corner of the towel over its small face to keep out the draft. She marched across to the barn, dumped the bundle of bedclothes at Bubba's feet, and held out the baby. Bubba recoiled. "I said I ain't no orderly, me."

Roz laid the baby on the bar and untied the splotched apron, added it to the pile. "All this needs to be washed."

"Here, take dis." Bubba warded her off with a five-dollar bill. He offered another from the cash box. "I'll double it, you get rid of da baby. Just get it outta here."

Roz snatched the ten dollars. "Get rid of it?"

"Drown it like a kitten, wring its neck like a chicken, I don't care. Get it outta here. It's bad for da business."

"I'll find a home for it."

"*Bonne chance* wit' dat. Kid is part nigger."

"And part DeVille."

"Like I say, *bonne chance* wit' dat."

Roz picked up Innocent and went back to her table.

"Someone give you a present?" Edna asked.

"Oh, dear, you have some sort of stain on your pretty dress." The widow dabbed at it with her hankie.

"I'm sorry to break up our party, but I have to take this child back to town."

Bernard Toomey blinked. Faye turned pale under her freckles. "A baby?" they said in unison.

"Yes, a baby. One of the girls back in the cribs gave birth. Bubba asked me to attend. She can't keep the child."

"Jeez, and we all thought you got lost trying to find the necessary," Edna marveled.

"*Cher* little heart." The widow peeped under the towel.

"As I said, the party's over." Roz led the way back to Bernie's auto that, like him, was small and immaculate. They crushed together in the back seat, Edna, the widow, and Roz. Faye sat in the front next to Bernard.

"Faye, would you take the baby? It's so crowded back here," Roz implored.

"No."

"Please."

"No."

"Faye, take the baby," Bernard Toomey ordered in his classroom voice. Reluctantly, the English teacher took the bundle, but she refused to look at the child, cuddle, or coo to it.

"Should we take it to the clinic?" the driver asked.

"No, I'll keep the baby overnight. She's normal and healthy enough not to need special care. Miz Purdue, would you have any rags we could use for diapers? If I could trouble you for some milk, we'll boil a formula in the morning. A sugar-tit should get her through the night."

"I have rags aplenty, all nice and clean. We'll make a little bed for her in the clothesbasket and put her in my room. Yours is far too drafty. If she cries, I'll get up and give her the sugar-tit. I used to make them for my son when he was cranky."

At the boarding house, they unloaded. Faye tapped her foot impatiently as Bernard ran around to open the door for her. She thrust the baby into his arms. "Here, you take a turn. I have a headache."

Faye marched up the steps and nearly tripped over the packages left on the doorstep. One was a large brown paper parcel addressed to Roz, the other a paper bag containing a re-used brown patent medicine bottle with its label peeled off and a fresh cork inserted.

"Looks like there's one for you and one for me." She tossed Roz the parcel, barely missing Bernie who, holding the baby as carefully as he would a test tube of volatile liquid, came slowly up the steps.

Faye entered the house and, leaving the door open behind her, ran up the stairs to her room. The rest of the group went into the kitchen where the widow dashed about pulling cloth for diapers from her ragbag and padding the wash basket to make a baby bed for the infant whom Bernard Toomey continued to hold. He flipped up the corner of the towel and ran his little finger down the baby's delicate cheek. Innocent turned her head toward the pinkie and rooted until she had it in her mouth. She sucked earnestly, then made little fretting noises.

"You is a miracle of biology, yes, you is. Miss Faye doesn't like you, don't know why, but Uncle Bernie does. Yes, he does."

Edna shook a cigarette from the pack in her purse, started to light it, put in back in the box after a glare from the widow. "Faye has been all kinds of moody lately. Maybe, she's trying to give up the smokes. That always makes me edgy."

Roz jerked her head up from where she attempted to cut diapers from a pair of faded red flannel long johns with a worn out flap. "Bernie, I can see you are fond of children. Are you that fond of Faye?"

The little man's face suddenly generated enough heat to melt his moustache wax. "It wouldn't be proper to discuss my feelings for Miss Faye with others," he said primly.

"I don't want you to tell me. I want you to tell her. Right now! Give Edna the baby and run up those stairs and tell her before it's too late. Go, go, go!"

At least, Edna got the message. She snatched up the baby with one arm and gave Bernard Toomey a push in the right direction with the other. He stumbled from his chair and, looking confused, bolted for the staircase. The baby, missing Bernard's fingertip, began to wail. Miz Purdue finished wrapping a lump of sugar in a wet rag. She twisted it into a nipple shape and popped the sugar-tit into Innocent's wide-open mouth. The baby clamped down and sucked.

For a moment, silence filled the house. Then, an upstairs door slammed, and two sets of feet thudded down the stairs. Bernie dragged Faye into the kitchen.

"Roz, she drank a bottle of poison...because of me," the chemistry teacher said in anguish and wonder. "Save her, Roz."

"Faye, go over to the sink and put your finger down your throat. Make it come up!" Roz commanded.

Faye gagged and wretched but only a small amount of brown fluid came out.

"Miz Purdue, do you have any syrup of ipecac?"

"I used to when my son was small. Boys, they'll eat anything on a dare, you know. Let's see. Here it is way back on this shelf, and all covered with dust." The widow shook the little bottle. "Think it's still good?"

"We'll have to try it. Drink it down, Faye."

"What if I cramp up? What if I lose—"

"You'll lose your dinner. Quickly."

Faye swallowed, making a face. The entire group waited as intently as tourists wait for Old Faithful to erupt. Suddenly, the teacher bent low over the sink. She spit out a volume of dark fluid, followed by a gin and tonic, birthday cake, that evening's rice and gravy, canned sweet peas, and pot roast. Bernie held her head and wrapped one arm around her waist. The retching seemed to go on long after the food was gone.

Through it all, Innocent, eyes closed, sucked her sugar-tit until she went to sleep.

The baby was tucked into her wash basket. Bernard helped wobbly-legged Faye up to her bed. He made it clear that, rules or no rules, he intended to sit beside her throughout the night. No one objected, evidently their secret not as well kept as Faye thought.

"If she cramps or bleeds, anything at all abnormal, come for me, Bernie," Roz told him. "We'll have to get her to the clinic if that happens."

Edna watched the couple go. "Jeez, where am I going to sleep? Who would have thought Faye would try to kill herself over someone like Bernard Toomey? I can't believe it. Sorry, Miz Purdue, I need a smoke right now."

"Very well, finish your cigarette, then take one of the rooms in the attic. With the rivers high and the roads bad, the drummers aren't coming through—but no smoking up there. You could burn us out. Roz, I'll take the baby to my room, *cher* little lamb. I suppose you'll take her to the nuns tomorrow. Why, you never opened your package. Here it sits on the table after coming all the way from New Orleans." The widow pointed out the abandoned parcel, the one Roz had been hoping for earlier and couldn't care less about now.

An envelope addressed to Roz Boylan—Purdue's Boarding House—was tucked under the string. She recognized Loretta's handwriting and Henri's artwork on the construction paper card it contained. Several green and purple dinosaurs grazed on giant yellow daisies, though the tyrannosaur appeared to have two hairy legs dangling from its jaws. The crayoned greeting read, "Have a Happy Birthday, Cousin Roz, from Henri and Mama." A folded five-dollar bill fell out into Roz's lap.

Some of my pin money will not be missed. Put it to good use. Love from Loretta, said a message, written with a fine-nibbed fountain pen that had blotted here and there on the thick paper.

Roz untied the string without enthusiasm. The parcel contained several boxes of sheer stockings, the latest popular novel, and a golden carton of expensive chocolates, all of them reminders of her past life, and none of them costly enough to hock.

Edna shook the box of chocolates. "Could I have one? It's been quite a night, and I could use the lift."

"No, sorry. I have other plans for the chocolates, but help yourself to a pair of the stockings."

"You mean it?"

"Certainly. Widow, would you like a pair?"

"Show my legs in sheer stockings, never!"

"Take a pair up for Faye when you go, Edna. That still leaves two for me. What I really want is some sleep. Tomorrow is going to be busier than I thought."

Chapter Thirty-One

Roz woke to the sound of rain slamming against the wall of her room and a dark, gray dawn showing through the small, high window. The boarding house remained quiet, but she finally had patients to check on. Roz dressed in her midwife clothes. She wanted to look as official as possible this morning.

In the kitchen, baby Innocent rested in her basket near the gas range where water boiled in a kettle. The coffeepot sat nearby ready to drip. Widow Purdue came in from the back porch on a gust of wind. She carried the milk pail and set it in the sink.

Seeing Roz bent over the basket, she remarked, "You're up early considering the night we had. Drip that coffee for me, dear, while I skim off the cream."

"We need to scald some of the milk for Innocent. We'll dilute it with some boiled water, add a little syrup, and let her suck it from a clean rag."

"No need for that. I found the nursing bottle I used last year to feed the runt puppy in my son's litter of German shepherds. Pup's as big as Rin Tin Tin now. In fact, they call him Rinny. I've washed it clean. You want to pour some of that hot water over it and the nipple?"

Roz sterilized the baby bottle. "You know more about this than I do, and I'm supposed to be an expert now."

"Experience, that's all it is."

Bernard Toomey stumbled into the room. Neither woman could recall ever seeing the man without a fresh shave and clean shirt. He'd lost the curl in his moustache, and last night's starched shirt hung limp and crumpled.

"Faye has the dry heaves. I thought tea and crackers might help her. I can make it in my room if you'd loan me a tea bag and put it on my tab."

"No need, Mr. Toomey. Just for today, coffee and tea are on the house. I can't recall when I last had such an interesting group of boarders—dancing at the Barn, bringing home abandoned babies, taking poison. You were all so quiet before Rosamond moved in."

"I seem to have that effect on people," Roz sighed. "I'll look in on Faye if you will keep an eye on the formula."

The widow nodded as she finished preparing a tray for her ill boarder and handed it to Roz. Innocent began to fret, and to Roz's surprise, Bernard picked her up. She made a small, wet spot on his already soiled shirt. "I think we need a dry diaper here."

"Stir the formula, Mr. Toomey." The widow efficiently unwrapped the bundle of joy on the kitchen table, held the tiny legs up as she washed the small private parts and sprinkled it with cornstarch. She had the clean diaper pinned before Innocent drew in a deep breath and began to squall. Bernard Toomey watched with fascination.

Upstairs, Roz knocked on Faye's door and backed in with the tray. Her friend stared up pale and woebegone under the covers.

"My stomach is still unsettled. What do you think

that means?" she asked Roz.

"I think it means you're still pregnant. No cramps or bleeding?"

"None. Yesterday, after you told me where to go, I rushed right out to find Miz Senegal before I lost my nerve. She said she didn't know what I was talking about, but since I was a friend of yours, maybe I might find a bottle of medicine to help me out on the doorstep later in the evening. I had to take it before I lost my nerve. That baby, she made me think twice. Then, Bernard knocks on my door, all nice and polite like he always is. I told him to go away, no sex tonight. He said he wanted to talk to me, just talk—about our future together. I still had the bottle in my hand, and I blurted out everything. You know the rest. I am so ashamed." Faye looked away.

"Oh, drink your tea and enjoy the crackers. It isn't often the widow gives anything away. Bernard was so pathetic she didn't even charge him. Right now, he's down there watching a diaper being changed as if the widow were teaching a class on French cookery. I think he'll make a good father, Faye, if you give him a chance."

"I know. It's just that a girl always thinks she's going to marry someone tall, dark and handsome like Lord Byron or Mr. Darcy, and Bernard is short, clean, and well-groomed."

"There's a lot to be said for the last two, and he can't help being short."

"Well, I hope this baby gets my legs, and Bernie's nice, straight brown hair. I don't think there's much chance of him being handsome."

"Does that mean there is going to be a wedding?"

"As soon as school lets out. If we do it during Lent, everyone will know. Besides, it's against my contract. Bernie said he'd get me an engagement ring even though he doesn't have to, and I won't be able to wear it in public. He's so sweet." Faye dabbed at her eyes with a corner of the blanket and took a sip of her tea.

"I'll send him back up."

"No! Let me primp a little. The last two times he's touched me, he's been holding my head over a basin. I want to erase that picture from his mind."

"Sure. I'll tell him you're getting dressed."

In the kitchen, Bernard Toomey, patting Innocent on the back, paced the planks as they waited for the milk to cool. Finally, the widow tested a few drops on her wrist and declared the formula ready. She tickled a corner of the baby's mouth with the bulbous nipple and watched the infant latch on like a starving Armenian.

"*Cher* poor heart, she's so hungry."

"May I feed her?" Bernard Toomey held out his arms, and the widow slipped the infant into them.

"Would you have a market basket I could carry her in?" Roz asked.

"Oh, surely she doesn't have to go so soon. You can't take a newborn out in a storm like this," the widow protested.

Roz wondered if they would be so fond of the child if they knew her skin might turn darker and her tight black curls become nappy as she grew, but she wasn't about to deprive the baby of some much-needed cuddling and attention by announcing its lineage.

"I'll wait for the rain to stop. Then, I intend to see she gets the home she deserves. Bernie, could you drive me over to the mayor's house around ten? I need to visit Anaise DeVille."

By ten, the rain had slowed to a drizzle, and Roz, holding a market basket with Innocent wrapped snuggly in red flannel and covered with a light cloth, dashed through the puddles to the car. In her other hand, she clutched her birthday chocolates. Bernard held both the door and an umbrella for her and the baby.

The trip was short, just a few blocks to the brick mansion painted white from its iron grillwork balcony to its tall, fluted columns. The DeVille ancestral town house sat on an artificial rise to prevent bayou flooding from entering the home. Two live oaks, a hundred years old if they were a day, flanked the walkway. Bernard Toomey parked, opened the wrought iron gate, also painted white, and held the umbrella over Roz and the baby as they walked up the gravel path skirted with the broad green leaves of aspidistra, the iron plant that grows so well in the deep shade of the oaks. They mounted the semi-circle of brick steps that jutted out from the portico. Roz thanked Bernie and told him to go home to Faye. She rang the bell.

A colored maid in full uniform of black dress, ruffled apron, and cap answered the ring. She took a good, long look at Roz in her white uniform with a basket over her arm and said, "Deliveries to the back."

Never had Rosamond St. Rochelle entered a house through its service entrance—unless she was sneaking in from an escapade. She raised her chin and skewered the maid with the glare honed by old French families for centuries and learned at her mother's knee. "Mrs. Rosamond Boylan to visit Mrs. Hector DeVille the Third. Please announce me."

The maid eyed the woman in white. "Miss Anaise

jus' had a baby and ain't seeing nobody who ain't invited."

"I'm aware of that as I was her midwife. I have a small gift for Mrs. DeVille and won't stay long. She'll be quite upset that you kept me waiting."

Knowing her employers would be more upset if she let a pushy stranger in the front door, the maid stared at the basket. Under the light covering, Innocent wiggled and let out a sharp cry followed by a small stinker.

"Better not be no kitten in there. Cats, they can smother a new baby."

"It's not a kitten. The gift is this box of chocolates all the way from New Orleans. I believe new mothers should be pampered," Roz continued in her starchiest manner. She hoped she sounded exactly like Nurse Emory, superior and undeniable.

"Better not be no puppy, neither. We got mo' dogs around here then we needs."

"Emmy Lou, who is at the door?" a high voice called from the parlor.

"Says she the midwife. Got a present for Miss Anaise."

"For heaven's sake, let her in. The draft alone is bad for the baby." The woman whom Roz had last seen in hysterical tears came to the door. "I'm the child's grandmother, Clarise Olivier. Do come in, but please limit your visit."

Lowering her voice, Mrs. Olivier added, "Anaise needed surgery to deliver, you know. She's still very weak and shouldn't be exposed to germs. I'll take you upstairs."

Roz followed a pair of narrow hips and long legs

remarkably like the daughter's up a graceful spindled staircase. Clarise Olivier tapped on a door at the far end of the hall. "Are you awake, dear? You have a guest, the midwife who attended you."

"Come in," Anaise answered in a remarkably strong voice. She lay propped up in a feather bed old enough to have been used by Jefferson Davis, covered with lace-edged sheets and a half canopy of pale blue and gold. Little Lionel DeVille sucked vigorously at one of her plump, blue-veined breasts protruding from a quilted silk bed jacket edged with ecru lace. The elder Mrs. Olivier averted her eyes from the sight.

"How are you, Anaise? Any problems? Any questions I can answer? I see you did decide to nurse. Good for you."

"Mama and Mother DeVille aren't too happy about it. I had to ask one of the nurses at the clinic to show me what to do since neither mother breastfed. Did you bring me chocolates?" Anaise's eyes turned greedy. "My appetite is simply voracious, and I feel sublime except for the sore tummy. They won't let me out of bed. I do tire easily, but it's nothing an afternoon nap won't fix."

"You look wonderful. Here." Roz opened the golden box, selected a morsel topped with a candied violet, and popped it into the mouth of the nursing mother.

"Yummy!" Anaise DeVille plucked Lionel from one breast with a small pop and gave him the other before he could whine.

"Don't eat too much at one time. Chocolate can have a laxative effect on babies."

"I'll try to restrain myself."

"Well, then, I'll let you two have a nice visit." Mrs. Olivier twisted her fine-boned hands together. She couldn't seem to take her dark and beautifully made-up eyes off the exposed breast that still dribbled milk. Finally, she handed Anaise an embroidered hankie and retreated from the room.

Anaise put the hankie over the leaking breast. "It is a messy business. Hector isn't too pleased about having the baby in the room, either, though he couldn't be prouder of his son—the next governor of Louisiana, he says—after the boy plays football for Tulane, of course."

Roz nodded her understanding. Her father had said similar things about his lost sons. His girls were going to be queens of the Mardi Gras. She didn't wish it on Roxie.

"Anaise, I need your help with a small problem." Roz took a seat on a little gold and white boudoir chair and lifted the basket onto her lap.

"I delivered this child last night to one of the girls out at Broussard's Barn." Roz parted the covering so the tiny, delicate face and tight curls of the baby could be seen. "Her name is Innocent DeVille."

Anaise's glowing color drained from her face. "Is it Heck's child? Did he betray me so soon?"

"No. I'm sorry I blurted it out that way. The baby belongs to Denny. The mother is colored, very light-skinned, barely eighteen. Her name is Kitty Brown. If I don't do something fast, she'll end up prostituting herself out at the Barn, and the child will have to go to the Children's Home. The mayor must have influence with old Wally Broussard. Could you ask him to find them a place? Every socialite needs a good cause to support, my mother always said."

"Couldn't mine be eradicating polio or some other awful disease?" Anaise shifted Lionel to her shoulder and patted his back until he released a manly belch.

"Young women forced into prostitution because they had an illegitimate child are worse than a disease. And, you might do something for Eloise Elmo, too, while you're at it. I think she'd like to get out of the business, but doesn't know how."

"How could I possibly help Eloise or this Kitty?"

"Didn't you say your father-in-law and husband would give me anything I asked right after your son was born? Are you going back on that?"

"No, of course not. The Oliviers and the DeVilles never renege on a promise," Anaise said with a hint of the old imperial attitude in her voice.

"Good. Then, here's something that will help them to do the right thing. Dennis DeVille was named as the father of this child, and that's the name I plan to file on the birth certificate. You know how gossip like this gets around in a small town. The sooner they settle Kitty and the baby elsewhere, the sooner the talk will die down. Now, I will leave Innocent here with you. There is a jar of formula and her nursing bottle in the basket. If you need more, call me."

"That won't be necessary. If the men balk, I'll threaten to nurse the child myself. I bet they won't be able to get out to the Barn fast enough to retrieve the mother."

"Why, you cunning rebel, you. I can just see it now—The Anaise DeVille Home for Unwed Mothers."

"How about the Anaise DeVille Sanctuary for Reformed Prostitutes?"

Roz threw back her head and laughed. The release of tension felt so good after the events of last evening. "That's the spirit. Call if you need reinforcements."

Roz left the DeVille mansion empty-handed. Feeling light and happy, she bounced along in her sensible white shoes and barely turned her head when a car stopped next to her. Pierre Landry leaned across the front seat and opened the door. "May I offer you a ride somewhere?"

"No. I'm only walking back to the boarding house, and the rain has stopped."

"I thought you might need to take that baby you delivered last night over to the Children's Home in Lafayette. I heard you cheated me out of a fee."

"Already? My, word does spread fast in Chapelle. Who told you—your favorite hooker, Eloise?"

"Get in the car."

"I think not. I have my reputation to consider."

"Get in the car if you want an explanation."

"No need to explain to me. Men have their needs is what I've always heard."

Pierre glanced up and down the street, empty on this dreary April day. He lowered his voice. "Yes, they do, and I was taught early to take mine to the kind of woman who got paid to take care of them after Papa caught me with Susu Theriot. If her baby hadn't been the image of Otto Muller when it was born, I might have been the youngest married man in all of Chapelle. As it was, I worked extra hard for Doc Spivey to earn a little pleasure money. As my mama said, any decent girl that gives it away is looking to trap a husband."

"Is that so? Then, I couldn't possibly ride with you. What would people say?"

"Forget I ever offered. Wally called me out to the Barn to examine the mother. He wanted to know when she would be fit to work."

"I hope you told him never."

"You did a good delivery, Roz. No tearing. No sign of infection."

"The baby was small. I'm arranging a home for her and the mother."

"That should cause a stir. The girls rarely escape from Broussard's Barn. I gave Eloise train fare once, and she returned it to me when I was called out to set her broken arm. Be very careful, Roz."

Roz shivered though the day wasn't particularly cold. "I don't think that's in my nature, Pierre, but thanks for your concern."

She slammed the door decisively and watched the doctor drive away without his knowing how much she had wanted to accept that ride.

Chapter Thirty-Two

Like a lady of leisure, Roz lay, fully dressed, on top of her covers taking an afternoon nap when a pounding fist nearly broke in her door. She scrambled for the little pistol she had unearthed from her trunk after talking to Pierre and pointed it at the door. Any second now, Bubba Broussard might smash the flimsy barrier off its hinges.

"Who's there? What do you want?"

"Ursin. Ursin Landry. You come wit' me right now. My woman say da baby, he comin' quick quick."

"Oh, Pierre's brother. Doesn't she want the doctor to do her delivery?" Relieved, Roz put down the gun.

"*Mais*, no. Mignon, she want da fancy white *chasse-femme,* not da old lady *traiteur*, not my brudder, not me, her own man, not my mama who tell her what to do too much, she say. 'If you love me, Ursin, you go fetch Miz Roz,' she say. The roads, dey is all *bourbeux*. What she t'ink, I can jus' fly here, me? Drive my boat down Main Street, huh? Come, come!"

Roz tied her shoes and pinned her veil in place. She considered the gun for a moment and finally strapped the purple satin holster to her thigh, sliding the pistol into place. She slung her midwife's big white bag over her shoulder and scurried out the door to follow the massive Ursin to his mud-coated truck.

They sped along the paved road, scattering flocks

of egrets and passing mule-drawn wagons poking along the highway. Ursin spun the wheel at a fork in the road and turned off on to a dirt and shell lane running between two water-filled ditches lined with chinaberries, tallow trees, and scrubby yaupon bushes. Beyond the tree line, cane fields spread out flat and flooded. The truck ran over a cottonmouth snake four foot long in the roadway and buried it with the mud splashed from its wheels as Ursin urged the old vehicle forward.

Roz hung on to the door handle as they bucketed along. "Where are we going?"

"We got a place out by Catahoula. The water, she high, no?"

"Yes, I hear the Mississippi is near flood level with all the rain and the snow melt from up North. I worry about my family in New Orleans, and I guess they worry about me."

"Da Teche ridge, she don't flood, even if da levee go. T'ings get too bad, we go by my papa's place outside Chapelle."

"How many children do you have?"

"*Sept.* Seven livin'. Mignon and me, we been married since we was seventeen, you know. You take good care of my old lady, huh? She *tetu*, likes her own way, but I don't want to lose her, no."

"I'll do my very best."

"*C'est bon.*"

They came to a small settlement where most of the homes were raised on cypress piles and connected to enormous, barrel-like fresh water cisterns. A small rain-swollen bayou fronted the houses and beyond that, the great, grassy wall of the levee held in the waters of the

Atchafalaya swamp. Ursin stopped the truck in front of one of the more substantial cabins, and two brindled black and white dogs with eerie blue eyes raced from the porch to greet him with muddy paws. He shouted them down, and without asking, scooped up the midwife all in white and carried her through the mud to his front steps.

"Your family does this very well, Ursin."

"But of course," he said so charmingly that Roz was convinced he had once been as slim and handsome as Pierre, despite his big belly and missing front tooth.

Inside the house, Mignon shouted, "Don't you let dem dogs in here, Ursin. Aaaa-eee, dis baby comin' fast, fast."

Roz rushed into the front room where a cauldron of hot water bubbled on the wood stove. The room was swept clean and dusted. A long table made from a single, untrimmed cypress plank three feet across filled much of the space, its benches neatly aligned. Rag rugs and rockers sat not too far from the stove. Crockery and pans gleamed on wall shelves beside a sink that emptied out under the house. A picture of the Blessed Virgin hung nailed to the whitewashed *bousillage* wall made of mud and moss. Beneath the picture on a small table burned a votive candle in a ruby glass holder. Someone had gone out into the wet to gather a bouquet of yellowtop and daisy fleabane and placed the bouquet in an old green bottle beside the flickering candle. The house had floor space enough for babies to crawl and children to play indoors on rainy days.

"You have a very pleasant home, Ursin," Roz said as she scrubbed up.

"Mignon, she been cleanin' all day. Da kids, she

sent over by her sister."

"Y'all comin', *Madame Chasse-femme*, 'cause dis baby, he ready to come out," Mignon called. "Ai-yai-yai!"

Roz hastened to the large bedroom where Mignon lay on a double bed with a plump moss mattress covered in boiled, bleached, and mended old sheets. Ursin's wife had fastened two rope handholds to the bars of the bedstead. She strained against them. Her belly heaved under the worn nightgown of flowered flannel. Her muscles bulged. She let out another cry.

"Dis one, he hurts more den all the rest."

"Let me take a look. Don't push. I see a foot."

"*Mais*, no!"

"This isn't your first. We have plenty of room to get him out, but I need to pull both legs down and make sure the cord isn't in the way. This will hurt, but don't push."

The strength of the contractions squeezed the pelvic muscles against her hands. Roz waited for an interval and quickly drew one leg down, fought the muscles again, found a small foot and paired it with the other. She moved the baby down the birth canal.

Mignon swore, "'*Cre tonnerre!*'"

"Definitely a boy, a big-headed boy."

"Ain't dey all. We was gonna call him Toussaint, but now maybe he be *Gros Tete*, eh," Mignon panted. She regarded the bloody, vernix-smeared baby with experienced and loving eyes. "He big all over."

"A big, clean afterbirth, too. Can you rub your belly to help stop the bleeding? This being your eighth child, we need to help your womb to contract."

"Tent'," said Mignon doing as she had been asked.

"What?" Roz attended to the baby, wiping him clean while he fussed and squirmed, and dressing him in a diaper and shirt almost too tiny for the nine pound boy. Mignon had laid out the clothes and blankets in the nearby crib.

"Toussaint, he my tent' child. *Diphterie* took my first born, and *La grippe* got one of my baby girls."

Roz snuggled the newborn next to his mama and arranged the rags that would catch the clots and the abundant lochia following the birth of such a big child. She rolled the large woman from side to side, changing the sheets, even the sweat-soaked pillowcase. At Mignon's direction, she found a clean nightgown in the big armoire and helped the woman put it on.

When everything and everybody was tidy, Roz went to look for Ursin. He wasn't far off. Ursin sat on the front steps, a dog on either side of him, a hand-rolled cigarette dangling from his lips, and a bouquet of wildflowers pulled up by their muddy roots in his hands.

"You done in dere? I heard da baby cry."

"Yes, you can go in and see your new son. He's big and healthy. Would you like me to put those flowers in a vase?"

"Yeah, sure. Women, dey like flowers. I give the Virgin some, too, for my woman's safety, you know."

"I know." Roz took the flowers and cut off the roots while Ursin went in for his visit. She found a jar to arrange them in and took the bouquet to Mignon, setting it on the table by her bedside.

Ursin held his son, but he stood, kissed his wife's forehead, and settled the baby back in her arms. "Best I go get da kids. My *belle-soeur*, she lives down da

Bayou Bouef levee road, got five of her own and one more due any time now. She probably crazy by now wit' twelve runnin' around."

Ursin shook a finger at his wife. "My mama, she gonna be *en colere,* you don't call her to come."

"Go get da kids." Mignon waved him away.

"I'll sit with you until he returns."

"Yeah, dis been good. No noise, all nice and quiet. No MawMaw Alida sayin' da water not hot enough, da house not clean enough. Havin' you take care of me and Toussaint, *c'est bon.* I gonna tell my sister, Cherie. She make her man come get you, end of May when she due. Don't care if MawMaw Alida don't like it. Ain't no one good enough for her boys. She want Pierre to marry some nice country girl. I say, he been to da city, won't no'ting but a city girl do now." She looked pointedly at Roz.

"That can't be. I'm married and in the midst of a divorce. Afterwards, I won't be welcome in the Church, and I refuse to buy an annulment. In fact, I'm thinking of joining the Methodist church permanently."

Mignon shrugged. "Won't dat jus' burn MawMaw Alida's tailfedders, huh? Pierre don't care about religion. Help me up. I got to get dinner on da stove."

"Oh, no. Let me do that for you." Roz spoke without thinking.

"You cook?"

"Ah, I can boil water."

"*Bon.* Put some rice in it. You stay to eat. Me, I give Toussaint da tit."

****

By the time Ursin returned with a truckbed load of children, a pot of gumbo and a pan of cornbread sent by

Cherie, the smell of scorched rice filled the house.

"T'aught da place was burnin' down, me," he grumbled, but he settled the children around the table even though they clamored to see the new baby.

"Hush, hush, he sleepin'. You get to hold him after supper."

Mignon, who insisted on getting up, dished rice from the center of the pot into bowls and ladled the still warm crawfish gumbo over it. She let Roz cut the cornbread into squares and pass the pan around the table. The children scooted over to let the midwife sit. A pitcher of cold milk from the icebox by the sink sat at the ready to be poured into tin cups, and the coffee pot was prepared for after the meal. Spoons remained down until they said grace with Ursin thanking *Le Bon Dieu* for the safe delivery of his wife, his fine new son, and his seven other blessings. "And Lord," he added, "Let da rains stop and da levee hold. Amen."

After the meal while the older children took turns holding the baby and the toddler crawled into his mother's lap looking for attention, Ursin set two pierced cans of sweeten condensed milk in hot water to make a treat for the family. While the milk caramelized, he drew Roz aside.

"I don't got much cash money, me, but I do got dese, a nice otter fur or dis alligator hide tanned soft as butter. Which you want?"

Roz ran her hand over the thick winter fur of the otter, but the long tail and little paws put her off. She accepted the alligator hide. Perhaps, she could send it to her mother and have a purse or shoes made in the city. People paid good money for that sort of thing. Maybe, Anaise would buy them. She tucked the rolled hide under her arm and slung her bag over her arm in preparation for leaving.

"What, you not stayin' for dessert?" Ursin asked.

She stayed and ate a bit of the taffy-like candy made from the milk and listened to Ursin play a lullaby on his squeezebox. When his wife had gone back to bed and the baby slept in his crib, Ursin sent his sons to the loft and settled his girls in the rear bedroom. "Now, we go," he announced.

The long road hemmed in by ditches and trash trees was dark as a tunnel. The dim lights of the truck scarcely penetrated the night as Ursin drove much more carefully than he had coming. Despite his caution, he ran down a slow-footed possum, stopped the vehicle, and slung the carcass into the rear of the truck.

"Makes good stew, you know how to cook it," he remarked as they went on their way.

Where the road turned onto the hardtop an obstruction sat in the way—a car, big and black. Two white men lounged against it and passed a bottle back and forth.

Ursin got down. "Come, come, Bubba, Gaston. What you blockin' da road for, eh?"

They pointed to Roz sitting the cab. "Dat midwife. Tell her come out."

"What your business wit' her? She jus' deliver my new son."

"She cost us a whore, dat's what. Mayor DeVille come out to our place and carried off dat little yeller gal. 'Course, he paid off her debt and promised da Old Man, he get one of us on da Police Jury some day, but we don't want her meddlin' no more. Got da mayor's *belle-fille* all upset over some quarter-nigger baby, dat midwife, and we paid her to get shut of it." Bubba pointed the neck of the bottle toward Roz.

"Won't kill her, jus' teach her a lesson, eh," Gaston added, reclaiming the bottle.

"You don't touch her, you. Dere's jus' as many Landrys as dere is Broussards 'round here. You don't want to start no feud wit' us. Y'all got soft makin' your livin' on whiskey and whores. I can take you bot'."

"All you Landrys is soft on your women. But, she ain't no Landry. Dis not your quarrel, Ursin."

Gaston took a blackjack from his pocket, smacked it into his palm, and started toward the truck. He jerked open the door and looked right into the barrel of a very small pistol. Something prodded his belly, the tip of a pair of scissors.

"No man will ever beat me again," Roz said steadily. "Tell your brother to move the car, or I'll shoot your eye out and gut you on the way down."

"Wooo-eeee." Ursin rocked back on his heels. "Bubba, I put you in da driver's seat, me." He opened the door to the sedan and heaved Bubba up by the back of his shirt.

"Don't go nowheres, Bubba, I can take her," Gaston called.

"It's your eye," Roz said and shrugged. "The bullet is small, but it might go right through to the brain."

"You know, she shot her husband, no?" Ursin said casually. "He beat her, and she shot him down. Bang, bang."

Gaston jumped. He stepped away from the scissors pricking his stomach. "*Merde*," he swore.

He shook a finger at Roz. "Jus' you don't meddle again, you hear?"

"I hear."

"*C'est bon*, no?" Gaston stomped to the car, slammed the door, and motioned to his brother to drive.

Ursin climbed in beside Roz and waited for a few moments to create some distance between them and the Broussard brothers. The frogs resumed singing in the ditches, rejoicing in all the rain.

"Thank you, Ursin. You didn't have to stick up for me." Roz rewrapped her sterile scissors and packed them in a pocket of her bag. She left the pistol in her lap.

"You know, Pierre, when he was a boy, he bring home everyt'ing hurt and watch over it 'til it strong and ready to go free. Mama and Papa, dey always say, wring dat bird's neck, shoot dat deer for da gumbo pot, but no, not Pierre. Den, he take dose creatures far, far out in da swamp where we don't hunt and let 'em lose when dey better. Me, I don't t'ink he want to set you loose, but you gettin' plenty strong."

"Pierre set me loose some time ago."

"Me, I don't t'ink so, or he wouldn't have said for me to watch out for you, and all my fam'ly, too."

Roz started to say she didn't need their help and no longer needed Pierre to lean on, but instead, she simply said, "*Merci.*"

****

Her wristwatch showed nine p.m. As far as Roz was concerned, it could have been midnight. She tried to slip quietly past the parlor, but Edna, enjoying an evening smoke, turned her way. "Roz, where have you been! You missed dinner. Come see Faye's engagement ring."

Bernie and Faye, appropriately cuddled together on

the Victorian love seat, called to her also. She had no choice but to enter the room and admire the tiny diamond, ornately set to make it look bigger, on Faye's freckled finger.

"We went this afternoon and picked it out at LeClerc's jewelry shop. I'm paying for it on time," Bernard announced proudly.

"I'll have to wear it on a chain until school lets out, or the School Board will fire me outright for getting engaged." Faye blushed. "But come June, I want you and Edna to walk in my wedding."

"Congratulations to both of you. I'd be honored to be in your wedding," Roz replied, going through the motions. Completely exhausted, she still felt pumped full of adrenaline from her encounter with the Brothers Broussard.

The widow entered with a coffee tray and set it on the low claw-footed table sitting between the love seat and the single chairs. "Your mother called, Roz. She wants you to call back no matter what the time. I'll be expecting repayment for the cost."

Evidently, coffee was still free, but out-of-town telephone calls were not. "Thanks, Miz Purdue. I'll do that immediately." Before I collapse on my ass.

"Here, dear. Take the coffee with you. You look all done in."

Roz nodded her thanks, stoking her cup with sugar before she took on her mother. The telephone in the hallway wasn't the best place to converse with her family. She knew all the ears in the parlor would be tuned her way.

"Hello, Mama. Yes, I did get your gift. Henri must have brought it over. I found it on the doorstep last night… No, I find country people to be very honest. This isn't the city, you know… Yes, I'm sure I'll enjoy the novel when I have the time to read it… Yes, I noticed the chocolates were from my favorite shop. One can always use stockings… No, Mama, I'm not unappreciative or lacking in manners. I've been very busy and would have called tomorrow."

"Busy doing what?" her mother said shortly. "Too busy to call your family when the river is threatening to burst the levees at any minute and flood the city?"

"The newspapers say there is no need to worry. The levees will probably breach to the north and drain off the excess, but if you are worried, why don't you come and stay with Loretta?"

"My home is one-hundred-fifty years old, Rosamond. I have never lived anywhere else, and I will not abandon it to flood waters and looters. I am grateful that my children are in safe places, however. We aren't allowing Roxanne to come home for Easter. She'll stay with the nuns at the Academy. The Teche area is supposedly out of danger as well. You can loll around eating chocolates and reading without fear, Rosamond, or go to Mass and pray for us."

"Mama, in the last twenty-four hours I've delivered two babies and prevented a miscarriage. I'm about to go to my drafty room, pull the sheet over my head and sleep until I feel like waking up. I have no intention of going to Mass, either. But please, if your situation is dangerous, leave the city."

Madame St. Rochelle sniffed. "People are fleeing New Orleans like the proverbial rats from the sinking ship, but your father will handle the matter. He's been meeting with the politicians and business leaders. Say nothing, but they will approach the River Commission on the eighteenth about dynamiting the levee in St. Bernard Parish to take the pressure off the city."

"What about the fishermen and trappers who live there? How terrible!" Roz exclaimed.

"The city will reimburse them for their losses and see they are given time to evacuate. Rosamond, you have no idea. I've never seen the river this angry. It's shored up with sandbags, and still the water leaks through. I've seen whole trees, dead cows, and pieces of houses washing by. If action isn't taken soon, New Orleans will be gone. Do you want that?"

"Of course not. The solution seems drastic, that's all. I have to hang up, Mother, the widow doesn't like us running up her bill. Please, you and Papa take care. Good-bye."

As Roz set down the receiver, she glanced toward the parlor. Her friends were no longer in their seats. They crowded in the archway listening to every word.

"What's happening in New Orleans? I thought the city was safe," Edna said.

"Let's just say if you have friends there or in Plaquemine and St. Bernard, urge them to leave. Be grateful the flood isn't coming here. If you'll excuse me, I'm going to bed."

It occurred to Roz as she went to her room that no one had asked about the babies delivered to poor folk. Now, the concern was all about the city and the coming flood.

Chapter Thirty-Three

While the citizens of New Orleans bargained to save their city and desperate men with shotguns patrolled the levees of St. Bernard Parish, Roz gained her first real client, one she could counsel and prepare for birth. Ursin Landry stopped by and drove her along the top of the Bayou Bouef levee to the home of Cherie Arton, his sister-in-law.

Cherie, unlike her big and bountiful sister, probably had been pretty and petite in her youth. Now, she'd turned stringy, thin arms and stick-like legs supporting her pregnant belly. She possessed a shy smile already becoming gap-toothed from the bearing of so many children, and big, dark eyes that still held a certain beauty. She wore her dark hair pulled back severely in a bun and was graying young.

Clearly, Cherie had married poorly. Her two-room cabin with an overhead loft stood upon rickety posts on the swamp side of the levee where squatters weren't required to pay property tax because the land belonged to the state. A boardwalk, also raised on stilts, connected the house to the crest of the levee. A wide gallery, boxed in all the way around with weathered gray boards to keep the children from tumbling off, gave the place the appearance of a houseboat that had grown legs. Ursin said that was actually the case.

Cherie insisted that her husband, Claude, stop

roaming the Basin when the first of the children grew old enough to attend school. He'd put his houseboat up on stilts for her. A boat came by daily to pick up the students and deliver them to the classroom for an elementary education.

The oldest child, a skinny girl of twelve with her mother's shy smile and long, dark brown hair that hung in her eyes, had finished with schooling and stayed home to help her mama with the babies and scrape hides and scale fish for her papa, Ursin explained. Muskrat skins stretched on hoops dangled from the eaves like soundless wind chimes and fishing nets draped the railings where the youngster bounced a three-year-old on her bony knees so her mother could have some peace to talk to the midwife.

Coffee was offered and poured. Roz sat at the homemade table aged as gray as the outside of the place and felt foolish talking about rest and good nutrition. Her eyes took in the reality of a twenty-pound sack of rice sitting in a corner next to a ten-pound sack of cornmeal, and a five-pound container of coffee beans. The shelves held canned goods—cane syrup, condensed milk, and peaches packed in sugary juice. The family had no china, only tin plates and cups stacked in an open cupboard by the wood stove. She suggested Cherie purchase tomato juice and canned vegetables and perhaps get a cow that could graze for free on the levee grass.

"Oh, I make da coffee-milk each day before da boys leave for school, cornbread and syrup, too. We get plenty milk. Claude, he say a cow too much trouble, always getting lost, always stuck in da mud. Canned vegetables, dey too dear. Mignon, she give me extra from her garden when she have it. Claude, he bring home fish and game. We got plenty meat." Cherie gestured to smoked venison haunches and strings of dried fish hung from the rafters.

"I can see that. He must be a very good hunter and fisherman. Well then, do you have old sheets for the bed? They should be boiled and very clean."

"*Cher*, everyt'ing I got is old, and I try to make it clean, but I got t'ree boys, you know. Mostly, we sleep right on da mattress." She gestured toward a bag of striped ticking stuffed with Spanish moss rolled up in one corner.

"I'll bring a rubber sheet and some old linens if you call me in plenty of time. Please don't wait 'til the last second like your sister did. Toussaint was a breach birth. She might have lost him if she'd waited much longer. I don't mind sitting with you."

"Mignon, she always t'inks it's gonna be *bon, bon, bon*. Me, I seen some bad in my time. Dat spring Claude lost his leg to a gator, t'ought we was gonna starve, but da Church and da fam'ly seen to us. *Le bon Dieu* watch out for us, and we take care of our own. More *café*?"

"No, thank you. Do you have lots of clean water?"

"We catch da rain water in da barrel outside. I boil it up. And, we got da indoor commode."

"Really?" Roz looked around the small space and saw no indication of a bathroom.

"Come see." Cherie led the way into the second room where the moss mattress lay on a bedframe covered with a blue and white striped cotton blanket. A corner of the bedroom had been boarded up and hung with a door. Cherie opened it with a flourish. There sat a porcelain toilet in all its glory. By its side hung a bucket of water to provide the flush and a Sears catalog hanging from a hook to supply the wipes.

Roz raised the lid and looked down. She could hear the water lapping against the stilts. She had no doubt where the sewage went. "You keep it very clean," she said.

"Dat I do. Put da lid back down. Wit' da water so high, da snakes come in."

Roz dropped the wooden cover with a bang, and Cherie laughed. "Heard Pierre Landry was *fou* for a city girl. Must be true."

"It's true I'm from the city. Snakes are not my favorite creatures."

"Oh, we got plenty snakes here." Cherie cocked her head. "Da school boat comin'."

She led the way out on to the deck where the girl urged the baby to wave to the children on the canopied launch. The boat nosed into the levee and lowered a plank. Three boys, aged ten, eight, and six, scrambled across the board and raced each other for the house. Roz noticed the oldest lad hung back and let the little ones win. "Nonc Ursin," they shouted in passing as they thundered across the deck past the man and into the kitchen.

The boys clapped down tin lunch buckets and schoolbooks on the table and clamored for food. Their mother brought out a plate of cold biscuits covered with a checkered cloth and placed a knife and jar of fig preserves beside it. The boys reached out.

"No, no! We got a guest. Miz Roz, will you eat a biscuit?"

"No, but thanks. We're almost finished talking. I

have to get back to town."

"Elise," Cherie called to her daughter. "Make a biscuit for da baby before da boys get dem all."

She poured four tin cups half full of coffee and punctured a tin of condensed milk to fill the rest of the cup. "Elise, you give da baby a sip of yours. Come outside. We can't talk wit' all dat noise."

Roz followed her. "You think you're in the eighth month, and the baby is due at the end of May. You have five living children. Any miscarriages, stillbirths, or difficulty with past labors?"

"No, no. We miss a year when Claude lost his leg, but den da one *between* his legs, it grow back when Claude see he can still trap and fish." Cherie pointed to her own crotch. "Da new leg and da old one, bot' made of wood, eh? Pierre, his like wood, too, no?"

"I can't say," Roz managed to get out as Cherie laughed some more at her flustration.

Ursin heaved himself off of a coil of rope where he had been sitting and enjoying the rare sunny afternoon with a smoke and his own cup of coffee. "Don't tease, Cherie. You finished? I got a delivery to make to Broussard's Barn today."

"Yes, we are. I'll come back and check your progress in a few weeks and see if you've begun to dilate."

Cherie raised her eyebrows. "*No comprendre.*"

"To see if the baby is getting ready to come, to see if the head is in position."

"*Bon.* We talk. We have some *café.*"

Cherie seemed totally unconcerned about giving birth in a cabin far from the nearest neighbor. Considering her own experiences, Roz admired the hardiness of the woman. Evidently, her husband had delivered all the others.

As the truck with three casks covered in burlap sloshing in the back turned toward Chapelle, Ursin ran through a list of relatives who were in some stage of pregnancy. Roz figured if she developed a clientele among all the Landrys, their in-laws, and more distant kin, she'd never want for rent money or alligator hides again.

When they arrived at the boarding house, Roz let herself out and leaned across the cab. "Will you be okay out at the Barn?"

"Sure. We got us a deal. Wally can't make enough hooch his own self to keep his customers happy. My cousin, Putt-Putt, he make da best white mule in da Atchafalaya Basin. Me, I deliver it. Dey ain't gonna do me not'ing, but you, stay clear of dem Broussards."

"I will. I have more serious things to worry about right now."

****

Wearing yet another of last year's white dresses and a straw hat trimmed with a pink grosgrain ribbon and a silk rose she'd clipped from another outfit, Roz attended Easter services at the Methodist church where the air was filled with the scent of the potted lilies that bedecked the altar. The boarding house stood empty when she returned, each of her friends having gone to have dinner with family, or in Bernard's case, to meet Faye's family in Crowley. Ignoring Roz's outcast status, Loretta had invited her to dine. She wasn't sure she could endure an entire afternoon with Loretta's oldest daughter, but the prospect of thick slices of ham, fresh green beans, fluffy biscuits, pecan pie and the inevitable plate of deviled eggs drew her to accept. The telephone in the hall rang as Roz prepared to leave for the feast.

Emmaline St. Rochelle called to wish Roz a happy holiday and tell the story of the dynamiting at Caernarvon. On Good Friday, her parents had taken a picnic lunch along for the noon event, joining a parade of cars, carriages, and boats venturing out to watch the destruction of St. Bernard Parish. They waited until past two p.m. for the show to begin. At last, the charges were set and fired. The earth heaved and settled back into place. A trickle of water flowed through a six-foot wide gap. More dynamite exploded. Divers went underwater with charges. Finally, thirty-nine tons of dynamite created a rift big enough to relieve the pressure of the river against its banks.

"Very anti-climatic, my dear," Madame St. Rochelle told her daughter.

"Very tragic for the small farmers and trappers. Sheriff Meraux said his parish was publicly executed, according to the newspapers."

"Meraux is a well-educated bootlegger and power-monger. Everyone knows that. He's angry because his trade has been interrupted. There's two million dollars set aside for reparations. Do you want to guess who will get most of it?" her mother asked in an irritated voice.

"I suppose you're right. I've been working with people who make their living off the land. They have so little. It doesn't seem right to take their livelihood."

"Cajuns and Negroes, you mean. They've always lived that way. It doesn't bother them, but I don't know how you could sink so low. Yes, I heard you took your classes with coloreds. Several people called to tell me.

Perhaps, we should have let you join a nursing order if you wanted to care for the poor. That would be more respectable than what you are doing now."

"Yes, Mama. I would have made a great nun," Roz replied with an edge of sarcasm in her voice.

"Give it up, Rosamond."

"And return to Buster?"

"Of course not. Apply for an annulment, and when the scandal dies down, remarry and be what you were born to be. If you continue to act outrageously, society will not accept you again."

"Perhaps, that's not what I want. I have clients now. You won't starve me out, Mama, even if you cut off the pittance I get from the bank. I can make my own way in life."

"You were always defiant, Rosamond. Keep consorting with lowlifes, and you'll never be able to return to New Orleans."

"Mama, the only reason I'd want to return now is to see you and Papa and Roxie and Uncle Laurence."

She rendered her mother speechless for a moment. The silence didn't last. "We love you, Roz. We only want what's best for you. Happy Easter."

"Give my love to everyone, Mama. Call again soon."

As she hung up the phone, Roz recalled how the nuns had taught the War Between the States. At the first battle, Manassas, residents of Washington had gone to view the fighting in their carriages with packed cold lunches in baskets. As the slaughter went on and on, the civilians fled back to the city and were overtaken by retreating Federal troops. The Yankees had committed a sin of pride, the nuns hinted, in regarding a tragedy as amusement. Maybe that's why the war had gone on and on, a sin of pride on both sides.

The next day, the Glasscock levee broke on the west bank of the river, bleeding off the floodwaters into the Atchafalaya Basin. There had been no need to inundate St. Bernard Parish at all.

Chapter Thirty-Four

One by one, the levees popped under a renewed deluge of floodwaters and endless rain. The Cabin Teele crevasse poured out over northern Louisiana seventy-five miles to the town of Monroe on May third. On May thirteenth, the levee at Bayou des Glaises melted away. The town of Melville, Louisiana, was totally destroyed by floodwaters at six a.m. on May seventeenth. Roz read the newspapers and wept.

Roz visited Cherie Arton. Her surly, unshaven husband sat at the table drinking coffee and playing bouree with Ursin while Roz examined his wife in the bedroom. His own truck, even older than Ursin's, sat parked on the levee, but Claude hadn't wanted to waste the gas driving the midwife to and fro.

His boat was tied to one of the stilts, the water level so high he could jump into it easily. Roz heard the dark flood lapping inches from the floorboards and suggested Cherie spend the last week or so of her pregnancy in town.

"You've dilated three fingers. The baby will be coming soon. You shouldn't be out here alone."

"Claude is here. Da water too high. All his traps, dey wash away. If da house flood, we go over to da backside of da levee."

Roz took her plea to Claude Arton. "Monsieur Arton, with the weather so uncertain, I think you should bring your wife into town until the baby comes."

Claude took a deep swallow of coffee and wiped the ends of the bushy moustache that topped his stubble free of condensed milk with the back of his hand. He looked at the midwife with eyes as small, dark, and feral as the muskrats he trapped, rattled off some rapid Cajun French and shrugged.

"Speak *l'anglais*, Clauce, to da midwife. She comp'ny," Cherie shouted from the bedroom.

Claude threw down his cards and shouted back. The ever-mellow Ursin translated. "Claude say if da road's too bad, he bring da baby like he done all the res'. Cherie, she don't need no fancy midwife. She jus' being *tetu*, stubborn, 'cause her sister is spoiled by me, Ursin."

More rapid French flew back and forth between the rooms. Finally, Claude stomped out on his wooden leg, jumped into his boat, and cast off, the putt-putt of the small engine fading into the distance. Cherie still shouted at him from the small window in the bedroom.

"She say she don't care if he never come back, but he will," Ursin continued.

In the corner, the girl, Elise, cowered, holding the toddler against her thin chest. Cherie Arton came into the room. Her face was flushed with yelling. She drew a hand down over her belly where the baby kicked furiously, making the front of her flowered dress look lumpy. "*Café?*" she offered as if nothing unusual had taken place.

"Not today, thank you. I have a meeting with another expectant mother in town. Perhaps, you know her, Marcelle Begnaud."

"*Oui*, cousin to Ursin and Pierre."

"Really? I didn't know that. If your pains begin or your water breaks, have Claude come for me at once, day or night."

Cherie nodded and walked them to the door of the cabin. Roz crossed the plank to the levee, and Ursin followed, the board bowing under his weight. In the truck, Roz interrogated him. "Is Pierre sending me clients? I don't need his help."

Ursin gave his favorite answer, a shrug. "Dere's lotsa Landrys to go 'round. One woman get somet'ing special, dey all want it, eh."

"Claude obviously doesn't want me here."

"Claude, he not so bad mos' times. He make good money. 'Rat hides going for t'ree dollars each right now, but he like to gamble. He take his pelts into town, get paid, stop at da Barn on da way back, and come home with nuttin'."

"Why on earth did Cherie marry him?"

"Claude, he raised in da swamp. Never went to no school. Jus' come to town to find a wife. Cherie, she t'ink she tame da wild man, yeah. Instead, he take her off into da Basin. Dey come back wit' a boatload of kids a few years later. Least now, he can sign his name and speak some of da English."

"He's a terrible man. Why doesn't she leave him?"

"Wit' going on six kids and a fort' grade education? Where she go? Mos' women, dey got to lie in da bed dey make. Not too many can get up out of it and run off. Besides, Claude, he yell, but he don't hit her." Ursin raised his eyebrows, and let that information sink in.

Roz remained quiet for the rest of the trip. As they parked before the boarding house, she was startled to see Pierre Landry and an older man sitting in the porch rockers. Both rose as she got down and thanked Ursin for the ride.

"Roz, let me introduce you to Dr. Leonard Spivey, home from the desert and fully recovered, he claims. This is the midwife I was telling you about, Len."

"I longed for lazy brown bayous and bearded oaks, my dear," Leonard Spivey said. Even in old age, he stood taller than Pierre but just as spare. His hair had gone white, but his blue eyes twinkled with mischief. He possessed the elegant, concerned manner that Pierre had adopted as his own.

"Truthfully, he heard about the flooding in Louisiana and came back to help. The Red Cross is setting up a camp on the ridge above Spanish Lake. More flooding is expected, and people are being called to evacuate the low-lying areas. They need medical personnel. We wanted to know if you would join in the effort. Stressful situations seem to bring on the births, you know."

"Doing me another favor, Pierre? I understand Marcelle Begnaud is your cousin."

"I don't think living in a tent in a muddy campground is doing you a favor, Roz. You could be of great help if you choose to be. The Red Cross will see you get paid."

"I'm not concerned about getting paid. I'm worried about being confined in a small area with you."

"I'm sure we'll both be too tired to follow our inclinations."

"I didn't know you still had any toward me. You keep your distance well enough."

"As do you!" Pierre's dark eyes flashed like the

lightning in the rain clouds.

However, Leonard Spivey's eyes twinkled. "The one that got away, Pierre? The one from New Orleans I was supposed to save you from, and here she is. Just shows old doctors shouldn't meddle. I told Gilbert St. Rochelle moving my retirement up wouldn't stop that freight train from rolling and now here we are, all parked in the same roundhouse."

Pierre turned on him. "You faked your retirement!"

"No, boy. I'm sixty-five years old, and I was exhausted. I might have exaggerated the weak ticker to get you here in a hurry, but I badly needed the rest. My apologies. Gilbert made it sound as if you were being pursued a by married woman who would give you nothing but grief, not a hard-working colleague."

"Thank you for calling me a colleague, Dr. Spivey," Roz said stiffly.

"She *has* given me nothing but grief," Pierre Landry said.

"Then stop looking after me. Stop being there for me. I'll take care of myself."

"Young people, please." Doc Spivey held up his hands. "We came to ask for your assistance in the camp, Miz Roz. Will you come?"

"If I can be of use, certainly. I have an appointment this afternoon, but after that I'll notify my landlady and pack a few things. Could you arrange transportation for me, Dr. Spivey?"

"I'll take you out to the camp, Roz. It's only a few miles from town," Pierre said wearily.

"I wouldn't want to cause you any more grief, Pierre."

"I'll take you to the camp as a professional

courtesy, Midwife Boylan."

"Then, I accept your offer, Dr. Landry."

Chapter Thirty-Five

Dozens of conical white tents with straight dropped sides blossomed on the hills above Spanish Lake as if some strange new tribe of Indians had taken over the area. Evacuated coloreds were housed lower down the slope in Camp McGlade, and below them, six-hundred head of stray cattle and lost mules tore at the rain-soaked grasses quickly turning pasture to mud. Around this haven from the flood, the National Guard patrolled on foot or rode fully armed on horseback.

Red Cross nurse, Judith Strictland, welcomed Roz and assigned her a tent and a cot. A sign affixed by the flap opening read, "Midwife Services." Below those words, Pierre wrote *Chasse-femme*, though those who couldn't read English probably couldn't read in French either. Considering, he drew an awkward line sketch of a cradle holding a bald-headed infant next to the words.

"Bravo!" Roz clapped.

"Another of my amazing talents." Pierre bowed. They smiled into each other's eyes.

Nurse Strictland looked from one to the other. She cleared her throat and thinned her unpainted lips. "Midwife Boylan, I think we should take a tour of the camp. I have a list of all the pregnant women admitted and their approximate due dates. We've tried to persuade those farthest along to evacuate to the maternity ward being set up at Southwestern Louisiana

Institute in Lafayette where they can give birth in a clean, dry environment, but these Cajuns are remarkably stubborn. No matter how loudly I shout, they simply shake their heads and pretend not to understand."

Nurse Strictland's plump, ruddy cheeks grew redder at the thought. She led the way in sturdy brown shoes because in no way could she keep her white footwear clean in the muck. She wore her white veil bearing its signature red cross pulled down over her forehead, not a wisp of hair showing. Judith Strictland's hands were broad, short-nailed, and totally competent. Nearing forty, she had thickered around the middle and thighs but still gave off an aura of boundless energy. She bore no wedding ring and reminded Roz of some of the sterner nuns at the Academy.

As they approached the mess tent, Nurse Strickland bemoaned the lack of local hygiene and abysmal dietary habits. "Perhaps, you could assist with lessons on tooth-brushing. We are giving every child and adult a new toothbrush, but the way they stare at them, I'm afraid they'll use them to polish their boots. We have the children line up with a container for milk every day, and provide three meals, but all we get are complaints. Oh, no! Here they come again, and I can't understand a word of their jibber-jabber."

Like hornets from a disturbed nest, women swarmed from the opening of the mess tent and buzzed angrily in Cajun French at the nurse. One held out a bowl containing a lump of cooked rice and a watery roux in which chopped wieners floated. The loudest of the women shoved the bowl under Roz's nose. "*C'est merde*!" she exclaimed.

Roz took two steps back. "She says it's sh—not tasty."

"I know the word *merde*. I served in France. Heard it all the time over there. You tell them that is perfectly good wiener gumbo. They can't expect chicken under the circumstances."

Appalled herself by the idea of gumbo made with hot dogs, Roz did her best to translate using her nun-instilled Parisian French and words she had picked up from Pierre's relations. The women were not appeased.

"They say if you will give them the rice and flour and let the children catch some crawfish, they will make you a good gumbo or a nice courtboullion with catfish from the lake. They cannot eat this sh—food."

"Explain that the water might be polluted, that the fish could be contaminated."

"*L'eau, c'est mal. Le poisson ne bon,*" Roz managed to get out before the angry wives buzzed again.

"They say they will cook the fish until it is good to eat. They are not stupid. Oh, and they want cornmeal to make bread and *coush coush* for breakfast and syrup to put on it, bigger coffee rations, and tobacco for the old folks." Ros hastened to remember all the demands.

"*Coush coush*? Whatever is that?" Nurse Strictland's face was growing redder by the minute.

"Fried cornmeal, sort of like a breakfast cereal."

"We are serving healthy bowls of oatmeal, and they keep demanding cornbread and syrup. No wonder half of them are toothless."

"But, you have to admit they do make a wonderful gumbo."

"That burns out the lining of my stomach. I've

been going into New Iberia for chocolate malteds at the drugstore merely to survive."

"Perhaps, the cayenne pepper kills the bacteria in the meat and seafood. I'm so used to the taste that other foods seem bland." Roz took another look at the wiener gumbo and smiled sympathetically at the women.

"Very well. I'll give them an opportunity to cook. We'll see how they manage."

"Oh, I think you'll be surprised. No one can stretch food like a Cajun and still make it taste good." Roz conveyed the excellent news to the crowd. The women gave her three rousing cheers, and the crowd dispersed.

"With your fair skin and light eyes, you're not one of them, are you?"

"My fine old Creole family would be outraged if you suggested I was a Cajun."

"I wouldn't have guessed you had Negro blood either."

"Creole—as in founding French families, Nurse Strictland."

"Then, when we have a free moment we will have to see if my ancestors got to New York before yours arrived in New Orleans."

"You'll have to meet Catherine Emory. I believe her family came over on the Mayflower, but please remember the Cajuns arrived here in the 1750s and have survived very well without our help. Keep that in mind and things will go more smoothly, I believe."

"Catherine Emory is a legend among public health nurses."

"She taught me my skills."

"Then, you have my regard. Now, that Dr. Landry, he looks like a Cajun."

"He is, the first of his family to go to high school and college."

"Those dark-eyed Frenchmen can get between your legs before you know what's happening—just a word of warning from someone who served at Marne and the Somme. In a camp such as this, we must set the moral example. You will see that I am right."

"I've promised myself to keep my knees together where Pierre is concerned."

"Good. I've observed far too much mischief of a sexual nature going on in the camp already without having to worry about the staff. Take those three girls who showed up yesterday and claimed a tent right by the boundary where the boys from the National Guard patrol. I intend to keep my eyes on them. No one fleeing high water has the time to have their hair freshly bleached or dyed that bright shade of red. None of them seems to own a dress without a hem six inches above the knees and a low dip across the chest."

"Would you happen to know their names?"

Nurse Strictland flipped over several sheets on her clipboard beneath the listing of pregnant women. "Laverne, Kiki, and Eloise. They claim to be waitresses from a local establishment that has taken on some water. Evidently, they live on the premises."

Without admitting that one name sounded familiar, Roz nodded. "Yes, I'd keep an eye on them."

****

Roz didn't lack for customers. Despite camp conditions, the women she assisted resisted being separated from their families in order to give birth in a hospital ward. They hid their pains until transport to Lafayette became out of the question. Most of the mothers were multipara, giving life to their sixth or seventh child with admirable stoicism and relatively short labors. The worst case so far had been a fourteen-year-old girl who had hidden her pregnancy for months. During the climax of her labor, female relatives quizzed her on the identity of the father. When the agony of transition hit after a long, grueling night, the girl finally cursed the boy by name. Before the newborn exited the birth canal, the male relatives had rounded up a wild-eyed seventeen-year-old and found Father Grainger. As soon as the girl could stand, the couple married. At the direction of the family, Roz waited until after the brief service to fill in the birth certificate.

Roz made time for a visit to the colored camp down the hill. She and Beulah Senegal sat on overturned buckets near the entrance and exchanged birthing stories.

"So business is good there?"

"Dey droppin' like fruit from a chinaberry tree, Peep. Sorrow brings 'em on."

"The body of the mother needs to be lightened to deal with crisis."

"Never heard it put so befo', but we sho' got our crisis now. De old ones is dyin' of de damp as fast as de new ones come."

"I bring them into the world. Dr. Landry sees them out of it."

"Y'all makes a good couple."

"We rarely see each other with more and more people crowding into the camps. It's for best."

"The Lawd gonna work his will wit' you and de doctor, Peep, one o' dese days. Jus' you wait."

"For what—my husband back in New Orleans to

vanish?"

"Maybe so, Peep, maybe so." Beulah looked up at a sight on the hill. "Look like you needed again. Dat a scared papa sliding in de mud if I ever seen one."

The wiry form of Claude Arton moved toward them so fast every other step he took on his wooden leg slipped in the mud. Beneath his walrus moustache, a steady stream of French burst forth, pebbled with curse words each time he lost balance.

"*Chasse-femme! Chasse-femme! Merde, merde, merde.*"

"Monsieur Arton, is Cherie having her baby? Have you brought her to the camp?"

"*Bebe, oui.* Cherie no come. She *tetu.* You come." Claude Arton tugged on her elbow.

"Better go, Peep." Beulah shooed her away. "Dey droppin' like chinaberries, didn't I just say?"

Roz hurried up the hill dislodging clumps of soggy grass as Claude hastened her on. At the gate of the camp, his old truck sat, its bed holding the skinny Elise who gripped the toddler and three wide-eyed little boys pointing excitedly at the tents and the soldiers. Their father rattled off French faster than Roz could translate it in her mind.

"Please, speak slowly. *No comprendre.*"

Claude looked over her shoulder and then pushed Roz aside. He latched one callused brown hand on to the dark-suited arm of Pierre Landry and gestured wildly with the other.

Calmly, Pierre translated. "He says Cherie wants to give birth in her own bed, not in some teepee like a wild Indian, but the water is still rising under their house. He brought the children to safety, and now he will take you back to his wife to deliver the baby. He has three good muskrat hides set aside for your fee, but you must come now."

"Tell him if he will trust me with his truck, I'll go persuade Cherie to come or deliver the baby, whichever seems best. He should stay here with his children and be assigned a tent so we can get his wife settled as soon as possible."

Pierre didn't repeat the message to Claude Arton. "Are you sure about this? The roads could be flooded by now. I didn't know you could drive. Even if you can, crossing a muddy levee won't be like cruising through City Park on a Sunday."

"I badgered our chauffeur to teach me when I came home from the Academy. Papa never knew. I may be rusty, but I'm sure I can do this. Claude should stay with his children in case anything goes wrong. No sense in making orphans of them. Tell him what I said."

Beneath his olive complexion, Pierre Landry paled. He repeated the words. Claude Arton, however, gripped her shoulders and kissed both of Roz's cheeks. He hoisted her into the driver's seat and shouted to his children to get down. They jumped to the ground and clustered around their father like a flock of chickens when a hawk flies over.

Claude pushed the children back and cranked the truck. Roz worked the gears. The chassis bucked forward and stalled. Roz began the process all over again until she was able to make a wide circle turning the vehicle toward the distant levee road. Her white veil fluttered in the windowless cab, and she shoved it behind her. Biting her lip Roz headed down the hill, picking up speed. Pierre Landry ran along side.

"Let me go with you," he shouted.

"They need you here, Pierre. I'll be just a few hours. Take over my deliveries, will you?" Roz didn't hear his answer. She clung to the wheel and rolled so fast she nearly missed the turn onto the main road. Afraid that stopping or slowing would stall the engine Roz sucked in her breath and pressed the gas pedal to the floor.

Chapter Thirty-Six

The closer Roz got to the levee road, the higher the water in the roadside ditches became. In some places, huge puddles covered the blacktop or packed shells making it impossible to judge what lay beneath. She bullied through them all in the same gear she'd been using since leaving the camp. Roz thanked God when she finally reached the high road running along the spine of the levee and could set the truck into the wheel ruts that would prevent it from sliding off into the high water of the swamp on one side or skidding down into the tilled farm land to the west. She was even more grateful when the weathered cabin came into view. The stilts on which it rested could no longer be seen beneath the flood.

With the sagging boardwalk awash with an inch of muddy water, Roz made her way across to the porch. Inside the cabin, Cherie groaned and called out for Claude. An iron pot of hot water had been left on the small stove. Roz ladled some into a metal basin and scrubbed with homemade brown soap while she told Cherie that she had come to take her back to the camp.

"The *bebe,* he come now," Cherie cried.

She knew. The crown of the baby's head bulged from the vagina when Roz lifted the covers. She had barely enough time to rotate the torso for the delivery of the shoulders before the infant, already screaming and

343

flailing his fists much like his daddy, slipped into the midwife's hands. Roz placed Cherie's fifth son on his mother's hip and scrambled for the scissors and thread to tie off the cord. The afterbirth followed, quickly and easily falling into the pan.

Roz cleaned the blood and cheesy vernix from the child, pinned him into a diaper, and pulled a tiny, hand-sewn shirt over his head. With the baby well-swaddled in a blanket Cherie had laid out along with the other clothes Roz placed the boy in the mother's arms. This was always the midwife's favorite moment of the birth, one that brought her a sense of peace and worthiness.

Roz bent to clean the mother. In the distance, she heard the noise of a freight train. The train moved closer as if someone had recently built tracks along the levee.

"Cyclone?" Cherie asked, holding tightly to her baby.

"I don't know. Let me go see." Roz moved toward the front door, but the sound overtook her.

Cherie screamed, "Crevasse!" as the wall of water hit, splintering the stilts beneath the cabin like the breaking of bones. Water skittered across the floor and into the bedroom, growing deeper by the minute. Clinging to the door, Roz watched the levee disappear beneath a force that made water run uphill. The wave topped the earthen barrier taking Claude's truck with it—and then the water returned, slamming the small house from the opposite side. The cabin, as if remembering its former life as a houseboat, rode the crest away from the shore. Roz waded to the bed. "We must go up to the loft. There's too much water down here. Can you walk?"

"*Oui*. I will do this."

Roz took the baby from the weakened woman and as an afterthought, snatched up the iron pot of hot water. Its weight anchored her as she crossed the swamped floor. Cherie, holding her nightgown above the filthy water, followed. They made their way to the outside stairs. Roz helped her patient up the first few steps, and when she was above the water, handed her the baby and made her own way into the loft. The house rode the surge.

In the dim *garconniere*, Roz settled Cherie on to one of the three pallets filled with cured Spanish moss. Small louvers set into either end of the loft to let in light and air allowed only a patch of gray sky to show and didn't block the terrifying sounds of the houseboat colliding with uprooted trees and bawling cattle trying to find footing before they drowned. The infant, feeling its mother's fear in her tight clutch, howled. Helpless in the flood, two women and a child rode the waters at the mercy of God.

The cabin came to a stop with a jolt that knocked Cherie off the pallet and Roz from her feet. Like Noah and the ark coming to rest on Mount Ararat, they could do nothing more than wait for the waters to receed and thank the Lord they were still alive. Roz made her way down the staircase as far as the water would allow.

The house had been caught in a copse of young cypress trees inundated up to their lower branches. Boards from barns and huge tree limbs ripped from live oaks piled up around them. Horrified, Roz watched the body of a black man floating facedown snag on their artificial island, then tear loose and spin away with other pieces of flotsam. They were no longer moving, it was true, but the pressure from debris pushed their refuge lower into the water. The waves lapped up the steps and licked at her toes.

Roz retreated into the loft. "I'm sorry, but we have to go up to the roof soon if we can find a way to get there."

"*La hache*," Cherie said from her pallet. She gestured toward the far wall of the loft. From hooks and nails hung an assortment of traps, nets, and knives ranging in size from a big machete to blades thin enough to fillet small fish. Muskrat furs lay stored in one corner and in the other leaned an ax.

"The boys sleep in the loft with all of these dangerous things?" Roz questioned when she should have been grateful Claude did store his his ax here.

Cherie gave a wan smile. She stilled her newest son by giving him a tit. "Papa say don't touch, believe you me, dey don't touch."

"Well, thank you, Claude." Roz drew a three-legged stool to a space between the roof beams. She dragged the ax, heavy enough to split logs, from its corner. The awkward slant of the roof, the weight of the ax, and her own weak muscles made the task go slowly, one chip, then another. Glancing at Cherie, who seemed amused by a woman who couldn't chop wood, Roz noticed the first trickles of water enter the loft.

She moved her hands higher up on the ax handle, drew back and swung a mighty blow into the small crack she had made. A gap opened in the shingles wide enough for her to chop downward, letting the weight of the ax do the damage to the roof. Roz gestured to Cherie who raised herself carefully from the lochia-stained pallet. She took the baby and placed him on the stack of furs, then boosted Cherie, thin as the wand of a willow tree except for her sagging belly, through the gap.

Roz surveyed the loft and snatched up a pile of cotton blankets before the spreading water reached them. She pulled a tarp from the gear along the wall and hung the machete from her wrist by its rawhide cord. These things, she shoved through the hole to Cherie. The cauldron of boiled water went up next, and then the tender newborn, wrapped for extra protection in the largest of the muskrat hides. Last of all, Roz clambered onto the roof. As her weight lifted, the stool floated away from her feet.

Cherie ruched down the roof ridge to give Roz some room to lay out the blankets and open the tarp. The rough cypress shakes destroyed Roz's white stockings, but her tennis shoes were a blessing on the slick shingles. She slipped only once, grazing her chin and having to scramble back up the roof before she slid into the sloshing mass of debris. The women settled on the blankets and wrapped themselves in the tarp. A light rain fell.

"Here, drink your fill. Then, set the pot out to collect rainwater. Both you and the baby need fluids." Roz scooped up a handful herself carefully making sure any spillage went back into the pot. No telling when help would come if it came at all.

Cherie, dehydrated by the birth, drank deeply and set the iron pot to one side when she finished. Its stubby feet straddled the peak of the roof. She knotted the skirt of her bedraggled nightgown near her thighs and placed her baby, muskrat hide and all, in the pouch formed by the bodice. Tired from being born, he snuggled against her breast and slept. Roz spread the tarp over the three of them.

"If you want to rest, lean on me. We'll take turns keeping watch for help."

"Our men, dey gonna come for us. You see."

"I haven't got a man," Roz said with some bitterness.

"Pierre, he come for you, and Claude for me. Dey come." With that certainty voiced, Cherie leaned against Roz and closed her eyes.

Roz had no intention of waking her patient to take a watch. As the gray light dimmed and turned into darkness, she tried to stay awake. She knew she dozed. Once, the whimpers of the baby made her sit up straighter. She heard Cherie say softly, "*Dodo, mon cher 'tite bete*," as she switched the child to her other breast.

The filmy light of dawn and the cries of swamp birds rising from a nearby roost woke Roz a second time. As the sun rose, the space beneath the tarp grew too warm, and she folded it back. Cherie opened her eyes. "You sleep. I watch."

"I don't think I can. We have company." Roz pointed a finger toward the mass of boards and branches below them.

Two thick, dark-scaled water moccasins stretched out along a broken limb to take in the morning sun. A stiff breeze came up and ruffled the surface of the endless lake into wavelets that doused the resting snakes. Disturbed, they sought higher ground. Curving and straightening, curving and straightening, the belly scales of the serpents propelled them along to the edge of the roof and up over the rough shakes.

The women sat still. Roz slowly moved her hand down to grip the handle of the machete whose rawhide thong had bitten into her wrist throughout the night. She was very glad she hadn't given in to the urge to toss it aside. One snake took a horizontal path across the shingles. The other kept climbing toward the roof ridge.

Reeking of musk, a muscular five feet long, the moccasin arrowed its triangular head toward the women. Its forked black tongue flicked in and out, sensing their presence, their size, their warmth. They were prey too big to devour but a definite danger.

The baby awoke with a wail and beat his small fists against the front of Cherie's gown. That quickly, the huge snake went into its coil, rose up and flashed the white lining of its mouth—cottonmouth, its other name—so appropriate, so apt. Cherie moved her hands to cover the child, and the serpent sprang.

Roz struck down with a two-handed grip on the machete, severing the reptile in the middle of its thick torso with the heavy blade. The broad head, lidless cat-like eyes staring, tumbled down the roof trailing two feet of torso. The tail end of the snake, oozing stinking brown feces from its pierced intestines, thrashed and curled, drawing the attention of the second moccasin.

The smaller cottonmouth turned, its body flowing in a wide U-shape as it slithered up the shingles. Roz didn't wait. She struck before the snake had a chance to go into its coil and heaved it off the roof with the tip of her knife. As the snake splashed into the water, a small log on the edge of the debris opened wide jaws and crunched down on the meal that had unexpectedly come its way. The alligator took its prey beneath the gray waters. Watching for the gator to resurface, Roz kicked the reeking body of the first moccasin into the branches below.

"What you doing? We coulda eat dat," Cherie protested.

"Maybe *you* could have."

The young gator crawled up on a broad board making up part of the raft of debris. The tail of the snake dangled from its mouth. With a few jerks of its head, reptile swallowed reptile. The alligator, content with its snack, stretched out in the sun and lowered its eyes to slits.

"I'll tell you what, Cherie. If that gator decides to come up the roof, you take the knife. Just save me a piece of the tail." With that comment said, Roz draped the tarp over them to provide a sun screen, surveyed the horizon, and seeing no sign of help, rested her head on Cherie's shoulder and went to sleep.

Chapter Thirty-Seven

"What do you mean they haven't come back?" Pierre Landry said as he set the leg of a man who had been trapped beneath a fallen tree. "I had to go into Chapelle to tend some of my patients there and didn't get back until very late. I thought Roz and Cherie would be asleep in their tents."

His arms gesturing, Claude Arton rattled on in rapid French. Nurse Strictland got between them and said loudly and slowly, "You can't be in this tent unless you have a medical emergency. Emergencies only. Do you understand?"

Dr. Landry smoothed the last layer of plaster bandages. "He says he understands, Nurse Strictland, and that he isn't deaf. His wife and Midwife Boylan did not return to the camp last night. Incoming refugees say there have been breaks in the levee near Henderson, more in Ste. Jeanne Parish. We need to go look for the women."

"He needs to stay here and take care of his family. Let some of those young National Guardsmen go. They seem to spend more time flirting with the women than working. I don't see why he is bothering you about this."

"Claude is my brother's brother-in-law. Ursin has gone to check on my parents, and Ursin's wife is watching the children. He wants me to help search."

"Tell him you are needed here. It's out of the question."

"I'll be back as soon as I can. Please fit this man with crutches."

"I said you can't go." Nurse Strictland puffed up to twice her normal size like an offended cat.

"I'm a volunteer here, and I said I'll be back. Wake Doc Spivey to take my place." Giving no more assurances, Pierre Landry followed Claude Arton from the medical tent.

"We can take my Ford, but we may need a boat, Claude."

"*Un bateau, oui.* I get, me."

At the base of the hill, Claude gestured toward a pile of surfboats brought in from the Atlantic coast and stacked up like a pile of turtles in the Louisiana mud. A youthful guardsman sat under a nearby oak tree, his Great War rifle propped against the trunk, his eyes half-closed with boredom until Claude and the doctor started to lift a boat from the heap.

"Hey, hey, you can't take those boats!"

"I'm a doctor. We need this boat to deal with an emergency." He and Claude muscled their unwieldy burden toward the car. As the guardsman grabbed his rifle and started toward them, the two men managed to heave the surfboat on to the roof of the Ford. It dwarfed the small car. Claude Arton disappeared beneath its overturned stern and searched the trunk for rope to tie the boat in place.

"You need written permission from the commandant to take a boat." The guardsman rapped on the stern. "You come out from under there."

Claude did. He came out low to the ground,

knocking the boy down. In seconds, he had the rifle with the bayonet pointed at the solider's throat. Men with wooden legs were always underestimated.

Casually, Pierre Landry took the rope Claude offered, threw it over the boat and drew it through the cab of the car. He translated as he worked. "He says his wife and baby are out in the flood, and your life isn't worth shit compared to theirs."

When he finished with the boat, the doctor borrowed the knife sticking out of the top of Claude's boot and cut off lengths of rope to tie up the guard. He used a wad of gauze from his bag for a gag. With the bulk of the auto and boat hiding them from view, they dragged the young man back to the shade of the oak tree and went on their way. Claude kept the rifle and helped himself to the man's canteen, sniffing it first to make sure it contained water, not booze.

Once they turned off the Teche ridge road, the water rushed to meet them. Where cane fields and pasture had filled the land, now there was the flood. Off in the distance, the broken levee held in water on both of its sides. Claude and Pierre found a gap in the submerged tree line and launched the surfboat. Rowing proved difficult as the oars snagged in barbed wire fences lurking below the surface of the opaque, muddy waters. A coffin that had popped from a graveyard bobbed by carrying a desperate possum as a second passenger. Claude crossed himself and muttered a prayer to ward off bad omens.

The men searched for landmarks, but the flood had erased them. Finally, skirting along the base of the levee, Claude cried out. The roof of a sunken truck broke the surface of the water. They rowed alongside and peered through the windshield. Both of them let out a breath when they found it empty.

"Your truck, Claude?"

The other man nodded. Getting wet to their waists, they beached the surfboat on the side of the levee and scrambled up the crumbling barrier. From its top, they could see the splintered stilts where the Arton cabin once stood.

"Let's get the surfboat and see if we can find them," Pierre said without any hope in his voice.

"No, no! Look!" Claude limped down the levee road. Stranded high and dry by the whim of the flood, his flat-bottomed swamp boat rested across the path. He was already bailing a few inches of water and muck when Pierre caught up with him. Grinning, Claude held up the gas can wedged under one of the seats.

"Incredible! Let's see if the engine is working. We can let the water take us wherever it took our women and use the gas to come back here."

Grinning, Claude bailed faster. They dragged his boat down the levee's east side and continued their rescue mission. They hadn't gone far when cries for help came from the top of an oak tree submerged to its bottom branches. A colored man in baggy overalls sat on a sturdy limb, his shoeless feet dangling inches from the water. Pierre fired the engine to cross the current to reach him.

"Been up here all night wit' de crawfish and a real nasty raccoon for company. Praise God you come for me 'cause I can't swim a stroke." As the Negro lowered himself into the boat, Claude argued with Pierre.

"We can't just leave him. We'll take you over to the levee. If you walk north a short way, you'll see some stilts sticking out of the water. On the other side of the levee is another boat. Wait for us there. If we aren't back by high noon, take the boat and get to a Red Cross shelter. Tell them Dr. Landry and Claude Arton are out here searching for family."

The black man eyed the army rifle Claude had slung over his shoulder. "Whatever you say, mistah. My brother and me, we was commandeered by de sheriff to sandbag de levee a couple of miles from here, but it broke somewheres else and washed us all away. I grabbed aholt of a wagon slat and rode it to dis here tree. My brother, I ain't seen him since. He gone. Da water and da Lawd done took him."

The flat-bottomed boat bumped against the levee, and the colored man jumped out and made his way up the bank with frequent backward glances at the silent Claude. He hadn't reached the top before Claude kicked the boat away from the levee and used the oars to regain the current. They drifted southward and saw nothing but wreckage and a bloated dead mule floating by.

Past noon, the sky clouded over, and the wind kicked up. Small whitecaps formed on the surface of the sullen gray water, but on the breeze came the cries of a baby and the voice of a woman shouting for help. They turned the skiff in that direction, took up the oars, and rowed with energy.

A homemade boat, gray and resting so low in the water it blended in with the sky and the flood, bobbed in the waves. A blonde woman, her hair straggling from its bun, waved frantically. A tow-headed two-year-old and a bald six-month old baby sat on her lap while her own feet rested in several inches of foul water. A pair of shabby shoes sat beside the woman on the bench, and a baby blanket draped the shoulder of her shapeless calico dress patterned with tiny blue flowers.

"Praise God you come for us! My man went into town for supplies. Said we was gonna hunker down and wait out the flood if it come our way, but the water started risin' fast. I just about had time to get the boys into the boat. Forgot the oars was in the house to keep people from stealin' it. Guess you could say we went up the crick without a paddle. We been drifting a day and a night, and the boat's been aleakin' bad. Been scooping out water with my hands and nursin' both my babies so they won't drink it. You got water? I'm so dry."

Pierre handed over the military canteen. The woman drank so rapidly, water dribbled from the side of her mouth. He had to pry the container from her hands. "Not so much, not so fast. You will be sick. We will take you over to the levee. Walk north if you can manage until you come to some stilts in the water. A Negro man should be waiting there with a boat. If we don't return by high noon, he'll take you to a camp."

"Don't know if my husband would like that. He said life would be easier here than in the Ozarks with no rocks in the soil and no snow on the ground come winter. So, here we are surrounded by niggers and Catholic Frenchies, no kin to take us in. Sorry!" She clamped her hands over her mouth.

"I know you're a Frenchie, but you speak English real good. I'm Lizzie McDonald, and these are my boys, Luther and Virgil."

Pierre Landry took the baby, handed him to Claude, and coaxed the shy toddler into his arms. He opened his medical bag and gave the child a lollipop while his mother crossed between the boats. He gave another lollipop to Lizzie McDonald.

"Ain't that sweet," she exclaimed. "Say your thanks, Virgil."

The little boy kept his eyes downcast and mumbled a single unintelligible word.

"He don't talk too good. It's his lip."

"I see. Virgil, would you like another lollipop for later? Let me take a look at your mouth, then."

The boy nodded and raised his face. He was a beautiful little boy except for the slash of a harelip marring his pale, freckled face.

"This can be fixed though there will be scar. Bring him to the camp at Spanish Lake if you can and ask for Dr. Landry."

"My husband says we don't take charity. We don't have no money for fancy doctoring."

"Madame McDonald, in times like these, everyone must take charity. You will repay it when you are able. Claude, start the engine."

Claude grumbled under his breath about the water wasted and the gas spent, but did as he was asked. He continued to hold the baby in the crook of his arm and let the child tug on his mustache. Finally, he sang a chorus of *Alouette* so boisterously that both children and their mother laughed.

Pierre helped Lizzie to climb the levee with her family while Claude steadied the boat. He pressed more suckers into her hand.

"They will keep your mouth from feeling so dry and give you some energy. Go this way. I hope to see you and Virgil again soon."

"Thank you. Mercy. Isn't that what you Frenchies

say—Mercy."

"Close enough, Madame McDonald. Close enough."

Back in the boat, Claude expressed his opinion that they could not save the entire world in one day.

"Here, I saved a cherry one for you." Pierre stuck the lollipop into Arton's mouth. "We can't forsake the living in favor of the—never mind." He chose a lemon sucker from the few left in his bag and put it in his own mouth.

A slow drizzle began to fall. They drifted on using the oars now and then to avoid clumps of debris caught in the trees as they entered a wooded area. In the distance, a large raft of boards and branches had accumulated around a copse of cypress trees. A whole house seemed to have come to rest there with only its roof above water. A lumpy tarp draped over the ridge, and a small iron pot straddled the beam.

"We might have to use the engine to steer around that mass. We don't want to get snagged, or our search will be over," Pierre said reasonably.

Claude ranted back that their search would be over if they ran out of gas or gave away more water or if they were caught in a hard rain because they had wasted time saving a nigger and a redneck. He raised his arms in the air and shouted into the doctor's face.

A voice shouted back. "*Claude, mon amour!*" The outburst was followed by the thin wail of a newborn. The men looked across the raft of debris. A nurse in a stained white uniform and a limp head veil sat next to a bare-legged woman wearing only a light nightgown. By the size of the bulge in her lap, the second woman appeared to be hugely pregnant, but the crying baby could be clearly heard. The tarp lay bunched around them.

The woman in white waved her arms and put her hands to her mouth. "Pierre, you came. My God, you came for me!"

The men started the engine and moved as close as they could come to the house. Slowly, carefully, Pierre Landry made his way over the mass of shifting debris. The women shinnied down the roof and sat on the eaves waiting for help. Pierre tied a rope under Cherie's arms and tossed the end to Claude. Balancing on her white, hairy legs and brown, sun-tanned feet, modesty forgotten, Cherie Arton took one wobbling step at a time, one arm outstretched, the other cradling the baby tied up in her nightdress. Pierre and Roz waited as she climbed into the boat and hugged herself to Claude.

Sighing, Cherie called back to the others. "Me, I don't swim. You want da rope, Pierre?"

"No, I think we'll be fine together." He took Roz's hand, and they started forward.

"Watch for da *cocodrie*," Cherie cautioned.

"*Cocodrie*?" said Claude.

Cherie pointed to the small alligator. Lying log still a moment before, it opened its jaws and hissed at her motion. Claude unslung the rifle, brought it up smoothly, and shot the gator through the eye. The small boat rocked and shifted the raft of debris. A hole of dark water opened under Pierre's next step. He went in and under.

Roz started to sink with him but caught herself on a branch of an uprooted basswood tree. The opening in the debris began to close over a hand groping upward. She grasped and pulled Pierre to the surface. He grabbed the trunk of the tree and, that quickly, a snake hidden in the branches struck his left hand. A second later, the snake was hacked in half by a machete that barely missed Pierre's fingertips. The blow tipped Roz into the water next to him.

"Eh, Pierre, you want dat rope now?" Cherie called.

"A rope would be helpful, yes."

Hand over hand, Claude towed Pierre with Roz clinging to his back to the skiff. He dragged Pierre in by his coat collar and Roz more gently with a grip under her arms. She forgot to thank him.

"My God, Pierre, you've been bitten." Roz bent over his hand. "Take my knife and cut it open. I'll suck out the venom." She offered him the massive machete still attached to her wrist by its cord.

"Thank you, dearest, but I'd like to keep my hand regardless of your Girl Scout training. That was only a water snake. See, no fang marks. But, it is good to know you'll come to my rescue if I ever need it."

"Always, Pierre."

"Claude, hand me my bag. No sense in getting blood poisoning. Who knows what bacteria lurked in that water, not to mention the snake's mouth."

Claude, however, ignored him and cooed over his new son who had been fished from the bodice of Cherie's nightgown. The small bundle shook his fists and kicked his legs as he lay with his head cupped in his father's palm.

"*Mon fils*, Bartolomé."

"No, no, Claude. Grandeau."

"Grandeau?"

"*Oui*, Grandeau Pierre Arton," Cherie said happily,

looking at her other savior, who had made a light cut across his snake bite with a sterilized scapel and was letting the wound bleed itself clean.

"*Allons*, Claude. We need to get back to the camp before dark."

Pierre gestured toward the motor, and Claude opened the throttle after he carefully maneuvered the boat close enough to the debris to sling the dead alligator into the bottom. Over the racket of the engine, Cherie and Claude continued to argue.

"I can't follow that. They speak too fast, but I gather she wants to name the baby High Water Pierre Arton," Roz said as Pierre swabbed his snakebite with alcohol.

Without looking up, he translated. "He says Grandeau is a crazy name. They agreed on Bartolomé after his grandfather. Why not Claude for his second name? Why Pierre? She says they already have a T-Claude. How many does he want? He says he wants a woman who is less trouble. Well, she says, he got trouble. This is a special baby delivered by a midwife during a flood, and he should have a special name to go on the birth paper they are going to get. This time, she isn't just going to write the name in the family Bible. Here, let me clean your wrist. That thong has rubbed it raw."

Roz sucked in her breath as the alcohol bit into the scrapes. Suddenly, silence reigned in the boat. Grandeau Pierre Arton had gone to sleep, but his mother sat with tears running down her face.

"My Bible, she is gone. My home, gone."

Claude put his free arm around his wife. He spoke to her again most gently.

"He is saying he will build her another house, a better house, on high ground, and if he can get the smell of baby piss out of the muskrat hide, he will trade it for a new Bible with colored pictures of the saints. She can write down the names of all their children in it, even the name of Grandeau Pierre Arton, crazy as it is."

"He does love her, then."

"It takes a hard man to make a living from the swamp, but yes, he does love his wife and children."

Pierre paused. He raised Roz's chin and swabbed the cut on her chin. "Yes, he does love her."

Looking into his eyes seemed to take the sting from her wound, but Roz quickly turned away. She lowered her voice even more. "I'm worried about Cherie. I did my best to keep her clean and hydrated, but what if infection sets in? She was able to nurse the baby and keep him warm and dry. I believe he will be fine, but what if he loses his mother?"

"You did all that you could for your patients and kept them safe as well. I suspect if we hadn't come along, you would have built a boat from the loose boards and paddled back to the levee when your water ran out, Peep. That's what the other midwives call you, isn't it? I like it."

"I think it was intended as sort of an insult implying that I was nothing but fluff and noise."

"Around here, if you are given a nickname, you have been accepted. Many of them are insulting. Consider Henri's friends, Tubbs and Boozoo."

"They call Henri, Bebe—the baby. He's dying for a better name."

"He may graduate to Bubba, but I doubt it. And I think you will always be Peep, one tough chick. You were right when you said you didn't need my help anymore."

"Your help, no, but I could use your shoulder to rest on. I'm so tired."

Pierre Landry tucked her head under his chin. She slept and slipped gradually down his chest until her head rested in his lap. Not the time or place for sexual feelings or even wishful thinking, but Claude leered at them and made an obscene comment that earned him a jab from his wife.

Cherie told the story of how Roz delivered the baby, chopped their way out of the sinking house, and killed two *serpents congo*. Yes, Claude agreed, the midwife was brave, but he was willing to bet she would not mind sleeping with the snake in Pierre's pants. Another argument started, but Roz slept through it all.

Pierre patted her awake when the boat nudged the levee. Roz sat up, still drowsy. "My mouth feels like cotton."

"Here, I saved the orange one for you. Cherie took the lime, and Claude got the last cherry." Pierre offered her the lollipop.

"Thank you, doctor. I feel better already. Where are we?"

"Back at the levee. The surfboat on the other side is gone. Hopefully, the others we rescued made good use of it. Claude and I need to pull this one over to the other side. We aren't home yet."

"Far from it."

Roz scrambled up the muddy bank and waited with Cherie and the baby as the men coaxed the bateau up the hill. It slid easily down the other side. Proceeding carefully so as not to snag the engine in barbed wire or clumps of vegetation, they made it halfway across the new lake before the gasoline gave out. The men took the oars and rowed. By the time they reached the end of the road where the Ford waited, the dead alligator, which Claude insisted on bring along, was giving off a ripe smell.

"I feel bad that you killed it after it ate the snakes. Can't we just ditch it here?" Roz suggested.

"Claude, he say it a nice, unscarred hide, bring good money. Hey, don't I say we eat his tail? Tonight, I make alligator sauce piquant," Cherie said.

"Tonight, you will have some soup, take a shower, and sleep in a clean cot."

"Okay. Mignon, she can make the sauce piquant, but I don't go to bed 'til I have some, me."

With the women and baby crammed into the back and nodding off, and Claude in the front seat with his foot resting on the gator, Pierre Landry drove the Lizzie back to the camp where they found the welcome none too cordial.

The guards at the gate marched the men, bayonets pricking their backs, to the commandant's tent. The women and little Grandeau followed, protesting and wailing like the chorus in a Greek tragedy. They were stopped by guards before the entry and caught only a glimpse of the commandant wearing jodpurs, a slouch hat and very shiny knee-high leather boots. He raised his bushy gray eyebrows and opened the thin lips under his large, aristocratic nose. "Dr. Landry, you are under military arrest for stealing a boat, assaulting a soldier, and taking his weapon and canteen. If I had a brig, I'd lock you up, but we need your services, so you are confined to the camp for the duration of this crisis. As for your accomplice, he will work at hard labor restoring the levees."

"But I have patients in town who need my care. We borrowed the boat for an emergency rescue and had no time to do paperwork."

The general beat his fist against a portable desk that quivered beneath the blows. "In the military, we always have time to do the proper paperwork. You stole that boat!"

"Sir," said one of the lads guarding the prisoners. "The boat has been returned. A nigger and a white lady with two kids were picked up walking toward the camp, and they told us where we could find it. Said Dr. Landry and Mr. Arton, here, rescued them."

Claude Arton shouted and gestured. He stripped the canteen from his shoulder and threw it down on the desk. More reluctantly, he slowly unshouldered the rifle and tossed it to one of the guards.

The commandant went purple in the face. "You greenies didn't even disarm the man before you brought him in here? A translator, I need a translator."

Cherie pushed in front of a young man in uniform who was reluctant to manhandle a desperate woman in a dirty nightgown and bearing a squalling newborn. She called out over the cries. "Me, I speak for Claude. He say he hit da guard and took da canteen. He say he made Dr. Landry tie up da soldier and help wit' da boat so he could come get me, his wife, and save da baby, his son. You let da doctor go. Him, Claude, he got no'ting better to do now da swamp flooded den fill da sandbags anyhow. Oh, and he only borrow da gun and canteen jus' like dat boat what already been returned."

"Can't you quiet that child? It's destroying my

concentration." The commandant pressed his hands against his temple.

Roz squeezed between the guards too busy listening to stop her. "I'll hold the baby. I delivered him yesterday in a house swept away by the flood. We were stranded on a rooftop until Dr. Landry and Mr. Arton came to our rescue."

Roz took Grandeau and patted his tiny back, but he would not be comforted.

"Mrs. Arton is still weak from childbirth and the ordeal she has been through. Now her husband is arrested for saving our lives. I wouldn't be surprised if she went into shock." Roz gave Cherie a sharp look.

Cherie put a hand to her bony chest above her milk-swollen breasts and crumpled to the ground. Pierre scooped her up and placed her, filthy nightgown and all, on the general's spotless, could bounce a dime on the covers, cot. He knelt by the woman and took her pulse. Roz thought the scene very affecting.

A stentorian voice penetrated the canvas walls and made Grandeau cry all the harder. Nurse Strictland had arrived. "Let me by, I say. You have no authority over me!"

The boys at the entry gave way. They had been raised to respect nuns and schoolteachers and other women with big voices.

"See here, General Emory. Dr. Landry is a civilian volunteer who is free to come and go as he pleases. We badly need his services, and I would not be at all surprised if he refused them after the way he is being treated for merely borrowing a boat to save lives."

She put her hands on her broad hips as Pierre Landry stared at her, astonished. Cherie moaned pitifully, and Claude rushed to her side. Grandeau continued to cry.

"My God, you remind me of my daughter. I haven't been able to tell her a thing since she got back from the war." General Emory raked a hand through his vigorous growth of steel gray hair.

"You scoot on in, Virgil. Mama and brother are right behind you. Well, I got to go after my boy, don't I?" a voice with an Arkansas twang explained to the guards.

A tow-headed two-year-old with angelic blue eyes and a deformed lip stared up at the intimidating face of the general and began to whimper. Lizzie McDonald in her shapeless calico dress drew the boy against her hip where he hid his face in her skirt. Bald-headed baby Luther on her shoulder heard Grandeau screaming and wailed in sympathy.

"There now," Lizzie said, "don't you cry, Lutie. We's safe now 'cause of Dr. Landry and Mr. Arton and that nice nigger man. Silas, nicest nigger I ever met, rowed us right to the road in that borrowed boat. He's down in t'other camp, but I'm just sure he'd like to say thankee, too, for being rescued. And pretty soon, Dr. Landry is going to fix brother's lip so he can talk better. Then, he'll say thankee right clear to these good, brave men who saved our lives."

"Water," Cherie said faintly. "Water."

Claude snatched a canteen hanging from the back of general's chair and put it to his wife's lips. The general appeared both shaken and embarrassed now.

"Brandy, dat's more better." Cherie smacked her lips. "I feel stronger now. Doctor, can you take me to my tent?" she asked weakly.

General Emory threw up his hands. "You are dismissed! You are all dismissed! Don't come to my attention again in any way. Do you understand?"

A round of yessirs, *oui-ouis*, thankees, and of courses issued from the crowd as they filed out of the tent. General Emory called in his guards for a good chewing out to let them know he was still totally in charge.

"What next?" Roz asked rhetorically, but she got an answer.

"Soup, shower, and the sack. That's an order," said Nurse Strickland.

Chapter Thirty-Eight

Roz slipped her practical spare white uniform over pink silk undergarments that felt wonderful against her newly washed flesh. She drew a comb through her cropped, damp hair. In a moment, she'd lay down fully clothed except for her shoes and veil, just in case someone needed her in the night. Most of the camp refugees were still up, sitting around small fires, having a last cup of coffee, swapping escape stories, puffing out tunes on a harmonica or playing checkers, but she was exhausted. Someone scratched on the tent flap that she'd lowered while changing her clothes. Another woman had gone into labor, no doubt.

"Come in."

"I came to examine your cuts and bruises. Medical professionals are notorious for neglecting their own health."

Pierre Landry entered the twilight of the tent. He lit a camp lantern and beckoned Roz to sit on a cot. His dark hair was slicked back and still damp like hers. He wore a fresh white shirt and one of his many dark jackets, but no tie. He smelled of soap and a lime-scented aftershave, like a boy come courting.

"I'm fine."

"Sit. Let me look at your knees. You have several small splinters that are going to fester."

He plucked them out with tweezers and, all the

while, Roz felt the warmth of his breath on her thighs as he knelt by her feet. The sensation distracted her from the pain as he probed her wounds and painted them red with a stinging tincture of iodine. Pierre took her hands and turned them palm up, dabbed on more iodine. He raised her chin and coated the raw scrape on the tip.

"Now I look like a red Indian about to go on the warpath. That's what my mother used to say. I was constantly getting scraped up doing things I shouldn't have done."

"I think you look beautiful. I haven't seen your hair for a long time. It's still so short but back to its natural color." His dark sheik's eyes shone in the lamplight.

Self-consciously, she patted her hair with her fingertips. "I can't afford the hairdresser, and this style is more practical."

"I always thought the color resembled sunlight shining through a jar of honey. Sit still. There is another abrasion on your forehead. Then I'm finished."

She hissed as he dabbed on the iodine. "What, no lollipop to take away the pain?"

"I gave them all away today. No more lollipops until I can get into town again. This will have to do." He applied his lips to hers as thoroughly as he had the iodine to her wounds.

Roz grasped his face between her hands, staining his cheeks with the red solution as she held him tightly and reveled in the softness of his moustache and the heat of his tongue gliding across her lips and entering her mouth. They paused for breath.

"Three times today, I thought you were dead and gone from me. Now, I know I can't give you up. I will always find you, Roz, no matter how often we are parted," he said.

"Six months ago, I was a silly girl who thought she could get over a bad marriage and a lost love by going to a party and getting drunk. You told me I had to heal myself. I think that I have. But Pierre, I will always want you no matter how strong I become. Stay with me tonight."

"The other nurses will be coming in soon."

"Then just hold me while I go to sleep, the way you did after I lost the baby."

"The way I did all night after I took you from Broussard's Barn."

"I don't remember."

"You don't need to." He drew a second cot close to hers and lay as near her side as he could get. Again, he kissed the nape of her neck, her hair, and matched his breathing to hers. They slept.

****

"Dr. Spivey, I need to bring a matter to your attention."

Nurse Strictland bore down on him in the mess tent where Leonard Spivey sat fortifying himself with more coffee. He was determined to allow young Landry a full night's sleep after today's ordeal.

"Please, come with me at once."

Doc Spivey brought his tin cup of dark roast along as they passed among the tents and came at last to the one used by the midwife and several other nurses. Nurse Strictland raised the flap with her fingertips and held it up so Doc could get a good long look at Roz Boylan entwined with Dr. Pierre Landry. Landry's face rested against the midwife's pale neck. His arms encircled her, and her hands lay atop his as if to keep him right there, pressed against her as tightly as possible. Nurse Strictland dropped the flap and stepped back a few paces.

"One of the other nurses said she wasn't comfortable coming to her own bed when they were in here like that. I knew the first day something was going on between those two. I warned her about propriety, about moral behavior in the camp."

"Nurse Strictland, I'm sure you did, but they are both fully clothed. Pierre still has his shoes on. I suspect they are both so exhausted the tent could fall on them, and they wouldn't notice. Why don't we let them have a few hours sleep, then I'll go in and wake them."

"We should do that now!"

"Nurse Strictland, I don't know your first name."

"Judith."

"Judith, you served in the Great War, did you not? I was too old to volunteer and the only doctor in Chapelle. I couldn't desert my patients, and my wife would have killed me, no battlefield wounds necessary. As it turned out, she was the first to go. Breast cancer—I didn't find it in time."

"I'm sorry."

"So am I, but we were speaking of the Great War. You must have been in your early twenties then."

"Late twenties."

"The war was a huge disaster, even greater than this one."

"Yes, it was. Bloody and terrible."

"And during those terrible times, didn't you ever give the comfort of your body to a soldier far from home or to an overworked surgeon?"

"I was much younger then." Nurse Strictland's

cheeks burned red in the light of a campfire they passed as Leonard Spivey guided her away from the midwife's tent.

"You blush like a redhead. I've been wondering what color your hair is beneath that veil," Doc said smoothly.

"Not red, heavens no! Just plain brown—though some people have told me I have auburn highlights."

"I'm sure your hair is as lovely as your compassionate brown eyes, Judy. I share a small tent with Dr. Landry. Perhaps, we could go there and wait. You could tell me about your experiences in the Great War, and I could tell you what I know of Pierre Landry and Roz Boylan. A few months back, I had a hand in tearing them away from each other. Now, I'm beginning to see that giving another person comfort in times like these is not so bad. What do you say, Judy, shall we go to my tent?"

Chapter Thirty-Nine

"What a pissant little burg!" Burke Boylan proclaimed as he steered the mud-splashed, white Mercedes toward Mt. Carmel Academy. "I can't believe you convinced me to risk my life driving up the River Road and crossing the Mississippi in full flood on the ferry so you could visit Rosamond's brat of a sister. I thought we were going to be washed out to sea."

"I paid you to bring me here, Buster. Don't pretend you didn't need the money. If the St. Rochelles hadn't given you that house outright as a wedding gift, you wouldn't have a roof over your head right now. Since they kicked you out of the law firm, your clients haven't been exactly the cream of society," Artemus Delamare shot back.

"Besides, the town of Rainbow is holy ground. Miracles happen here every day. If you don't want to attend the tea, you can visit some of the shrines and pray for your blackened soul," Artie continued.

"I make my own fate, Artie. I may be finished in New Orleans, but once I get my hands on Rosie again, I'm going to drag her back to Philly and show my family there isn't going to be a divorce. She'll stay home and crank out babies and write letters to her family saying how happy she is to be my wife."

"Give it up, Boylan. Even the servants couldn't be bribed to tell where Roz is hiding out. I know you tried.

Most of them have worked for the St. Rochelles for three generations. They aren't going to let you beat up their Mardi Gras queen any more."

"Oh, I know where she is—with lover boy Landry. His hometown is Chapelle, just down the road. All that tender care he gave her in the hospital, and then he threatens my life. I know they slept together while I was out earning a living, so Roz deserved what she got. The baby was his, I'm certain. Maybe we'll pay the doctor and the adulteress a little visit after we finish here since we've come this far."

"Look, if you don't want to visit the Academy, fine. I didn't pay for any side trips. Here's a ten-spot. Go find some gas for the trip home, and buy yourself some lunch."

"You're up to your neck in dough since you passed the bar exams," Burke replied resentfully.

"My success did open the parental purse strings. Too bad I hate practicing law. Let me out at the gates, Boylan."

"I'm not your fuckin' chauffeur, Artie."

"Today, you are. Get lost for a few hours. The poor kid is going to have to stay here all summer getting the spirit knocked out of her by the nuns because her parents don't feel it's safe to have her come home. After three months of good works and Latin study, they'll have Roxie all softened up for the convent, and that would be a damned shame."

"I always said you were a pervert, Delamare."

Burke skidded to a stop before the tall iron gates of Mt. Carmel Academy, open today for Saturday visitation. The marigolds and red cannas surrounding the statue of the Virgin Mary centered in front of the ancient columned buildings glowed through the miserable drizzle. Holding his gift for Roxie tightly under his arm, Artie pulled his hat down and the collar of his trench coat up as he trudged the gravel path toward the visitor's reception room where he had visited his numerous female cousins in the past.

"Meet me back here in two hours, Buster," he called over his shoulder.

"Yeah, your wish is my command."

Burke revved the engine and sped off toward the nearest and only gas pump in Rainbow. Red and rusting, it sat before a false-fronted frame general store that named itself Plato Grocery in flaking yellow letters. The owner had shoveled a pile of oyster shells into the wheel ruts by the pump, but Buster had to slog through the mud, sullying the cuffs of his white linen suit, to reach the two board steps leading up to the entry. On the sagging porch running the length of the building, he removed his hat and shook the rain droplets from the pristine vanilla-colored felt.

Inside, a colored man, old, judging by the ring of white hair encircling a shining bald pate the color of polished pecan wood, but without a wrinkle on his face, sat behind a tall brass register and read the *Times-Picayune*. The front page news was all about the flood.

"Glad we got these holy hills protecting us," the proprietor said to his customer.

Burke slapped the ten-dollar bill on to the counter. "Fill her up, Sambo."

"The name is Plato, and my grandson does the filling. Leon, get out here. We got a customer."

A teenaged boy, skinny and closer to white than his granddaddy, slouched from the back room and sent

Burke a resentful stare as he headed out into the rain to crank up the gas for the Mercedes.

"Mud, miracles, and uppity niggers in a nowhere town. Shit, I could use a drink."

A sly look passed over Plato's smooth face. "Would you be wanting buttermilk, a pop, or something stronger? Plato Grocery has it all."

"I might be interested in the something stronger." Burke studied a po-boy menu written on a slate hanging from the wall. "Catfish po-boys any good?"

"Fresh caught and fried to order. Come fully dressed on a French loaf."

"That and whatever you got under the counter."

Plato had a loaded shotgun under the counter. Sometimes, white people passing through thought they could take advantage of an old colored man. Right beside the weapon sat sealed Mason jars of clear, potent liquid that burned the throat and warmed the belly. Plato set one jar on the counter.

"Might want to keep that under your coat in case any teetotalers from the Baptist Church drop by," he suggested. "Leon, put together a catfish po-boy for our customer," Plato ordered as the boy returned from the pump.

Ignoring the warning, Buster twisted the seal off the jar and took a few sips. From the back room, the sound and smell of seasoned, floured catfish hitting hot grease filled the air. In minutes, the sandwich came out still smoking, the tomato, lettuce, onion rings, and dressing spilling over the sides of the loaf of bread on to a thick china plate that also held a split dill pickle. Burke took the lunch to a table that seemed clean enough and hunched over his meal. He washed the bread and fish down with gulps of liquor from the jar. When he finished, he went to the counter to get his change. Plato handed over five ones.

"You trying to cheat me, nigger?"

"The po-boy is fifty cents. The gas come to two-fifty. The drink, it come dear."

"Then I got enough for two more. Pass them over and keep the change."

Buster snatched his jars never knowing how close old Plato's hand hovered to the shotgun. A big white man like that could be big trouble. Plato exhaled deeply when the customer left and went back to reading his paper.

Burke drove to the Academy and parked under one of its famous oak trees. He sipped and simmmered and watched the water drip from the leaves as he waited for Artie.

****

Inside the reception room, Artemus Delamare dined on dainty watercress sandwiches and delicate madeleines under the watchful eyes of a nun who never removed her hands from the wide sleeves of her habit. When Roxie greeted him with a squeal, a huge hug, and a kiss right on the lips, the visitor had been placed under instant surveillance by Sr. Gertrude, who said in her thick German accent, "Roxanne, we do not greet our guests in such a manner, not even the close cousins. You do not haf so close a resemblance to Mr. Delamare."

"Oh," said Artie, covering for Roxie's lie, "these old New Orleans families are all inter-related. Cousin Roxanne comes from the pretty side."

Roxie blushed and stared at her sturdy Oxford

shoes. Her homely, waistless plaid jumper hung just above mid-calf, and the white blouse beneath it had popped a few buttons when she flung herself on Artie. He couldn't see she had real breasts now, but maybe he felt them. She'd wanted to wear something nicer, but a spring growth spurt had made her Sunday skirts too short and her bodices too tight, according to Sr. Gertrude who sent her back to her room to change.

While she liked being taller and more shapely, Roxie lived in fear of growing bigger than Artie. She may have gotten her mother's dark hair and eyes, but definitely had her father's long legs. Why couldn't she be petite like Roz? Guilt made her squirm on the horsehair sofa left over from the last century.

"May I get you more tea, Cousin Artie?" she asked very properly.

Artie glanced at the china cup hand-painted with yellow roses that held both cream and a lemon slice curdled together in an unappetizing manner. "Sure, kiddo, but just lemon and sugar this time, okay?"

With Roxie gone, he made friendly with Sr. Gertrude. "Nice cup. Did you nuns paint them?"

"The students, they are encouraged to learn useful arts such as china painting. We don't believe in idle hands. Our sisters do very good needlework. We haf for sale on the large table." Delivered without a smile, this was more of a command to buy than an invitation to browse.

"You know, Sr. Gertrude, my mother would love a set of these teacups. How many would a twenty buy?' Artie pulled a bill from his money clip.

"*Vier.* Four."

"Expensive."

"Hand-painted, Mr. Delamare. Each cent goes to goot works."

"Then, give me six." He peeled off another twenty. "And keep ten for charity, but could you wrap them really well? I have a long, bumpy ride back to New Orleans."

Artie watched Sr. Gertrude stride away with his twenties while Roxie bounced toward him, spilling tea into the saucer in her exuberance. He noticed some bounce beneath her hideous jumper, too, and she'd let her boyish crop grow out into soft curls that had a jiggle all their own. She'd gotten so tall in the last six months she didn't need to stand on her toes to kiss him. How old was Roxanne now? Fourteen? Maybe, he really was a pervert.

Roxie set the teacup down with a clatter that drew the attention of several nuns and a senior student playing the *Moonlight Sonata* on a baby grand donated by a grateful alumnus who had married well—as did all their girls.

"More sandwiches, Artie?" she asked, eager to serve him.

"No, thank you. Open your present. I emptied every music store in the city."

Roxie tore off the brown paper and string. "Sheet music! All the latest songs."

She fanned them out across the table. The covers showed flappers smoking cigarettes in long holders, a movie starlet in a long gown leading wolfhounds on a leash, and nearly naked Ziegfeld girls wearing more feathers in their headdresses than clothes on their bodies. Expressing her joy was another reason to hug Artie tightly. He picked up one of the booklets, placed it on his lap, and pretended to study the music. Across the room, he could see Sr. Gertrude blocking the view of the tea table with her broad shoulders as she picked up six of the teacups and went in search of a box.

"Let me ask Margie if I may use the piano. We can sing together like we used to when I was a kid." Roxie rushed across the room.

Oh God, she had hips now, too, small but nicely rounded and pressed against a uniform a little tight on her. Artie covered his eyes with his hands. In a place like Rainbow with its reputation for holy interventions, he might be struck blind.

Roxie sat on the piano bench, long enough for two, and beckoned him from afar. Artie sucked in several deep breaths, took his hat off the arm of the sofa, placed it over his crotch, put on a smile, and joined her at the instrument.

"Here, I'll play. Sing this one for me, Artie."

"Ah, kiddo. That's not my style."

"Please, please, please!"

Before he knew it, the ham in his nature had him belting out *All of Me—why not take all of me*—hat over his heart, then arms spread wide as he went for the big finish. The young Catholic girls, who looked like they wanted to swoon, applauded along with their terribly polite parents. He handed Roxie the sheets for *Ain't She Sweet*. He added dance steps. The young nun left in charge while Sr. Gertrude wrapped the teacups looked distressed. Her hands had come out of her sleeves and clenched together in her lap. Perhaps she was praying. Artie went into his encore. A cardboard box crashed on to the top of the piano with a sound like china breaking.

"Ach so, now we know how this jass music comes

here. We find it in the girls' rooms. It is *verboten*. You must go, Mr. Delamare, and take it *mit* you."

Roxie's pink lips quivered as if she were about to cry. Artie gathered up the music. "Sorry, sorry, my fault. Don't blame the girl."

"Please, Sr. Gertrude. Don't send him away. I never get to see Artie, I mean Cousin Artie."

"And no wonder. No, he must go."

"May I walk him to the gate? I'll only be gone five minutes, I swear on the head of the little baby Jesus."

"We do not swear, Roxanne. Five minutes you can haf to say good-bye. No more."

Artie put on his hat and bundled the sheet music, his trench coat, and a box of broken teacups under his arms. Roxie held the door for him. Sadly, they trudged down the gravel walk together. The eyes of Sr. Gertrude bore into their backs from the front steps.

"I'm sorry, Artie. I know the music and the cups cost you a lot of money."

"Forget it, kiddo. Since I passed the bar, all I have to do is sit in Burke's old office and pretend to care about the law for a nice fat slice of the pie."

"You passed! Roz said you never would. I'd like to tell her that to her face." The girl frowned. "She wrote to me at Christmas from Cousin Loretta's house, but I didn't answer back. I blamed her for my being sent here. I thought I'd never see you again, but you wrote and called and now here you are."

"I'd never forget my best buddy." Artie cuffed her gently on the arm. "Can't let them make a nun of you."

"Oh, Sr. Gertrude says I have even less of a vocation than my sister, so I don't think that will happen. I worry about Roz though. My parents won't tell me anything about her except that she's well, but I had a letter just the other day from Cousin Loretta's youngest daughter. She promised she'd write as soon as she got home. She says Roz doesn't live with them anymore."

They had come to the gate. Taking a quick look over her shoulder and seeing Sr. Gertrude had been distracted by a pair of parents taking leave, she slipped outside the grounds.

"I'll just walk you to your car. Is that it under the oak tree? It looks exactly like Buster's Mercedes."

"Well, I—"

Roxie leaned up against the muddy side of the machine and assumed the languid sexy stance she'd seen on some of sheet music covers. "As I was saying, my second-cousin wrote from Chapelle that Roz is staying at Purdue's Boarding House and working for a living. My parents have cut her off entirely because they don't approve. Isn't that dreadful?"

"Hmmm, dreadful. Would you move over Roxie, so I can put this stuff inside?"

Suddenly, she became a little girl again, sulking because he wasn't paying enough attention to her. "I guess you are in a big hurry to leave. Maybe you have a hot date back in the city."

"Hot date? Me? No. Oh, well, let's see what's left of the teacups. No reason to carry shards all the way to New Orleans."

Each cup rested in a newspaper nest, but despite that, all but two had cracks running up their sides from Sr. Gertrude's harsh handling. Artie lifted out the intact pair.

"Look, Roxie." He held a cup in each hand with his

pinkie raised and did a shuffle step in the oak duff. *"Tea for two, and two for tea. You for me, and me for you— alone!"*

He coaxed a smile from her with his dance. Bowing, he presented her with a teacup. "A souvenir of my visit, princess. The other I shall cherish all my days in remembrance of you."

Artie kissed the back of Roxie's free hand. She would have stepped into his arms hoping for more, but a voice thick with sarcasm and bootleg liquor interrupted. Burke Boylan stepped out from behind the bole of the oak and zipped up his pants as he spoke.

"Maybe if I'd acted like a fool instead of a real man, your sister wouldn't be hiding out in Chapelle. Purdue's Boarding House, you said. Come on, Artie. Let's pay my precious Rosie a visit."

"Buster, I'm the one who paid for this trip. I say we head for New Orleans."

"Get in the Mercedes, Artie." Burke Boylan picked up the smaller man, heaved him into the front seat and smashed him down on the broken china.

"Jesus, Buster. I have glass in my ass."

"Don't make me shove it down your throat. Shut the door."

The last sight Artemus Delamare had of Roxanne St. Rochelle for many years to come was that of a very young woman, her dark brown eyes wide with fright, slipping a delicate china teacup painted with yellow roses into the bodice of her jumper. Over the roar of the Mercedes engine as it pulled them toward Chapelle, he could hear the bass voice of Sr. Gertrude calling, "You haf left the grounds, you naughty girl. You must do penance. Ach, St. Rochelle girls, too much trouble."

Roxanne ran through the gates and past the glowering Sr. Gertrude. She crossed the lawn and plowed through the marigolds and cannas planted at the feet of the statue of the Virgin Mary. She fell to her knees and pressed her forehead against the cold plaster base.

"Holy Mother, hear my prayer. Keep my sister, Rosamond, safe from Burke Boylan, now and forever more. I'll be good. I'll do what I should. I won't write Artie or try to see him again. I swear."

"*Und* that will be a pleasant change for us all, *nicht*? Tomorrow, you replant the flowers when the rest are riding. Go change. You are *schmutzig mit* mud."

Chapter Forty

Burke pushed through the town of Lafayette with one hand on the Mercedes' horn. He terrified mules taking wagonloads of Negro evacuees to the camp at the fairgrounds. He recklessly passed military trucks full of troops as he whizzed past the red brick buildings of Southwestern Louisiana Institute. When the road dipped into a swampy area just outside the tiny village of Cade, Burke forced the vehicle through a foot of standing water. He and Artie arrived in Chapelle before dark. Burke pounded on the door of Purdue's Boarding House.

A stout woman dressed in black opened the door. "Sorry, we're full up with relief workers. I should have put up the No Vacancy sign."

"We don't want a room. We're here to visit Rosamond Boylan. Isn't that so, Artie? Tell her she has guests from New Orleans."

"Oh my! In all the time Roz has lived here, no guests have ever come from New Orleans to visit. She'll be so sorry to have missed you, but she's working at the Red Cross camp above Spanish Lake. You passed it on your way here, most likely. Go back toward Cade and turn on Lady of the Lake Road. It will take you right there."

The small, nervous man who had taken off his hat in the landlady's presence said, "Is there any way you could call ahead and tell her Buster and Artie are coming?"

"Shut up, Artie," the muscular young man, whose breath reeked of alcohol, growled.

"I do have a telephone, and I'm sure they must have strung wires to the camp, but I don't know the number. If you'd like, come in and try asking the operator."

"No, I want to get there as soon possible. Come on, Artie."

The big bruiser shoved his friend away from the door. The smaller man looked back over his shoulder and mouthed, "Call her!"

"Young man, young man, do you know your britches are torn? I think I see some blood, too. If you would just take a moment, I could—"

"He's fine, old lady. Don't bother calling Rosie. We want our visit to be a big surprise."

Widow Purdue watched the men leave in their fancy car. People had been asked not to call the camp unless an emergency occurred, and this was only a social visit, though an odd one, to be sure. Rosamond certainly possessed many strange friends: Negroes and swamp Cajuns, and now rough young men from the city, gangsters, perhaps. And here she was with no one to tell.

****

The white Mercedes stopped at the gates of Camp Roy as an early gray dusk descended. The guardsmen crossed their rifles and explained that the camp kept an 8:00 p.m. curfew and no one without proper identification would be admitted.

"My wife is in there, Rosamond Boylan. You know

her?" Burke demanded.

"Sure, she's the camp midwife. Dr. Landry rescued her from a flooded house a few days ago. She doesn't wear a ring, so we all thought she was widowed or on her own. Not that anyone else has a chance with the doc around. You sure you're her husband? Anyhow, we can't let you in. Try back in the morning."

Burke's alcohol-flushed face went a shade redder. He put the powerful engine into gear and stomped on the gas. The gates parted before his chrome grill like a levee breaking. The guardsmen jumped to either side and watched the car climb the hill. They were impressed.

"Wish I had me an auto like that."

"Better wish you had wings and could fly away from the ass-chewing General Emory is going to give us. Call headquarters."

Burke reached the summit and spun to a stop by the mess tent. He grabbed the shirt of a man exiting with a cup of hot coffee. "Rosamond Boylan. They said she's the midwife. Where's her tent?"

"Man, I t'ink you need dis coffee more dan me. Babies, dey don't come dat fast."

Burke bunched his thick fingers into a large fist and cocked back his arm. "Where is she?"

"Da nurses' tent down dere if she ain't out bringing a baby." The chosen informant pointed the way. Burke dropped the smaller man, sloshing coffee over both of them, and charged away. Artie Delamare limped after him.

"Buster, the guards are coming. We need to leave here right now."

"Shut your trap, Artie. I'm taking my wife out of

here."

Buster reached the designated tent and tore down the midwife's sign. "Now she's out of business."

He pitched the sign and walked into the tent to be met with the squeals and shrieks of nurses in various stages of undress. None of them were Roz.

"Rosamond Boylan. Where is she?"

A disapproving nurse pursed her lips and said snidely, "Probably with Dr. Landry in his tent down by the infirmary. Who wants to know, another one of her boyfriends?"

"Her husband, her still lawful husband." Burke turned on his heel and weaved between the tents. In the distance, he could hear the Cajun man he had accosted jabbering in French to the guards. Artie lagged far behind still calling to him to stop. The nurses clustered in the entry to their tent.

One of the women said, "You shouldn't have told him, Dorcas. He looks like he wants to kill her."

Damn right, he wanted to kill her—and her lover. Catch them together and strangle them both, a crime of passion. No jury would hang him for that. Burke Boylan lumbered toward the doctors' tent.

****

In the intimacy of the small tent he shared with Doc Spivey, Pierre Landry held Roz close. The tent flap was down, giving them some scant privacy in the crowded camp. Leonard Spivey told Pierre he wouldn't enter if he closed the flap, giving his fellow doctor a wink like a randy college boy—and he expected the same favor in return. Spivey was most certainly joking, Pierre thought, until he nearly lifted the flap after returning from dinner. Low but unmistakable sounds of mating stopped him from entering.

"Len, Len, Len, oh, Len," a woman, husky-voiced, whispered.

Len, you old dog. Strange to think of his mentor that way. Obviously, Doc Spivey's heart condition had been greatly exaggerated.

But this evening, the tent belonged to Roz and Pierre. They shared the long kisses and the deep caresses that brought them both some satisfaction. Roz wanted more. She tore at his clothes, but was calmed at last by her own climax. *Frottage*. The act sounded so much better given its French name, but he thought he might go insane having to make love in this way for seven more months.

Surrounded by disaster, unwilling to be apart, they talked in the dark about the life they might build together. He wanted Roz to get nurses' training in Lafayette, perhaps study for an M.D. They'd open a proper medical office and work together every day. Children would come, and they could raise them in a house built on the bayou. He didn't care what religion they practiced, but he did want to stay in Chapelle near his kin and the people who needed him

Roz, pleasantly drowsy, leaned her head against his shoulder. "Fine. I could develop an appetite for alligator sauce piquant. It tasted more like pork than fish, don't you think?"

"Best alligator I ever had." Pierre kissed the top of her head. "I want to give you something." He released her long enough to find his medical bag. Cool and rubbery, a pair of surgical gloves landed in Roz's lap. She regarded their long, limp fingers.

"How lovely. Just what I've always wanted."

"I know they're thick and clumsy, but I want you to wear them during deliveries until your hands heal completely. There's an outbreak of acute gonococcus infections in the camp, mostly among the soldiers and young men, but it's bound to spread among the women. I broke the news to General Emory this morning. He's outraged by the moral turpitude of his troops but did agree to distribute prophylatics to the men. The Catholic boys think it's a sin to use a rubber. Me, my brothers, we always washed down with white mule after we'd been with a woman. No sin in that, but it burned like the devil. Maybe, that's why it worked so well."

"Nurse Strictland told me about the outbreak. She was amazingly mellow about it." Roz sighed heavily. "We're supposed to give lectures to the unmarried girls about pick-ups and petting being like the first leaks in a levee that will lead them to an uncontrollable crevasse."

"I know that feeling."

"Pierre, we could make use of those condoms."

"We can wait the seven months until your divorce is final. If we made a mistake and conceived a child during that time, the town's people and my family would have an even harder time accepting you."

"People will talk about me anyhow." Giving up, Roz straightened. "I could use some extra silver nitrate if you have any. I refuse to allow any of my babies to be blinded because the National Guard boys have nothing better to do with their time. Have you traced the source of the infection?"

"Straight to Eloise and her pals. I suspected they were plying their trade when I drove past the Barn the other day and noticed the yard wasn't flooded. They've been passing their earnings to one of the men on the work crews. He hands it off to Bubba or Gaston Broussard for a small cut of the take. The girls are being shipped to Lafayette for treatment in the morning. The general posted a guard on their tent for the night. I hope he picked some geezers for the job, but then I know one geezer who can still get it up—which accounts for a mellow Nurse Strictland."

"Pierre, really? I can't believe—"

People shouted. Heavy footsteps ran their way. A commotion started outside the tent. Probably another brawl as tempers grew short among evacuees impatient to return home. He would have more broken heads to stitch, but hopefully no knife wounds. Pierre stood up and tucked in his shirt. Roz smoothed her wrinkled midwife's uniform with her hands.

Someone pushed the tent flap aside letting in the glare of the camp lighting. A bulky form filled the entry. Before Roz could react, a large, all too familiar hand grabbed her by the wrist and jerked her upward. Pierre Landry, caught off guard as he searched in his bag for the silver nitrate, fell to the ground with a blow to the jaw.

Buster shoved Roz out into the light. He pinched her face between his hands and raised it so that her wide, terrified blue eyes had to look into his. He ran a rough thumb over the scab on her chin.

"Did you give Landry a hard time, too? Did he have to put you in your place? No matter, I'll adjust your attitude once we get out of here. We can catch a train in Lafayette and be on our way to Philly before daylight. We can reconsummate our marriage in a sleeper car—if I decide to wait that long, Rosie."

Roz struggled, beating on Buster with her fists. Out of the corner of her eye she could see Artie Delamare being chased in their direction by a weedy young guardsman whose face was covered with the acne of adolesence.

"Let her go, Burke! You've had too much to drink. You'll hurt someone," Artie panted.

The soldier came up behind them and assumed a fighting stance behind his rifle and bayonet. "Halt! I say halt! Y'all can't come in here after curfew. Y'all got to move outta here."

"Just visiting my wife, Private. Merely ending a long separation." Buster lowered his face toward Roz's lips. He held her in place with a grip that bruised her jaw and bit her upper lip, drawing blood, when she kicked him in the shin.

"Halt! Don't look like Miz Roz wants to go with you." The private looked over his shoulder, hoping his fellow guard would arrive soon to help take on this brute. His buddy, having slipped in the mud and sprained an ankle, was making his way slowly to the fracas using his rifle as a crutch. When the soldier glanced back at Burke, the situation had changed.

An arm wrapped around Buster's neck exposing his throat. The big man didn't move because a slim, shiny blade pressed against the side of his thick neck. Dr. Landry spoke into the man's red ear. "Do you remember what I told you would happen if you ever hurt Roz again? Now, my brothers, they would use a hunting knife across the jugular and windpipe to kill a brute like you. Me, I'd rather make a deep cut, severing the carotid artery with a scalpel. It's easy, quick, and relatively painless. You'll be dead before you notice,

Boylan."

"Uh, Dr. Landry, sir. I don't think the commandant would like it if you killed this fella," the private said, his hands shaking the rifle a little.

"Then, why don't you restrain him and escort him out of the camp, soldier? Tell him not to come back."

"That what you want, Miz Roz?" the guardsman asked.

"Yes." She rubbed the marks on her jaw with her small, white hand.

A crowd of men, who had nothing better to do than start fights or watch them since the brothel tent had been closed down, gathered round. One offered a long rawhide string that might have been a bootlace to the soldier. The guardsman couldn't decide what to do with his rifle and the string at the same time.

"I'll tie him up," Artie offered.

"Don't touch me, Artie. I'll kill you if you touch me," Burke ground out between his teeth as he tried to keep his jaw muscles from scraping against the scalpel.

"Hold him steady, Doctor. Buster, I'm going to drive us out of here. I'll let you go when we're a few miles out of town." Artie wound the rawhide lace so tightly around Boylan's wrists that it cut into the flesh.

"Sorry, Roz. I'm so sorry—again. Oh, Roxie is worried about you. Try writing her again, would you? She's a good kid, just a little mixed up about what she wants right now."

Artie finished his task. The private poked the subdued Burke in the back with the tip of his bayonet. As they turned, Roz called out. "Artie, you're bleeding."

"Yeah. I sat on some glass."

"Let us take care of that before you go."

"We'll see Mr. Boylan gets to his car and stays there if you need a doctor, sir," the guard offered, his thin chest puffed out a little, as he prodded Buster along.

"Thanks. It hurts like hell."

So did the removal of a two-inch shard of china from his slim white ass, the disinfecting of the wound and the eight stitches needed to close the cut. Artie sang out in his fine tenor voice a few times before the ordeal ended. Roz taped a thick pad of gauze over the injury.

"There, that should get you back to New Orleans. Take care, Artie."

Artemus Delamare looked at Roz and the doctor. He regarded how they stood close together. He figured they itched to put their arms around each other once he left. Thanks to him, Roz had gotten a bum deal with Buster.

"Yeah. You, too. Take care of each other."

He bumped into a courier as he left the tent. "Dr. Landry," the man said, "We had a call that one of your patients in town may have suffered a stroke. Here's the address. You're needed in Chapelle at once."

"Coming," he heard Pierre reply.

On his way back to the Mercedes, he passed a gaunt country woman, swollen breasts wobbling beneath beneath a loose dress. She had a newborn slung over one shoulder. The baby startled when its mama bellowed, "We need da midwife, tent turty-four."

Burke waited in the passenger seat of the Mercedes when Artie returned to the car. The guards had given him a few snorts from one of the jars of liquor. Some spilled down the front of Buster's shirt, filling the air with the redolence of alcohol.

"Figured if he passed out he'd be easier to handle, but the guy sure can hold it," the private remarked, looking longingly at the empty container.

"He's an ugly drunk, I can tell you that." Artie turned over the engine. Burke gave an animal-like growl drowned out when cylinders fired. They rolled down the hill and through the crumpled gates of Camp Roy.

The waters of Spanish Lake pushed against the narrow road all the way back to the main highway. In the night, the spillover seemed closer, darker, deeper. When Artie took the Mercedes over the small hill and down into the dip that Burke had powered through before, he discovered more was at work than his imagination. The big vehicle refused to brake and fishtailed down the incline into water swollen to a depth of several feet. It flowed over the floorboards and into the car. The huge engine stalled as Burke thrashed his feet in the rising water.

"Untie me, you idiot, before I drown!"

"Sure, Burke. Don't get excited. You're getting the knots wet. Makes them harder to untie."

Both of them wet to the waist now, Artie fumbled with the rawhide lace. Burke jerked his hands free as the thong loosened. He used them to shove Artie from the car.

"Get the hell out and push, fool."

"Buster, we need to leave the machine behind and get out of here."

"I just lost my wife for the second time. I won't lose the Mercedes. I said push!"

Artie started to wade away toward the slope of the

small hill, but Burke sprang from the car and jerked him back.

"Push, I said, you puny pervert. What did you think—that taking Roz's side would help you hook up with the baby sister? I saw how you looked at that little girl in her school uniform. If I hadn't interrupted, you would have had her in the backseat."

"Shut up, Buster. You can push your own damned car up the hill. I'm gone."

The water was on the move, rising higher, carrying with it branches and old boards that scratched the paint of the white Mercedes and piled up along one side. Burke yanked Artie by his coat collar and turned him toward the car. "Bend over and push, I said!"

"It's not moving, Buster. The gears are locked. Be reasonable. We can still get out of here alive."

"You're not trying hard enough, child molester."

Burke eyed the debris marring his sleek, white vehicle. Dark as the night was, Buster's cold, pale eyes glittered. He worked a plank from the pile. The end of it bore a stubble of rusty nails.

"What you need is more incentive. Artie, the pervert, needs a goose in the ass."

Burke smashed the board against Artie's rear. The nails missed his flesh, but the impact on the wound in his backside wrenched a scream from deep in the wounded man's gut. Artie stood up, the water now past his waist.

"Don't hit me, Buster, and never call me a pervert again! If Roz can fight you, so can I."

"Come on, Artie. Let's see how close you can get."

Burke swung the studded board in a wide arc, all his muscle behind it. Artie, remembering the lithe

Italian fighter who had taken a toll on Buster at the Holland House, launched himself under the swing and knocked Boylan off his feet. They went down into the water, Artie on top. He stood on the big man's chest and wrested the board away while Burke gulped muddy water. The body beneath him bucked and fought.

Artie jumped backwards and raised the board high as Buster came up coughing and choking, Artemus surprised that he could actually see murder in a man's eyes. Burke's large hands moved toward his throat. He swung the board against Boylan's head with all the strength of accumulated anger. One rusty nail pierced a pale, mad eye. It was Buster's turn to scream.

Artie tossed the board and scrambled away. The water rose faster now, chest high. He pushed against the current, finally gaining a grip on a sapling by the side of the road. Pulling himself out of the dip, he crawled up the side of the hill. From the top, he watched the blinded Burke struggling, slipping, going down. Boylan emerged again covered in mud and slime, more monster than man now, a Cyclops in the throes of death, defeated by his puny enemy.

Buster grasped at the spare tire mounted on the side of the Mercedes, tried to pull himself onto the hood, but his strength was drained away by the flood. The waters plucked his thick fingers, one by one, from the wires of the fancy wheel and bore Burke Boylan away. Artie stood, turned his back, and began the long walk to Camp Roy.

Chapter Forty-One

"Thank heaven, you're back!"

Roz had been waiting since dawn at the top of the hill for Pierre Landry's Ford to make the turn into the camp. As it was, he surprised her by entering through the rear gate. The early light revealed clear evidence that somewhere another levee had broken. Water coursed down the railway cut along the main road, adding volume to Spanish Lake, eating away at the old levee that prevented the lake from spilling into an abandoned canal and flooding the drained farm lands beyond.

"I'm ashamed to admit I fell asleep at the wheel and almost did for myself last night. Old Mrs. Fruge died of a massive brain hemorrhage before I arrived. At eighty-six, she would have been severely paralyzed had she lived. Her death was a blessing, quick and painless. I sat with the family and filled in the death certificate while waiting for the hearse to come. I didn't realize how fatigued I'd become until I jerked awake on the road and saw an oak tree coming up fast."

Pierre got down from his Ford and took his black bag from the rear seat. Not caring who saw after yesterday's scene with Boylan, he put his arm around Roz's waist. "I pulled over, planning to take a short nap and before I knew it, the sun rose over the cane fields. By that time, the Lizzie was mired in. I had to push her

399

out of the mud. *Bon chance* that I parked on higher ground because I could see water to the northeast all the way back to Chapelle and St. Martinville. I had to come in through Cade and back the Ford up that last big hill to get into camp."

At the tent, Pierre set his bag on the cot and brushed at the mud on his clothes, all the while taking a good look at Roz. Pausing, he raised her chin with his fingertips. "You seem tired yourself," he said.

"A young woman lost her first child at six months, not a stillbirth, but the infant lived only a few hours. The mother was frantic to have the child baptized, going on about not wanting her baby's soul to wander the night as a *feu-follet*. Reverend Grant offered to do the baptism, but the mother insisted on a priest. By the time Fr. Grainger arrived, the little girl had died. We all pretended otherwise."

Roz sank on the cot next to the bag. "After the baptism, the two men of God got into an argument. Fr. Grainger claimed the Baptists and the Methodists are preaching in the camps and trying to lure his people away from the Catholic Church. I thought they'd have to douse them with pails of water to put an end to it, but they finally stomped off in opposite directions. It would have been funny if it weren't so sad."

"I've lived with these beliefs all my life, Roz. Do you think you will be able to bear it?"

"If we are together, Pierre."

He would have liked to kiss her, but the camp was coming full awake, and bored, restless people seethed everywhere looking for a diversion. Instead, he laid a gentle, guiding hand on her shoulder. "Lie down here and rest. My place is quieter than the nurses' tent."

"If I lie in your bed, I won't be thinking of sleeping." She watched his slow smile spread showing his white teeth, then fade again.

"I need to clean up and get to the infirmary. Doc Spivey is probably there already. So far, we've been lucky to avoid any epidemics of typhoid or dysentery. Pneumonia is carrying off the elderly, but at least we do have a chance to see the children receive their smallpox innoculations."

"So said Nurse Strictland who runs a very tight and clean ship. I have to say she has been almost friendly lately."

"Evidently, Leonard's heart conditon wasn't as bad as we were told." They laughed together.

He wished he could have ignored the voice calling, "Dr. Landry, you're wanted in the commandant's tent."

"I need to change my clothes, soldier. Please tell the general I'll be along in a few minutes."

"Begging your pardon, sir, the general says right away. Miz Boylan, you're wanted, too."

"Would you know what's going on?" Roz asked the private whose upper lip was covered with downy fuzz masquerading as a moustache.

"I shouldn't say, ma'am, but..." He lowered his voice. "A big ole nigger brought a body up to camp just now. Maybe they need the doc to do an autopsy. Don't know why they want you, Miz Boylan. Please come along and don't give me no trouble."

The usual crowd had formed outside the general's tent. Above the heads, Roz could see the long ears of two mules and below their feet, a spreading puddle of water.

"Make way for the doctor," their escort shouted,

using the butt of his rifle to open a path.

As they got nearer, they could see a brawny colored man holding the reins of the mules. "Don't need no doctor. He dead. Dressed like a king or a politician, but dat won't get him into heaven, nossir. Might be his family would want to give dis nigger a reward for bringin' him in."

General Emory stood at the foot of the wagon close to a tarp-covered form, the source of the growing puddle. "Mrs. Boylan, several people have told me already this man caused trouble in camp last evening and attempted to force you to come with him. He was threatened with bodily harm by Dr. Landry, removed by the camp guards, and remanded to the company of a friend. Jasper, here, found the corpse half lodged under a railway crossing when he was walking the tracks into town. As a medical professional, I expect your stomach is strong enough to identify the body."

He pulled back the tarp, revealing the bloated face of the corpse. One eye nothing but a black and sunken hole, but the other stared straight up, so pale a blue it was almost white. People who could see crossed themselves. Roz swallowed. "It's Burke Boylan, my husband. We've been separated since January. Yesterday was the first I'd seen him in five months."

"Dr. Landry, would you say he died from drowning or from that injury to his eye and side of the head?"

"An autopsy would be needed to determine that."

"Just so. I understand you left camp right after Mr. Boylan and stayed out all night."

"Yes, I drove to Chapelle to see a patient and returned around midnight but nearly drove off the road. I parked to get some rest and came back to camp this morning."

"You were alone from midnight on? No one could testify to your whereabouts?"

"I don't know. I was asleep. I didn't see anyone until I approached the camp. The water came up during the night. No one would have passed me coming from Chapelle or St. Martinville. I stopped near Cade."

"And the trestle where you found the body was near Cade, Jasper?"

"Yes, suh. Had to go way back to my cabin to get a hook and some rope to draw him up. My mules was up to dere knees in water bringin' him here. I figured on a reward and a hot meal, leastways."

"Go down the hill to the colored camp. Tell them General Emory said to feed you. Stay there in case we need you."

"Whose gonna be givin' me my reward and takin' care of my mules, Mistah General, suh?"

General Emory did not answer the question, but his glare had Jasper jumping from the wagon and heading down the hill. All eyes followed his broad back for a moment before turning back toward the corpse and the desperate face of Rosamond Boylan.

She'd worked so hard to gain respect, but here in the close quarters of the camp, unable to ignore Pierre any longer, she'd tossed some of that reputation into the floodwaters and might be unable to retrieve it. Why not dive in all the way and save the person who had saved her? Roz took a deep breath. "Dr. Landry was with me. We arranged to meet at midnight outside the rear gate so we could be together in privacy."

"No! Mrs. Boylan stayed here in camp all night assisting with a birth." Pierre Landry scanned the crowd and picked out Cherie Arton. "You came for her, Cherie. Tell the general Roz never left the camp."

Cherie opened her mouth and clamped it shut again. A solid cannonball of a woman standing next to her had given her a pinch on the hip and pushed to the front of a group of women. "Don't you say nuttin', Cherie Arton."

"Mama," Pierre said with exasperation. "When did you get here?"

"Las' night. Da water, she come up in da house. Your papa and me, we get out da pirogue and paddle, paddle, den walk, walk, walk 'til we get here, and las' night, I don't see dat woman nowheres." She pointed a finger at Roz.

"I offered to take you to Euclide's out in Carencro three times last week, but you wouldn't come, Mama."

"Makes no never mind now." Alida Landry turned on the general even though her head barely came up to his last row of medals. She shook a finger in his face. "You tryin' to say my boy, he killed dis man over dat woman. I tell you, me, my son, he never killed nobody. Always, he fixin'up birds and dogs when he was tee-tiny. He got da gift, you know. He don't even hunt and fish. But wit' da ladies, dey say he can go all night. I hear what his brudders say about my Pierre, so how come you don't believe her?"

Roz watched Pierre color under his dark morning stubble. The general's face appeared to be getting ruddier, too. "Ma'am, I understand you are trying to defend your son, but even if he were with Mrs. Boylan last night, they might have performed an act of collusion."

"Well, I never heard it called dat before, but my

Pierre, he's a doctor and knows all ways to do it. He wouldn't have no time to kill nobody."

Acutely embarrassed, Pierre Landry broke into his mother's speech about his sexual prowess. "Mama, please go to your tent. You're making matters worse. General, I swear I didn't kill this man, nor was I with Mrs. Boylan last night."

Pacing with his hands clasped behind his back, General Emory tried to restore order to the situation. "Regardless of the aforesaid, I see a man covered in mud who didn't return to camp until daylight. I know this same man stole—or borrowed a boat as he claims—and neglected his duties to search for this woman, the wife of the victim. Camp rumors say that you, Dr. Landry, and Mrs. Boylan are lovers."

"We are in love. We haven't been lovers since Roz married Burke Boylan, but yes, we planned to marry when her divorce became final," Pierre asserted.

Alida Landry sucked in her breath at that announcement. She opened her mouth, but General Emory took his turn at shaking a finger. "No, ma'am, you've had your say. There is enough suspicion to hold your son under arrest until the sheriff can be contacted and an autopsy is completed."

"My patients in Chapelle—"

"Doctor Spivey will have to tend to them. Private, you will guard Dr. Landry with your life. If he attempts to leave the camp, shoot to kill. That's an order!"

The lad turned pale under his peach fuzz. "Yessir!"

"As for you, Mrs. Boylan, you will go to your tent where I will place another guard. You will not go out unless called on to perform your duties. There will be no more collusion—I mean plotting—with Dr. Landry.

Understood?"

"But I gave Pierre an alibi. Burke was with Artemus Delamare. Do you think we killed them both?"

The general drilled Roz with his gaze. "Possibly. Perhaps, the body of Mr. Boylan's companion will be found later."

A ripple went through the crowd. Those being pushed aside grumbled.

"Make way! Let me through! I got all the answers. Make way!"

A gap opened near the wagon, and Artie Delamare tumbled through it. His wide pants hung soggy on his slight frame, his bow tie was wilted, and his checked coat thoroughly ruined. Only his hair held in place with pommade and perfectly parted in the middle still looked presentable. He limped forward, shaking like a wet dog.

"Artie! Thank God! You can clear this up."

The way Roz looked at him, Artie felt like some kind of god holding another person's fate in his hands. Roxie gazed at him that way sometimes. He hung his head and took a deep breath. "Could someone bring me a blanket and a cup of hot coffee? I've been up in a live oak all night with a hostile possum and a family of raccoons for company. Thought I could find my way back here, but water was every which way I went. Some men in a boat picked me up and set me down at the base of the hill. Looks like Burke got here before me."

"Private, get this man a blanket and coffee," General Emory ordered.

"Sir, I thought I was supposed to guard and shoot Dr. Landry."

"I'll shoot the both of you if you don't get a move

on, Private. Your story, sir." The general gave Artie a curt nod and a disapproving glance at his college boy clothing.

"I drove when we left the camp last night. The guards had tied Boylan's hands when he became violent. It was dark, and I couldn't prevent the Mercedes from sliding into some deep water. The vehicle stalled. Burke, he wouldn't leave the car. He wanted me to help push it out, but the water rose fast. I refused and started up the hill."

Artie took another breath and glanced around. An avid audience hung on his every word. "Brush, boards with nails, dead animals washed up against the Mercedes."

Artie raised his arms and smashed them down. "A tree limb hit Buster on the head. He fell face forward onto a board full of nails. The water carried him away."

He paused dramatically. He'd stopped shaking. "I couldn't save him. Burke Boylan caused his own death."

Artie buried his face in his hands. One or two people applauded. The rest stood in silence.

"You'll sign a statement to that effect?"

Artie nodded without taking his hands away from his face.

"The sheriff still might want to investigate. I know I'll need to see the results of an autopsy myself."

The private had returned with an army blanket over one arm and a tin cup of coffee clutched in the hand not holding on to his rifle. Roz tucked the cover around Artie's shoulder and gave him the warm drink. The man shivered again.

"Do you think you pulled out your stitches, Artie?"

"Yes-s-s."

"General, do we have your permission to tend to this man?"

"Go, but don't leave the camp until I've collected statements from everyone involved in this sorry accident. Once again, Landry, no more incidents involving you and this woman, or I'll have to bar you from the camp, doctor or no doctor."

"I understand perfectly, *mon general.*"

****

The lamplight shone down on Artemus Delamare's naked backside like the sun on a California beach. As ridiculous as he felt in the open hospital gown, he was as warm and dry as a newly diapered baby. He could have dozed off if Pierre Landry would quit picking splinters from his butt, but the worst was over. His wound had been cleaned and resutured. Roz held his hand. Artie gave her a brave smile.

"You're badly bruised, Delamare. Were you hit by some trash in the water?"

"Yeah, I was hit by trash all right. Say Roz, are you and the doctor going to live happily ever after now—because I owe you one for introducing you to Boylan."

"I hope so. He rescued me, Artie. Life is too short to wait for happiness. I want to marry Pierre before the end of June."

The doctor looked up. "Roz, people will say you are dancing on Buster's grave."

"Perhaps that's just what I want to do."

"I'd join you in a Charleston," Artie offered. "But I need to give my statement and get back to New Orleans before I lose my reputation as a spiffy dresser."

He eyed the package of new underwear sent for

flood victims by a Wisconsin women's auxilliary. A checked flannel shirt and black trousers with knees so shiny they must have belonged to a shoe salesman or a priest had been plucked from the Red Cross donation bags by Roz. A brown cordouroy jacket with threadbare elbows hung off the back of a chair.

"I can tell you they aren't going to let me sit in first class on the train back to New Orleans, and me, a high class lawyer now."

"You passed the bar, Artie! Your family must be pleased."

"Yeah, like your family loved it when you married Burke. He wasn't right for you, and the law isn't right for me, Roz. As soon as I can pack my bags, I'm heading for Hollywood. You said it—life is too short not to make a quick grab at happiness. Tell Roxie I'll send her a postcard when I get there."

"My sister isn't speaking to me."

"And she feels bad about that. Call. Hell, invite her to the wedding. The only reason all this happened was because I paid Buster to drive me to the Academy for a visit. Roxie seemed so low in her letters. I only wanted to cheer her up. That's all there was to it, I swear. I had no idea he'd come after you."

"It's over now, Artie. No need to say anything more. I'll step out while you dress."

With Roz removed from the tent, Pierre Landry gave Artemus Delamare's bruised backside one last inspection. "Did Burke Boylan really die the way you said, Artie?"

"Close enough. I pray to God that he drowned. You take care of Roz. She's a great gal."

Artie finished buttoning his pants and shrugged

himself into the cordouroy jacket. He held out a hand to the doctor. "I won't be seeing you two again unless I come back as a movie star."

"*Bon chance,* Artemus."

Artemus Delmare attempted a grand exit with a few quick dance steps. He winced and settled for tipping an imaginary hat. Roz got a whopper of a kiss on the cheek. As if that weren't enough, he paused and said, "Adieu, adieu, adieu," and imitated Roxie's bobbing curtsy from Christmas Eve, 1925. The couple watched Artie limp down the hill in search of a way out of Louisiana.

Roz leaned into Pierre's arms. "Did he say anything more about Burke's death?"

"No. Either it happened as he said, or Artemus Delamare is a better actor than anyone suspected."

Chapter Forty-Two

Rosamond St. Rochelle Boylan married Dr. Pierre Boniface Landry in a simple Methodist ceremony atop the hill in Camp Roy the third week in June. They had planned to wed at sunrise and in secret with Reverand Grant presiding, Leonard Spivey and Judith Strictland witnessing, but word escaped and reached the ears of Alida Landry.

Her future mother-in-law cornered Roz in the nurses' tent. Shaking a finger in her face, Madame Landry ranted, "You t'ink I don't know you gonna marry my Pierre, eh, wit' no banns, no priest. Well, I tell you, me, we got to wait for dat water to go down some so dat all my fam'ly can come. Any woman who would make her name black and lie to save my son, she gonna make a good Landry. Fam'ly first, always fam'ly first. It don't matter so much my next grandbebes gonna be Met'odist."

Roz was struck speechless. She nodded her agreement to wait two weeks and marry at noon. The decision was a good one. With the sun shining down and the waters receding, the bride and groom took their vows in front of four thousand witnesses. Colored well-wishers watched through the fence. The Widow Purdue had come, bringing Roz one of her many white dresses, now dyed a pale rose, and a large straw hat trailing a veil of tulle. Loretta arrived with an enormous bouquet

411

made of all her garden flowers that had survived the flood, and three passengers—an excited Henri who couldn't wait to tell Roz how he'd rowed a boat down Main Street, Loretta's youngest daughter, and Roxanne St. Rochelle fresh from the Academy. Roxie held the bouquet while the bride and groom exchanged thin bands of gold.

Faye wept into her handkerchief as she clung to Bernard Toomey. The pregnancy, nearly disguised by a high-waisted dress, made her an emotional mess. Their own wedding was set for the next weekend, come hell or high water, according to Bernie. Edna looked on, wondering if she'd still be single and teaching at the age of sixty-five.

Yes, there had been talk about the swiftness of the nuptials following Burke Boylan's now confirmed accidental death by drowning, but only Verna Harkrider had been outraged. No one in Chapelle had known Boylan, but they heard he was a brutal man and halfway divorced from his wife anyhow. The Methodist women brought trays and trays of cookies, but they didn't bring Verna.

The Red Cross volunteers came up with turkey dinners and enough sheet cake covered in vanilla icing to feed both camps. The Landrys supplied the gumbo, so spicy it brought tears to the eyes of Nurse Strictland. At least, she claimed it was the gumbo.

Pierre's brothers formed up a band. Exiled musicians were plentiful enough in the camp for the dancing to last all day and all night without a stop, first under the shade of the mess tent with its tables pulled aside, and later under the stars where a light wind kept off the mosquitoes on this blessed day.

When Roz, her veil and dress aflutter with dollar bills pinned to the bride for a dance, sat down to drink a cup of lemonade, Roxie took a seat beside her. Shyly, she held out a postcard of the California sun setting over endless rows of orange trees.

On the back, it read, "Hey, Kiddo! I'm out in Hollywood. Everyone here is talking about a new flicker with its own sound called *The Jazz Singer*. Could be a big break for a guy with a great voice like mine if they make any more of them. Don't let the Sisters turn you into a nun, and don't take any wooden nickels. Artie."

"I guess my love for Artie was just a silly crush. I won't write back. Sorry I blamed you for everything."

"Roxie, honey, I'd be the last one to point out mistakes others have made. Look, here comes Pierre. He's up to something. I can tell by that sly smile."

"There's a photographer here taking pictures of the camp for a magazine. He's willing to make a wedding portrait of me with the queen of the Mardi Gras Ball."

"You mean Doctor and Midwife Landry."

"But of course."

The photographer took one picture of the bride and groom and another with the gathering of family and friends. Roz pulled Roxie close to her side, and Alida Landry, dressed in her Sunday best polka dot dress, put an arm around her son. He gave the newlyweds his card and took down their address, his mind already on the next poignant shot that would tell the story of the Great Flood of 1927 to the reader's of *National Geographic* magazine.

Pierre had another surprise. He showed his key to the apartment over the hospital to his bride. "It's not the

Paris Ritz, but we'll have more privacy than here in a tent. Doc Spivey said he'd cover all calls tonight as a wedding gift. He's still guilty about lying to bring me home."

"Let's take advantage of that while we can. If he and Judy continue on as they are, they might want to use the place themselves. As for me, I know I'll be happier staying over the hospital than I ever was at the Ritz." Roz smiled into his eyes.

"Leonard has a nice house in town. It's too big and empty for him since his wife died and his children moved away. We could rent it. One day, we'll build our own place on the bayou and raise our family there— after you finish nursing school."

"Yes, yes, yes, but there is only one thing I want to finish now, a whole night with you. No waiting for people to accept me, no shunting me off to the nurses' tent, no holding off for one more hour!"

They thought they were slipping quietly from the gathering, but the Tin Lizzie had been moved to a spot under one bright light. The Ford trailed an assortment of tin cans and old shoes tied to the bumper. A "Just Married" sign hung over the spare tire, and a throng of rice throwing well-wishers lay in wait. The newlyweds drove off to the sound of cheers and Cajun yells. Roz shook the rice from her hat.

"I think we have enough rice on the floor of the car to make gumbo," Roz said, laughing.

"It's not gumbo we're going to be making tonight, *ma cherie.*"

Pierre carried her up the stairs to the apartment. She had a vague memory that he might have done that before. Roz reached down to turn the key in the lock allowing her husband to take her all the way to the bed. They didn't bother to turn down the covers. Roz flung her hat at the snake lamp and missed. She didn't get up to retrieve it.

Pierre took off her shoes and slowly rolled down her stockings, one by one, trailing a finger along her soft thighs, over her slim calves, all the way to her toes. She could feel her silk step-ins growing damp between the legs. By the time he'd stopped fiddling with every button on her dress and teasing the breasts beneath her camisole before releasing them from their band, Roz had grown impatient. She pushed away his jacket, flung his tie after her hat, and tore open his shirt. Buttons pinged off the iron headboard. She had his pants down to his ankles in less than ten seconds, and they were flesh to flesh within a minute.

"You know I hate long waits, *mon amour*."

"Are you sure you're ready, *cher* heart?" He was teasing her again.

Roz drew his face to hers and reveled in the feel of his soft moustache, the warmth of his mouth, the play of his tongue with hers. She seized his lean flanks and urged him to enter, now, now, now. Lent had passed and for Rosamond St. Rochelle, Mardi Gras had come again.

Epilogue

Chapelle, Louisiana, 2004

Doretha Robertson looked at the skinny white boy the agency sent as a replacement to tend Miz Roz while the nurse took a personal day for her annual checkup. Hypertension and heart disease had killed the women in her family for three generations, but they weren't going to get her. Sure, she needed to lose weight. Her big, black body stored up fat like a bear preparing for winter, but Dorey tried to eat healthy, took her pills religiously, and never missed her checkup. Still, she wasn't all too sure she wanted to leave her frail ninety-seven-year-old patient with this man-child who wore rings in both ears and had a tattoo of a peace symbol peeking out from under the short sleeves of his blue scrubs.

"Now listen here. I got her all cleaned up, and she's in her chair. Soon as she gets bored with CNN, she'll want to go outside and sit facing the bayou. You make sure the morning chill is off the air before you allow any such thing. She'll sit out there and tell you she's waiting for Pierre—that's her deceased husband, and sometimes she talks to him—but she's not really senile. Around noon, you make her come in and eat whether she has an appetite or not. Heat up the Chunky Chicken Soup and make her a turkey sandwich cut in quarters, then she can feed herself. There's applesauce with plenty of cinnamon for dessert if she wants it, and she can have coffee or tea. You make sure she takes all the pills in this cup. You got all this?"

"Yes, ma'am." The young man nodded his blond head, the hair shaved close to his scalp, respectfully.

"Afterwards, you help her to the bathroom, put on a clean Depends. She might take a nap, but most likely, she'll want to go out and wait for Pierre some more. Usually, she dozes in her chair. I should be back in time to give her dinner. You got my beeper number by the phone."

"Yes, ma'am. I'll take good care of Mrs. Landry."

"She'll tell you to call her Roz, but you say 'Miz Roz' out of respect, you hear. She likes to talk about the old days, and it wouldn't do you no harm to listen for a while. I used to bring my own kids here to sit at her feet and hear how it was. Come on then. I'll introduce you before I get going."

The young man in scrubs followed Nurse Robertson's bulky body in its snug white uniform out of the kitchen and into a sunroom that had been made over as a bedroom when the elderly woman could no longer manage the stairs in the rambling bayouside home. Her family installed a downstairs bath at the same time. More often than not, one of them would come to spend the weekend in one of the three upstairs bedrooms. The great-grandson, one of the many Pierres, kept his houseboat docked on the river below. They watched out for their own, the Landrys did.

"Miz Roz, this is Nurse Chad Duhon. He's going to stay with you today while I go for my checkup."

The old woman turned her attention from the CNN

417

news reports on the television. The fluff of white hair and the thin, pale skin of her face made Mrs. Landry's eyes seem very blue and piercing. Her cataracts had been removed years ago because she couldn't be without her books and her television.

"How terrible that people are still killing each other over religion, but how wonderful more men are going into nursing. I used to be a nurse, you know, and a midwife. Back in the Sixties, the nursing school at the university asked me to speak to a group of young women interested in becoming midwives. They must have been appalled at how quickly we were trained and how little equipment we had at our disposal. Still, we were a godsend to rural women during the Depression. After World War II, everyone wanted to give birth in a hospital, and better medical care for the poor allowed that. Did I ever tell you Fr. Grainger threatened to excommunicate me for giving out information on birth control, Dorey? I told him it was good thing I'd gone over to the Methodists years ago."

"Yes, you might have mentioned that to me once or twice, but Chad, here, he hasn't heard any of your stories. You behave now. I'm going."

"Fresh meat for my grinder!" The old lady's laugh was surprisingly youthful, as if she were still a careless flapper in the Twenties. "Take me outside, Nurse Duhon. Pierre might come to find me today."

Chad checked to make sure the lap blanket wouldn't catch in the wheels of the chair and that his patient's feet were positioned properly. He pushed his charge out through the living room and kitchen to a deck overlooking the bayou and reset the brake when he reached a spot where the late autumn sun shone neither too hot nor too glaring.

"Sit down, kiddo. That's what Artie always called my sister, Roxie, even when they were old and gray. Well, Roxie never let herself go gray, but you know what I mean. Have you ever heard of Artie Delaware, singer and comedian extraordinaire?"

"No, Mrs. Landry. I can't say that I have." Chad brushed a hand over his bristle. Maybe, he should go change the sheets on her bed instead of sitting out here listening to the lady go on.

"Call me Roz, no matter what Dorey said. Delaware, Artie took that as his stage name. His family never got over the shame, but they should have. He could sing like a blackbird in the cane fields and make a whole room full of people smile. Artie was a big name in Hollywood in his day. He got to be Grand Marshal of Rex. That was during the Depression, so the floats and entertainments weren't as fine as in my time, but he came. When he left, he took Roxie, queen of Hercules that year, with him. What a marvelous scandal even if they did get married in Vegas on the way to California! He was thirty, and she just turned eighteen."

"That doesn't seem too strange for Hollywood."

"It wouldn't have been strange for New Orleans if he'd been a banker or an attorney, but the Old Guard didn't approve of an entertainer even if he was one of them once. To think he knew the Marx Brothers and did all those USO shows during the war, even appeared on *Lucy* during the Fifties, and now no one remembers him."

"I remember Groucho Marx," Chad said, trying to keep up his end of the conversation.

"Artie was better friends with Harpo. They both

loved music so. To think, I told Roxie that Artie would never amount to anything. I guess I was as bad as my parents. That Hollywood marriage lasted until Artie passed away in 1965 from too much of the good life. Roxie didn't re-marry. She had her children, a son and two darling daughters. They're quite old now, but the girls do come to visit when they're in the area."

Chad smiled.

"Oh, I know you think I'm old, but that's just on the outside. When Pierre comes for me, I'll be as young and fresh as a college girl at Mardi Gras. Don't look at me that way. I know my Pierre is dead. Don't I go put flowers on his grave every week? Don't I have my headstone already set up next to his—Rosamond St. Rochelle Landry, nurse, midwife, mother, and beloved wife of Pierre, 1907 -? All they have to do is fill in the end date. Do you think it's too pretentious?"

"No, ma'am."

"Call me Roz, I said. Well, I am proud of what I became. I could have been buried in the family vault in New Orleans if I'd taken another path. Then, they would have buried me as Rosamond St. Rochelle Boylan, Queen of Hercules, 1926, and probably dead by 1927. I was divorcing Boylan when he died, you know. What a brutal man."

"No, I didn't know that, Miz Roz."

"Another family scandal. Divorce is no big deal today. I escaped from an abusive husband, came here, made something of myself, and married Pierre. We had forty-five wonderful years together and four children, the boys, Pierre Junior and Laurence and my two girls. That's small for a Cajun family. They were all born during the Depression. Pierre insisted I finish my nurses' training before we started our family. That always annoyed Junior. He said if we'd started right away like most Cajuns, he could have gotten in on World War II. As it was, he served as a marine in Korea. Oh, how angry he got when his son, Perry, protested the war in Vietnam, and he wasn't too happy with me for joining in the picketing either. I lost my cousin, Henri, during World War II, a pilot shot down over France. His death killed his mother, Loretta. I barely slept the whole time Junior spent in Korea. I just couldn't let Perry be sent off to die in a senseless war and sit by doing nothing. Junior is gone now. It's terrible to outlive your children."

Chad thought Miz Roz might cry. Her eyes had gone watery, but then she smiled. Down on the bayou, a very hairy man with a bushy beard and long dark mane drawn back in a ponytail emerged from the houseboat cabin, stretched, and waved. He started up the hill.

"My great-grandson, Pete. I admit I'm partial to Junior's family. They seem to have inherited my wild streak, for better or worse. You won't believe this but under all that hair, Pete looks just like my Pierre except for the dimples. The ladies love him. Come here, boy, and sit with your Granny Roz."

"Just what I planned to do." Instead of taking the steps, the young man vaulted over the deck railing. He held out a hand to Nurse Chad.

"Pierre Boniface Landry the Fourth, Cajun entertainer, my card." A business card appeared from somewhere under the chest-covering beard. "I do parties."

Chad shoved the card into a pocket of his scrubs. "Can I get you and Mr. Landry anything, Miz Roz?"

"Oh, do bring us coffee with brown sugar. Make enough for yourself."

"I'll sit with my favorite lady while you do that. Where's Dorey?"

"I'm subbing while she takes a personal day. I'm Chad Duhon."

"I admit I like nurses to be female and bodacious, but as long as you take good care of Granny Roz, you're okay in my book."

"I'll go make that coffee."

Chad took advantage of the visit to put clean sheets on Miz Roz's bed and get a start on her lunch. As he made the turkey sandwich and cut it in quarters, he could hear her chiding her great-grandson.

"When are you going to shave and get married, boy?"

"I tried both once, didn't work. If I ever find a woman as tough and beautiful as you, Gran, I might give marriage another try. Since I suspect God only made one of you, I might be alone forever."

"That would be tragic, *cher* heart. Family is everyt'ing, as my mother-in-law used to say. She even got over having Methodist grandchildren. Junior was so like his Cajun uncles, while your father had my Pierre's gentleness."

"And don't forget his Cajun pride. My dad did a lot of the research that led to the Cajun Renaissance even if he does hates to hunt and fish. Got to go, Gran. I have to see a man about some ducks. Might have a gig as a hunting guide." Pierre Boniface Landry the Fourth gulped down the last of his coffee. "I'll bring you a big bag of beignets from Pommier's on my way home."

Pete brushed her papery cheek with his whiskers

and waved as he bounded up the hill toward an old truck parked in the shade of the pecan trees. Roz looked after him, shaking her head. Chad came to wheel her in for lunch.

"He's a wild child, that one," she remarked to her nurse, "But then, so was I."

"More coffee or some iced tea, Miz Roz?"

"The tea, I suppose. I need a new diaper, but coffee with my great-grandson was worth the humiliation. We'll take care of it after lunch. Make yourself a sandwich and sit with me. I enjoy the company of young people."

Chad took his lunch sack from the refrigerator and poured himself some tea. He took a place next to Miz Roz.

"Dorey usually eats with me, a Lean Cuisine meal, but I know she sneaks cookies when I'm napping. I stock up on the sugar-free, low-fat varieties just for her. They've taken all the joy out of cookies, you know. There was a time when I was criticized for eating with black people—coloreds we used to say, oh so politely. Now, they're called African-Americans. I like that one the best. I think the term was Afro-Americans when I marched to desegregate the university up in Lafayette. I was egged, but I caught enough of them to make an omelet for me and Pierre that evening. You could call it my tribute to Martin Luther King, Jr. and passive resistance that I didn't throw them back. A very tasty omelet, as I recall."

"My grandfather on my mom's side is sort of a redneck. I think he used to be in the Klan. Maybe he still is," Chad confessed. "He used to brag about going out nigger bashing."

"Yes, and there were lynchings. Even during the '27 flood, the Red Cross camps were segregated. I marched proudly with Beulah Senegal's great-grandchildren in the Sixties. We midwifed together, Beulah and me, in the early days. She died of a stroke just after World War II. At least, she lived to see the victory and her grandson come home. Dorey is her great-great grandchild, and look at her, a nurse educated at the university. Her brother is a dentist, and the rest of the family owns a big trash collection company. The Senegals have done well for themselves."

"Yeah, I went to high school with some of the Senegals. My grandfather hates that I have a few black friends. He hates my earrings, my tats, and my profession. I guess the only thing he likes is my short hair. He wanted me to join the military."

"Just because I said 'family first' doesn't mean you shouldn't find your own way in life. What I mean is family should stand by you and support your decisions. Maybe that's why I'm still here after all these years, thirty plus years without my Pierre, to say what needs to be said to the younger generations."

Her eyes filled again. Chad Duhon rushed to change the subject. "I'll bet you were something when you were my age."

"That I was, queen of the Mardi Gras ball—and I danced on a table out at Broussard's Barn."

"That dive! They do have good music going all the time, but it's not a safe place for gays."

"It's never been a safe place, dear, for anyone. You do practice safe sex, I hope. I wouldn't want to have to give you one of my lectures. I preached that message all my adult life. Still, my great-granddaughter, Celine, got pregnant at the age of seventeen. She knew better but was too shy to tell that slick college boy to put on a condom. I guess he thought all girls were on the pill. She decided to have the baby, and I told her to stand strong and make something of herself. Then, she could provide for her child and look anyone in the eye. She's a teacher now, and her little boy is just wonderful. I never pushed anyone toward abortion, but Lord, I saw enough rape and incest victims in my day not to be against it."

Chad collected their dishes and put them in the washer. "Let me make you comfortable. Then, maybe, you'd like to nap."

"Bring on the Depends, then, but I want to go outside again and wait for Pierre."

Nurse Duhon did his duty, checking for bedsores and chafed areas along the way. He made sure she took her pills, checked her heart and blood pressure, and then suggested Miz Roz might want to stretch on the chaise lounge. He could put it in the shade and bring her a pillow and light blanket.

"You're just hoping I'll doze off and not keep talking. Well, fine. Sit with me for a while though. I hate being alone. All my old friends are gone. Faye and Bernie Toomey—they raised a nice family over in Crowley. Edna, my teacher friend, taught for forty-five years, never married, but she didn't die a virgin. Leonard Spivey, that tricky old goat, married Judith Strictland, one of the Red Cross nurses, and didn't pass on until the age of eighty-five. They had a lovely daughter, too, a second family for him. Claimed he had a bad heart—my ass!"

Chad Duhon laughed. He didn't know a single one

of these people, but he could listen to this lady go on all day.

"My Pierre died at the age of seventy-two. He's the one who had the heart attack. He was always so lean and active. No one suspected. He went too suddenly, too soon. People used to ask him if he couldn't control his wife when I'd go out crusading for one of my causes. He'd just smile and say his life would be too dull if he did. His only causes were fighting disease and poverty, and he did it every day of the week. He was one of the last doctors still doing house calls, and he never got rich like they do today. Still, we had a good life working together, raising our children. We built this fine house on the part of the Landry farm he inherited. Split up among so many children, we only got a few acres going down to the bayou. That was enough."

"It's a beautiful place, Miz Roz."

"Yes, old but beautiful."

"Like its owner."

"You flatter me, boy, but thank you. I want the place to go to Perry. I'll make it up to the rest with money. I did inherit a bundle from my parents despite the stock market crash, the one in '29. My papa's bank didn't go under, and bankers always thrive. Of course, I was disinherited for a while for marrying beneath myself, but after Roxie ran off with Artie, my parents realized they could accept our lives or die alone. I was expecting Junior that year. Grandchildren have a way of making things right."

Miz Roz caught her breath for a moment, then continued. "Forgiveness is important, Chad. Remember that. Junior forgave his own son everything once he had a grandson in Pete to take fishing and hunting. When

Pete left a career in Wildlife and Fisheries to be a Cajun comedian, Junior wept, but he got over it. They were still close at the end. I believe I do feel tired. You may go inside. I'll rest now."

Chad tucked in her covers and adjusted her pillows. "Nurse Robertson will soon be back. I just want to say, it's been a privilege to know you, Miz Roz, even for one day. I won't let my grandfather put me down anymore."

"Good. That's good."

Nurse Duhon went indoors and cleaned up the bathroom. On his way back to the kitchen, he heard the crunch of shells in the driveway and the thump of the afternoon newspaper hitting the front door. He brought the paper in and sat down with a cup of coffee in the kitchen. Through the open door, he could hear Miz Roz talking to herself. Maybe she wasn't as clear of mind as Nurse Robertson claimed.

"Yes, it's a beautiful day to go walking, *mon amour*. You've made me wait for you again—far too long—Pierre, but I knew you would come."

Chad shook his head. Old people did strange things. She was talking to her dead husband. He got up and looked at the lounge and saw Miz Roz slept now, her frail chest barely lifting under the pink, quilted robe. When she woke, he'd take her vital signs again and note them on the chart for Nurse Robertson, along with a report on how much lunch the patient had eaten—most of her soup and half the sandwich, a glass of tea, saving the applesauce for later.

Chad read the sports page. Baseball, one of the few things he could talk to his grandfather about without getting into an argument and the World Series was in full swing. Another car pulled into the shell drive and stopped.

Doretha Robertson bustled in declaring, "A miracle of God just happened. The doctor ran on time today, so here I am back earlier than expected. How's our lady doing?"

"She ate a fairly good lunch and chatted all day."

"Nothing new about that."

"I didn't mind, but, well, she was talking to Pierre a little while ago."

"Usually, she tells him what their children and grandchildren are up to."

"Not today. They were going walking. I thought she might try to get up on her own and checked on her, but she had closed her eyes and gone to sleep."

Doretha Robertson knew. She knew without going out to the porch and lifting that small, lifeless hand to check for a pulse. Pierre Landry had come for his beloved Roz.

Other books in the Mardi Gras Series

MARDI GRAS MADNESS—Anything can happen on Mardi Gras day in a small town.

Seeking to escape the memory of her husband's tragic death, Laura Dickinson leaves the North and takes a job as a librarian in the small town of Chapelle, Louisiana. She soon finds herself embroiled with the family of Robert LeBlanc. Owner of Chateau Camille and single father to a little girl badly in need of a mother, Robert sees everything through the lens of the past and local custom. Strongly attracted to him, Laura scoffs at the old tales. In tiny Chapelle, however, history is very much alive, but mad women and disturbed children are no longer locked in attics.

Forced to face her feelings for Robert on Mardi Gras day, Laura unwittingly unleashes a series of terrible events. Some will not survive as one person seeks to destroy the past with fire and bloodshed.

~*~

COURIR DE MARDI GRAS—Anything can happen on Mardi Gras day in the countryside.

Fleeing an obsessive boyfriend, Suzanne Hudson arrives in tiny Port Jefferson, Louisiana, to inventory the antiques of an antebellum home. Full of moonlight and magnolia dreams, she soon finds her job boring and the master of the manor, George St. Julien, dull.

Everything changes during the Mardi Gras ride when Suzanne is playfully abducted by a masked man on a white horse and the famous Magnolia Hill silver disappears shortly thereafter. Determined to discover the rider's identity and solve the mystery of the lost silver, Suzanne unearths small town secrets that might be better left alone and finds her life in jeopardy.

A word about the author...

Once a librarian, now a writer of romance, Lynn Shurr grew up in Pennsylvania Dutch country. She attended a state college and earned a very impractical B.A. in English Literature. Her first job out of school really was working as a cashier in a burger joint. Moving from one humble job to another, she traveled to North Carolina, Germany, then California where she buckled down and studied for an M.A. in Librarianship.

New degree in hand, she found her first reference job in the Heart of Cajun Country, Lafayette, Louisiana. For her, the old saying, "Once you've tasted bayou water, you will always stay here" came true. She raised three children not far from the Bayou Teche and lives there still with her astronomer husband.

When not writing, Lynn likes to paint, cheer for the New Orleans Saints and LSU Tigers, and take long road trips nearly anywhere. Her love of the bayou country, its history and customs, often shows in the background for her books.

You may contact Lynn at www.lynnshurr.com, lynn.shurr@yahoo.com, or visit her blog—lynnshurr.blogspot.com

~*~

Other Lynn Shurr titles
available from The Wild Rose Press, Inc.

Goals for a Sinner, *Wish for a Sinner*, *Kicks for a Sinner*, *Paradise for a Sinner*, *Love Letter for a Sinner* (The Sinners sports romances), *The Convent Rose*, *A Wild Red Rose*, *Always Yellow Roses* (The Roses series), *Mardi Gras Madness*, *Courir de Mardi Gras* (Mardi Gras series), and *A Trashy Affair*